THE DIVINE COMEDY OF DANTE ALIGHIERI

III PARADISO

uniform with this volume

INFERNO

PURGATORIO

THE DIVINE
COMEDY OF
DANTE ALIGHIERI

WITH

TRANSLATION AND

COMMENT BY

JOHN D. SINCLAIR
III PARADISO

OXFORD UNIVERSITY PRESS   NEW YORK

OXFORD UNIVERSITY PRESS

London   Oxford   New York
Glasgow   Toronto   Melbourne   Wellington
Cape Town   Ibadan   Nairobi   Dar es Salaam   Lusaka   Addis Ababa
Delhi   Bombay   Calcutta   Madras   Karachi   Lahore   Dacca
Kuala Lumpur   Singapore   Hong Kong   Tokyo

First published, 1939
First issued as an Oxford University Press paperback by special
arrangement with THE BODLEY HEAD, 1961

This reprint, 1972

Printed in the United States of America

PREFACE

WITH many things of more consequence, the completion of my work on *The Divine Comedy* has been held up by the war, and these years of delay have allowed me the more opportunity for applying and testing the principles of interpretation by which I have chiefly sought to be guided. These are, first, that all the imagery of the poem has its value, not merely or chiefly in its ingenuity nor even in its incidental beauty, but in its consistent and sustained relevancy to the spiritual interests concerned—Dante's *sì come*'s not only illustrate, they confirm and clinch his meaning; and, second, that the poem, and not least the *Paradiso*, is thoroughly autobiographical. Fundamentally and obviously, all art is autobiography, 'marked clearly with the internal stamp' and reporting of its maker; but this is peculiarly true of the art of Dante, not merely in its fictional form, but in its intimate spiritual veracity, in its passionate and convincing utterance of the deepest currents of his life, the pulse of his lines keeping time always with his heart. On these principles I have tried to read Dante with Dante continually in mind and to find the significance of every passage in its consonance with Dante's temper and outlook and experience. With these principles in view, I may have strayed into some far-fetched glosses; without them, I could not hope to be right. The question, where there is a question, is partly how far Dante, being Dante and medieval, may fairly be taken to have fetched his meaning.

The enforced delay in the publication of this volume has given me, too, the great advantage of much consultation—in the *Paradiso*, where I had most need of it—with my friend Professor Bickersteth of Aberdeen, whose knowledge and understanding of Dante, of Aquinas and of Virgil have tempted me to lay a heavy tax on his patience and generosity, both, in

7

my experience, inexhaustible. So far as my comments are justified they owe much to him, and for the rest he is not to be held responsible.

Charles Williams's recently-published *The Figure of Beatrice* is a full and imaginative study of the place of Beatrice in Dante's writings, and not least in the *Paradiso*. Without committing myself to all its interpretations, I have welcomed especially its strong support for the actual personal devotion of Dante to Beatrice's memory and for her profound and lasting influence on his spiritual life.

I have to acknowledge the kindness of my fellow-student, the Rev. D. T. Robertson, who has read the English text and Notes and given me the benefit of his criticisms.

Of my wife's share in all three volumes I do not begin to speak; it is incalculable.

As in the earlier volumes, I have used—by permission of the publishers, Messrs. Ulrico Hoepli, of Milan—the Italian text of the Società Dantesca Italiana, revised by G. Vandelli, with a few readings from the texts of Moore and Casella. In one line only I have ventured to differ from all of these, reading in *Par.* xvi, 38 *tre fïate* instead of *trenta fiate*. The latter reading has the great preponderance of both MS. and editorial support; but the former was expressly preferred by Dante's son Piero, and in a line which dates the birth of the most distinguished ancestor of the family Piero's authority for the family tradition seems to me decisive against that of any copyist or editor.

The names of some of the authors quoted in the Notes are followed by 'L.D.,' which means that the quotation in each case is taken from one of the *Lecturae Dantis* given by Dante scholars from time to time in Florence and elsewhere in Italy.

The references in the Index of Persons and Places are, for simplicity, references to the Italian text in the three volumes, from which the English reader will readily find the relevant passages in the opposite pages.

J. D. S.

EDINBURGH
April 1946

CONTENTS

9

CONTENTS

CONTENTS

CONTENTS

DANTE'S PARADISE

FOLLOWING the Ptolemaic astronomy of his time Dante con-
ceived of the earth as stationary and central in the universe,
with the sun and moon and the five visible planets revolving
about it at various speeds. Each of these seven heavenly bodies
has its own sphere, or 'heaven'; beyond them is the sphere of
the fixed stars, and beyond that the ninth and last of the
material heavens, called the Crystalline because it is transparent
and invisible, or the Primum Mobile because from its infinite
speed the other lower heavens take their slower motions.
These nine spheres are severally moved and controlled by the
nine orders of the angels, and all the spheres and the heavenly
bodies in them have certain spiritual significances and certain
influences on human life and character. As Dante passes
upward with Beatrice the souls of the blessed appear to them
in the successive heavens according to their corresponding
predominant character in their earthly lives. Beyond the nine
material spheres is the Empyrean, outside of time and space,
the heaven of God's immediate presence and the only real
home of the angels and the redeemed, whose blessedness
consists in their eternal vision of Him.

THE SYSTEM OF DANTE'S PARADISE

The Ten Heavens

10. The Empyrean: the Holy Trinity, the Virgin, the Angels and the Saints

9. The Crystalline, or Primum Mobile: the Angelic Orders

8. The Fixed Stars: the Church Triumphant

7. Saturn: Temperance; Contemplatives

6. Jupiter: Justice; Rulers

5. Mars: Courage; Warriors

4. The Sun: Wisdom; Theologians

3. Venus: Love marred by wantonness

2. Mercury: Service marred by ambition

1. The Moon: Faithfulness marred by inconstancy

PARADISO

PARADISO

LA gloria di colui che tutto move
  per l'universo penetra e risplende
  in una parte più e meno altrove.
Nel ciel che più della sua luce prende
  fu' io, e vidi cose che ridire
  nè sa nè può chi di là su discende;
perchè appressando sè al suo disire,
  nostro intelletto si profonda tanto,
  che dietro la memoria non può ire.
Veramente quant' io del regno santo   10
  nella mia mente potei far tesoro,
  sarà ora matera del mio canto.
O buono Apollo, all'ultimo lavoro
  fammi del tuo valor sì fatto vaso,
  come dimandi a dar l'amato alloro.
Infino a qui l'un giogo di Parnaso
  assai mi fu; ma or con amendue
  m'è uopo intrar nell'aringo rimaso.
Entra nel petto mio, e spira tue
  sì come quando Marsïa traesti   20
  della vagina delle membra sue.
O divina virtù, se mi ti presti
  tanto che l'ombra del beato regno
  segnata nel mio capo io manifesti,
venir vedra' mi al tuo diletto legno,
  e coronarmi allor di quelle foglie
  che la matera e tu mi farai degno.

CANTO I

The appeal to Apollo; the ascent from the earth; the order of the universe

THE glory of Him who moves all things penetrates the universe and shines in one part more and in another less. I was in the heaven that most receives His light[1] and I saw things which he that descends from it has not the knowledge or the power to tell again; for our intellect, drawing near to its desire, sinks so deep that memory cannot follow it. Nevertheless, so much of the holy kingdom as I was able to treasure in my mind shall now be matter of my song.

O good Apollo, for the last labour make me such a vessel of thy power as thou requirest for the gift of thy loved laurel. Thus far the one peak of Parnassus has sufficed me, but now I have need of both,[2] entering on the arena that remains. Come into my breast and breathe there as when thou drewest Marsyas from the scabbard of his limbs.[3] O power divine, if thou grant me so much of thyself that I may show forth the shadow of the blessed kingdom imprinted in my brain thou shalt see me come to thy chosen tree and crown myself then with those leaves of which the theme and thou will make me worthy. So seldom, father, are they

Sì rade volte, padre, se ne coglie
   per triunfare o cesare o poeta,
   colpa e vergogna dell'umane voglie,   30
che parturir letizia in su la lieta
   delfica deità dovrìa la fronda
   peneia, quando alcun di sè asseta.
Poca favilla gran fiamma seconda:
   forse di retro a me con miglior voci
   si pregherà perchè Cirra risponda.
Surge ai mortali per diverse foci
   la lucerna del mondo; ma da quella
   che quattro cerchi giugne con tre croci,
con miglior corso e con migliore stella   40
   esce congiunta, e la mondana cera
   più a suo modo tempera e suggella.
Fatto avea di là mane e di qua sera
   tal foce quasi, e tutto era là bianco
   quello emisperio, e l'altra parte nera,
quando Beatrice in sul sinistro fianco
   vidi rivolta e riguardar nel sole:
   aquila sì non li s'affisse unquanco.
E sì come secondo raggio suole
   uscir del primo e risalire in suso,   50
   pur come pellegrin che tornar vuole,
così dell'atto suo, per li occhi infuso
   nell' imagine mia, il mio si fece,
   e fissi li occhi al sole oltre nostr' uso.
Molto è licito là, che qui non lece
   alle nostre virtù, mercè del loco
   fatto per proprio dell'umana spece.
Io nol soffersi molto, nè sì poco,
   ch' io nol vedessi sfavillar dintorno,
   com ferro che bogliente esce del foco;   60
e di subito parve giorno a giorno
   essere aggiunto, come quei che puote
   avesse il ciel d'un altro sole adorno.
Beatrice tutta nell'etterne rote
   fissa con li occhi stava; ed io in lei
   le luci fissi, di là su remote.

gathered for triumph of Caesar or of poet—fault
and shame of human wills—that the Peneian bough
must beget gladness in the glad Delphic god when
it makes any long for it.[4] A great flame follows a
little spark. Perhaps after me prayer will be made
with better words so that Cyrrha may respond.

The lamp of the world rises on mortals by differ-
ent entrances; but by that which joins four circles
with three crosses it issues on a better course and
in conjunction with better stars and tempers and
stamps the wax of the world more after its own
fashion.[5] Its entrance near that point had made
morning there and evening here and that hemisphere
was all white and the other dark, when I saw Beatrice
turned round to the left[6] and looking at the sun—
never eagle so fastened upon it; and as a second ray
will issue from the first and mount up again,[7] like
a pilgrim that would return home, so from her
action, infused by the eyes into my imagination,
mine was made, and beyond our wont I fixed my
eyes on the sun. Much is granted there that is not
granted here to our powers, by virtue of the place
made for possession by the race of men. I had not
borne it long, yet not so briefly as not to see it
sparkling like iron that comes boiling from the
fire; and of a sudden it seemed there was added day
to day, as if He that is able had decked the sky
with a second sun. Beatrice stood with her eyes
fixed only on the eternal wheels, and on her I fixed
mine, withdrawn from above. At her aspect I

Nel suo aspetto tal dentro mi fei,
   qual si fè Glauco nel gustar dell'erba
   che 'l fè consorte in mar delli altri Dei.
Trasumanar significar per verba   70
   non si porìa; però l'essemplo basti
   a cui esperïenza grazia serba.
S' i' era sol di me quel che creasti
   novellamente, amor che 'l ciel governi,
   tu 'l sai, che col tuo lume mi levasti.
Quando la rota che tu sempiterni
   desiderato, a sè mi fece atteso
   con l'armonia che temperi e discerni,
parvemi tanto allor del cielo acceso
   della fiamma del sol, che pioggia o fiume   80
   lago non fece mai tanto disteso.
La novità del suono e 'l grande lume
   di lor cagion m'accesero un disio
   mai non sentito di cotanto acume.
Ond'ella, che vedea me sì com' io,
   a quïetarmi l'animo commosso,
   pria ch' io a dimandar, la bocca aprìo,
e cominciò: 'Tu stesso ti fai grosso
   col falso imaginar, sì che non vedi
   ciò che vedresti se l'avessi scosso.   90
Tu non se' in terra, sì come tu credi;
   ma folgore, fuggendo il proprio sito,
   non corse come tu ch'ad esso riedi.'
S' io fui del primo dubbio disvestito
   per le sorrise parolette brevi,
   dentro ad un nuovo più fu' inretito,
e dissi: 'Già contento requïevi
   di grande ammirazion; ma ora ammiro
   com' io trascenda questi corpi levi.'
Ond'ella, appresso d'un pio sospiro,   100
   li occhi drizzò ver me con quel sembiante
   che madre fa sovra figlio deliro,
e cominciò: 'Le cose tutte quante
   hanno ordine tra loro, e questo è forma
   che l'universo a Dio fa simigliante.

was changed within, as was Glaucus when he tasted of the herb that made him one among the other gods in the sea.[8] The passing beyond humanity cannot be set forth in words; let the example suffice, therefore, for him to whom grace reserves the experience. If I was only that part of me which Thou createdst last, Thou knowest, Love that rulest the heavens, who with Thy light didst raise me.[9] When the wheel which Thou, being desired, makest eternal held me intent on itself by the harmony Thou dost attune and distribute,[10] so much of the sky seemed then to be kindled with the sun's flame that rain or river never made a lake so broad. The newness of the sound and the great light kindled in me such keenness of desire to know their cause as I had never felt before; and she who saw me as I saw myself, to quiet the agitation of my mind, opened her lips before I mine to ask. And she began: 'Thou makest thyself dull with false fancies so that thou canst not see as thou wouldst if thou hadst cast them off; thou art not on earth as thou thinkest, but lightning flying from its own place[11] never ran so fast as thou returnest to thine.'

If I was freed from my perplexity by the brief words she smiled to me I was more entangled in a new one and I said: 'I was content already, resting from a great wonder, but now I wonder how I should be rising above these light substances.'[12]

She, therefore, after a sigh of pity, bent her eyes on me with the look a mother casts on her delirious child, and she began: 'All things whatsoever have order among themselves, and this is the form that makes the universe resemble God; here the higher

23

Qui veggion l'alte creature l'orma
   dell'etterno valore, il qual è fine
   al quale è fatta la toccata norma.
Nell'ordine ch' io dico sono accline
   tutte nature, per diverse sorti,   110
   più al principio loro e men vicine;
onde si muovono a diversi porti
   per lo gran mar dell'essere, e ciascuna
   con istinto a lei dato che la porti.
Questi ne porta il foco inver la luna;
   questi ne' cor mortali è permotore;
   questi la terra in sè stringe e aduna:
nè pur le creature che son fore
   d' intelligenza quest'arco saetta,
   ma quelle c' hanno intelletto ed amore.   120
La provedenza, che cotanto assetta,
   del suo lume fa 'l ciel sempre quïeto
   nel qual si volge quel c' ha maggior fretta;
e ora lì, come a sito decreto,
   cen porta la virtù di quella corda
   che ciò che scocca drizza in segno lieto.
Vero è che come forma non s'accorda
   molte fïate all' intenzion dell'arte,
   perch'a risponder la materia è sorda;
così da questo corso si diparte   130
   talor la creatura, c' ha podere
   di piegar, così pinta, in altra parte;
e sì come veder si può cadere
   foco di nube, sì l' impeto primo
   s'atterra, torto da falso piacere.
Non dei più ammirar, se bene stimo,
   lo tuo salir, se non come d'un rivo
   se d'alto monte scende giuso ad imo.
Maraviglia sarebbe in te, se, privo
   d' impedimento, giù ti fossi assiso,   140
   com'a terra quïete in foco vivo.'
Quinci rivolse inver lo cielo il viso.

creatures see the impress of the Eternal Excellence, which is the end for which that system itself is made.[13] In the order I speak of all natures have their bent according to their different lots, nearer to their source and farther from it; they move, therefore, to different ports over the great sea of being, each with an instinct given it to bear it on: this bears fire up towards the moon,—this is the motive force in mortal creatures,—this binds the earth together and makes it one. And not only the creatures that are without intelligence does this bow shoot, but those also that have intellect and love. The providence that regulates all this makes forever quiet with its light the heaven within which turns that of greatest speed,[14] and thither now as to a place appointed the power of that bowstring is bearing us which aims at a joyous mark. It is true that, as a shape often does not accord with the art's intention because the material is deaf and unresponsive, so sometimes the creature, having the power, thus impelled, to turn aside another way, deviates from this course, and, as fire may be seen to fall from a cloud, so the primal impulse, diverted by false pleasure, is turned to the earth.[15] If I am right, thou shouldst no more wonder at thy ascent than at a stream falling from a mountain-height to the foot; it would be a wonder in thee if, freed from hindrance, thou hadst remained below, as on earth would be stillness in living flame.'

Then she turned her face again to the sky.

1. The Empyrean.

2. Cyrrha, one of the two peaks of Parnassus, was regarded as sacred to Apollo, the other to the Muses.

3. Challenged by the satyr Marsyas to a musical contest, Apollo defeated him and flayed him for his presumption.

4. 'The Delphic god', Apollo; 'the Peneian bough', a branch of laurel.

5. The spring equinox, when the sun rises at the point where the celestial equator, the zodiac, and the equinoctial colure intersect on the horizon, and when the sun is in the Ram, is the most propitious time of the year,—the time of the creation (*Inf.* i). It is now a few days past the equinox, so the sun rises 'near that point'.

6. They have been facing east, and Beatrice turns left to the noonday sun north from them.

7. By reflection.

8. The fisherman Glaucus, seeing the fish revive by eating a certain herb, ate it himself and was moved to plunge into the sea, where he became a sea-god.

9. 'Whether in the body . . . or out of the body, I cannot tell: God knoweth' (2 *Cor.* xii. 2). 'The Lord God formed man of the dust of the ground, and breathed into his nostrils the breath of life; and man became a living soul' (*Gen.* ii. 7). Compare the account of human generation in *Purg.* xxv. The soul was 'created last'.

10. The Primum Mobile, the outermost physical sphere, spins with infinite speed from the desire of every part of it to be in contact with the Empyrean, the divine presence, and gives their motions to the lower spheres; the notes of the music of the spheres are kept in tune and 'distributed' among the spheres by that divine influence.

11. Lightning's 'own place' is the sphere of fire, between the earth and the moon. The soul's 'own place' is with God.

12. Passing through the regions of air and fire.

13. The divine order of the universe is its 'form'—the scholastic term for its essential formative principle; that which makes it to *be* a universe is this likeness to God, its realization of God's thought.

14. The Empyrean, containing the Primum Mobile.

15. It is the nature of fire to rise, but lightning, against its nature, falls; so the soul, against its nature, may fall to the earth.

NOTE

The subject of the *Paradiso* is the whole and consummation of things. It departs more completely from earthly experience than either the *Inferno* or the *Purgatorio*, and its matter, at least in its upper reaches, is, in strictness, inconceivable. 'Beginning the other two canticas the poet spoke of himself ("I found myself"—"the little boat of my wit"); beginning the third he speaks of God' (*F. Torraca*). The *Inferno* is realistic and dramatic and the *Purgatorio* human and sacramental; the *Paradiso* is largely dogmatic, with a constant urge to become visionary and lyrical. Its meaning is summed up in its first and last lines, —'The glory of Him who moves all things' and 'The Love that moves the sun and the other stars'. 'The background and the starting-point of everything in Dante is the *intelletto d'amore*, the genius of love' (*G. Santayana*). In the stately music of the opening lines he declares the unspeakableness of his matter, and many times in the course of the *Paradiso* he takes this way of telling the infinite quality of its subject; the matter is always greater than the song. Entering Hell he declared his confidence in his memory,—'O memory that noted what I saw, here shall be shown thy worth', and his memory, with its grim storage, did not fail him; but now memory and language alike fall short of his great experience.

Here he does not appeal merely to the Muses, as he has done repeatedly before (*Inf.* ii and xxxii and *Purg.* i and xxix), but to their leader Apollo, god of the sun, of light itself. Mere skill in verse will not serve him now, for this 'last labour' he must be filled with a divine breath; only such afflatus will save him from the presumption and the shame of Marsyas and gain for him, it may be, the true laurel, 'the Peneian bough', which is the gift of Apollo himself. It is a language which is echoed, perhaps deliberately, by Milton's 'Fame is no plant that grows

27

on mortal soil', and it is in such terms that Dante claims his place as a poet. 'For the first time in our literature the name of poet was used by Dante for a writer of vernacular verse, a title that was reserved solely for the Greeks and Latins, while modern writers were merely rhymers. Dante is conscious of himself and of his work, not only raising the Italian vernacular to the height of the classical tongues, but in the Italian vernacular raising poetry high above the range of transitory personal feelings to that of sublime doctrine and eternal things. For that reason he takes the name of poet' (*G. Mazzoni, L.D.*).

All the celestial conditions are favourable and the scientific details give concreteness to the situation; it is high noon, the perfect hour, and the day is in the year's perfect season, the vernal equinox, the time of creation, when 'God saw every thing that he had made, and, behold, it was very good'. Virgil, in his last words to Dante, spoken on the last stairway of Purgatory, had said: 'That sweet fruit which the care of mortals goes to seek on so many boughs shall today give peace to thy hunger.' 'And what a wondrous day it was to be, heralded by the dream of Rachel and Leah, followed by the glorious pageant of the Church and Empire! He had mounted the last steps as the sun rose; it was midday as he stooped to drink of Eunoe, but Dante was to see no evening of that day. The sun of the last day of his pilgrimage rose on the Earthly Paradise, but the Poet passed beyond it into eternity' (*E. G. Gardner*). It is a part of the studied coherence of Dante's narrative that he entered Hell, the place of despair, at nightfall—, he came forth at the foot of Purgatory, the place of hope, and entered its gate, and reached the Earthly Paradise, in the early morning of three successive days—, and now at noon he rises with Beatrice into the heavens, the place of fulfilment; and it is plain, though here he makes no reference to it, that he intended these times to correspond with the death of Christ and His descent into Hell on the evening of Good Friday, His resurrection on the morning of the first day of the week, and His ascension, according to the accepted tradition, at noon.

At the opening of the narrative we find Dante standing with Beatrice on the summit of Purgatory, 'pure and ready to ascend to the stars' and looking at the sun. There he sees the glory of

things as unfallen man could bear to see it; but it is only when
he looks again at Beatrice while she is gazing above—the strong
word *fissare* is used four times for that intense absorption—
that he is suddenly aware of the music of the spheres and of a
'great light' and comes, without his knowledge, nearer to the
sun, brought into a new contact with heavenly realities. It is a
bewildering and incommunicable experience, and for illustration
of it he can only recall the story of Glaucus and the language of
St Paul. At her aspect he 'was changed within', he says, and
in the words he sums up the *Vita Nuova* and continues it. For
the *Paradiso* does, in fact, complete Dante's love-story, up to
the point when, in the Empyrean, 'she, so far off as she seemed,
smiled and looked at me' (*Par.* xxxi). Beatrice is the truth of
God for him, and she is still Beatrice, and still, 'through hidden
virtue that came from her, [he] felt old love's great power'.
His love, sublimated, is not lost but fulfilled, and it is fulfilled
as it can only be, in the fulfilment of his life itself. For that
sublimation of love is a thing that happens, as, if we are to
believe him, it happened to Dante. 'The *Paradiso* is above all
the cantica of Beatrice. That one of the blessed should watch
with particular care over the well-being of individuals living the
hard and perilous earthly life was a prevalent idea of the time,
but the Poet's choice of Beatrice for that office is an invention
that gives to this third cantica a beautiful note of humanity
and affection. . . . During his journey through the heavenly
spheres he depends on her shining eyes—the eyes that had
power to move Virgil to give his immediate succour (*Inf.* ii);
and her smile, becoming ever more joyous, is the sign of their
continual ascent from the lower heavens to the divine presence.
. . . There are those who look askance at the "theological"
Beatrice and talk of "a cold creation", but that arises from a
cold preconception and reconstruction of Dante's vision.
Beatrice enlightens Dante, from time to time, without putting
on the doctor's cap; she is one of the blessed and speaks of that
which all the blessed know naturally in their constant vision
of God' (*M. Barbi*). Beatrice exists for us wholly in what Dante
tells us of her, and for him she is, in very fact, sacramental,
'an outward and visible sign of an inward and spiritual grace'.
Her lessons to him as they pass through the spheres are not so

29

much themselves the revelation as the exposition of it, and she is herself more than all her lessons. Such a conception of Beatrice is vital to the *Paradiso*.

When Dante questions her about their ascent she smiles at his 'false fancies', his measuring and limiting of experience by the conditions of the flesh, and she tells him of the divine order of things by which the soul, 'freed from hindrance' rises to 'its own place' in God. It is an idea which has been steadily prepared for in the *Purgatorio* by the increasing lightness of his steps as he climbs. Beatrice's account, here and later, is the statement in scholastic terms of the conception of the universe as a spiritual and comprehensive order working to spiritual and final ends. 'In this world and in the next, on earth, in the depths of hell, in the infinitude of heaven, from the motes in the sunbeam to the mighty spirits who sway the spheres in their courses, all are parts of one sovereign design, the work of one supreme intelligence and will, created in all their relations for a single end, and accomplishing that end by law, immutable and eternal. This root idea, the immortal tradition of the Church, developed and systematized by the great Schoolmen in Dante's childhood and in the generation before, is the soul of the *Divine Comedy*. The poem is one great hymn to the spiritual and moral order of the universe, in which is seen at every moment the impress of the God who unceasingly informs and upholds it all' (*The Times Dante Supplement*, 14.9.21). 'The moral world is engrafted into the physical in that stupendous concord of all things. . . . All things move, not drifting like flotsam at the mercy of the waves, but like ships steering their course to different ports on the great sea of being' (*G. Mazzoni, L.D.*).

O VOI che siete in piccioletta barca,
  desiderosi d'ascoltar, seguiti
  dietro al mio legno che cantando varca,
tornate a riveder li vostri liti:
  non vi mettete in pelago, chè, forse,
  perdendo me, rimarreste smarriti.
L'acqua ch' io prendo già mai non si corse;
  Minerva spira, e conducemi Apollo,
  e nove Muse mi dimostran l'Orse.
Voi altri pochi che drizzaste il collo   10
  per tempo al pan delli angeli, del quale
  vivesi qui ma non sen vien satollo,
metter potete ben per l'alto sale
  vostro navigio, servando mio solco
  dinanzi all'acqua che ritorna equale.
Que' glorïosi che passaro al Colco
  non s'ammiraron come voi farete,
  quando Iason vider fatto bifolco.
La concreata e perpetüa sete
  del deïforme regno cen portava   20
  veloci quasi come 'l ciel vedete.
Beatrice in suso, e io in lei guardava;
  e forse in tanto in quanto un quadrel posa
  e vola e dalla noce si dischiava,
giunto mi vidi ove mirabil cosa
  mi torse il viso a sè; e però quella
  cui non potea mia cura essere ascosa,

CANTO II

The Sphere of the Moon; the spots on the Moon;
the influences of the heavens

O YE who in a little bark, eager to listen, have
followed behind my ship that singing makes her
way, turn back to see your shores again; do not put
forth on the deep, for, perhaps, losing me, you
would be left bewildered. The waters I take were
never sailed before. Minerva breathes, Apollo pilots
me, and the nine Muses show me the Bears.

Ye other few that reached out early for the angels'
bread by which men here live but never come from
it satisfied,[1] you may indeed put forth your vessel
on the salt depths, holding my furrow before the
water returns smooth again. Those glorious ones
who crossed the sea to Colchis were not amazed
as you shall be, when they saw Jason turned
ploughman.[2]

The inborn and perpetual thirst for the godlike
kingdom bore us away, swift, almost, as your
glance to heaven. Beatrice was gazing upward,
and I on her, and in the time, perhaps, that a bolt
strikes and flies and looses from the catch I saw
that I had come where a marvellous thing drew my
sight to itself. She, therefore, from whom my

volta ver me, sì lieta come bella,
  'Drizza la mente in Dio grata' mi disse,
  'che n' ha congiunti con la prima stella.'   30
Parev' a me che nube ne coprisse
  lucida, spessa, solida e pulita,
  quasi adamante che lo sol ferisse.
Per entro sè l'etterna margarita
  ne ricevette, com'acqua recepe
  raggio di luce permanendo unita.
S' io era corpo, e qui non si concepe
  com' una dimensione altra patìo,
  ch'esser convien se corpo in corpo repe,
accender ne dovrìa più il disio   40
  di veder quella essenza in che si vede
  come nostra natura e Dio s'unìo.
Lì si vedrà ciò che tenem per fede,
  non dimostrato, ma fia per sè noto
  a guisa del ver primo che l'uom crede.
Io rispuosi: 'Madonna, sì devoto
  com'esser posso più, ringrazio lui
  lo qual dal mortal mondo m'ha remoto.
Ma ditemi: che son li segni bui
  di questo corpo, che là giuso in terra   50
  fan di Cain favoleggiare altrui?'
Ella sorrise alquanto, e poi 'S'elli erra
  l'oppinïon' mi disse 'de' mortali
  dove chiave di senso non diserra,
certo non ti dovrìen punger li strali
  d'ammirazione omai, poi dietro ai sensi
  vedi che la ragione ha corte l'ali.
Ma dimmi quel che tu da te ne pensi.'
  E io: 'Ciò che n'appar qua su diverso
  credo che fanno i corpi rari e densi.'   60
Ed ella: 'Certo assai vedrai sommerso
  nel falso il creder tuo, se bene ascolti
  l'argomentar ch' io li farò avverso.
La spera ottava vi dimostra molti
  lumi, li quali e nel quale e nel quanto
  notar si posson di diversi volti.

thought could not be hid turned to me, as happy as she was fair, and said to me: 'Direct thy grateful mind to God, who has brought us to the first star.'[3]

It seemed to me that a cloud covered us, shining, dense, solid and smooth, like a diamond that is smitten by the sun; the eternal pearl received us into itself, as water receives a ray of light and remains unbroken. If I was body—and here we cannot conceive how one bulk admitted another, which must be if body enters into body—it should the more kindle our desire to see His being in whom is seen how our nature was joined to God. There will be seen that which we hold by faith, not demonstrated but known in itself, like the primal truth that man believes.[4]

I replied: 'My Lady, with all the devotion of my heart I give thanks to Him who has taken me from the mortal world. But tell me, what are the dark marks on this body which make men on earth below tell the tale of Cain?'[5]

She smiled a little, then said to me: 'If the judgement of mortals errs where the key of sense fails to unlock, surely the shafts of wonder should not prick thee henceforth, since even following after the senses thou seest that reason's wings are short.[6] But tell me what thou thinkest of it thyself.'

And I: 'That which appears to us diverse up here I suppose to be caused by rare and dense matter.'

And she: 'Assuredly thou shalt see thy belief to be sunk deep in error if thou listen well to the reasons I bring against it.

'The eighth sphere shows you many lights, which both in quality and in magnitude can be seen to be of different aspects, and if rarity and density

Se raro e denso ciò facesser tanto,
   una sola virtù sarebbe in tutti,
   più e men distribuita e altrettanto.
Virtù diverse esser convegnon frutti   70
   di principii formali, e quei, for ch' uno,
   seguiterìeno a tua ragion distrutti.
Ancor, se raro fosse di quel bruno
   cagion che tu dimandi, od oltre in parte
   fora di sua materia sì digiuno
esto pianeta, o sì come comparte
   lo grasso e 'l magro un corpo, così questo
   nel suo volume cangerebbe carte.
Se 'l primo fosse, fora manifesto
   nell'eclissi del sol per trasparere   80
   lo lume come in altro raro ingesto.
Questo non è: però è da vedere
   dell'altro; e s'elli avvien ch' io l'altro cassi,
   falsificato fia lo tuo parere.
S'elli è che questo raro non trapassi,
   esser conviene un termine da onde
   lo suo contrario più passar non lassi;
e indi l'altrui raggio si rifonde
   così come color torna per vetro
   lo qual di retro a sè piombo nasconde.   90
Or dirai tu ch'el si dimostra tetro
   ivi lo raggio più che in altre parti,
   per esser lì refratto più a retro.
Da questa instanza può deliberarti
   esperïenza, se già mai la provi,
   ch'esser suol fonte ai rivi di vostr'arti.
Tre specchi prenderai; e i due rimovi
   da te d'un modo, e l'altro, più rimosso,
   tr'ambo li primi li occhi tuoi ritrovi.
Rivolto ad essi, fa che dopo il dosso   100
   ti stea un lume che i tre specchi accenda
   e torni a te da tutti ripercosso.
Ben che nel quanto tanto non si stenda
   la vista più lontana, lì vedrai
   come convien ch' igualmente risplenda.

alone produced this, one single virtue would be in them all, distributed more and less and equally; different virtues must needs be fruits of formative principles, and it would follow from thy reasoning that these, except one, would be annulled.[7] Again, if rarity were the cause of that dimness of which thou askest, either this planet would be lacking of its matter right through in parts, or else, just as fat and lean are distributed in a body, this would alternate the pages in its volume. In the former case it would be evident in eclipses of the sun by the light showing through as when it is brought into any other rare medium; this is not so, therefore we must look at the other case, and if then I destroy that, thy view will be proved false. If it be that this rarity does not go through, there must be a limit at which its opposite does not let it pass farther, and from that the other's ray is thrown back just as colour returns through glass that conceals lead behind it. Now thou wilt say that the ray shows dim there more than in other parts from being reflected there farther back, and from this objection experiment, if ever thou try it, may free thee,—the spring always of the streams of your arts. Take three mirrors and put two of them at an equal distance from thee, and let the other, farther off, meet thy eyes between the first two; then, turned to them, have a light set behind thy back which kindles the three mirrors and returns to thee struck back by them all. Although the light seen farthest off is not of the same size thou wilt see then that it must shine with equal brightness.[8]

Or come ai colpi delli caldi rai
    della neve riman nudo il suggetto
    e dal colore e dal freddo primai,
così rimaso te nell' intelletto
    voglio informar di luce sì vivace,   110
    che ti tremolerà nel suo aspetto.
Dentro dal ciel della divina pace
    si gira un corpo nella cui virtute
    l'esser di tutto suo contento giace.
Lo ciel seguente, c' ha tante vedute,
    quell'esser parte per diverse essenze,
    da lui distinte e da lui contenute.
Li altri giron per varie differenze
    le distinzion che dentro da sè hanno
    dispongono a lor fini e lor semenze.   120
Questi organi del mondo così vanno,
    come tu vedi omai, di grado in grado,
    che di su prendono e di sotto fanno.
Riguarda bene omai sì com' io vado
    per questo loco al vero che disiri,
    sì che poi sappi sol tener lo guado.
Lo moto e la virtù de' santi giri,
    come dal fabbro l'arte del martello,
    da' beati motor convien che spiri;
e 'l ciel cui tanti lumi fanno bello,   130
    della mente profonda che lui volve
    prende l'image e fassene suggello.
E come l'alma dentro a vostra polve
    per differenti membra e conformate
    a diverse potenze si risolve,
così l'intelligenza sua bontate
    multiplicata per le stelle spiega,
    girando sè sovra sua unitate.
Virtù diversa fa diversa lega
    col prezïoso corpo ch'ella avviva,   140
    nel qual, sì come vita in voi, si lega.
Per la natura lieta onde deriva
    la virtù mista per lo corpo luce
    come letizia per pupilla viva.

'Now, as the substance of the snow, smitten by the warm rays, is left bare both of its former colour and its cold,[9] so I would inform thee, left thus bare in thy mind, with a light so living that it will sparkle in thy sight.

'Within the heaven of the divine peace spins a body in whose virtue lies the being of all that it contains;[10] the next heaven, which has so many sights, distributes that being among different existences, distinct from it and contained in it;[11] the other spheres, by various differences, direct the distinctive qualities which they have in themselves to their ends and fruitful working.[12] These organs of the universe proceed thus, as thou seest now, grade by grade, each receiving from above and operating below. Observe well now how I pass by this way to the truth thou seekest, so that then thou mayst know how to take the ford alone. The motion and the virtue of the holy wheels must derive from the blessed movers,[13] as the craft of the hammer from the smith; and the heaven that so many lights make fair takes its stamp from the profound mind that turns it, and of that stamp becomes itself the seal; and as the soul within your dust is diffused through different members that are adapted to various faculties, so the Intelligence unfolds its bounty, multiplied through the stars, itself wheeling on its own unity.[14] Diverse virtue makes diverse alloy with the precious body which it quickens and with which, even as life in you, it is bound;[15] by the joyous nature whence it springs the mingled virtue shines through the body as

Da essa vien ciò che da luce a luce
par differente, non da denso e raro:
essa è il formal principio che produce,
conforme a sua bontà, lo turbo e 'l chiaro.'

joy through the living pupil. From this comes that difference which appears between light and light, not from density and rarity; this is the formative principle which produces, according to its excellence, the dark and bright.'

1. 'That food which, satisfying with itself, for itself makes appetite' (*Purg.* xxxi).

2. Jason, leader of the Argonauts (*Inf.* xviii), yoked two fire-breathing bulls and ploughed with them.

3. The moon.

4. Axiomatic truth, as: Nothing can be and not be at once.

5. Cain, condemned to carry his bundle of thorns forever, is still to be seen in the moon's marks.

6. Neither the senses nor the flight of reason working on their evidence are able to comprehend heavenly things.

7. If the differences of the stars were only in magnitude, owing to density and rarity, there would be no difference of quality, 'virtue', in them, or in the 'formative principles' shown in their virtues; but they do differ in quality, as their 'different aspects' (such as colours) show.

8. Therefore the spots on the moon are not due to the more distant reflection of the sun's light within it, and the whole theory of 'rare and dense' is mistaken.

9. 'The substance', the matter of the snow 'under-lying' its qualities, i.e. water, snow stripped of the 'accidents' of colour and cold.

10. From the Primum Mobile, spinning within the Empyrean, all the lower spheres and through them all earthly things, derive their natures.

11. The Starry Sphere differentiates the 'virtue' of the Primum Mobile in the constellations and 'distributes' it in the planetary spheres.

12. The influence of the stars and planets on the earth.

13. The angelic orders, 'intelligences', each order controlling one of the heavens, transmit the powers and purposes of the Divine Intelligence to the whole creation, as the hammer derives its force from the smith who wields it.

14. The eighth sphere, that of the fixed stars, is controlled by its 'Intelligence', the Cherubim, who distribute its virtues variously among its stars, while maintaining its unity.

15. The virtues of the constellations make an 'alloy' with the virtue of each planet.

NOTE

The opening lines of the second canto recall the beginning of the *Purgatorio*: 'The little boat of my wit now lifts her sails'. Here, Dante's readers are said to have been following in *their* little bark 'my ship that singing makes its way'. He speaks now with a new assurance and warns those that are still to follow him of the greatness of the enterprise. For in the *Paradiso* he faces his greatest task and imposes their greatest task on his readers. It is a voyage in untracked seas with Dante for its Jason, undertaken with greater daring and for a better prize and showing greater wonders than that for the Golden Fleece. For it he needs and dares to claim the qualifications of wisdom (Minerva), inspiration (Apollo), and artistry (the Muses).

The primal impulse of which Beatrice had spoken and which is here described as 'thirst for the godlike kingdom', quickened in him by the light from Beatrice's eyes, bore them swiftly upward to the sphere of the Moon, and their speed is likened to the instantaneous leap of vision to the sky and to the course of a bolt from the cross-bow; the release, flight, and striking of the mark, being named in reverse order, as if all happened in the same moment. Dante does not, so to speak, *move* from the earth into the heavenly sphere; he *finds himself* in it by an apprehension in which distance is annihilated, 'swift, almost, as your glance to heaven'.

It belongs to the conventions of the *Paradiso* that on each arrival in a new sphere Beatrice and Dante enter not merely the sphere but the heavenly body itself, so that here 'it seemed to me that a cloud covered us'. The account of their interpenetration with the body of the Moon, as of a strange and happy dream, gives the impression of an experience at once unreal and undeniable, at once supernatural and natural to the new conditions; and the newness of it, realizing what was not even conceivable before, seems to him a promise that the last mystery of the Word become flesh will at last be plain as faith passes into sight. For the whole ascent in the *Paradiso* is essentially an account of the perfecting of the soul's vision, and this is indicated here in Dante's characteristic diction—the word *see* three times within three lines, in deepening significance: 'Our desire to see, . . . in whom is seen, . . . there will be seen'. In this first ascent the ultimate Beatific Vision is anticipated and the whole story is one.

Dante's question immediately on their reaching the Moon: 'What are the dark marks on this body?' strikes us as oddly naïve, as if it were merely an irrelevant expression of scientific curiosity. In reality it is far more than that. The discussion of the spots on the Moon becomes a demonstration of the spiritual nature of the universe, which is the meaning of all Dante's astrology. The view that they are caused by density and rarity in the Moon's matter, which he had himself maintained in the *Convito*, is in the first place carefully controverted by Beatrice, by divine truth; then, the ground being cleared, she explains the phenomena by the 'virtues', the powers that operate through the stars, which are in fact the power of God making the heavens, in all their manifoldness, one. The material universe, or any part of it, cannot itself give account of itself; that must come from beyond it, and, especially in these early cantos of the *Paradiso*, Dante needs correction of his measuring of heavenly things by earthly standards.

By the speech of Beatrice in the first canto: 'All things whatsoever have order among themselves', he was instructed in the comprehensive order that is in the nature of things and that works variously in the nature of each thing. Then, in the first part of her speech here: 'The eighth sphere shows you many lights', she disposes of the theory which must now seem to him unwarranted and unspiritual and no better than materialistic; and in the latter part: 'Within the heaven of the divine peace', she gives an account of the universe which derives from the intellectual tradition of Plato and Aristotle, of St Augustine, and of the thirteenth-century schoolmen Albertus Magnus and his greater pupil Aquinas. That is the 'light so living' which she promises him. The three discourses are, characteristically, of almost identical length, and together they offer a typical example of medieval dialectic. The last of them 'is like the remaining part of the hymn which the Poet began to sing in the first canto. There he had celebrated the order of being and the ascent of the creature towards God; here he sings how God descends towards nature. . . . The lines are of doctrine, but Dante's fervour, moved as he shows himself to be before the loftiest mysteries of existence, impresses on them a sense of religious solemnity and of vastness without bound' (*E. G. Parodi, L.D.*).

The being of all creation in its ideal unity is held, as it were, in the Primum Mobile, the sphere which is the frontier of time and space, the sphere of the angelic circles under the immediate divine control; and that unity of being is distributed in the multiplicity of the next heaven, that of the fixed stars, these then 'mingling' their virtues with those of the several planets in their lower spheres and co-operating by conjunction with them. 'All heavenly phenomena are direct utterances of God and of His angels. The undivided power of God, differentiated through the various heavenly bodies and agencies, shines in the diverse quality and brightness of the fixed stars, of the planets, and of the parts of the moon, as the vital principle manifests itself diversely in the several members of the body' (*P. H. Wicksteed*). The angelic orders control by their divine enlightenment the moving heavens, 'these organs of the universe', each higher heaven dispensing its proper influence on the heaven beneath it, and all the various heavenly influences operating variously on earthly creatures and on the temperaments and the lives of men. These starry influences are never regarded by Dante as mere magical or mechanical forces, and he is always on guard against the unspiritual astrological fancies and practices of his time. 'The motion and the virtue of the holy circles must derive from the blessed movers, as the craft of the hammer from the smith', the 'Intelligence'—the controlling angelic order—'unfolding its bounty' in each heaven, as the soul animates our dust. Thus all things have their essential being and quality from above themselves and ultimately from God. The shining of the stars and planets is the utterance and reflection of God's joy in His creation, 'as joy shines

45

through the living pupil', and it is so that the heavens declare the glory of God. It is a great discourse on a small text, and the correction of Dante's old error seems to us strangely disproportionate. But it means that a great part of Dante's—that is, of Everyman's—spiritual recovery is to think spiritually of the whole of things and to know creation as the seamless garment of God. This conception of the universe, at once spiritual and physical, conditions the whole story of the *Paradiso*, and the poet is concerned that his reader should have it clearly before his mind from the beginning.

In the closing lines we are quietly brought back to 'the dark and bright' of the Moon and recalled to the point of the narrative from which we set out.

It is notably characteristic of Dante that more than a third of the canto is occupied with the discussion of a purely scientific question in purely, and prosaically, scientific terms, with the careful account of an experiment with mirrors, and that it is only *after* this negative demonstration that Beatrice rises to her greater subject, the divine order of the universe. This is the first among many illustrations in the *Paradiso* of the doctrine— which Dante owed to Aquinas and Aristotle—that knowledge based on sensible experience and reached by a strictly rational process from that must logically precede all greatness of conception, all assurance of heavenly realities and of the ultimate values which prompt our aspiration and move our hearts to love. It is the same doctrine which is summarily stated by Beatrice in Canto xxviii: 'The state of blessedness rests upon the act of vision, not of love, which follows after.' The doctrine is highly disputable and was, indeed, much disputed in Dante's day, and it was, perhaps, the more stoutly defended by him as the first condition of intellectual integrity and as the manifest teaching of the very order of the heavens. The spots on the moon are, for Dante, Tennyson's 'flower in the crannied wall' to understand which is to 'know what God and man is'.

PARADISO

Quel sol che pria d'amor mi scaldò 'l petto,
 di bella verità m'avea scoverto,
 provando e riprovando, il dolce aspetto;
e io, per confessar corretto e certo
 me stesso, tanto quanto si convenne
 leva' il capo a proferer più erto;
ma visïone apparve che ritenne
 a sè me tanto stretto, per vedersi,
 che di mia confession non mi sovvenne.
Quali per vetri trasparenti e tersi,   10
 o ver per acque nitide e tranquille,
 non sì profonde che i fondi sien persi,
tornan di nostri visi le postille
 debili sì, che perla in bianca fronte
 non vien men tosto alle nostre pupille;
tali vid' io più facce a parlar pronte;
 per ch' io dentro all'error contrario corsi
 a quel ch'accese amor tra l'omo e 'l fonte.
Subito sì com' io di lor m'accorsi,
 quelle stimando specchiati sembïanti,   20
 per veder di cui fosser, li occhi torsi;
e nulla vidi, e ritorsili avanti
 dritti nel lume della dolce guida,
 che, sorridendo, ardea nelli occhi santi.
'Non ti maravigliar perch' io sorrida'
 mi disse 'appresso il tuo pueril coto,
 poi sopra 'l vero ancor lo piè non fida,
ma te rivolve, come suole, a voto:
 vere sustanze son ciò che tu vedi,
 qui rilegate per manco di voto.   30

CANTO III

Faithfulness marred by inconstancy; Piccarda Donati;
the Empress Constance

THAT sun which first warmed my breast with love
had discovered to me, by proof and refutation, fair
truth's sweet aspect, and I raised my head—but
not higher than was need for speech—to confess
myself corrected and assured; but a sight appeared
to me which held me so fast to itself to see it that
of my confession I had no remembrance. As
through smooth and transparent glass, or through
limpid and still water not so deep that the bottom
is lost, the outlines of our faces return so faint that
a pearl on a white brow does not come less quickly
to our eyes, many such faces I saw, eager to speak;
at which I ran into the opposite error to that which
kindled love between the man and the spring.[1]
The moment I was aware of them, taking them for
reflected semblances, I turned my eyes to see whose
they were, and saw nothing, and turned them
forward again straight into the light of my sweet
guide, whose holy eyes were glowing with a
smile.

'Do not wonder' she said to me 'that I smile at
thy childish thought, since it does not yet trust its
foot on the truth but turns thee back, as it is wont,
on vacancy. These are real beings that thou seest,
assigned here for failure in their vows; therefore

Però parla con esse e odi e credi;
   chè la verace luce che li appaga
   da sè non lascia lor torcer li piedi.'
Ed io all'ombra che parea più vaga
   di ragionar drizza'mi, e cominciai,
   quasi com' uom cui troppa voglia smaga:
'O ben creato spirito, che a' rai
   di vita etterna la dolcezza senti
   che, non gustata, non s' intende mai,
grazïoso mi fia se mi contenti   40
   del nome tuo e della vostra sorte.'
   Ond'ella, pronta e con occhi ridenti:
'La nostra carità non serra porte
   a giusta voglia, se non come quella
   che vuol simile a sè tutta sua corte.
I' fui nel mondo vergine sorella;
   e se la mente tua ben sè riguarda,
   non mi ti celerà l'esser più bella,
ma riconoscerai ch' i' son Piccarda,
   che, posta qui con questi altri beati,   50
   beata sono in la spera più tarda.
Li nostri affetti che solo infiammati
   son nel piacer dello Spirito Santo,
   letizian del suo ordine formati.
E questa sorte che par giù cotanto,
   però n'è data, perchè fuor negletti
   li nostri voti, e vòti in alcun canto.'
Ond' io a lei: 'Ne' mirabili aspetti
   vostri risplende non so che divino
   che vi trasmuta da' primi concetti: 60
però non fui a rimembrar festino;
   ma or m'aiuta ciò che tu mi dici,
   sì che raffigurar m'è più latino.
Ma dimmi: voi che siete qui felici,
   disiderate voi più alto loco
   per più vedere e per più farvi amici?'
Con quelle altr'ombre pria sorrise un poco;
   da indi mi rispuose tanto lieta,
   ch'arder parea d'amor nel primo foco:

speak with them and hear and believe, for the true light that gives them peace does not let them turn their steps from itself.'

And I directed myself to the shade that seemed most desirous of speech, and began, all but overcome with excess of eagerness: 'O spirit made for bliss, who in the beams of eternal life knowest the sweetness which, not tasted, never is conceived, it will be a kindness to me if thou satisfy me with thy name and with your lot.'

Then she, eager and with smiling eyes: 'Our charity does not shut the doors against right will, any more than His who wills all His court to be like Himself. In the world I was a virgin sister, and if thou search well in thy memory my being more fair will not hide me from thee, and thou wilt know me again for Piccarda,² who am put here with these other blest and am blest in the slowest of the spheres. Our affections, which are kindled only in the pleasure of the Holy Ghost, rejoice in being conformed to His order, and this lot which seems so low is given us because our vows were neglected and in some part void.'

Then I said to her: 'In your wondrous aspects there shines forth I know not what of divine which transforms you from our former knowledge; that is why I was not quick to remember, but now what thou sayest helps me so that I more clearly recall thy features. But tell me, do you who are happy here desire a higher place, that you may see more and become more dear?'³

With the other shades there she first smiled a little, then answered me with such gladness that she seemed to burn in the first fire of love: 'Brother,

'Frate, la nostra volontà quïeta   70
   virtù di carità, che fa volerne
   sol quel ch'avemo, e d'altro non ci asseta.
Se disïassimo esser più superne,
   foran discordi li nostri disiri
   dal voler di colui che qui ne cerne;
che vedrai non capere in questi giri,
   s'essere in carità è qui *necesse*,
   e se la sua natura ben rimiri.
Anzi è formale ad esto beato esse
   tenersi dentro alla divina voglia,   80
   per ch' una fansi nostre voglie stesse;
sì che, come noi sem di soglia in soglia
   per questo regno, a tutto il regno piace
   com'allo re ch'a suo voler ne invoglia.
E'n la sua volontade è nostra pace:
   ell'è quel mare al qual tutto si move
   ciò ch'ella cria e che natura face.'
Chiaro mi fu allor come ogni dove
   in cielo è paradiso, etsi la grazia
   del sommo ben d'un modo non vi piove.   90
Ma sì com'elli avvien, s'un cibo sazia
   e d'un altro rimane ancor la gola,
   che quel si chere e di quel si ringrazia,
così fec' io con atto e con parola,
   per apprender da lei qual fu la tela
   onde non trasse infino a co la spola.
'Perfetta vita e alto merto inciela
   donna più su' mi disse 'alla cui norma
   nel vostro mondo giù si veste e vela,
perchè fino al morir si vegghi e dorma   100
   con quello sposo ch'ogni voto accetta
   che caritate a suo piacer conforma.
Dal mondo, per seguirla, giovinetta
   fuggi'mi, e nel suo abito mi chiusi,
   e promisi la via della sua setta.
Uomini poi, a mal più ch'a bene usi,
   fuor mi rapiron della dolce chiostra:
   Iddio si sa qual poi mia vita fusi.

the power of charity quiets our will and makes us will only what we have and thirst for nothing else. Did we desire to be more exalted, our desire would be in discord with His will who appoints us here, which thou wilt see cannot hold in these circles if to be in charity is here *necesse*[4] and if thou consider well its nature. Nay, it is the very quality of this blessed state that we keep ourselves within the divine will, so that our wills are themselves made one; therefore our rank from height to height through this kingdom is pleasing to the whole kingdom, as to the King who wills us to His will. And in His will is our peace. It is that sea to which all things move, both what it creates and what nature makes.'[5]

It was clear to me then that everywhere in heaven is Paradise, although the grace of the Supreme Good does not rain there in one measure. But as it happens, when of one food we have enough and the craving for another still remains, that we ask for this and give thanks for that, so I did with speech and gesture, to learn from her what was the web through which she had not drawn the shuttle to the end.[6]

'Perfect life and high desert' she said to me 'place in a higher heaven a lady by whose rule in your world below they take the robe and veil,[7] so that till death they may wake and sleep with that Bridegroom who accepts every vow that charity conforms to His pleasure. To follow her I fled, a young girl, from the world and wrapped me in her habit and promised myself to the way of her order. Then men more used to evil than to good snatched me from the sweet cloister. God knows what my life was then.

E quest'altro splendor che ti si mostra
 dalla mia destra parte e che s'accende   110
 di tutto il lume della spera nostra,
ciò ch' io dico di me di sè intende:
 sorella fu, e così le fu tolta
 di capo l'ombra delle sacre bende.
Ma poi che pur al mondo fu rivolta
 contra suo grado e contra buona usanza,
 non fu dal vel del cor già mai disciolta.
Quest'è la luce della gran Costanza
 che del secondo vento di Soave
 generò il terzo e l'ultima possanza.'   120
Così parlommi, e poi cominciò 'Ave
 Maria' cantando, e cantando vanìo
 come per acqua cupa cosa grave.
La vista mia, che tanto la seguìo
 quanto possibil fu, poi che la perse,
 volsesi al segno di maggior disio,
e a Beatrice tutta si converse;
 ma quella folgorò nel mïo sguardo
 sì che da prima il viso non sofferse;
e ciò mi fece a dimandar più tardo.   130

'And this other splendour that appears to thee on my right and is kindled with all the light of our sphere applies to herself my own story. She was a sister, and in like manner there was taken from her head the shade of the holy wimple; but even after she was turned back to the world against her will and against right custom she was never loosed from the veil on the heart. It is the light of the great Constance, who bore to the second blast of Swabia the third and last potentate.'[8]

She spoke thus to me, then began singing *Ave Maria* and singing vanished, like a weight through deep water. My sight, which followed her as long as it was possible, turned, when it lost her, to the mark of its greater desire and bent itself wholly on Beatrice; but she so flashed on my gaze that at first my eyes could not bear it, which made me slower to question her.

1. Narcissus' error in taking his own reflection in the spring for another person.

2. The sister of Forese and Corso Donati.

3. For closer vision of God and deeper experience of His love.

4. Logical necessity.

5. Direct creations, as human souls, and things produced by nature; both have their final purpose in God.

6. What vow she had neglected.

7. St Clare (early 13th century), founder of the Franciscan Order of the Poor Clares.

8. Constance, presumptive heiress to the crown of Sicily, wife of Henry, the son of the Emperor Frederick Barbarossa and himself afterwards Emperor; their son was Frederick II, who died in 1250 and was regarded by Dante in 1300 as the last true Emperor. These three constituted the Swabian Dynasty.

NOTE

The first line of the canto, 'That sun which first warmed my breast with love', recalls the beginning of *Purgatorio* xxxii, where Dante tells of his eyes 'satisfying their ten years' thirst' with the sight of Beatrice; and both passages are evidence of the spiritual integrity of his experience through the years—except for the period of his forgetfulness—from the time when 'about the end of my ninth year I saw her' and 'love had the lordship of my soul' to this time when, in his impassioned imagination, she was his teacher in heavenly things.

The souls in this sphere, perfected up to the measure of their nature, appear dimly in the Moon's shining substance like reflections in still water, corresponding to something vague and limited in their personalities. And as Narcissus, too credulous, took his reflected face for real, so Dante, too slow of heart to believe, did not know real spirits when he saw them, and he is again corrected for his failure in spiritual perception. He still limits new experience by old and has yet to learn to trust his foot on the truth.

Piccarda Donati was of the family of which we already know something from *Purgatorio* xxiii and xxiv. Forese Donati was Dante's intimate friend with whom he talked on the terrace of gluttony in Purgatory, and Corso Donati was a leader of the Blacks in Florence and Dante's enemy. Piccarda, like Forese, refers to their brother, who had forced her into a hated marriage which she did not long survive, but both Piccarda and Forese, significantly, avoid Corso's name. In reply to Dante's question, 'Where is Piccarda?' Forese had said: 'My sister, of whom I know not if she was more fair or good, already triumphs in high Olympus, blissful in her crown.' The words suggest the glory of a Greek goddess and might almost seem intentionally paradoxical when applied to the gentle and gracious spirit we meet here, 'a fragile white flower from a harsh and blood-stained waste' (*V. Capetti, L.D.*). Piccarda inevitably recalls two earlier figures in the poem, Francesca (*Inf.* v) and La Pia (*Purg.* v). All three were victims of unhappy marriage ending in tragedy, all three were gentle and loving natures brought to their death by the cruelty and violence of a barbarous age, and nowhere else in the whole poem is Dante's lyric sweetness more compelling than in their words. 'The stories of all three are dramatic rather by what they leave for thought than by what they tell, and are so much the more moving in their few lines in which the record of the three unhappy women lives forever and makes eternal the passion of tears in Francesca, the distress and agitation of La Pia, the exultant charity of Piccarda' (*V. Capetti, L.D.*). It is to Piccarda that Dante gives his best-remembered line: 'And in His will is our peace.'

It should be noted that both here and in *Purgatorio* xiii, xiv and xv, on the purgation of envy, Dante uses repeatedly the word *charity*, which is quite infrequent elsewhere in the *Comedy*, rather than the much more familiar *love*. '*Caritas* in medieval theology and philosophy connotes love of God even before love of our neighbour, in so far as the two can be separated' (*G. G. Coulton*). It is love's breadth and inclusiveness, an ardour of affection that is not limited by personal and individual relations, the extreme opposite of envy as of private ambition and personal rivalry. In *Purgatorio* xv we read that 'there'—in the highest sphere—'the more they are who say *ours* the more of good does each possess and the more of charity burns in that cloister', and 'the more charity extends the more does the eternal goodness increase upon it'; and here, 'Brother, the power of charity quiets our will and makes us will only what we have and thirst for nothing else', and 'to be in charity is here *necesse*'.

Another feature in Piccarda's language, as in that of Beatrice in the next canto, is that it harps on the word *will* and its derivatives; they occur eleven times in Piccarda's short speeches here. The limitation, and the temptation, of these souls has been an infirmity of will, by their yielding to which there has been some failure in their vows. Now, 'it is the very quality of this blessed state'—that which makes it to *be* a blessed state—'that we keep ourselves within the divine will'. That is now their will's security. In this order of souls it is 'the King who wills'—more precisely, 'in-wills'—'us to His will. And in His will is our peace.' The last words may well have been suggested by a sentence in St Augustine's *Confessions*: '*In bona voluntate pax nobis est*', itself an echo of the angels' song in *Luke* ii. 14: '*Pax hominibus bonae voluntatis*.' Dante's adaptation of St Augustine—an adaptation with which St Augustine would have no quarrel—is that which is required by Piccarda and, as much, by the whole tenor of the *Paradiso*. Not in the goodness, or rightness, of our will do we find our peace, but only in our will being 'in His'. Dante betters what he borrows.

'The great Constance', Empress a hundred years before Piccarda's time, was the mother of Frederick II (*Inf.* x) and the grandmother of Manfred (*Purg.* iii). The three, like the three Donati, are severally in Hell, Purgatory and Paradise. The story of Constance is obscure, and Dante may have wished to counter the less favourable version of it that was current among the Guelfs. For them, Frederick was another name for Antichrist, and some of the odium was reflected back on his mother.

'With Piccarda we have breathed the air of the convent. Her canto is full of the purest poetry of the medieval cloister, impregnated with the mystical aroma of the fire that burned from Assisi and the Umbrian mountains' (*E. G. Gardner*). Singing *Ave Maria*, the first of the many songs we hear in the *Paradiso*—and Dante's lines sing too—she disappears as strangely and as gently as she had first appeared to him.

INTRA due cibi, distanti e moventi
  d'un modo, prima si morrìa di fame,
  che liber'uomo l'un recasse ai denti;
sì si starebbe un agno intra due brame
  di fieri lupi, igualmente temendo;
  sì si starebbe un cane intra due dame:
per che, s' i' mi tacea, me non riprendo,
  dalli miei dubbi d'un modo sospinto,
  poi ch'era necessario, nè commendo.
Io mi tacea, ma 'l mio disir dipinto   10
  m'era nel viso, e 'l dimandar con ello,
  più caldo assai che per parlar distinto.
Fè sì Beatrice qual fè Danïello,
  Nabuccodonosor levando d'ira,
  che l'avea fatto ingiustamente fello;
e disse: 'Io veggio ben come ti tira
  uno e altro disio, sì che tua cura
  sè stessa lega sì che fuor non spira.
Tu argomenti: "Se 'l buon voler dura,
  la vïolenza altrui per qual ragione   20
  di meritar mi scema la misura?"
Ancor di dubítar ti dà cagione
  parer tornarsi l'anime alle stelle,
  secondo la sentenza di Platone.
Queste son le question che nel tuo velle
  pontano igualmente; e però pria
  tratterò quella che più ha di felle.

CANTO IV

Dante's questions; the souls appearing in the spheres really in the Empyrean; violence no excuse for failure of the will; the intellect's demand for truth

BETWEEN two foods at equal distance and equally tempting a free man would die of hunger before he brought either to his lips—so a lamb would stand between the cravings of two fierce wolves, in equal fear of both—so would a hound stand between two does; therefore if I kept silence, urged equally by my doubts, I neither blame nor commend myself, since it was of necessity. I was silent, but my desire was painted on my face, and with it my question, far more warmly than in plain words.

Beatrice did as did Daniel when he appeased the wrath of Nebuchadnezzar that made him cruelly unjust,[1] and she said: 'I see well how one desire and another draw thee, so that thy eagerness itself binds itself and does not get breath. Thou reasonest: "If the right will endures, on what ground does another's violence lessen the measure of my desert?" Also, it gives thee perplexity that the souls seem to return to the stars, in agreement with Plato's teaching. These are the questions that press equally on thy will. First, then, I shall deal with that which has more poison in it.[2]

De' Serafin colui che più s' india,
    Moïsè, Samuèl, e quel Giovanni
    che prender vuoli, io dico, non Maria,   30
non hanno in altro cielo i loro scanni
    che questi spirti che mo t'appariro,
    nè hanno all'esser lor più o meno anni;
ma tutti fanno bello il primo giro,
    e differentemente han dolce vita
    per sentir più e men l'etterno spiro.
Qui si mostraron, non perchè sortita
    sia questa spera lor, ma per far segno
    della celestïal c' ha men salita.
Così parlar conviensi al vostro ingegno,   40
    però che solo da sensato apprende
    ciò che fa poscia d' intelletto degno.
Per questo la Scrittura condescende
    a vostra facultate, e piedi e mano
    attribuisce a Dio, ed altro intende;
e Santa Chiesa con aspetto umano
    Gabrïel e Michel vi rappresenta,
    e l'altro che Tobia rifece sano.
Quel che Timeo dell'anime argomenta
    non è simile a ciò che qui si vede,   50
    però che, come dice, par che senta.
Dice che l'alma alla sua stella riede,
    credendo quella quindi esser decisa
    quando natura per forma la diede;
e forse sua sentenza è d'altra guisa
    che la voce non suona, ed esser puote
    con intenzion da non esser derisa.
S'elli intende tornare a queste ruote
    l'onor della influenza e 'l biasmo, forse
    in alcun vero suo arco percuote.   60
Questo principio, male inteso, torse
    già tutto il mondo quasi, sì che Giove,
    Mercurio e Marte a nominar trascorse.
L'altra dubitazion che ti commove
    ha men velen, però che sua malizia
    non ti porìa menar da me altrove.

'Not he of the Seraphim that is most made one with God, not Moses, Samuel, or whichever John thou wilt—none, not Mary herself, have their seat in other heaven from these spirits that have now appeared to thee, nor for their being have more years or fewer; but all make fair the first circle and hold sweet life in different measure as they feel more and less the eternal breath.[3] These have shown themselves here, not that this sphere is allotted to them, but in sign of the heavenly rank that is least exalted. It is necessary to speak thus to your faculty, since only from sense perception does it grasp that which it then makes fit for the intellect.[4] For this reason Scripture condescends to your capacity and attributes hands and feet to God, having another meaning, and Holy Church represents to you with human aspect Gabriel and Michael and the other who made Tobit whole again.[5] What Timaeus argues about the souls is not like that which we see here; for what he says he seems to hold for truth. He says the soul returns to its own star, from which he believes it to have been separated when nature gave it for a form;[6] but perhaps his view is other than his words express and may have a meaning not to be despised. If he means the return to these wheels of the honour and the blame of their influence, his bow perhaps strikes on a certain truth. This principle, ill-understood, once misled almost the whole world, so that it went astray, naming them Jupiter and Mercury and Mars.[7]

'The other doubt that troubles thee has less poison, because its mischief could not lead thee away from me. That our justice appears unjust in

63

Parere ingiusta la nostra giustizia
   nelli occhi de' mortali, è argomento
   di fede e non d'eretica nequizia.
Ma perchè puote vostro accorgimento   70
   ben penetrare a questa veritate,
   come disiri, ti farò contento.
Se vïolenza è quando quel che pate
   nïente conferisce a quel che sforza,
   non fuor quest'alme per essa scusate;
chè volontà, se non vuol, non s'ammorza,
   ma fa come natura face in foco,
   se mille volte vïolenza il torza.
Per che, s'ella si piega assai o poco,
   segue la forza; e così queste fero,   80
   possendo rifuggir nel santo loco.
Se fosse stato lor volere intero,
   come tenne Lorenzo in su la grada,
   e fece Muzio alla sua man severo,
così l'avrìa ripinte per la strada
   ond'eran tratte, come fuoro sciolte;
   ma così salda voglia è troppo rada.
E per queste parole, se ricolte
   l' hai come dei, è l'argomento casso
   che t'avrìa fatto noia ancor più volte.   90
Ma or ti s'attraversa un altro passo
   dinanzi alli occhi, tal, che per te stesso
   non usciresti, pria saresti lasso.
Io t' ho per certo nella mente messo
   ch'alma beata non porìa mentire,
   però ch'è sempre al primo vero appresso;
e poi potesti da Piccarda udire
   che l'affezion del vel Costanza tenne;
   sì ch'ella par qui meco contradire.
Molte fïate già, frate, addivenne   100
   che, per fuggir periglio, contra grato
   si fè di quel che far non si convenne;
come Almeone, che, di ciò pregato
   dal padre suo, la propria madre spense,
   per non perder pietà, si fè spietato.

the eyes of mortals is evidence of faith, not of heretical wickedness; but since your understanding is well able to enter into this truth I shall content thee as thou desirest.[8] If violence is when he that suffers takes no part with him that enforces, these souls were not excused on that account. For will, if it will not, is not quenched, but does as nature does in fire though violence wrench it aside a thousand times; therefore if it bends much or little it seconds the force, and these did so when they might have fled back to the holy place. If their will had been unbroken, like that which kept Lawrence on the grid and made Mucius stern to his own hand,[9] then, as soon as they were free, it would have driven them back on the path from which they had been dragged; but will so firm is rare indeed. And by these words, if thou hast rightly taken them in, the reasoning is quashed that would often have troubled thee still.

'But now another hard place lies across the way before thine eyes, such that thou wouldst not get past it by thyself before being exhausted. I have set it surely in thy mind that a soul in bliss cannot lie, since it is always near the primal truth, and then thou couldst hear from Piccarda that Constance kept her love for the veil; so that here she seems to contradict me. Many a time ere now, brother, has it happened that unwillingly, for escape from danger, that has been done which ought not to have been done; as Alcmaeon, urged by his father, slew his own mother and, not to fail in piety, turned pitiless.[10] At this point, I would have thee

65

A questo punto voglio che tu pense
 che la forza al voler si mischia, e fanno
 sì che scusar non si posson l'offense.
Voglia assoluta non consente al danno;
 ma consentevi in tanto in quanto teme,   110
 se si ritrae, cadere in più affanno.
Però, quando Piccarda quello spreme,
 della voglia assoluta intende, e io
 dell'altra; sì che ver diciamo inseme.'
Cotal fu l'ondeggiar del santo rio
 ch' uscì del fonte ond'ogni ver deriva;
 tal puose in pace uno e altro disio.
'O amanza del primo amante, o diva,'
 diss' io appresso 'il cui parlar m' inonda
 e scalda sì, che più e più m'avviva,   120
non è l'affezïon mia sì profonda,
 che basti a render voi grazia per grazia;
 ma quei che vede e puote a ciò risponda.
Io veggio ben che già mai non si sazia
 nostro intelletto, se 'l ver non lo illustra
 di fuor dal qual nessun vero si spazia.
Posasi in esso come fera in lustra,
 tosto che giunto l' ha; e giugner pòllo:
 se non, ciascun disio sarebbe frustra.
Nasce per quello, a guisa di rampollo,   130
 a piè del vero il dubbio; ed è natura
 ch'al sommo pinge noi di collo in collo.
Questo m' invita, questo m'assicura
 con reverenza, donna, a dimandarvi
 d'un'altra verità che m'è oscura.
Io vo' saper se l'uom può sodisfarvi
 ai voti manchi sì con altri beni,
 ch'alla vostra statera non sien parvi.'
Beatrice mi guardò con li occhi pieni
 di faville d'amor così divini,   140
 che, vinta, mia virtute diè le reni,
e quasi mi perdei con li occhi chini.

reflect, force mixes with the will and they so
operate that the offences cannot be excused. The
absolute will does not consent to the wrong, but
the will consents in so far as it fears, by drawing
back, to fall into more trouble; Piccarda, therefore,
in what she says, means the absolute will, and I the
other, so that we both speak truth.'[11]

Such was the rippling of the holy stream that
issued from the fount from which springs every
truth, and it set at rest the one desire and the
other.

'O beloved of the First Lover,' I said then 'divine
one whose speech so floods and warms me that
I am quickened more and more, not all the depth
of my affection is sufficient to render you grace
for grace; but may He recompense it who sees and
can. I see well that our intellect is never satisfied
unless the truth enlighten it beyond which no truth
can range.   In that it rests as soon as it gains it,
like a beast in its lair; and it can gain it, else every
desire were vain. Doubt, therefore, like a shoot,
springs from the root of the truth, and it is nature
that urges us to the summit from height to height.
It is this, Lady, that invites and emboldens me to
ask you with reverence of another truth that is
obscure to me; I would know if a man can so
satisfy you with other good works for vows unful-
filled that in your balance they will not come
short.'

Beatrice looked at me with eyes so full of the
sparkling of love and so divine that my power,
overcome, took flight and, with eyes cast down,
I was almost lost.

1. Daniel told Nebuchadnezzar both his dream and the interpretation of it (*Dan*. ii. 24–45).

2. More danger of heresy.

3. The angels and all redeemed souls are in the Empyrean, 'the first circle', for eternity.

4. According to Aquinas all human knowledge derives from sense impressions, images formed from which are then handled by the intellect.

5. The archangel Raphael, who enabled Tobias to cure his father Tobit's blindness (*Tob*. xi. 2–15).

6. In Plato's myth of creation in the *Timaeus* he teaches that the soul leaves its native star when, at its birth on earth, nature gives it to *inform* the body, and at death, if it has lived well, it returns to its star again. For 'form' cp. *Par*. i, Note 13.

7. The truth that men are influenced by the stars led them, all but the Hebrews, to identify the planets with the false gods.

8. 'Mortals would not trouble themselves concerning the justice of God unless they had faith in it. These perplexities are then arguments or proofs of faith' (*C. E. Norton*).

9. St Lawrence, who was roasted to death on a gridiron, and Mucius Scaevola, who held his right hand in the flames because it had failed to stab Lars Porsena, the enemy of Rome.

10. Alcmaeon avenged his father Amphiaraus's death on his mother Eriphyle; cp· *Inf*. xx and *Purg*. xii. *Pietà* may mean either piety—here, filial loyalty—or pity.

11. Aristotle and Aquinas distinguish between the absolute and the conditioned will. With her absolute will Constance still chose the cloister, even when, with her conditioned will, she yielded to violence against it.

NOTE

The fourth and part of the fifth canto are largely occupied with questions which concern the liberty, the autonomy, and the destiny of the soul, and in a sort of pedantic playfulness Dante, perplexed with questions, begins with the logical dilemma of the equally divided will, a dilemma as ancient as Aristotle and as modern as Aquinas and popularly known as the problem of Buridan's ass—the ass that cannot decide between two bundles of hay. This preface to his subject, of an apparently disproportionate length, may well represent the reflections in which humanity finds excuses for the failure of its will. Can we be blamed on account of 'others' violence'? Can we shake from us the yoke of inauspicious stars to which we belong by birth and destiny and which stamp us with our temperament as with a seal? They are real questions, and not least when they are unspoken. Beatrice tells him both his questions and their answers—the truth *justifies* his questioning—and she takes first that which most directly concerns the nature of the 'free man', the question of the soul's liberty, which is its life. No subject is more central in Dante's thinking.

Plato's doctrine, as Dante understood it, making human souls begin and end in the stars and seeming to put them in bonds to a material universe, is a part of that unspiritual teaching against which the whole of the *Divine Comedy* is Dante's contention. With a solemn emphasis ('Not he of the Seraphim that is most made one with God', etc.) Beatrice declares to him that the appearance of these souls in the Moon's sphere, so far from confirming Plato's teaching, corrects it; that they appear there only by way of accommodation to Dante's human limitations and in sign of their lower rank of blessedness; and that in reality they are now and forever in the Empyrean along with the greatest of the angels and the saints and 'Mary herself', in the eternal divine presence in which they have their life. Redemption is never less than redemption, the final fellowship, a blessedness which fills each soul up to the measure of its capacity, greater or less.

Dante's attitude to Plato is interesting. He was familiar with the tradition of Plato's greatness, and Plato himself, Socrates his master, and Aristotle his pupil, are named in Limbo first among the great thinkers of antiquity (*Inf.* iv); but he knew very little of Plato's writings, perhaps only the *Timaeus*, the dialogue on natural science, and that only through an imperfect Latin version, at a time when very few in western Christendom knew more. (It would be tempting, if it were not quite vain, to try to imagine what Dante would have been if he had known Plato—his far nearer kinsman—as he knew Aristotle.) It is with something of deference and diffidence that Beatrice differs from Plato, and in spite of that difference it was on the suggestion of the Platonic teaching that Dante laid out a great part of the scheme of his Paradise, making the souls of the redeemed appear in the successive material heavens. He 'makes use as a poet of the Platonic theory which he attacks as a Christian. . . . That which in Plato is set down as a fact is in Dante a symbolical appearance, but as background or underlying device it comes to the same thing' (*G. Albini*, *L.D.*). 'It is thus that Dante has been able to reconcile his theology and his art. The theological Paradise is spirit, beyond sense and imagination and intellect; Dante gives it a human aspect, rendering it sensible and intelligible. The souls smile, sing, talk, as men, and this renders Paradise accessible to art' (*F. de Sanctis*). In effect, it is the souls themselves in their after-life that Dante meets with from heaven to heaven, while he never allows us to forget that these are in their final bliss, the immediate presence of God. It has been suggested that 'the concern which Dante shows here to excuse his own invention betrays the suspicion of accusations to which it might lend itself' (*N. Zingarelli*).

'The souls appear to us in the spheres as we have been able to judge of them in the world according to our human knowledge of them, the artificers, by their virtues and vices, of their own destiny; in the Empyrean there rules essentially the work and the will of God. . . . Human will, not having a bodily organ, is immune from the influences of the heavens and is able to contend with nature, to dominate it, to raise itself high above it, but not to destroy it, not to cause that I become another I, that the psychological constitution of the individual change its congenital and indelible character. Individuality—in Dante's philosophical system, which is that of Aristotle and Aquinas—is given by the body, that is by nature, that is, in the last analysis, by the stars; and the souls, appearing in the stars, tacitly affirm that they owe to these their individual imprint, manifested in their particular virtues. . . . In the spheres man is, as it were, analysed into his three fundamental elements' (*E. G. Parodi*). These fundamental elements are: *nature*, his original individual temperament, his given psychological outfit, *freewill*, God's direct gift to man in his creation, and *grace*, divinely co-operating with the rightly-disposed will and at last wholly dominating the obedient soul. Man, therefore, in his essential freedom and in his capacity for the divine fellowship, is the creature, not of nature, but of God. 'To a greater power and to a better nature you, free, are subject' (*Purg*. xvi).

The other questions raised in Dante's mind, of the responsibility of these souls for their yielding to violence, and of the faithfulness of Constance in spite of her failure, are really one, and both are occupied, like the first question, with the fundamental nature of the soul's freedom. The reply to them, elaborated by Beatrice in the scholastic fashion, is summed up in a single characteristic stanza: 'Will, if it will not, is not quenched, but does as nature does in fire though violence wrench it aside a thousand times.'

It is his sense of the height of this doctrine of the free and erect will as the divine and dominant element of the soul that moves Dante to his outburst of praise and thanks to Beatrice, the 'beloved of the First Lover', whose speech floods and warms him.

In the closing passage of the canto the autonomy of the will is linked with the equally sacred autonomy of the mind in its persistent quest after 'the truth beyond which no truth can range'—the all-inclusive truth of God—and Dante multiplies his images (and mixes his metaphors!) to repeat and enforce his meaning. The striving intellect, reaching the truth, 'rests like a beast in its lair', and meantime it carries in itself the assurance that it can reach it; its ever-new doubts spring from the truth, like the shoots from a tree-trunk, by its very vitality; it is driven by its nature, like a mountain-climber, from one height to another up to the great summit. And at his further question, Beatrice, the truth itself, shines on him with a new splendour.

'S'ɪo ti fiammeggio nel caldo d'amore
 di là dal modo che 'n terra si vede,
 sì che delli occhi tuoi vinco il valore,
non ti maravigliar; chè ciò procede
 da perfetto veder, che, come apprende,
 così nel bene appreso move il piede.
Io veggio ben sì come già resplende
 nell' intelletto tuo l'etterna luce,
 che, vista, sola e sempre amore accende;
e s'altra cosa vostro amor seduce,   10
 non è se non di quella alcun vestigio,
 mal conosciuto, che quivi traluce.
Tu vuo' saper se con altro servigio,
 per manco voto, si può render tanto
 che l'anima sicuri di letigio.'
Sì cominciò Beatrice questo canto;
 e sì com' uom che suo parlar non spezza,
 continuò così 'l processo santo:
'Lo maggior don che Dio per sua larghezza
 fesse creando ed alla sua bontate   20
 più conformato e quel ch'e' più apprezza,
fu della volontà la libertate;
 di che le creature intelligenti,
 e tutte e sole, fuoro e son dotate.
Or ti parrà, se tu quinci argomenti,
 l'alto valor del voto, s'è sì fatto
 che Dio consenta quando tu consenti;
chè, nel fermar tra Dio e l'uomo il patto,
 vittima fassi di questo tesoro,
 tal quale io dico; e fassi col suo atto. 30

CANTO V

*The sanctity of vows; the Sphere of Mercury;
service marred by ambition*

'If I glow on thee with the flame of love beyond
all that is seen on earth so that I overcome the
power of thine eyes, do not marvel, for it comes
from perfect vision, which, as it apprehends,
moves towards the apprehended good. I see well
how there shines now in thy mind the eternal light
which, seen, alone and always kindles love; and if
aught else beguile your love it is nothing but some
trace of this, ill-understood, that shines through
there. Thou wouldst know if with other service
it is possible so to make good for a vow unfulfilled
that the soul is secure from challenge.'

Thus Beatrice began this canto and, like one who
would not interrupt his speech, continued thus her
holy theme: 'The greatest gift that God in His
bounty made in creation, the most conformable
to His goodness and the one He accounts the most
precious, was the freedom of the will, with which
the creatures with intelligence, all and only these,
were and are endowed. Now will appear to thee,
reasoning from this, the high worth of the vow, if
it be such that God consents when thou consentest;
for in the establishing of the compact between God
and man this treasure, being such as I have said,
becomes the sacrifice, and that by its own act.

75

Dunque che render puossi per ristoro?
 Se credi bene usar quel c' hai offerto,
 di mal tolletto vuo' far buon lavoro.
Tu se' omai del maggior punto certo;
 ma perchè Santa Chiesa in ciò dispensa,
 che par contra lo ver ch' i' t' ho scoverto,
convienti ancor sedere un poco a mensa,
 però che 'l cibo rigido c' hai preso,
 richiede ancora aiuto a tua dispensa.
Apri la mente a quel ch' io ti paleso   40
 e fermalvi entro; chè non fa scïenza,
 sanza lo ritenere, avere inteso.
Due cose si convegnono all'essenza
 di questo sacrificio: l'una è quella
 di che si fa; l'altr' è la convenenza.
Quest' ultima già mai non si cancella
 se non servata; ed intorno di lei
 sì preciso di sopra si favella:
però necessità fu alli Ebrei
 pur l'offerere, ancor ch'alcuna offerta   50
 si permutasse, come saver dei.
L'altra, che per materia t'è aperta,
 puote ben esser tal, che non si falla
 se con altra materia si converta.
Ma non trasmuti carco alla sua spalla
 per suo arbitrio alcun, sanza la volta
 e della chiave bianca e della gialla;
e ogni permutanza credi stolta,
 se la cosa dimessa in la sorpresa
 come 'l quattro nel sei non è raccolta.   60
Però qualunque cosa tanto pesa
 per suo valor che tragga ogni bilancia,
 sodisfar non si può con altra spesa.
Non prendan li mortali il voto a ciancia:
 siate fedeli, e a ciò far non bieci,
 come Ieptè alla sua prima mancia;
cui più si convenìa dicer "Mal feci",
 che, servando, far peggio; e così stolto
 ritrovar puoi il gran duca de' Greci,

What then can be given in its place? If thou think to use well that which thou hast offered, thou wouldst do good works with ill-got gains.

'Thou art now assured on the chief point; but since Holy Church gives dispensations in this matter—which seems contrary to the truth I have declared to thee—thou must sit a little longer at the table, for the tough food thou hast taken requires more help for thy digestion of it. Open thy mind to what I lay before thee and hold it fast there, for to have heard without retaining does not make knowledge. Two things belong to the essence of this sacrifice; the one is that of which it is made, the other is the compact itself. This last is never annulled except by fulfilment, and it is of this I spoke just now so precisely; therefore necessity was upon the Hebrews still to make an offering, though some offerings might be changed, as thou must know.[1] The other part, explained to thee as the matter of the vow, may indeed be such that there is no fault if it is exchanged for other matter; but let no one shift the burden on his shoulder by his own choice without the turning of both the white and the yellow key;[2] and let every exchange be reckoned vain unless the thing laid down is contained in that taken up as four in six. Whatever, therefore, is of such worth that it weighs down every balance cannot be made good by other outlay.[3] Let not mortals take vows lightly. Be faithful, and with that be not perverse, like Jephthah in his first offering,[4] who ought rather to have said "I did ill" than, keeping faith, to do worse; and thou canst find the same folly in the great leader of the Greeks because of which Iphigenia lamented

onde pianse Ifigenia il suo bel volto,   70
   e fè pianger di sè i folli e i savi
   ch' udir parlar di così fatto colto.
Siate, Cristiani, a muovervi più gravi:
   non siate come penna ad ogni vento,
   e non crediate ch'ogni acqua vi lavi.
Avete il novo e 'l vecchio Testamento,
   e 'l pastor della Chiesa che vi guida:
   questo vi basti a vostro salvamento.
Se mala cupidigia altro vi grida,
   uomini siate, e non pecore matte,   80
   sì che 'l Giudeo di voi tra voi non rida!
Non fate com'agnel che lascia il latte
   della sua madre, e semplice e lascivo
   seco medesmo a suo piacer combatte!'
Così Beatrice a me com' ïo scrivo;
   poi si rivolse tutta disïante
   a quella parte ove 'l mondo è più vivo.
Lo suo tacere e 'l trasmutar sembiante
   puoser silenzio al mio cupido ingegno,
   che già nuove questioni avea davante;   90
e sì come saetta che nel segno
   percuote pria che sia la corda queta,
   così corremmo nel secondo regno.
Quivi la donna mia vid' io sì lieta,
   come nel lume di quel ciel si mise,
   che più lucente se ne fè 'l pianeta.
E se la stella si cambiò e rise,
   qual mi fec' io che pur da mia natura
   trasmutabile son per tutte guise!
Come 'n peschiera ch'è tranquilla e pura   100
   traggonsi i pesci a ciò che vien di fori
   per modo che lo stimin lor pastura,
sì vid' io ben più di mille splendori
   trarsi ver noi, ed in ciascun s' udìa:
   'Ecco chi crescerà li nostri amori.'
E sì come ciascuno a noi venìa,
   vedeasi l'ombra piena di letizia
   nel fulgor chiaro che di lei uscìa.

her own fair face and made lament for her both wise and simple who heard the tale of such a rite.[5] Be graver, Christians, in your undertakings. Be not like feathers in every wind, and think not that every water will wash you clean. You have the New Testament and the Old, and the Shepherd of the Church to guide you; let that suffice for your salvation. If wicked greed call to you aught else, be men, not senseless sheep, that the Jew in your midst make not a jest of you.[6] Be not like the lamb that leaves its mother's milk and, silly and wanton, fights with itself at its pleasure.'

Thus, in the words I write, Beatrice spoke to me, then turned, full of longing, to the part where the universe is brightest.[7] Her falling silent and her changed look imposed silence on my eager mind, which already had new questions before it; and, like an arrow that strikes the mark before the cord is still, we sped into the second realm. Here I saw my Lady so joyful when she passed into that heaven's light that the planet turned brighter for it; and if the star changed and smiled, what did I become who by my very nature am subject to every kind of change?

As in a fish-pool that is calm and clear the fish draw to that which comes from outside, taking it to be their food, so I saw plainly more than a thousand splendours draw towards us, and in each I heard: 'Lo one who will increase our loves!'[8] And as each shade came near it appeared to be full of happiness, by the bright effulgence that came forth from it.

Pensa, lettor, se quel che qui s' inizia
   non procedesse, come tu avresti   110
   di più savere angosciosa carizia;
e per te vederai come da questi
   m'era in disio d'udir lor condizioni,
   sì come alli occhi mi fur manifesti.
'O bene nato a cui veder li troni
   del triunfo etternal concede grazia
   prima che la milizia s'abbandoni,
del lume che per tutto il ciel si spazia
   noi semo accesi; e però, se disii
   di noi chiarirti, a tuo piacer ti sazia.'   120
Così da un di quelli spirti pii
   detto mi fu; e da Beatrice: 'Dì dì
   sicuramente, e credi come a dii.'
'Io veggio ben sì come tu t'annidi
   nel proprio lume, e che delli occhi il traggi,
   perch'e' corusca sì come tu ridi;
ma non so chi tu se', nè perchè aggi,
   anima degna, il grado della spera
   che si vela a' mortai con altrui raggi.'
Questo diss' io diritto alla lumera   130
   che pria m'avea parlato; ond'ella fessi
   lucente più assai di quel ch'ell'era.
Sì come il sol che si cela elli stessi
   per troppa luce, come 'l caldo ha rose
   le temperanze di vapori spessi;
per più letizia sì mi si nascose
   dentro al suo raggio la figura santa;
   e così chiusa chiusa mi rispose
nel modo che 'l seguente canto canta.

Think, reader, if this beginning went no further how keenly thou wouldst crave to know the rest, and thou shalt see for thyself what desire I had to hear from them of their state as soon as they were plain to my eyes.

'O born for good, to whom grace has given to see the thrones of the eternal triumph before thy warfare is ended, we are kindled by the light that extends through all heaven; therefore if thou desire to be enlightened about us, satisfy thyself at thy pleasure.' This was said to me by one of those devout spirits; and by Beatrice: 'Speak, speak with confidence, and trust them even as gods.'

'I see well how thou nestest in thine own light, and that thou drawest it from thine eyes, since it sparkles whenever thou smilest;[9] but I know not who thou art, nor why, good spirit, thou hast thy rank in the sphere that is veiled to mortals in another's beams.'[10] I said this, directing myself to the radiance that had first spoken to me, and it then became far brighter than before. Like the sun, which itself conceals itself by excess of light when the heat has gnawed away the dense tempering vapours, so with increase of happiness the holy form hid itself from me within its own beams and thus all enclosed answered me in the manner the next canto chants.

1. 'If a man will at all redeem ought of his tithes, he shall add thereto the fifth part thereof' (*Lev.* xxvii. 31).

2. The silver key of priestly wisdom and the golden of priestly authority; cp. *Purg.* ix.

3. As in vows of monastic celibacy and obedience.

4. 'And Jephthah vowed a vow unto the Lord, and said, If thou shalt without fail deliver the children of Ammon into mine hands, then it shall be, that whatsoever cometh forth of the doors of my house to meet me . . . I will offer it up for a burnt offering. . . . And, behold, his daughter came out to meet him' (*Jud.* xi. 30–34).

5. Agamemnon, to gain favouring winds for the expedition against Troy, offered Iphigenia his daughter in sacrifice to Diana.

6. 'If ignorant and unauthorized "pardoners" and others tempt you to lighthearted vows and offer you easy terms of remission, do not be so senseless as to be misled by them' (*P. H. Wicksteed*).

7. To the sun and the Empyrean.

8. 'The more souls that are enamoured there above the more there are to be rightly loved and the more love there is and like a mirror the one returns it to the other' (*Purg.* xv).

9. 'What is a smile but a sparkling of the soul's delight, a light appearing without according to what is within?' (*Convito*).

10. The planet Mercury, hidden in the light of the sun.

NOTE

Between Dante's question about the commutation of vows near the end of the fourth canto and the reply of Beatrice in the fifth there occurs an account of the increased brightness of her eyes which might seem merely a picturesque interlude. But her shining look follows immediately on his question as if it were itself the reply to it, and the whole intervening passage is pointedly connected with her answer; she continued, 'like one who would not interrupt his speech'.

Dante has asked 'if a man can so satisfy you with other good works for vows unfulfilled that in your balance they will not come short', where 'your balance' means the standard of the heavenly court, the measure of divine truth; and of divine truth the eyes of Beatrice are the demonstration. They shine now with what she is now to tell, and she first establishes 'the high worth of the vow'—a vow to which 'God consents'—as no mere bargain between layman and churchman, but a 'compact between God and man', a grave and significant committal of the will, whose significance springs from the nature of the soul and from God's greatest gift in creation, the gift of freewill. Shocked by the 'wicked greed' of the 'pardoners' who accept and cancel the vows of the faithful for their own profit, on the one hand, and by the childish and helpless superstitions of the people, on the other—'Be men, not senseless sheep'—, she sets the whole question of vows and their authority in 'the eternal light which, seen, alone and always kindles love'. It is in that context and reference that the new brightness of Beatrice is to be understood. She is the light of God in whom Dante sees light. It is that light that 'kindles love'; for the essential priority of knowledge to love is a presupposition of the whole scheme of the *Paradiso*. 'Vision, as it apprehends, moves towards the apprehended good.'

In a religious vow, particularly in a monastic vow, the will gives up the will, as the victim's life is laid down on the altar, and the will cannot will itself back to itself, and all light vowing and light remission of vows is an impiety against this most sacred gift.

Dante's plea is for reality and reasonableness in religious practice, and it is noteworthy that, with all the rigour of his teaching on the sanctity of a vow rightly made and accepted, he is in one respect more liberal and more reasonable than his master Aquinas. 'Notwithstanding his deep veneration for St Thomas, Dante, endowed as he was with a spirit of independence and with a mind devoted in the extreme to ratiocination, did not always agree with him. . . . He dissents from St Thomas, for whom the doing of a thing by vow was better and more meritorious than the doing of the same thing without a vow, and he insists that vowing is not necessary to salvation and that in the making of vows men should proceed with the utmost caution. . . . Living in the world and seeing the wretched consequences of the extreme facility with which vows were made, he regards the matter on its practical side; while Aquinas, living between the walls of the cloister, regarded it purely as a matter of theory' (*A. Zardo, L.D.*). Arguing in the *Convito* that matrimony is no bar to the devout life, Dante says: 'In religion, God requires nothing of us but the heart.'

Choosing his examples, as usual, from Scripture and from paganism, Dante finds a 'perverse' faithfulness in Jephthah's and Agamemnon's keeping of their bad vows. Under the conditions of his time and the inevitable limitations of his outlook, he takes the subject of vows, commonly regarded as a mere matter of ecclesiastical arrangement, and bases upon it his high argument for reverence, for plain human values, and for moral realism in religion. How strongly Dante felt on such subjects is plain in the accumulated brief imperatives of Beatrice and in the emphasis in the lines immediately following: 'Thus, in the words I write, Beatrice spoke to me, then turned, full of longing, to the part where the universe is brightest.'

The ascent to the second sphere will be considered with the next canto.

PARADISO

'Poscia che Costantin l'aquila volse
  contr' al corso del ciel, ch'ella seguìo
  dietro all'antico che Lavina tolse,
cento e cent'anni e più l' uccel di Dio
  nello stremo d' Europa si ritenne,
  vicino a' monti de' quai prima uscìo;
e sotto l'ombra delle sacre penne
  governò 'l mondo lì di mano in mano,
  e, sì cangiando, in su la mia pervenne.
Cesare fui e son Giustinïano,   10
  che, per voler del primo amor ch' i' sento,
  d'entro le leggi trassi il troppo e 'l vano.
E prima ch' io all'ovra fossi attento,
  una natura in Cristo esser, non piùe,
  credea, e di tal fede era contento;
ma il benedetto Agapito, che fue
  sommo pastore, alla fede sincera
  mi dirizzò con le parole sue.
Io li credetti; e ciò che 'n sua fede era,
  vegg' io or chiaro sì, come tu vedi   20
  ogni contradizione e falsa e vera.
Tosto che con la Chiesa mossi i piedi,
  a Dio per grazia piacque di spirarmi
  l'alto lavoro, e tutto 'n lui mi diedi;
e al mio Belisar commendai l'armi,
  cui la destra del ciel fu sì congiunta,
  che segno fu ch' i' dovessi posarmi.

CANTO VI

Justinian; the flight of the Eagle; Romeo

AFTER Constantine turned back the Eagle against
the course of heaven which it had followed behind
him of old that took Lavinia to wife, for two hundred
years and more the bird of God remained on the
bounds of Europe, near the mountains from which
it first came forth;[1] and there it ruled the world
under the shadow of the sacred wings, passing from
hand to hand, and, so changing, came into mine.
I was Caesar and am Justinian, who, by will of the
Primal Love which moves me, removed from the
laws what was superfluous and vain.[2] And before
I had put my mind to the work I believed that there
was but one nature, and not a second, in Christ,
and with that faith I was satisfied;[3] but the blessed
Agapetus, who was Chief Shepherd, directed me
by his words to the true faith. I believed him, and
what he held by faith I now see as clearly as thou
seest that every contradiction is of false and true.[4]
As soon as I took my way beside the Church it
pleased God, of His grace, to inspire me with the
high task; and I gave myself wholly to it and com-
mitted arms to my Belisarius, with whom the right
hand of heaven was so joined that it was a sign for
me to rest from them.[5]

Or qui alla question prima s'appunta
 la mia risposta; ma sua condizione
 mi stringe a seguitare alcuna giunta, 30
perchè tu veggi con quanta ragione
 si move contr'al sacrosanto segno
 e chi 'l s'appropria e chi a lui s'oppone.
Vedi quanta virtù l' ha fatto degno
 di reverenza; e cominciò dall'ora
 che Pallante morì per darli regno.
Tu sai ch'el fece in Alba sua dimora
 per trecento anni e oltra, infino al fine
 che i tre e tre pugnar per lui ancora.
E sai ch'el fè dal mal delle Sabine 40
 al dolor di Lucrezia in sette regi,
 vincendo intorno le genti vicine.
Sai quel che fè portato dalli egregi
 Romani incontro a Brenno, incontro a Pirro,
 incontro alli altri principi e collegi;
onde Torquato e Quinzio che dal cirro
 negletto fu nomato, i Deci e' Fabi
 ebber la fama che volontier mirro.
Esso atterrò l'orgoglio delli Arabi
 che di retro ad Annibale passaro 50
 l'alpestre rocce, Po, di che tu labi.
Sott'esso giovanetti triunfaro
 Scipïone e Pompeo; ed a quel colle
 sotto 'l qual tu nascesti parve amaro.
Poi, presso al tempo che tutto 'l ciel volle
 redur lo mondo a suo modo sereno,
 Cesare per voler di Roma il tolle.
E quel che fè da Varo infino al Reno,
 Isàra vide ed Era e vide Senna
 e ogne valle onde 'l Rodano è pieno. 60
Quel che fè poi ch'elli uscì di Ravenna
 e saltò Rubicon, fu di tal volo,
 che nol seguiterìa lingua nè penna.
Inver la Spagna rivolse lo stuolo,
 poi ver Durazzo, e Farsalia percosse
 sì ch'al Nil caldo si sentì del duolo.

'Here ends, then, my reply to the first question; but its tenor constrains me to make some addition to it, so that thou mayst see with what reason they act against the most holy standard, both those that take it for their own and those that oppose it.[6] See what valour has made it worthy of reverence, beginning from the hour when Pallas died to give it sway.[7] Thou knowest that it made its stay in Alba for three hundred years and more, till at the last, still for its sake, the three fought with the three;[8] and thou knowest what it did under seven kings, from the wrongs of the Sabine women to the woe of Lucrece, conquering the neighbour peoples round about. Thou knowest what it did when borne by the illustrious Romans against Brennus, against Pyrrhus, against the other princes and communes, so that Torquatus and Quinctius, named from his unkempt locks, the Decii and the Fabii, had the fame I rejoice to embalm.[9] It brought low the pride of the Arabs[10] who behind Hannibal passed the Alpine crags from which, Po, thou fallest. Under it, as youths, Scipio and Pompey triumphed, and to that hill beneath which thou wast born it showed itself bitter.[11] Then, near the time when heaven willed to bring all the world to its own state of peace,[12] Caesar, by the will of Rome, laid hold of it; and what it did from Var to Rhine, Isère saw and Loire and Seine and every valley from which the Rhone is filled. What it did when it issued from Ravenna and leapt the Rubicon was such a flight as no tongue or pen might follow. Towards Spain it wheeled the host, then towards Durazzo, and smote Pharsalia so that grief was felt on the burning Nile. Antandros and the Simois,

Antandro e Simoenta, onde si mosse,
  rivide e là dov' Ettore si cuba;
  e mal per Tolomeo poscia si scosse.
Da onde scese folgorando a Iuba;   70
  onde si volse nel vostro occidente,
  ove sentìa la pompeana tuba.
Di quel che fè col baiulo seguente,
  Bruto con Cassio nell' inferno latra,
  e Modena e Perugia fu dolente.
Piangene ancor la trista Cleopatra,
  che, fuggendoli innanzi, dal colubro
  la morte prese subitana e atra.
Con costui corse infino al lito rubro;
  con costui puose il mondo in tanta pace,   80
  che fu serrato a Iano il suo delubro.
Ma ciò che 'l segno che parlar mi face
  fatto avea prima e poi era fatturo
  per lo regno mortal ch'a lui soggiace,
diventa in apparenza poco e scuro,
  se in mano al terzo Cesare si mira
  con occhio chiaro e con affetto puro;
chè la viva giustizia che mi spira,
  li concedette, in mano a quel ch' i' dico,
  gloria di far vendetta alla sua ira.   90
Or qui t'ammira in ciò ch' io ti replico:
  poscia con Tito a far vendetta corse
  della vendetta del peccato antico.
E quando il dente longobardo morse
  la Santa Chiesa, sotto le sue ali
  Carlo Magno, vincendo, la soccorse.
Omai puoi giudicar di quei cotali
  ch' io accusai di sopra e di lor falli,
  che son cagion di tutti vostri mali.
L'uno al pubblico segno i gigli gialli   100
  oppone, e l'altro appropria quello a parte,
  sì ch'è forte a veder chi più si falli.
Faccian li Ghibellin, faccian lor arte
  sott'altro segno; chè mal segue quello
  sempre chi la giustizia e lui diparte;

whence it set out, it saw again, and the place where
Hector lies; then roused itself—the worse for Pto-
lemy. From there it fell like lightning on Juba,
then turned to your west, where it heard Pompey's
trumpet.[13] Of what it wrought with its next bearer
Brutus and Cassius bark in Hell, and Modena and
Perugia were in grief. Still weeps because of it
the wretched Cleopatra, who, flying before it, took
from the viper sudden and dreadful death. With
him it ran as far as the Red Sea shore. With him
it set the world in such peace that Janus's shrine
was locked.[14]

'But what the standard that moves my speech
had done before and was yet to do throughout the
mortal kingdom that is subject to it, comes to seem
small and dim if with clear eye and right affection
we look at it in the hand of the third Caesar; for
the Living Justice that inspires me granted to it,
in his hand of whom I speak, the glory of doing
vengeance for His wrath. And now marvel at
what I unfold to thee: that afterwards it ran with
Titus to do vengeance on the vengeance for the
ancient sin.[15] Then, under its wings, when the
Lombard tooth bit Holy Church, Charlemagne
won victory and succoured her.[16]

'Now thou canst judge of such men as I accused
before, and of their offences, which are the cause
of all your ills; the one opposes to the public stan-
dard the yellow lilies[17] and the other claims it for
a party, so that it is hard to see which offends the
more. Let the Ghibellines carry on their arts under
another standard, for of this he is always a bad
follower who severs it from justice; and let not this

e non l'abbatta esto Carlo novello
   coi Guelfi suoi; ma tema delli artigli
   ch'a più alto leon trasser lo vello.
Molte fïate già pianser li figli
   per la colpa del padre, e non si creda   110
   che Dio trasmuti l'arme per suoi gigli!
Questa picciola stella si correda
   di buoni spirti che son stati attivi
   perchè onore e fama li succeda:
e quando li disiri poggian quivi,
   sì disvïando, pur convien che i raggi
   del vero amore in su poggin men vivi.
Ma nel commensurar di nostri gaggi
   col merto è parte di nostra letizia,
   perchè non li vedem minor nè maggi.   120
Quindi addolcisce la viva giustizia
   in noi l'affetto sì, che non si puote
   torcer già mai ad alcuna nequizia.
Diverse voci fanno dolci note;
   così diversi scanni in nostra vita
   rendon dolce armonia tra queste rote.
E dentro alla presente margarita
   luce la luce di Romeo, di cui
   fu l'ovra grande e bella mal gradita.
Ma i Provenzai che fecer contra lui   130
   non hanno riso; e però mal cammina
   qual si fa danno del ben fare altrui.
Quattro figlie ebbe, e ciascuna reina,
   Ramondo Beringhieri, e ciò li fece
   Romeo, persona umile e peregrina.
E poi il mosser le parole biece
   a dimandar ragione a questo giusto,
   che li assegnò sette e cinque per diece.
Indi partissi povero e vetusto;
   e se 'l mondo sapesse il cor ch'elli ebbe   140
   mendicando sua vita a frusto a frusto,
assai lo loda, e più lo loderebbe.'

new Charles strike at it with his Guelfs,[18] but let him fear its claws, which have torn the hide from a greater lion. Many a time ere now have the children wept for the father's fault, and let him not think God will change arms for his lilies.[19]

'This little star is adorned with good spirits whose deeds were done for the honour and glory that should follow them; and when desires mount there thus deviously then the rays of the true love must needs mount upwards with less life. But in the measuring of our reward with our desert lies part of our happiness, for we see it to be neither less nor more; thus the Living Justice sweetens our affections so that they can never be warped to any evil. Diverse voices make sweet music, so diverse ranks in our life render sweet harmony among these wheels.

'Within this same pearl shines too the light of Romeo,[20] whose great and noble work was ill rewarded; but the Provençals who wrought against him do not have the laugh, and indeed he takes an ill road who makes of another's well-doing a wrong to himself. Raymond Berenger had four daughters, each of them a queen, and Romeo, a man of low birth and a stranger, did this for him. And when crafty tongues moved him to call to account this just man, who rendered him seven and five for ten, Romeo left there poor and old; and if the world knew the heart he had, begging his bread by morsels, much as it praises him it would praise him more.'

1. Constantine, two centuries before Justinian's time (A.D. 350–527), changed the seat of the Empire from the west to the east, 'against the course of heaven', reversing the journey of Aeneas from Troy to Italy. Aeneas married the Latin princess, Lavinia.

2. Justinian reduced and codified Roman Law.

3. Justinian was supposed to have held the Eutychian heresy, that Christ was only divine, not also human.

4. Of any two contradictory propositions, as 'A is B', 'A is not B', one must be true, the other false.

5. Justinian's general Belisarius recovered Italy from the Goths for the Empire.

6. Ghibellines and Guelfs, the Imperial and the Papal parties.

7. Pallas, a Latin prince who fought for Aeneas.

8. The three Horatii, champions of Rome, defeated the three Curiatii, champions of Alba.

9. Roman victories in Italy, Gaul and Greece.

10. Carthaginians, here called Arabs because they came from Africa.

11. Fiesole, on the hill above Florence, was believed to have been destroyed by the Romans under Caesar.

12. The *Pax Romana* at the time of the birth of Christ.

13. Caesar's campaigns in Gaul; the beginning of the Civil War, when he seized Rome; his defeat of Pompey's forces in Spain and Greece, and Pompey's death in Egypt; his campaigns in Mysia, Egypt and Numidia and defeat of Pompey's sons in Spain.

14. The victories of Augustus at Philippi and in Italy; his defeat of Cleopatra and her death; world peace under Augustus. The temple of Janus in Rome was kept closed in time of peace.

15. Under Tiberius, 'the third Caesar', Christ was crucified by Roman authority, bearing the penalty of human sin, God's 'vengeance for His wrath'; later, Titus, afterwards Emperor, destroyed Jerusalem, avenging the crucifixion, which was itself 'the vengeance for the ancient sin'.

16. Charlemagne delivered the Church from Lombard persecution, and he was crowned Emperor by the Pope in Rome in A.D. 800.

17. The fleur-de-lis of France, which was also the Guelf arms, was opposed to the Imperial Eagle, which was appropriated by the Ghibellines.

18. Charles II of Apulia, the degenerate son of Charles of Anjou (*Purg.* xx).

19. Let Charles not think that God is to give France the Empire, which belongs to Rome.

20. The story of Romeo is legendary. His master Raymond Berenger was Count of Provence in the first half of the 13th century.

NOTE

The last third of the fifth canto is, in effect, a summons to
Dante's reader to give his mind to the speech of Justinian
which 'the next canto chants' and it is to be understood in
relation to what follows. We are to pass from the sphere of
monastic calm, of prayer and contemplation, into the sphere of
battles for the Empire; and the joy of Beatrice, 'when she
passed into that heaven's light', is transmitted to the planet
itself and to Dante, and the reader is counted on to share
Dante's eagerness to know of the souls there. In the Moon the
souls were clearly seen with their human features; here in
Mercury they are hidden in their own light by their access of
happiness, and in the whole passage the related ideas of light
and joy are stressed by repetition. Beatrice bids Dante speak to
the souls and 'trust them even as gods'. The words are strange
to us and singular for Dante, but justified to his mind by the
language of Scripture: 'I have said, Ye are gods; and all of you
are children of the most High' (*Ps.* lxxxii. 6, confirmed in
John x. 34), and, 'that ye might be partakers of the divine
nature' (2 *Pet.* i. 4). They are words chosen and deliberate.
For it is expressly of the *divine* authority of the Empire that
Justinian is to speak, of God's making, through its victorious
history, of an earthly order in which men may find their public
justice and peace. In nothing was God's providence and pur-
pose in the world's affairs more plain and sure to Dante. For
nothing had he contended with a more passionate committal.
It was for him the essential framework of the story of human
redemption. 'The *preparatio evangelica* took its finest form in
Dante's conception of the provision of the Roman Empire
by the Father, with its universal peace as a cradle for His Son'
(*F. M. Powicke*). To set forth its meaning and its claims on

95

men's allegiance he had written the *De Monarchia*, and the *De Monarchia* has its consummation in the *Paradiso*.

The spirits in the Moon's sphere appeared to Dante like reflections in limpid and still water; those in Mercury are compared to fish, in water that is calm and clear, which dart to one point for food and are distinguished from the others by their movement and swift energy. Their natural temper has been such as to lead them to action and achievement, and to tempt them, as gentler natures are not tempted, through personal ambition and the world's praise. Once eager for a place in men's eyes, they are now in 'the sphere that is veiled to mortals with another's beams', hid from the world's reckoning in the light of God. They have sought men for fame; now they seek men's fellowship for increase of their loves, and with that increase their persons are cloaked and hidden in light, 'kindled by the light that extends through all heaven'. The same energy of character that is expressed in their flashing forms and swift decisive motions is exercised in the eagerness of their love and in their zeal for the divine purpose in world-history which inspires Justinian's story of Rome. Dante had experience of public life and was always an observer of it, and though his experience often made him harsh and bitter, it never made him cynical. He knew how rare is wholly disinterested public service and how great is the service that may be given to the world by those who find their motive and reward in men's praise. 'Fame is the spur that the clear spirit doth raise.'

This is the only canto of the *Divine Comedy* that is entirely occupied by a single speaker, so central to Dante's purpose is its main subject. It is the canto of Imperial Rome, and it begins with the name of the first Christian Emperor and with Aeneas the father of Rome, who is indicated by the marriage that founded the royal line. The first thing to note in Justinian's rapid review —in which are some inaccuracies which need not here concern us—is that it is spoken by the Empire's greatest law-giver. The first thing he says of himself is that he 'removed from the laws what was superfluous and vain'. 'The vain titles of the victories of Justinian are crumbled into dust; but the name of the legislator is inscribed on a fair and everlasting monument. . . . The public reason of the Romans has been silently or studiously transfused into the domestic institutions of Europe, and the laws of Justinian still command the respect or obedience of independent nations' (*Gibbon*). Justinian represents, not Roman arms, but Roman law; for not arms but law, and arms only for the sake of law, was Rome's glory and its gift to the world, the *Pax Romana*, the boon of world-order and peace. 'Not force, but reason, and that divine,' Dante said in the *Convito* 'was the origin of the Roman Empire'. On earth Justinian was Emperor, valuing chiefly name and fame—'I was Caesar, and am Justinian'; in Paradise he is a soul content in this low star, rejoicing in the justice that appoints it to him and gives him his due part in the harmony of the heavens, still subject to 'the Primal Love'—the Holy Spirit—that moved him to his task on earth.

It may seem a curious irrelevancy that Justinian had first to be corrected in his theology before he was qualified to codify the law, and that the fact is emphasized, in Dante's way, by the insistent repetition, 'faith—faith—faith', to note Justinian's stages of conviction. For Dante, all earthly order comes by divine ordinance. Just law belongs to the context of the Gospel. The Empire is the Empire of God's intention only when it is in harmony with the Church, both Church and Empire respecting with a mutual loyalty the other's province. So the Emperor was instructed by the Chief Shepherd in the true faith—the faith that Christ was human as well as divine, and therefore concerned with the earthly order—, and it was only when the Emperor 'took his way beside the Church' that he was inspired to his 'high task'. So Augustus made peace on earth for the birth of Christ; so Tiberius and Titus were the authorized instruments of divine judgement in the Crucifixion and in the destruction of Jerusalem; and so Charlemagne delivered the Church from the Lombard tooth. The theological thinking of the time was, of course, dominated by purely juridical conceptions, which are peculiarly fitted to Justinian and which produce the strange sophistication about the double vengeance which is discussed in the next canto. The victorious flight of the Eagle, 'the bird of God', from land to land and from age to age, following 'the course of heaven' from Troy to Rome and from Rome to the ends of the earth, was the divine preparation for the Christian Gospel and the appointed co-operation with it. The great leap of seven centuries—including Justinian's own time—from Titus to Charlemagne is significant. It is Dante's assertion that the Medieval Empire dating from Charlemagne was indeed, as by that time it was called, the Holy Roman Empire, differing only from the sway of Caesar and Augustus in that it was Christian. So far from his imperial authority deriving from his coronation by the Pope, as the Guelfs argued, Charlemagne, acting 'under the wings' of the Roman Eagle *before* the Pope had crowned him, 'won victory and succoured' the Church. 'The ideal of the Medieval Empire, the fundamental institutions of medieval society both in Church and State, and the incorporation of the classical tradition in medieval culture, all have their basis in the history of the Carolingian period. . . . The Carolingian Empire was a theocratic power, the political expression of a religious unity.' In it—that is, in the ninth century—'the ecclesiastical party stood for the ideal of a universal Empire as the embodiment of the unity of Christendom and the defender of the Christian faith. . . . The Emperor was an almost sacerdotal figure, who had been anointed by the grace of God to rule over the Christian people and to guide and protect the Church. . . . The State could no longer be identified with the world and regarded as essentially unspiritual; it becomes itself an organ of the spiritual power in the world' (*C. Dawson*). It was this lofty and religious ideal of the Empire that seized Dante's mind and imagination, an Empire, as he contends continually, not subordinate to the Church, but co-ordinate with it.

If we are to follow Dante's thought in this matter, 'we must keep constantly in mind the parallelism between the spiritual and the temporal power, between the history of Palestine and the history of Rome, between their outcome in the Gospel and in the system of Roman Law respectively. The Roman Empire existed for the development and promulgation of Roman Law, as the chosen people for the preparation of the Gospel. Thus the proof that the Roman people were specially appointed by God for this purpose and were specially protected by Him in its execution carries with it the permanent authority of Roman Law and of its appointed guardian, just as the miracles of the

Old Testament are taken as giving divine authority to the Gospel dispensation and to its ministers. . . . It is the kind of argument that depends for its value entirely upon the antecedent conviction that the series of events in question was intended by God to be significant. . . . This antecedent conviction was in Dante's mind with respect to Roman history just as clearly as it was in the minds of the writers of the New Testament with respect to Israelitish history' (*P. H. Wicksteed*).

In Ravenna, where Dante's last years were spent, San Vitale, its most beautiful church, was enriched by Justinian after the recovery of Italy from the Goths by Belisarius in A.D. 539; and its gorgeous contemporary mosaic of the Emperor, wearing the imperial crown and robes, with soldiers in attendance on one side, and on the other the archbishop and priests to whom he makes his gift of gold for the building, would be very familiar to Dante. It is a fair conjecture that the train of thought in this canto may have come to him in San Vitale while he looked at the portrayal of the Emperor at the summit of earthly majesty and in the service of the Church.

The purpose of the historical discourse is 'essentially political, not historical' (*O. Bacci, L.D.*)—to show that 'they act against the most holy standard, both those that take it for their own and those that oppose it', and to prove how it was 'made worthy of reverence'. It is impossible to reproduce the contrast in line 100 between the plain force of *il pubblico segno* and the contemptuous jingle of *i gigli gialli*. In the voice of the Emperor who represents Roman law and world-order when he speaks of the warring factions of Italy, in his accents of scorn and indignation, we hear the very tones of the *De Monarchia:* 'With derision, and not without a certain grief, I may cry on behalf of the glorious people and of Caesar, with him who cried on behalf of the Prince of Heaven, "Why do the nations rage, and the people imagine a vain thing?" ' It has been noted that the language of Justinian here about the two parties is substantially identical with that of the Emperor Henry VII in Dante's own day: 'What is the meaning of this rivalry? The one brings hatred on the name of the Empire and the other on the name of the Church by using them as blinds at the instigation of that Lucifer who fell.'

Dante was born and bred a Guelf and in his youth he fought in the ranks for the Guelf—which was the Florentine—cause; but he acknowledged later in the *Convito* the error of his earlier views, and there, as in the *De Monarchia* and in the *Divine Comedy*, he set forth the glory and the providential authority of the Empire. Yet he never became, in the party sense, a Ghibelline, a mere Imperialist. His ideal, of a world with its parts respecting each other's liberties and together submissive to justice and at peace, an Empire and a Church in harmony and co-operation, was beyond the clamour of party faction and outside the range alike of those who claimed the Eagle as their standard and those who set the lilies of France against it. The only justice for men—this was Dante's lesson—is justice for all men, and the only peace for men on earth is peace with God. 'The canto celebrates, not this man or that, but the Eagle, the divine cause, greater than anyone that served it. Even Caesar is incidental, a bearer of the standard. The wonder lies, not in this or that man's doings, but in the course of the Eagle, and it is so that Justinian tells its story, forgetting his own greatness, having learned his lesson. The Empire is God's business and care, "the will of the Primal Love" ' (*U. Cosmo*).

It is an instance of the harmony among the saints that the great Emperor tells Dante of Romeo, the mere Seneschal of the Provençal court, 'a man of low birth and a stranger'. But more, it is a demonstration that 'great and noble service' may sometimes be given in all sincerity to a cause that little deserves it. Provence offered no allegiance to the divine world-order which is the Empire. The Provençals' 'crafty tongues' made of Romeo's well-doing an offence to themselves and they contrived his ruin. But Romeo, who had served 'for the honour and glory that should come to him', showed a nobler spirit in his poverty and exile and deserved, what he did not get, a greater praise. Since souls are judged above not according to the world's judgement but by their intention and deserving, his light shines here along with that of Justinian himself. It is hard to suppose that Dante, when he wrote of Romeo—going out of his way, as it were, to speak of him—, did not have thought of himself, of his own ill-rewarded service of Florence—it also disloyal to the Empire—of his own ambitions there, of the bitter cure of them, and of 'the heart he had' during his wandering years, 'begging his bread by morsels', and when he signed his letter to the Florentines within: 'Dante Alighieri, Florentine, exile undeservedly'.

PARADISO

'*Osanna, sanctus Deus sabaoth,*
  superillustrans claritate tua
  felices ignes horum malacoth!'
Così, volgendosi alla nota sua,
  fu viso a me cantare essa sustanza,
  sopra la qual doppio lume s'addua:
ed essa e l'altre mossero a sua danza,
  e quasi velocissime faville,
  mi si velar di subita distanza.
Io dubitava, e dicea 'Dille, dille!'   10
  fra me: 'dille,' dicea 'alla mia donna
  che mi disseta con le dolci stille';
ma quella reverenza che s' indonna
  di tutto me, pur per *Be* e per *ice*,
  mi richinava come l' uom ch'assonna.
Poco sofferse me cotal Beatrice,
  e cominciò, raggiandomi d'un riso
  tal, che nel foco farìa l' uom felice:
'Secondo mio infallibile avviso,
  come giusta vendetta giustamente   20
  vengiata fosse, t' ha in pensier miso;
ma io ti solverò tosto la mente;
  e tu ascolta, chè le mie parole
  di gran sentenza ti faran presente.
Per non soffrire alla virtù che vole
  freno a suo prode, quell' uom che non nacque,
  dannando sè, dannò tutta sua prole;

CANTO VII

The divine vengeance; the plan of salvation

'*Osanna, sanctus Deus sabaoth,*
Superillustrans claritate tua
Felices ignes horum malacoth!'[1]

—thus, wheeling to his own notes, that spirit, on whom a double light is joined,[2] was seen by me to sing, and he and the others moved in the dance and like swiftest sparks were veiled to me by sudden distance.

I was in doubt, and 'Tell her, tell her!' I said within myself 'Tell my Lady who slakes my thirst with sweet drops.' But that reverence which wholly masters me even with *Be* or *ice*[3] bowed me down like one that falls asleep.

Beatrice did not long leave me thus, but began, shining on me with a smile that would make a man happy in the fire: 'By my judgement, which cannot err, how just vengeance should be justly avenged has set thee pondering;[4] but I will quickly free thy mind, and do thou hearken, for my words shall put before thee great doctrine.

'By not enduring for his good a rein on his will, the man that was never born,[5] condemning himself, condemned all his progeny; therefore mankind

onde l'umana specie inferma giacque
   giù per secoli molti in grande errore,
   fin ch'al Verbo di Dio discender piacque   30
u' la natura, che dal ṣuo Fattore
   s'era allungata, unì a sè in persona
   con l'atto sol del suo etterno amore.
Or drizza il viso a quel ch'or si ragiona.
   Questa natura al suo Fattore unita,
   qual fu creata, fu sincera e bona;
ma per sè stessa fu ella sbandita
   di paradiso, però che si torse
   da via di verità e da sua vita.
La pena dunque che la croce porse   40
   s'alla natura assunta si misura,
   nulla già mai sì giustamente morse;
e così nulla fu di tanta ingiura,
   guardando alla persona che sofferse,
   in che era contratta tal natura.
Però d'un atto uscir cose diverse:
   ch'a Dio ed a' Giudei piacque una morte;
   per lei tremò la terra e 'l ciel s'aperse.
Non ti dee oramai parer più forte,
   quando si dice che giusta vendetta   50
   poscia vengiata fu da giusta corte.
Ma io veggi' or la tua mente ristretta
   di pensiero in pensier dentro ad un nodo,
   del qual con gran disio solver s'aspetta.
Tu dici: "Ben discerno ciò ch' i' odo;
   ma perchè Dio volesse, m'è occulto,
   a nostra redenzion pur questo modo."
Questo decreto, frate, sta sepulto
   alli occhi di ciascuno il cui ingegno
   nella fiamma d'amor non è adulto.   60
Veramente, però ch'a questo segno
   molto si mira e poco si discerne
   dirò perchè tal modo fu più degno.
La divina bontà, che da sè sperne
   ogni livore, ardendo in sè, sfavilla
   sì che dispiega le bellezze etterne.

lay sick below in great error for many ages, till it pleased the Word of God to descend where the nature that was separated from its Maker He united with Himself in His own person by sole act of His Eternal Love. Now direct thy sight on what follows from that. This nature, thus united to its Maker, was pure and good, even as it was created; yet in itself, by its own act, it was banned from Paradise[6] because it turned aside from the way of truth and from its life. If, then, the penalty that was wrought by the cross is measured by the nature assumed, none ever stung so justly; so also none was so great a wrong, having regard to the Person who suffered, in whom that nature was bound up. From one act, therefore, came diverse effects, for the same death was pleasing both to God and to the Jews; because of it earth quaked and heaven opened. No longer, now, should it seem hard to thee when it is said that just vengeance was afterwards avenged by a just court.[7]

'But now I see thy mind entangled from thought to thought in a knot from which it waits with eagerness for release: thou sayest, "I follow clearly what I hear, but why God willed this sole way for our redemption is dark to me." This decree, brother, lies buried from the eyes of everyone whose mind is not matured in the flame of love; but since there is much aiming at this mark and little discernment, I shall tell how that way was the most fitting.

'The Divine Goodness, which spurns all envy from itself, burning within itself so sparkles that it displays its eternal beauties. That which imme-

Ciò che da lei sanza mezzo distilla
   non ha poi fine, perchè non si move
   la sua imprenta quand'ella sigilla.
Ciò che da essa sanza mezzo piove   70
   libero è tutto, perchè non soggiace
   alla virtute delle cose nove.
Più l'è conforme, e però più le piace;
   chè l'ardor santo ch'ogni cosa raggia,
   nella più somigliante è più vivace.
Di tutte queste dote s'avvantaggia
   l'umana creatura; e s'una manca,
   di sua nobilità convien che caggia.
Solo il peccato è quel che la disfranca,
   e falla dissimile al sommo bene;   80
   per che del lume suo poco s' imbianca;
ed in sua dignità mai non rivene,
   se non rïempie dove colpa vota,
   contra mal dilettar con giuste pene.
Vostra natura, quando peccò tota
   nel seme suo, da queste dignitadi,
   come di paradiso, fu remota;
nè ricovrar potìensi, se tu badi
   ben sottilmente, per alcuna via,
   sanza passar per un di questi guadi: 90
o che Dio solo per sua cortesia
   dimesso avesse, o che l'uom per sè isso
   avesse sodisfatto a sua follia.
Ficca mo l'occhio per entro l'abisso
   dell'etterno consiglio, quanto puoi
   al mio parlar distrettamente fisso.
Non potea l'uomo ne' termini suoi
   mai sodisfar, per non potere ir giuso
   con umiltate obedïendo poi,
quanto disobediendo intese ir suso;   100
   e questa è la cagion per che l'uom fue
   da poter sodisfar per sè dischiuso.
Dunque a Dio convenìa con le vie sue
   riparar l'omo a sua intera vita,
   dico con l'una, o ver con amendue.

diately derives from it has thenceforth no end, since its imprint, once stamped, does not pass away. That which rains down from it immediately is wholly free, since it is not subject to the power of changing things. It is more conformed to that Goodness and therefore more pleasing to it; for the Holy Ardour that irradiates all things is brightest in that which is most like itself.[8] Of all these gifts the human creature has the privilege, and if one of them is lacking he must needs fall from his noble estate. Sin alone it is that disfranchises him and makes him unlike the Supreme Good so that he is little illumined by its light; and he never returns to his dignity unless he fills up again the void made by his fault, with just penalties for sinful pleasure. Your nature, when it all sinned in its seed,[9] was parted from these dignities, as from Paradise; nor could they be recovered—if thou consider carefully—by any way except the passing of one of these fords: either that God, of His own sole clemency, had pardoned, or that man, of himself, had given satisfaction for his folly. Fix thine eyes now within the abyss of the Eternal Counsel and give thy closest heed to my words. Man could never, within his limits, give satisfaction, for he could not go so low in humility, by a later obedience, as, by disobedience, he had thought to go high;[10] and this is the cause by which man was debarred from the power of giving satisfaction by himself. It was needful, therefore, that by His own ways God should restore man to his full life,—by one way, that is, or by both.[11] But since the deed gratifies

Ma perchè l'ovra è tanto più gradita
   dall'operante, quanto più appresenta
   della bontà del core ond'ell'è uscita,
la divina bontà, che 'l mondo imprenta,
   di proceder per tutte le sue vie   110
   a rilevarvi suso fu contenta.
Nè tra l'ultima notte e 'l primo die
   sì alto o sì magnifico processo,
   o per l'una o per l'altra, fu o fie:
chè più largo fu Dio a dar sè stesso
   per far l'uom sufficiente a rilevarsi,
   che s'elli avesse sol da sè dimesso;
e tutti li altri modi erano scarsi
   alla giustizia, se 'l Figlíuol di Dio
   non fosse umilïato ad incarnarsi.   120
Or per empierti bene ogni disio,
   ritorno a dichiarare in alcun loco,
   perchè tu veggi lì così com' io.
Tu dici: "Io veggio l'acqua, io veggio il foco,
   l'aere e la terra e tutte lor misture
   venire a corruzione, e durar poco;
e queste cose pur furon creature;
   per che, se ciò ch'è detto è stato vero,
   esser dovrìen da corruzion sicure."
Li angeli, frate, e 'l paese sincero   130
   nel qual tu se', dir si posson creati,
   sì come sono, in loro essere intero;
ma li elementi che tu hai nomati
   e quelle cose che di lor si fanno
   da creata virtù sono informati.
Creata fu la materia ch'elli hanno;
   creata fu la virtù informante
   in queste stelle che 'ntorno a lor vanno.
L'anima d'ogne bruto e delle piante
   di complession potenzïata tira   140
   lo raggio e 'l moto delle luci sante;
ma vostra vita sanza mezzo spira
   la somma beninanza, e la innamora
   di sè sì che poi sempre la disira.

the doer more the more it manifests of the goodness of the heart from which it springs, the Divine Goodness which puts its imprint on the world was pleased to proceed by all its ways to raise you up again; nor between the last night and the first day[12] was or will be a procedure by the one way or the other so lofty or so glorious. For God was more bounteous in giving Himself so as to make man able to raise himself again than if, simply of Himself, he had pardoned; and all other means came short of justice save that the Son of God should humble Himself to become flesh.

'Now to give full satisfaction to all thy wishes, I go back to explain one point, that thou mayst see it as clearly as I do. Thou sayest: "I see water, I see fire and air and earth[13] and all their mixtures come to corruption, having little endurance; and yet these things were created, so that, if what was said is true, they should be secure from corruption."

'The angels, brother, and the pure country where thou art may be said to be created just as they are in their entire being; but the elements thou hast named and those things that are made from them are given their form by created power. Created was the matter that is in them, created was the informing virtue in these stars that wheel about them.[14] The soul of every beast and of the plants is drawn from a potential complex by the shining and motion of the holy lights;[15] but your life the Supreme Beneficence breathes forth immediately, and He so enamours it of Himself that it desires

E quinci puoi argomentare ancora
vostra resurrezion, se tu ripensi
come l'umana carne fessi allora
che li primi parenti intrambo fensi.'

Him ever after. And from this thou canst also argue
your resurrection, if thou recall how human flesh
was made, at the time of the making of both the
first parents.'[16]

1. 'Hosanna, holy God of hosts, making more resplendent with Thy brightness the happy fires of these realms.'

2. Earthly and heavenly greatness.

3. Fragments of the name of Beatrice.

4. If the crucifixion was 'just vengeance' on human sin, how could it be 'justly avenged'?

5. Adam, not being of human descent, did not inherit human sinfulness.

6. The Garden of Eden.

7. The crucifixion was 'just vengeance' on human nature, borne by Christ, and at the same time a wrong done to Christ which was 'justly avenged' by Titus. The 'just court' is the Imperial jurisdiction in the punishment of the Jews. 'The good Titus, by help of the King Most High, avenged the wounds from which poured the blood sold by Judas' (*Purg.* xxi).

8. Angels and human souls are immediate creations of God and therefore not subject to 'changing things' (literally, 'new things'), i.e. secondary causes; they have the 'privileges' of immortality, freedom, and likeness to God.

9. 'As by one man sin entered into the world, and death by sin; so death passed upon all men, for that all have sinned' (*Rom.* v. 12).

10. 'The serpent said, . . . In the day ye eat thereof, then your eyes shall be opened, and ye shall be as gods, knowing good and evil' (*Gen.* iii. 4–5). The primary sin was pride.

11. 'All the paths of the Lord are *mercy* and *truth*' (*Ps.* xxv. 10).

12. Between the Last Judgement and the Creation.

13. The four 'elements' of which all material things are formed.

14. The elements have their 'form', their specific nature, not by direct creation, but by the created angelic powers operating through the stars on the primal undifferentiated stuff of the material universe, that stuff itself being created.

15. Animal and vegetable life come into being by the operation of the stars on 'complexes' of the elements having the necessary potentiality; and the elements and plants and animals, not being of immediate creation, are corruptible.

16. The human body, like the soul, was originally a direct creation, and therefore immortal. 'The Lord God formed man of the dust of the ground, and breathed into his nostrils the breath of life. . . . And the rib, which the Lord God had taken from man, made he a woman' (*Gen.* ii. 7, 22).

NOTE

In the parting song of Justinian there is a curious instance of Dante's use of verbal device and of its relevancy and significance in his hands. The song is a mixture of Latin and Hebrew, for which Dante, being ignorant of Hebrew, would find the words *hosanna* and *sabaoth* in the Vulgate and *malacoth* (mis-spelled for *mamlacoth*) in St Jerome's Preface to the Vulgate. Why should he depart here, and only here, from the established convention that the language of praise for the saints in Paradise is Latin, the language of the Church? May it be that he reckoned it fitting that Justinian, with his world-outlook and after his survey of the divine working and convergence of events through the ages, should praise God in the languages, through the same ages, of Jerusalem and Rome, as it were the two sacred tongues of history? If that is so it is the more fitting at the beginning of the canto of the scheme of human redemption, a redemption without bounds of time or race.

We have already noted the contrast between the first appearance of the souls in the Moon and of those in Mercury, and we find now a similar contrast, as of character and temperament, in their disappearance—Piccarda, the gentle, monastic spirit, singing *Ave Maria* and vanishing 'as a weight sinks through deep water', Justinian, Emperor and law-giver, chanting the glory of the God of Hosts, and then, with the rest, veiled like a swift spark by sudden distance. In Paradise the personality is perfected, as in Hell it is lost.

Dante is left to his own reflections and to perplexities which, in other terms, have occupied many minds in many ages. He is absorbed and bowed down before the truth, which he has known only 'in part'—in '*Be* or *ice*', and yet thrilled by that part, like any lover at any hint of his lady's name. His words to himself: 'Tell her, tell her! Tell my Lady', introduced with such abruptness and breaking out with such eagerness, are a reminiscence of old insistent questions, such as he acknowledged in the *De Monarchia*, about the meaning of history, if it has a meaning; and the words follow so instantly on the apotheosis of Justinian, the spokesman of historic public justice, that it seems as if Dante felt a sudden challenge to his mind. He has heard, and has accepted, Justinian's great theodicy in the story of the Empire as the supreme authority for men in the world's affairs. But what is to be made of that story at its most crucial and challenging point, the crucifixion of Christ and the destruction of Jerusalem, and is Justinian's solution—'vengeance on the vengeance'—any solution or only a statement of the enigma? The question was central and unescapable for Dante. No man was ever made more conscious of the moral paradoxes of history; and yet history was for him, essentially, the sphere and the setting of human redemption, its meaning and its use nothing else but redemption, the fulfilment of creation, and it was through life's tragedy that he sought and believed that he saw the victory of love.

In maintaining his doctrine of providence in the *De Monarchia* Dante expounds the view, apparently peculiar to himself, that Christ acknowledged the authority of the Empire by being born under its jurisdiction and included in its census, and that the validity of the crucifixion as a penalty on the sin of humanity rests on its having been inflicted on Christ by an Empire in principle universal, a 'just', or valid, authority. There is something of the same implication in the elaborate imagery of the Empire in *Purgatorio* xxxii and xxxiii; and the statement here —not very suitable to its immediate context—that, in his uncertainty and suspense, he was 'like one that falls asleep' recalls the quite similar language of these scenes in Purgatory: 'I fell asleep'—'like one that dreams'—'thy wits sleep', each time with a reference to the Empire and to Dante's own attitude to it. The characteristic repetition seems to indicate how persistently such questions pressed on Dante's mind and how often he had been baffled by them and had given them up when he had not yet awakened to the Empire's significance. To count it a part of the 'glory' of the Empire that it crucified Christ and that in so doing it 'did vengeance' on behalf of the Divine

Justice is indeed a singular historical judgement, and it shows to what paradoxical extremes an ostensibly logical process may lead. But it is really incidental to Dante's great contention, that justice is one in heaven and earth, for God and man, and that, essentially and ultimately, history is just. Divine 'vengeance', here and elsewhere in the *Divine Comedy*, means always penal justice; the word, in Italian as in English, is nearly related to *vindication*, the reassertion and maintenance of a broken law, and Dante's whole treatment of the subject is a part of the medieval attempt to comprehend in one view the divine purpose in creation and in the actual course of world-events.

It was fitting that Justinian's account of the Empire should be followed by Beatrice's reasoned discourse on human redemption. For redemption, the deliverance of mankind from its own perversity and its consequences, is at once historical and beyond history. It is not man himself, but his Maker, that 'makes man able to raise himself again', and all his worth comes of a divine creative goodness which is beyond himself. Justinian's 'God of Hosts' becomes, for Beatrice's better knowledge, 'the Divine Goodness'—the phrase occurs twice—, 'the Supreme Goodness', 'the Supreme Beneficence'; and in one sentence the three Persons of the Godhead are named, 'the Word of God— Maker—Eternal Love'. The whole manner of the discourse is academic and scholastic, with the formal statement of question and answer and the dialectic handling of abstract terms which was common in the schools; but however unreal we must find much of the argument, it is shot through and sustained by a high and simple doctrine of the soul: 'Your life the Supreme Beneficence breathes forth immediately, and He so enamours it of Himself that it desires Him ever after.'

It is characteristic of the Christian teaching of the time that the closing note of the canto should be on the resurrection of the body, as it were the final completeness and individual stamp of the soul's immortality; while it is to be admitted that the argument here for bodily resurrection is not easily reconciled with the account of human generation in *Purgatorio* xxv. If we consider the whole motive and substance of Beatrice's words to Dante it will not seem strange that she began by 'shining on him with a smile that would make a man happy in the fire'.

PARADISO

S O L E A creder lo mondo in suo periclo
  che la bella Ciprigna il folle amore
  raggiasse, volta nel terzo epiciclo;
per che non pur a lei faceano onore
  di sacrificio e di votivo grido
  le genti antiche nell'antico errore;
ma Dïone onoravano e Cupido,
  questa per madre sua, questo per figlio;
  e dicean ch'el sedette in grembo a Dido;
e da costei ond' io principio piglio   10
  pigliavano il vocabol della stella
  che 'l sol vagheggia or da coppa, or da ciglio.
Io non m'accorsi del salire in ella;
  ma d'esservi entro mi fè assai fede
  la donna mia ch' i' vidi far più bella.
E come in fiamma favilla si vede,
  e come in voce voce si discerne,
  quand'una è ferma e l'altra va e riede,
vid' io in essa luce altre lucerne
  muoversi in giro più e men correnti,   20
  al modo, credo, di lor viste eterne.
Di fredda nube non disceser venti,
  o visibili o non, tanto festini,
  che non paressero impediti e lenti
a chi avesse quei lumi divini
  veduti a noi venir, lasciando il giro
  pria cominciato in li alti Serafini;

CANTO VIII

*The Sphere of Venus; love marred by wantonness;
Charles Martel; diversities of temperament*

THE world once believed, to its peril, that the fair
Cyprian, wheeling in the third epicycle, rayed forth
mad love, so that the ancient peoples in their ancient
error not only did honour to her with sacrifice
and votive cry but honoured also Dione and Cupid,
her as her mother, him as her son, and told that he
lay in Dido's bosom; and from her with whom
I take my start they took the name of the star that
woos the sun, now from behind, now in front.[1]

I was not conscious of rising into it, but of being
within it my Lady gave me full assurance when
I saw her become more fair. And as within a flame
a spark is seen, and within a voice a voice is dis-
tinguished when one holds the note and the other
comes and goes,[2] so I saw within that light other
lights in circling movement swifter and slower, in
the measure, as I believe, of their eternal vision.
From a cold cloud winds never descended, visible
or not,[3] so swiftly as not to seem hindered and slow
to one that had seen these divine lights come to us,
leaving the dance first begun among the high

e dentro a quei che più innanzi appariro
   sonava 'Osanna' sì, che unque poi
   di rïudir non fui sanza disiro.   30
Indi si fece l'un più presso a noi
   e solo incominciò: 'Tutti sem presti
   al tuo piacer, perchè di noi ti gioi.
Noi ci volgiam coi Principi celesti
   d'un giro e d'un girare e d'una sete,
   ai quali tu del mondo già dicesti:
"*Voi che 'ntendendo il terzo ciel movete*";
   e sem sì pien d'amor, che, per piacerti,
   non fia men dolce un poco di quïete.'
Poscia che li occhi miei si fuoro offerti   40
   alla mia donna reverenti, ed essa
   fatti li avea di sè contenti e certi,
rivolsersi alla luce che promessa
   tanto s'avea, e 'Deh, chi siete?' fue
   la voce mia di grande affetto impressa.
E quanta e quale vid' io lei far piùe
   per allegrezza nova che s'accrebbe,
   quand' io parlai, all'allegrezze sue!
Così fatta, mi disse: 'Il mondo m'ebbe
   giù poco tempo; e se più fosse stato,   50
   molto sarà di mal, che non sarebbe.
La mia letizia mi ti tien celato
   che mi raggia dintorno e mi nasconde
   quasi animal di sua seta fasciato.
Assai m'amasti, e avesti ben onde;
   chè s' io fossi giù stato, io ti mostrava
   di mio amor più oltre che le fronde.
Quella sinistra riva che si lava
   di Rodano poi ch'è misto con Sorga,
   per suo segnore a tempo m'aspettava,   60
e quel corno d'Ausonia che s' imborga
   di Barí, di Gaeta e di Catona
   da ove Tronto e Verde in mare sgorga.
Fulgìemi già in fronte la corona
   di quella terra che 'l Danubio riga
   poi che le ripe tedesche abbandona.

Seraphim; and among those that appeared in front sounded a *Hosanna* such that I have never since been without the desire to hear it again.

Then one drew nearer us and began alone: 'We are all ready at thy pleasure, that thou mayst have joy of us. We circle in one orbit, at one pace, with one thirst, along with the heavenly Princes whom thou didst once address thus from the world: *Ye who by understanding move the third heaven*;[4] and we are so full of love that, to do thee pleasure, a little quiet will be not less sweet to us.'

After my eyes had been raised with reverence to my Lady and she had satisfied them with assurance of her consent, they turned back to the light that had made such promise of itself, and 'Tell me, who are you?' I said, my voice showing that I was deeply moved. Ah, how much I saw it increase in size and brightness when I spoke, by new joy that was added to its joys! Thus changed, it said to me: 'The world held me but a short time below, and had it been longer much evil that will be would not have been. My happiness keeps me hid from thee, for it rays about me and conceals me like a creature swathed in its own silk. Thou didst love me much, and hadst good cause; for had I been below I would have shown thee much more of my love than the leaves. The left bank that is washed by the Rhone after it mingles with the Sorgue[5] awaited me for its lord in due course, and that horn of Ausonia which has on its borders Bari and Gaeta and Catona, from where Tronto and Verde discharge in the sea.[6] Already shone on my brow the crown of the land which the Danube waters after quitting its German banks;[7] and fair Trinacria,

E la bella Trinacria, che caliga
   tra Pachino e Peloro, sopra 'l golfo
   che riceve da Euro maggior briga,
non per Tifeo ma per nascente solfo,   70
   attesi avrebbe li suoi regi ancora,
   nati per me di Carlo e di Ridolfo,
se mala segnoria, che sempre accora
   li popoli suggetti, non avesse
   mosso Palermo a gridar: "Mora, mora!"
E se mio frate questo antivedesse,
   l'avara povertà di Catalogna
   già fuggirìa, perchè non li offendesse;
chè veramente proveder bisogna
   per lui, o per altrui, sì ch'a sua barca   80
   carcata più di carco non si pogna.
La sua natura, che di larga parca
   discese, avrìa mestier di tal milizia
   che non curasse di mettere in arca.'
'Però ch' i' credo che l'alta letizia
   che 'l tuo parlar m' infonde, signor mio,
   là 've ogni ben si termina e s' inizia,
per te si veggia come la vegg' io,
   grata m'è più; e anco quest' ho caro
   perchè 'l discerni rimirando in Dio.   90
Fatto m' hai lieto, e così mi fa chiaro,
   poi che, parlando, a dubitar m' hai mosso
   com'esser può di dolce seme amaro.'
Questo io a lui; ed elli a me: 'S' io posso
   mostrarti un vero, a quel che tu dimandi
   terra' il viso come tieni 'l dosso.
Lo ben che tutto il regno che tu scandi
   volge e contenta, fa esser virtute
   sua provedenza in questi corpi grandi.
E non pur le nature provedute   100
   sono in la mente ch'è da sè perfetta,
   ma esse insieme con la lor salute:
per che quantunque quest'arco saetta
   disposto cade a proveduto fine,
   sì come cosa in suo segno diretta.

which between Pachynus and Pelorus, on the gulf that is most vexed by the Sirocco, is darkened—not by Typhon but by rising sulphur[8]—, would still have looked for its kings born through me of Charles and Rudolph, if bad rule, which always exasperates subject peoples, had not moved Palermo to cry "Death, death to them!"[9] And if my brother foresaw this he would already shun the rapacious poverty of Catalonia that it may not make trouble for him; for truly there is need that he or another should look to it that on his loaded bark is not laid a still heavier load. His nature, a mean one descended from a generous, would need a knighthood who do not make it their business to fill their chests.'[10]

'Because I believe, my lord, that, as plainly as it is plain to myself, the deep joy with which thy words have filled me is seen by thee where every good has its end and its beginning, it is the more welcome to me; and I hold it dear too that thou discernest this in gazing upon God.[11] Thou hast made me glad; so too do thou enlighten me, for thy words have raised the question in my mind how from sweet seed can come bitter fruit.'[12]

I spoke to him thus, and he replied: 'If I can show thee one truth,[13] thou wilt then have before thine eyes the answer to thy question which is now behind thy back. The Good that revolves and satisfies the whole kingdom thou art climbing makes its providence to be power in these great bodies; and not only is the nature of things provided for in the Mind which has perfection in itself, but along with their nature their well-being, so that whatever this bow shoots falls fitted for a provided end, as a shaft directed to its mark. If it were not so the

Se ciò non fosse, il ciel che tu cammine
   producerebbe sì li suoi effetti,
   che non sarebbero arti, ma ruine;
e ciò esser non può, se li 'ntelletti
   che muovon queste stelle non son manchi,   110
   e manco il primo, che non li ha perfetti.
Vuo' tu che questo ver più ti s' imbianchi?'
   E io: 'Non già; chè impossibil veggio
   che la natura, in quel ch'è uopo, stanchi.'
Ond'elli ancora: 'Or dì: sarebbe il peggio
   per l' uomo in terra, se non fosse cive?'
   'Sì' rispuos' io; 'e qui ragion non cheggio.'
'E può elli esser, se giù non si vive
   diversamente per diversi offici?
   Non, se 'l maestro vostro ben vi scrive.'   120
Sì venne deducendo infino a quici;
   poscia conchiuse: 'Dunque esser diverse
   convien di vostri effetti le radici:
per ch'un nasce Solone e altro Serse,
   altro Melchisedèch e altro quello
   che, volando per l'aere, il figlio perse.
La circular natura, ch'è suggello
   alla cera mortal, fa ben sua arte,
   ma non distingue l'un dall'altro ostello.
Quinci addivien ch' Esaù si diparte   130
   per seme da Iacòb; e vien Quirino
   da sì vil padre, che si rende a Marte.
Natura generata il suo cammino
   simil farebbe sempre a' generanti,
   se non vincesse il proveder divino.
Or quel che t'era dietro t'è davanti:
   ma perchè sappi che di te mi giova,
   un corollario voglio che t'ammanti.
Sempre natura, se fortuna trova
   discorde a sè, com'ogni altra semente   140
   fuor di sua regïon, fa mala prova.
E se 'l mondo là giù ponesse mente
   al fondamento che natura pone,
   sequendo lui, avrìa buona la gente.

heavens in which thou journeyest would produce such effects as would not be things of art but of confusion; and that cannot be unless the Intelligences that move the stars are defective, and defective also the Primal Intelligence which has not made them perfect.[14] Wilt thou have this truth made clearer to thee?'

And I: 'No, truly, for I see it to be impossible that nature should fail in what is needful.'

He continued therefore: 'Now tell me, would it be worse for man on earth if he were not a citizen?'

'Yes,' I replied 'and here I ask no proof.'

'And can he be unless men below live in diverse ways for diverse tasks? Not if your master[15] writes well of this.'

When he had brought the argument to this point, he then concluded: 'The roots of your activities, therefore, must be diverse, so that one is born Solon and another Xerxes, one Melchizedek and another he that flew through the air and lost his son.[16] Circling nature, which is a seal on the mortal wax, plies its art well, but does not distinguish one house from another; whence it happens that Esau differs in the seed from Jacob, and Quirinus comes from so base a father that he is ascribed to Mars.[17] The begotten nature would always take a like course with its begetters if Divine Providence did not overrule.

'Now what was behind is before thee. But that thou mayst know the pleasure I have in thee, take a corollary for a cloak about thee. Always, if nature meets with fortune unsuited to it, like any kind of seed out of its own region, it has ill success, and if the world below gave its mind to the foundation that nature lays and followed it, it would be well

Ma voi torcete alla religïone
tal che fia nato a cignersi la spada,
e fate re di tal ch'è da sermone:
onde la traccia vostra è fuor di strada,'

for its people. But you wrest to religion one born
to gird on the sword, and you make a king of one
that is fit for sermons, so that your track is off
the road.'

1. Venus, born in Cyprus, is here identified with the planet, which was supposed, like all the planets, to gyrate in 'epicycles' about its main orbit, its motion bringing it sometimes ahead of the sun, sometimes behind it, as morning or evening star.

2. In '*canto fermo*', or plain-song, the main melody might be sung by one voice and accompanied in harmony by others.

3. As lightning or wind.

4. An early poem of Dante's addressed to the angelic order of Principalities who control this 'third heaven'. The speaker is Charles Martel (1271–1295), the oldest son of Charles II of Naples, titular King of Hungary, and heir to Naples and Provence. He visited Florence in 1294.

5. The County of Provence.

6. The Kingdom of Naples, occupying the south of Italy; Ausonia, the ancient name of the district.

7. The Kingdom of Hungary.

8. Sicily, once called Trinacria ('three-cornered'), gets the smoke of Etna and the storms of the Sirocco on its south-east coast; Typhon, a monster supposed to be buried under Etna and to be the cause of its eruptions.

9. Charles Martel's descendants, uniting the lines of Charles II of Anjou, his father, and of the Emperor Rudolph, his father-in-law, would have inherited the throne of Sicily, if the oppressions of Charles I had not provoked the slaughter of the French there—the 'Sicilian Vespers'—and their expulsion in 1282.

10. Robert, Charles's younger brother, afterwards King of Naples, had a following of rapacious and unruly Spaniards, whose greed was added to his own.

11. The two friends rejoice mutually in their meeting and recognition, and Dante rejoices to find Charles in Paradise.

12. How can a mean nature descend from a generous one, i.e. Robert from Charles II?

13. The truth that congenital character is not hereditary, but comes by divine appointment through the stars.

14. Through the celestial 'Intelligences' controlling the spheres God, 'the Primal Intelligence', gives to all things and all souls the qualities suited to their uses in His providence.

15. Aristotle.

16. A legislator, a warrior, a priest, and a craftsman; Daedalus, the mythical inventor of human flight, the father of Icarus (*Inf.* xvii).

17. The stars give souls their individual temperament without regard to their family; so Esau differed in the womb from Jacob, and Romulus (Quirinus), a peasant's son, became the founder of Rome and was believed to be the son of Mars.

NOTE

The sphere of Venus is the last of the three that are touched by
the shadow of the earth, the spirits in which have yielded to the
sins that most easily beset them. The gentle Piccarda under
constraint had failed in her vows; the active energy of Justinian
had led him to overvalue and to seek too much the praise of
men; and the ardent affections of the spirits in Venus had made
them yield to the love that is a kind of madness. Each soul is
tempted through its own temperament, while its temperament
is the work and the gift of the heavens and through its tempera-
ment, disciplined and used, the soul has its place in Paradise.
The gentle nature, once yielding to wrong, now rejoices in
perfect obedience—'In His will is our peace'; the adventurous
spirit, once eager for glory, now glories in God's cause on
earth, the flight of the Eagle; and souls born amorous, when
they are chastened and deepened, do not lose their ardour
and tenderness but live now in the fellowship of 'the high
Seraphim', the appointed spirits of love. It is as himself, in
God's making of him, that a man is saved. His temperament,
with his bodily features, is given him by 'nature', by the divine
operation of the stars; but *merely* to yield to it is to lose his
soul.

The opening lines, about 'the fair Cyprian', are an example
of Dante's double attitude to the nature-myths of the ancient
world,—on the one hand, his sense of their imaginative truth,
and, on the other, his deeper sense of their perilous falsehood,
the essential heathenism of regarding the soul as the mere
product and plaything of natural forces that may drive it to
destruction, as Cupid drove Dido. Here, telling of the redemption
of the amorous, he stresses the 'peril' and 'ancient error' of
paganism. For the planet to which Dante has now risen is quite
other than the wanton goddess to whom the old world did honour

with sacrifice and votive cry, honouring, too, even her mother and her son. From her this planet takes merely *il vocabol*— as if to say, only the sound of its name. Here is no 'mad love', but love as the soul's sanity and perfection. The first thing that Dante saw in the sky when he reached the shore of Purgatory before dawn had been 'the fair planet that prompts to love, making all the east to smile'; and the whole ascent of the mountain had been the setting of love in order in his soul.

When Dante and Beatrice rose to the Moon, he set his sight on her, 'and at her aspect I was changed within'; when they entered Mercury, 'I saw my Lady so joyful when we passed into that heaven's light that the planet turned brighter for it'; and here his first assurance of being in Venus was from his Lady, 'when I saw her become more fair'. One of Dante's most significant and beautiful inventions in the *Paradiso* is that each ascent from height to greater height is marked by the increasing beauty of Beatrice in his eyes; the truth of God, more known, becomes always more glorious. It is an allegorical device, a poet's version of justification by faith; and it is also much more. It is the sublimation of his old life and love in Florence, a repetition in deeper terms of the language of the *Vita Nuova*:

> 'What seems she when a little she doth smile
> Cannot be kept in mind, cannot be told,
> Such strange and gentle miracle is wrought'
> > (*D. G. Rossetti's Version*).

The affectionate ardour of the souls here is represented in the lightning speed of their first appearance to Dante, and their discipline and deliverance from wandering lusts in their accord with the angelic powers that control their sphere—'in one orbit, at one pace, with one thirst'. 'The dance that comes to rest here in the heaven of Venus begins in the Empyrean in the highest of the angelic orders, that of the Seraphim, and is drawn out in a luminous line across the immensities of starry space' (*L. Rocca, L.D.*).

Dante's ode, referred to by Charles Martel, seems to have been written, according to Dante's own account in the *Convito*, just about the time of Charles's visit to Florence. It is occupied with

Dante's divided love after the death of Beatrice of which he tells in the *Vita Nuova*, and the mention of it in this context may fairly be taken as his confession that at one time the light of this star had overcome him too. It is as if Charles had said to him: 'You are one of us', for Charles's place in this heaven tells of one aspect of his character,—love marred by wantonness.

The reference here to Dante's meeting with Charles Martel is a reminiscence, twenty years or more after the event, of his happier years in Florence. In Dante's childhood and youth Charles I, grandfather of Charles Martel and the first of his line in Italy, brother of Saint Louis, Count of Anjou and Provence, and King of Sicily and Naples—'he of the manly nose' in the Valley of the Princes (*Purg.* vii)—, was the most powerful champion of the Guelf cause in Italy and the chief friend and protector of the liberties of Florence; and even in 1294, after Charles I had lost Sicily by his misrule and his weaker son Charles II had succeeded to the Kingdom of Naples, Florence gave a great reception to Charles II's oldest son Charles Martel when he came, with a retinue of two hundred knights, to meet his father and mother there, and spent three weeks in the city. Dante was in his twenty-ninth year, the recognized leader of the notable group of Florentine poets, ardent, romantic, public-spirited, confident. Charles, six years Dante's junior, already King of Hungary, heir to the Kingdom of Naples and the County of Provence, and son-in-law of the late Emperor Rudolph, handsome, musical, popular, was expected to take a great place in the world's affairs. Nothing is known but what is told us here of the personal relations between Charles and Dante; but the language of the canto is enough to prove a warmth of attachment which is in accord with all we know of both and from which we may guess something of Dante's grief for the death of the young prince from plague in the following year.

When he wrote these lines Dante was a different man living in a different world, an exile and a refugee whose dearest hopes had been defeated, and defeated largely by that house of Anjou which in his youth he had learned to trust and which in recent years had been the main force against his hero, the young Emperor Henry VII, in his great stroke for public order—as

Dante conceived it—in Italy. 'From the midst of the gloomy shadows which now involve the Angevin princes there shines still in the eyes of the Poet a figure of pure light, that of Charles Martel, the gentle youth who had vanished in the white aureole of his early years, full of hopes and promises. His fair image was preserved blameless in Dante's mind as it had been impressed on him in the spring of 1294, with the memory of their mutual affection, of exchange of confidences, and—who knows?—perhaps of generous promises, of bold designs, and of vague and distant ideals, an image bright in proportion as the other memories of the Angevins had become dark about it. The Poet recalled it among the dearest recollections of his Guelf youth, alongside of that, equally lamented, of the gentle Judge Nino, in the Florence of old Ser Brunetto, of his friend Casella, and of Forese, a Florence proud of its Guelf victories, "the fair sheepfold where I slept as a lamb" ' (*L. Rocca, L.D.*).

It is natural that talk about so diversified a family as the Angevins should raise the question of human diversity in general, and Dante finds its reason and its cause in a Providence —*provedenza, provedute, proveduto*, in the course of six lines— which operates through the stars and overrules them for its own ends so as to give men their temperaments and aptitudes for the various needs of an ordered society. In the failure of his earthly hopes it is his first concern to justify the ways of God to men.

The 'corollary' at the end of the canto seems to be an afterthought by way of practical application, beginning as it does, like the other corollary in *Purgatorio* xxviii, on the second line of the stanza, after the completion of the rhyme with which the canto might have ended. 'That is God's providence in the making of men,' Charles seems to say 'see now what men have made of themselves.' The corollary consists of his gibe at two of his brothers, which is the sharper because it comes from him and because he does not name them,—Louis, who refused the prospect of a crown and turned priest, and Robert, who plumed himself on his learning and eloquence and produced some hundreds of sermons, an occupation, his brother suggests, for which he was at least more fit than for the throne he usurped from his nephew, Charles Martel's son.

The geographical account which Charles gives of Provence, the Kingdom of Naples, and Hungary, is characteristic as showing Dante's marked interest in rivers—for which we may recall, for example, the source and course of the Mincio in *Inferno* xx and of the Arno in *Purgatorio* xiv and the account of Rome's conquests in *Paradiso* vi. With his concrete, three-dimensional mind, he conceives of rivers, not merely as defining lines on the map, but as forces carving out the kingdoms in material fact.

PARADISO

D A poi che Carlo tuo, bella Clemenza,
  m'ebbe chiarito, mi narrò li 'nganni
  che ricever dovea la sua semenza;
ma dísse: 'Taci, e lascia volger li anni';
  sì ch' io non posso dir se non che pianto
  giusto verrà di retro ai vostri danni.
E già la vita di quel lume santo
  rivolta s'era al Sol che la rïempie
  come quel ben ch'a ogni cosa è tanto.
Ahi anime ingannate e fatture empie,   10
  che da sì fatto ben torcete i cori,
  drizzando in vanità le vostre tempie!
Ed ecco un altro di quelli splendori
  ver me si fece, e 'l suo voler piacermi
  significava nel chiarir di fori.
Li occhi di Beatrice, ch'eran fermi
  sovra me, come pria, di caro assenso
  al mio disio certificato fermi.
'Deh, metti al mio voler tosto compenso,
  beato spirto,' dissi 'e fammi prova   20
  ch' i' possa in te refletter quel ch' io penso!'
Onde la luce che m'era ancor nova,
  del suo profondo, ond'ella pria cantava,
  seguette come a cui di ben far giova:
'In quella parte della terra prava
  italica che siede tra Rïalto
  e le fontane di Brenta e di Piava,
si leva un colle, e non surge molt'alto,
  là onde scese già una facella
  che fece alla contrada un grande assalto.   30

CANTO IX

*Cunizza; Folco; repentance transformed to
praise; Rahab*

AFTER thy Charles, fair Clemence,[1] had enlightened
me, he told me of the treacheries his seed was to
suffer, but said: 'Be silent, and let the years revolve';
so that I can say nothing but that deserved sorrows
shall follow on your wrongs. And already the living
soul of that holy light had turned to the Sun that
fills it, as to the good that is sufficient for all things.
Ah, souls beguiled, creatures without reverence,
who from such a good turn away your hearts,
directing your brows to vanity!

And lo, another of those splendours moved
towards me and by brightening without signified
its wish to please me; and the eyes of Beatrice,
which rested on me as before, gave me assurance
of her dear assent to my desire.

'Pray, bring to my wish speedy fulfilment, blest
spirit,' I said 'and give me proof that what I think
I can reflect on thee.'[2]

The light, therefore, which was yet strange to
me, continued from out of its depth where it was
singing before, as one rejoicing to do a kindness:
'In that part of the depraved land of Italy that lies
between the Rialto and the springs of the Brenta
and the Piave rises a hill of no great height from
which once descended a firebrand that made a

D' una radice nacqui e io ed ella:
   Cunizza fui chiamata, e qui refulgo
   perchè mi vinse il lume d'esta stella;
ma lietamente a me medesma indulgo
   la cagion di mia sorte, e non mi noia;
   che parrìa forse forte al vostro vulgo.
Di questa luculenta e cara gioia
   del nostro cielo che più m'è propinqua,
   grande fama rimase; e pria che moia,
questo centesimo anno ancor s' incinqua: 40
   vedi se far si dee l'uomo eccellente,
   sì ch'altra vita la prima relinqua.
E ciò non pensa la turba presente
   che Tagliamento e Adice richiude,
   nè per esser battuta ancor si pente;
ma tosto fia che Padova al palude
   cangerà l'acqua che Vicenza bagna,
   per essere al dover le genti crude;
e dove Sile e Cagnan s'accompagna,
   tal signoreggia e va con la testa alta,   50
   che già per lui carpir si fa la ragna.
Piangerà Feltro ancora la difalta
   dell'empio suo pastor, che sarà sconcia
   sì, che per simil non s'entrò in Malta.
Troppo sarebbe larga la bigoncia
   che ricevesse il sangue ferrarese,
   e stanco chi 'l pesasse a oncia a oncia,
che donerà questo prete cortese
   per mostrarsi di parte; e cotai doni
   conformi fieno al viver del paese.   60
Su sono specchi, voi dicete Troni,
   onde refulge a noi Dio giudicante;
   sì che questi parlar ne paion boni.'
Qui si tacette; e fecemi sembiante
   che fosse ad altro volta, per la rota
   in che si mise com'era davante.
L'altra letizia, che m'era già nota
   per cara cosa, mi si fece in vista
   qual fin balasso in che lo sol percuota.

great assault on the country round. I and he sprang
from one root. Cunizza I was called,[3] and I shine
here because the light of this star overcame me;
but I gladly pardon in myself the reason of my lot,
and it does not grieve me,—which may seem
strange, perhaps, to your crowd. Of this brilliant
and precious jewel of our heaven that is beside
me great fame was left, and before it dies away this
hundredth year will come again five times;[4] con-
sider then if man should not make himself excel
so that the first life may leave another after it. Of
this the present rabble enclosed by the Taglia-
mento and the Adige have no thought, nor for all
their scourgings do they yet repent; but the time
will soon be here when Padua, because her people
are obstinate against their duty, will stain at the
marsh the waters that bathe Vicenza,[5] and where the
Sile and the Cagnano flow together one lords it
and goes with his head high for whom is made
already the net to take him.[6] Feltre shall yet bewail
the perfidy of her godless shepherd, which shall be
so foul that for the like none ever entered Malta.
Great indeed would be the vat that should receive
the blood of the Ferrarese and weary he that should
weigh it out ounce by ounce, which this courteous
priest will pay to show himself of the Party; and
such gifts will suit the country's ways.[7] Above are
mirrors—you call them Thrones— and from them
God in judgement shines upon us, so that we think
it right to say such things.'[8]

Here she was silent and appeared to me to have
turned to other things as she joined the ring where
she was before.

The other joy, which was already known to me as
precious, became in my sight like a fine ruby on
which the sun is striking; there above brightness

Per letiziar là su fulgor s'acquista,   70
  sì come riso qui; ma giù s'abbuia
  l'ombra di fuor, come la mente è trista.
'Dio vede tutto, e tuo veder s' inluia,'
  diss' io 'beato spirto, sì che nulla
  voglia di sè a te puot'esser fuia.
Dunque la voce tua, che 'l ciel trastulla
  sempre col canto di quei fuochi pii
  che di sei ali fatt' han la coculla,
perchè non satisface a' miei disii?
  Già non attendere' io tua dimanda,   80
  s' io m' intuassi, come tu t' inmii.'
'La maggior valle in che l'acqua si spanda'
  incominciaro allor le sue parole
  'fuor di quel mar che la terra inghirlanda,
tra' discordanti liti, contra 'l sole
  tanto sen va, che fa meridïano
  là dove l'orizzonte pria far suole.
Di quella valle fu' io litorano
  tra Ebro e Macra, che per cammin corto
  parte lo Genovese dal Toscano.   90
Ad un occaso quasi e ad un orto
  Buggea siede e la terra ond' io fui,
  che fè del sangue suo già caldo il porto.
Folco mi disse quella gente a cui
  fu noto il nome mio; e questo cielo
  di me s' imprenta, com' io fe' di lui;
chè più non arse la figlia di Belo,
  noiando e a Sicheo ed a Creusa,
  di me, infin che si convenne al pelo;
nè quella Rodopea che delusa   100
  fu da Demofoonte, nè Alcide
  quando Iole nel core ebbe rinchiusa.
Non però qui si pente, ma si ride,
  non della colpa, ch'a mente non torna,
  ma del valor ch'ordinò e provide.
Qui si rimira nell'arte ch'adorna
  cotanto effetto, e discernesi 'l bene
  per che 'l mondo di su quel di giù torna.

is gained by joy, as laughter here, but below the shade darkens outwardly when the mind is sad.

'God sees all,' I said 'and thy seeing, blest spirit, is in Him, so that no wish can hide itself from thee. Why then does thy voice, which ever delights heaven together with the song of those devout fires that have made their cowl of six wings,[9] not satisfy my desires? I would not await thy question if I were in thee as thou art in me.'

'The greatest valley into which the water spreads from the sea that encircles the world' he began then 'extends so far between its discordant shores against the sun's course that it makes the meridian at the place where before it made the horizon.[10] I was a dweller on that valley's shore between the Ebro and the Magra, whose short course separates the Genoese from the Tuscan; and with almost the same sunset and sunrise lie Bugia and the city whence I came, which once made the harbour warm with its own blood.[11] Folco the people called me to whom my name was known, and this heaven bears the stamp of me as I did of it; for the daughter of Belus did not burn more, wronging both Sychaeus and Creusa, than I, as long as it befitted my locks, not she of Rhodope who was deceived by Demophoon, nor Alcides when he clasped Iole to his heart.[13] Yet here we do not repent; nay, we smile, not for our fault, which does not come back to mind, but for the Power which ordained and foresaw. Here we contemplate the art that makes beautiful the great result, and discern the good for which the world above wheels about the world below.

Ma perchè tutte le tue voglie piene
 ten porti che son nate in questa spera,   110
 procedere ancor oltre mi convene.
Tu vuo' saper chi è in questa lumera
 che qui appresso me così scintilla,
 come raggio di sole in acqua mera.
Or sappi che là entro si tranquilla
 Raab; e a nostr'ordine congiunta,
 di lei nel sommo grado si sigilla.
Da questo cielo, in cui l'ombra s'appunta
 che 'l vostro mondo face, pria ch'altr'alma
 del tríunfo di Cristo fu assunta.   120
Ben si convenne lei lasciar per palma
 in alcun cielo dell'alta vittoria
 che s'acquistò con l'una e l'altra palma,
perch'ella favorò la prima gloria
 di Iosuè in su la Terra Santa,
 che poco tocca al papa la memoria.
La tua città, che di colui è pianta
 che pría volse le spalle al suo fattore
 e di cui è la 'nvidia tanto pianta,
produce e spande il maladetto fiore   130
 c' ha disvïate le pecore e li agni,
 però che fatto ha lupo del pastore.
Per questo l'Evangelio e i dottor magni
 son derelitti, e solo ai Decretali
 si studia, sì che pare a' lor vivagni.
A questo intende il papa e' cardinali:
 non vanno i lor pensieri a Nazarette,
 là dove Gabriello aperse l'ali.
Ma Vaticano e l'altre parti elette
 di Roma che son state cimitero   140
 alla milizia che Pietro seguette,
tosto libere fien de l'adultèro.'

'But, that thou mayst take with thee all the desires fulfilled that are born in this sphere, I must continue still further. Thou wouldst know who is in this radiance that so sparkles here beside me, like a sunbeam in clear water. Know then that within it Rahab is at peace,[14] and, since she is joined by our order, it is sealed with her in its highest rank; by this heaven, where the shadow ends that is cast by your world, she was taken up before any other soul of Christ's triumph. It was indeed fitting to leave her in some heaven as a trophy of the lofty victory that was gained with the one and the other palm,[15] because she favoured Joshua's first glory in Holy Land—a place that little touches the Pope's memory.[16]

'Thy city, which is a plant of his who first turned his back on his Maker and from whose envy comes such lamentation, brings forth and spreads the accursed flower that has led astray the sheep and the lambs, for it has made a wolf of the shepherd.[17] For this the Gospel and the great Doctors are neglected and only the Decretals[18] are studied, as may be seen by their margins. To this Popes and Cardinals devote themselves. Their thoughts do not go to Nazareth, whither Gabriel spread his wings. But the Vatican and the other chosen parts of Rome which were the burial-place of the soldiery that followed Peter will soon be freed from that adultery.'

PARADISO

1. Charles Martel's widow; their son was deprived of the succession to the crown of Naples by the usurpation of Robert, Charles Martel's younger brother, in 1309.

2. 'That my thought can be reflected from God to thee.'

3. The 'firebrand' was Ezzelino (*Inf.* xii), a cruel tyrant in the hill-country north of Venice in the first half of the 13th century; Cunizza, his sister, was the mistress of Sordello (*Purg.* vi), who was a minstrel at her brother's court, and of other men.

4. Centuries will pass. This is spoken in 1300.

5. Can Grande of Verona, representing the Imperial cause, defeated the Guelf Paduans near Vicenza in 1314.

6. Richard, the oppressive Lord of Treviso, was murdered in 1312.

7. The Bishop of Feltre betrayed some Ferrarese Ghibellines who had taken refuge with him to their enemies in Ferrara, where they were executed, in 1314. 'Malta' was the name of a Papal prison. The Guelfs were known as 'the Party'.

8. The Thrones are the third of the angelic orders, after the Seraphim and the Cherubim; they are the spirits of divine judgement.

9. The Seraphim (*Is.* vi. 2).

10. 'The greatest valley' is the basin of the Mediterranean, into which the ocean pours at Gibraltar; it reaches so far eastward that the celestial horizon from the west is from the east end the zenith, the Mediterranean being supposed to cover 90 degrees of longitude.

11. Marseilles, in almost the same longitude as Bugia on the coast of Africa, was taken with great slaughter by Caesar in the Civil War.

12. Folco (d. 1231), a famous troubadour and lover who became a monk and later a bishop and a leading persecutor of the Albigenses.

13. Belus's daughter Dido, becoming the mistress of Aeneas, wronged the memory of his wife Creusa and of her own husband Sychaeus (*Inf.* v); 'she of Rhodope', a Thracian princess abandoned by her lover, killed herself; Alcides (Hercules) paid for his love of Iole with his life.

14. Rahab the harlot (*Josh.* ii.).

15. Christ's triumph in the Harrowing of Hell, gained by His hands being nailed to the cross.

16. The Pope neglected to send a crusade to Palestine, where the last Christian government was destroyed by the loss of Acre to the Saracens in 1291 (*Inf.* xxvii).

17. Florence, the Devil's plant, produced the 'florin', stamped with the fleur-de-lis, which became the standard currency of Italy; it corrupted priests and people.

18. The books of Canon Law, profitable for the gaining of florins.

NOTE

At the beginning of the canto Charles Martel is called 'the life'
—*la vita*, here rendered 'the living soul'—'of that holy light'.
This singular use of the word occurs six times in the *Paradiso*
and nowhere else in the *Divine Comedy*. It is apparently Dante's
device by which to impress on the reader from time to time that
the spirits that are hidden in their own radiance are not thereby
reduced to a mere uniform saintliness, as they might appear to
be, but that they have in Paradise their full and individual
personality, their 'life'. The word in this sense does not occur
in the sphere of the Moon, where the features of Piccarda
and the other saints are visible, nor in the spheres of Mercury
and Mars, where Justinian and Cacciaguida are, respectively,
the only speakers and give a full account of themselves, but in
all the other five spheres, in which the souls are concealed in
their own light. It is an example of the sustained significance
and consistency of Dante's diction.

With the marriage of Charles Martel, the heir of the Angevins,
to Clemence, the daughter of the Emperor Rudolph, in 1291,
there was great hope of a reconciliation through their joint
line of the Guelfs and Ghibellines in Italy, a hope quickly
destroyed by the death of Charles in 1295, and later by his
brother's usurpation of the crown of Naples; and the disappoint-
ment would be bitter to Dante not less for public than for
personal reasons. Clemence died in 1301, so that she was still
living at the assumed date of Dante's vision, and it was natural
that he should, in imagination, declare to her his sympathy
in 'your wrongs', although she was dead long before he wrote
these lines.

The cruelties of Ezzelino, Ghibelline Lord of the March of
Treviso for thirty-four years, had become a legend of horror
in Italy, especially among the Guelfs; and with these cruelties

were associated the equally notorious love-affairs of his sister Cunizza. Dante had seen Ezzelino, 'that brow with the hair so black', in 'the red boiling' of Phlegethon among the 'tyrants who gave their hands to blood and plunder' (*Inf.* xii), and here we have another example of the division of destiny between members of the same family. Cunizza spent her last years in Florence as a guest of the Cavalcante family, with whom, at any rate later, Dante was intimate. She died there in Dante's fifteenth year, and whether he met her in her old age or not he was certainly in the way of knowing much about her from his friends who had been hers. Here, her 'splendour', as if recognizing him, 'moved towards me and by brightening without signified its wish to please me'. Her warm reference to Folco and to his lasting fame—not obviously called for in the narrative—may well be a reminiscence of her talk in Florence. She had the reputation of showing kindness to some of the victims of her brother's cruelty, and, as the last survivor of the family, she had liberated the family serfs. There is an impersonal reserve in her words to Dante and a composed sternness of judgement on her own degenerate and turbulent country, as of one who delivers an oracle from heaven, which are suited to the great lady of much experience in her graver years in Florence. There she would doubtless be regarded by the Guelf burghers, 'your crowd', with more interest for her glamorous and well-known story than for her repentance, and she would be all the more wrapped up in her own thoughts, like one that has 'turned to other things'.

The elaborate geographical account of his native city with which Folco begins may be in effect a correction of Cunizza's praise of him as 'this brilliant and precious jewel of our heaven', as if to say that from this height Marseilles could be made out only by such a calculation and that his name is now forgotten —'the people to whom my name was known'; and the same humbleness may explain his unreadiness to talk of himself to Dante. He compares his own earthly passion with that of famous lovers in antiquity whose loves ended in disaster. Then, as befits a monk and a bishop, he explains at more length what Cunizza had merely told as a matter of experience, that the reason of their lot, their old wantonness, did not now grieve them. There, he says, they 'smile for the Power which ordained and foresaw' and at the divine 'art that makes beautiful the great result', the art which operates in the moving heavens for God's purposes on earth. In the heaven of Venus it would seem that Dante is especially conscious of the strangely opposite possibilities of the same natural temper in men—in this case the amorous flame which may burn up the soul and leave it ashes, or may qualify it for a selfless passion for God and His will. Cunizza 'brightens without'; Folco 'becomes like a fine ruby on which the sun is shining'; Rahab—as it were the extreme case—'sparkles like a sunbeam in clear water'. In their redemption their native temper is itself redeemed, and their old repentance, cleansed of its bitterness in Lethe, is lost in thanksgiving. How much thought Dante had of himself in this context, who can say? 'It was human passion, purified and sublimated, that created the holy ardour by which, according to Christ's words to the Pharisees, "the harlots go into the kingdom of heaven before you". . . . In comparison with the lukewarm and the cowardly, whom Dante brands more severely than he does actual sinners, only the daring, the passionate in the nobler sense, are capable of the impulses that make saints and heroes. The ideal transfiguration of human passion, purged from fault, is the profound motive of these two cantos, and one of those daring souls, and one of the sublimest, was the Poet of the *Comedy*' (*C. Grabher*).

The last lines in Dante's appeal to Folco to speak to him are translated by Norton: 'I should not wait for thy request if I in-theed myself as thou thyself in-meest', rendering literally Dante's coinages *m'intuasse* and *t'inmii*; and on that analogy the first line in the same speech should be rendered: 'Thy sight, blest spirit, in-Hims itself', *s'inluia*. These expressions, as strange in Italian as such renderings would be in English, are Dante's bold and most characteristic way of telling of the soul's inner fellowship, divine and human, as of a mystery that cannot be told in common speech, no loss of personality but the fulfilment of it in an immediacy of intercourse, thought with thought, which belongs to the life of Paradise. In the first canto Beatrice is 'she who saw me as I saw myself' and in the second 'she from whom my thoughts could not be hid'; and in the seventh, when she sees him struggling with a question which he dared not utter, she knows and speaks it, 'by my judgement, which cannot err'. But it is in the heaven of Venus that we discover that this power of spiritual telepathy belongs to the vision of God which is the enlightenment of all the saints in Paradise. Dante rejoices that his own 'deep joy' at their meeting is 'seen' by Charles, and seen in his 'gazing upon God'; and now, as if testing a new experience, he asks Cunizza to 'give me proof that what I think I can reflect on thee', and, because Folco's seeing is 'in' God who 'sees all', he is sure that Folco knows his thoughts and can answer them. From this point on, that intuitive and unfailing perception on the part of the redeemed is taken for granted as a feature of the perfect life.

Folco is here as a great penitent and saint, and Dante cannot have been ignorant that he had been also a great persecutor in the savage 'crusade' against the Albigensian heretics a hundred years before Dante wrote, a crusade which Dante was too much a child of his age to condemn. It is not referred to here, unless it be by implication in Folco's words about 'Joshua's first glory in Holy Land', the capture of Jericho from the heathen by the people of God and the reproach cast, by contrast, on 'the Pope's memory'. But it is for his flaming zeal for the Church, the spiritual order of humanity, that Dante honours him. Not only the Old Testament story of Rahab the harlot's deliverance of the Hebrew spies, but also the singular place given to her in the New Testament—as an ancestress of Christ (*Matt.* i. 5), as one that acted 'by faith' (*Heb.* xi. 31), and as one 'justified by works' (*Jam.* ii. 25), and in the Church's teaching—as the type of the Church, saved by Joshua who was the type of Christ; all this explains Folco's language about her as sparkling 'like a sunbeam in clear water' and as 'a trophy of the lofty victory' of Christ. As Cunizza commends Folco, so Folco commends Rahab; both Cunizza and Folco receive Dante with a welcome that shines from them; and Dante eagerly claims of both that they should read his thoughts and respond to them. The whole heaven of Venus is filled with an intimate and impassioned fellowship of souls all whose fellowship is in God.

Folco was known on earth first as a troubadour, then as a

bishop, and something of both these contrasted characters has been noted in his long speech here, on the one hand in the picturesque elaboration of the account of his native place and the comparison of his own wantonness with that of the great lovers in antiquity, on the other in the close-knit energy of his judgement on Florence and the Church, 'springing from the force of a shaping and creative passion,—Lucifer, the root sunk in the earth's centre,—Florence, the plant from that root, confronting the world,—the florin, the flower of that plant,—the Pope, a wolf hungry for that flower and heedless of good pasture. *Le style c'est l'homme*. In Folco are two men, and two styles' (*Porena*, quoted by *Vandelli*).

It is fitting to Folco's character that he should be Dante's mouthpiece in the denunciation of Florence, whose money was the instrument of the Church's present corruptions. His last words doubtless refer to the death of Pope Boniface in 1303 and the removal of the Papacy to Avignon in 1305.

PARADISO

GUARDANDO nel suo Figlio con l'Amore
  che l'uno e l'altro etternalmente spira,
  lo primo ed ineffabile Valore,
quanto per mente e per loco sí gira
  con tant'ordine fè, ch'esser non puote
  sanza gustar di lui chi ciò rimira.
Leva dunque, lettore, all'alte ruote
  meco la vista, dritto a quella parte
  dove l'un moto e l'altro si percuote;
e lì comincia a vagheggiar nell'arte   10
  di quel maestro che dentro a sè l'ama,
  tanto che mai da lei occhio non parte.
Vedi come da indi si dirama
  l'oblico cerchio che i pianeti porta,
  per sodisfare al mondo che li chiama.
E se la strada lor non fosse torta,
  molta virtù nel ciel sarebbe in vano,
  e quasi ogni potenza qua giù morta;
e se dal dritto più o men lontano
  fosse 'l partire, assai sarebbe manco   20
  e giù e su dell'ordine mondano.
Or ti riman, lettor, sovra 'l tuo banco,
  dietro pensando a ciò che si preliba,
  s'esser vuoi lieto assai prima che stanco.
Messo t' ho innanzi: omai per te ti ciba;
  chè a sè torce tutta la mia cura
  quella materia ond' io son fatto scriba.

CANTO X

The Sphere of the Sun; the wise; the First Circle;
St Thomas Aquinas

LOOKING on His Son with the Love which the One
and the Other eternally breathe forth, the primal
and ineffable Power made with such order all that
revolves in mind or space that he who contemplates
it cannot but taste of Him.[1] Lift up thine eyes with
me then, reader, to the lofty wheels, directing
them on that part where the one motion strikes the
other,[2] and from that point take thy pleasure in the
art of the Master, who so loves it in His heart that
His eye never leaves it. See how from there the
circle branches obliquely that bears the planets
to satisfy the world which calls for them. And
if their track were not aslant much virtue in the
heavens would be vain and almost every potency
down here dead, and if it parted farther or less far
from the straight course much would be lacking
both above and below[3] in the order of the world.

Stay now, reader, on thy bench, thinking over
this of which thou hast a foretaste, and thou shalt
have much delight before thou art weary; I have
set before thee, now feed thyself, for the theme of
which I am made the scribe bends to itself all my
care.

Lo ministro maggior della natura
  che del valor del ciel lo mondo imprenta
  e col suo lume il tempo ne misura,   30
con quella parte che su si rammenta
  congiunto, si girava per le spire
  in che più tosto ognora s'appresenta;
e io era con lui; ma del salire
  non m'accors' io, se non com' uom s'accorge,
  anzi 'l primo pensier, del suo venire.
È Beatrice quella che sì scorge
  di bene in meglio sì subitamente
  che l'atto suo per tempo non si sporge.
Quant'esser convenia da sè lucente   40
  quel ch'era dentro al sol dov'io entra'mi,
  non per color, ma per lume parvente!
Perch' io lo 'ngegno e l'arte e l'uso chiami
  sì nol direi, che mai s' imaginasse;
  ma creder puossi e di veder si brami.
E se le fantasie nostre son basse
  a tanta altezza, non è maraviglia;
  chè sopra 'l sol non fu occhio ch'andasse.
Tal era quivi la quarta famiglia
  dell'alto Padre, che sempre la sazia,   50
  mostrando come spira e come figlia.
E Beatrice cominciò: 'Ringrazia,
  ringrazia il sol delli angeli, ch'a questo
  sensibil t' ha levato per sua grazia.'
Cor di mortal non fu mai sì digesto
  a divozione ed a rendersi a Dio
  con tutto il suo gradir cotanto presto,
come a quelle parole mi fec' io;
  e sì tutto 'l mio amore in lui si mise,
  che Beatrice eclissò nell'oblio.   60
Non le dispiacque; ma sì se ne rise,
  che lo splendor delli occhi suoi ridenti
  mia mente unita in più cose divise.
Io vidi più fulgor vivi e vincenti
  far di noi centro e di sè far corona,
  più dolci in voce che in vista lucenti:

The greatest minister of nature, which stamps the world with heavenly worth and with its light measures time for us, being in conjunction with the part I have noted, was wheeling through the spirals in which it presents itself earlier every day;[4] and I was with it but was not aware of the ascent any more than one is aware of the beginning of a thought before it comes. It is Beatrice who thus leads from good to better so instantly that her action has no measurement in time.

How shining in itself must have been that which was within the Sun as I entered it, showing not by colour but by light! Were I to summon genius and skill and practice I should never tell of it so that it might be imagined, but we can believe it, and let us long for the sight; and if our imagination is too low for such a height it is no wonder, for never did eye see light greater than the Sun. Such was there the fourth family of the Father on high, who ever satisfies it, showing how He breathes forth and how begets.[5]

And Beatrice began: 'Give thanks, give thanks to the Sun of the angels, who to this visible one has raised thee by His grace.'

Never was heart of mortal so ready for worship or so swift to yield itself to God with its whole assent as I became at these words, and all my love was so set on Him that it eclipsed Beatrice in forgetfulness; nor did this displease her, but she smiled at it so that the splendour of her smiling eyes broke up the absorption of my mind and divided it on many objects. I saw many flashing lights of surpassing brightness make of us a centre and of themselves a crown, sweeter in their voices than shining in their aspect; thus girdled we some-

così cinger la figlia di Latona
   vedem tal volta, quando l'aere è pregno,
   sì che ritenga il fil che fa la zona.
Nella corte del cielo, ond' io rivegno,   70
   si trovan molte gioie care e belle
   tanto che non si posson trar del regno;
e 'l canto di quei lumi era di quelle;
   chi non s' impenna sì che là su voli,
   dal muto aspetti quindi le novelle.
Poi, sì cantando, quelli ardenti soli
   si fuor girati intorno a noi tre volte,
   come stelle vicine a' fermi poli,
donne mi parver non da ballo sciolte,
   ma che s'arrestin tacite, ascoltando   80
   fin che le nove note hanno ricolte;
e dentro all'un senti' cominciar: 'Quando
   lo raggio della grazia, onde s'accende
   verace amore e che poi cresce amando,
multiplicato in te tanto resplende,
   che ti conduce su per quella scala
   u' sanza risalir nessun discende;
qual ti negasse il vin della sua fiala
   per la tua sete, in libertà non fora
   se non com'acqua ch'al mar non si cala.   90
Tu vuo' saper di quai piante s' infiora
   questa ghirlanda che 'ntorno vagheggia
   la bella donna ch'al ciel t'avvalora.
Io fui delli agni della santa greggia
   che Domenico mena per cammino
   u' ben s' impingua se non si vaneggia.
Questi che m'è a destra più vicino,
   frate e maestro fummi, ed esso Alberto
   è di Cologna, e io Thomàs d'Aquino.
Se sì di tutti li altri esser vuo' certo,   100
   di retro al mio parlar ten vien col viso
   girando su per lo beato serto.
Quell'altro fiammeggiare esce del riso
   di Grazïan, che l'uno e l'altro foro
   aiutò sì che piace in paradiso.

times see Latona's daughter when the air is charged
so that it retains the thread that makes her zone.[6]
In the court of heaven from which I have returned
many gems are found of such worth and beauty
that they may not be taken out of the kingdom, and
of these was the song of those lights. He that does
not take wings to fly up thither may wait for news
thence from the dumb! When, singing thus, these
burning suns had circled round us three times, like
stars near the steadfast poles, they appeared to me
like ladies not freed from the dance, but pausing
in silence and listening till they have caught the
new strain;[7] and within one of them I heard
begin: 'Since the beam of grace by which true love
is kindled and which then grows by loving shines so
multiplied in thee that it brings thee up that stair
which none descends but to mount again, he that
should refuse to thy thirst the wine from his vessel
would be no more at liberty than water that does
not fall to the sea. Thou wouldst know what plants
are these that bloom in this garland which surrounds
with looks of love the fair lady who strengthens
thee for heaven. I was of the lambs of the holy flock
that Dominic leads on the path where there is good
fattening if they do not stray; he that is next beside
me on the right was my brother and master, and he
is Albert of Cologne and I Thomas of Aquino. If
thou wouldst be thus informed of all the rest,
follow after my words with thine eyes, going round
the blessed wreath. That next flame comes from the
smile of Gratian, who served the one and the other
court so well that it gives pleasure in Paradise; the

L'altro ch'appresso adorna il nostro coro,
    quel Pietro fu che con la poverella
    offerse a Santa Chiesa suo tesoro.
La quinta luce, ch'è tra noi più bella,
    spira di tale amor, che tutto 'l mondo   110
    là giù ne gola di saper novella:
entro v'è l'alta mente u' sì profondo
    saver fu messo, che se 'l vero è vero
    a veder tanto non surse il secondo.
Appresso vedi il lume di quel cero
    che giù, in carne, più a dentro vide
    l'angelica natura e 'l ministero.
Nell'altra piccioletta luce ride
    quello avvocato de' tempi cristiani
    del cui latino Augustin si provide.   120
Or se tu l'occhio della mente trani
    di luce in luce dietro alle mie lode,
    già dell'ottava con sete rimani.
Per vedere ogni ben dentro vi gode
    l'anima santa che 'l mondo fallace
    fa manifesto a chi di lei ben ode:
lo corpo ond'ella fu cacciata giace
    giuso in Cieldauro; ed essa da martiro
    e da essilio venne a questa pace.
Vedi oltre fiammeggiar l'ardente spiro   130
    d'Isidoro, di Beda e di Riccardo,
    che a considerar fu più che viro.
Questi onde a me ritorna il tuo riguardo,
    è 'l lume d'uno spirto che 'n pensieri
    gravi a morir li parve venir tardo:
essa è la luce etterna di Sigieri,
    che, leggendo nel vico delli strami,
    sillogizzò invidïosi veri.'
Indi, come orologio che ne chiami
    nell'ora che la sposa di Dio surge   140
    a mattinar lo sposo perchè l'ami,
che l'una parte l'altra tira e urge,
    tin tin sonando con sì dolce nota,
    che 'l ben disposto spirto d'amor turge;

other who next adorns our choir was that Peter who, like the poor widow, offered his treasure to Holy Church. The fifth light, which is the most beautiful among us, breathes from such a love that all the world below hungers for news of it; within it is the lofty mind to which was given wisdom so deep that, if the truth be true, there never arose a second of such vision.[8] Beside it see the light of that candle which below in the flesh saw farthest into the nature and the ministry of the angels. In the little light that is next smiles that defender of Christian times of whose treatise Augustine made use. If now thou art bringing thy mind's eye from light to light after my praises, thou art already left eager for the eighth. Within it rejoices in the vision of all good the holy soul who makes plain the world's deceitfulness to one that hears him rightly; the body from which he was driven lies below in Cieldauro, and he came from martyrdom and exile to this peace. See, flaming beyond, the glowing breath of Isidore, of Bede, and of Richard who in contemplation was more than man. This one from whom thy look returns to me is the light of a spirit to whom, in his grave thoughts, death seemed slow in coming; it is the eternal light of Siger, who, lecturing in the Street of Straw, demonstrated invidious truths.'[9]

Then, like a clock that calls us at the hour when the bride of God[10] rises to sing matins to the Bride-groom that he may love her, when one part draws or drives another, sounding the chime with notes so sweet that the well-ordered spirit swells with

così vid' io la glorïosa rota
   muoversi e render voce a voce in tempra
   ed in dolcezza ch'esser non pò nota
se non colà dove gioir s' insempra.

love, so I saw the glorious wheel move and render voice to voice with harmony and sweetness that cannot be known but there where joy becomes eternal.

1. Divine Power, the Father, with Divine Wisdom, the Son, expresses Divine Love, the Spirit, in the creation of the spiritual and natural worlds.

2. The Ecliptic, the apparent annual path of the Sun, Moon and planets round the earth, cuts obliquely through the celestial equator, so that the Sun, moving in spirals between north and south, produces the changing seasons of natural life on the earth.

3. In the northern and southern hemispheres.

4. After the spring equinox.

5. The Father begets the Son, and the Father and Son breathe forth the Spirit.

6. Diana, the Moon, surrounded by the halo.

7. A reminiscence of a popular dance of the time, in which a company of women danced to their own singing, then stopped silent till the leader gave them the next stanza, when they took up the refrain again.

8. If Scripture be true: 'God said unto him, . . . Lo, I have given thee a wise and an understanding heart; so that there was none like thee before thee, neither after thee shall any arise like unto thee' (1 *Kings* iii. 11-12).

9. Albert and Thomas, both Dominicans, were the most influential theologians of the 13th century; Gratian's chief work was the harmonizing of the civil and the canon law; Peter the Lombard wrote a compendium of the theology of the early Fathers, in which he likened his own work to the widow's mite; Solomon's *Song* was regarded as the marriage-song of Christ and His Church,—the question of Solomon's salvation was much debated; Dionysius the Areopagite (*Acts* xvii. 34) was supposed to be the author of *The Angelic Hierarchy*—written in the 5th century—, the standard authority on angels; 'that defender of Christian times' was Orosius, 5th century historian; Boethius, statesman and philosopher in Theodoric's service, was unjustly disgraced and died in prison, where he wrote *The Consolation of Philosophy*,—he was buried in the Church of the Golden Roof (*Cieldauro*) in Pavia (A.D. 525); Isidore, an encyclopaedist; Bede, 'the Venerable', English monk, theologian and historian; Richard of St Victor, mystical theologian; Siger, professor in Paris in Aquinas's time, who expounded the philosophy of Averroes and was charged with heresy.

10. The Church.

NOTE

The tenth canto begins with a total change of subject and something like a new prologue to another section of the poem. Dante is now beyond the shadow of the earth and among souls that shine even against the brightness of the Sun. Their greatness was in their knowledge of God, and in putting them in the heaven of the Sun he may have had in mind the language of Scripture: 'They that be wise shall shine as the brightness of the firmament' (*Dan*. xii. 3). He had written in the *Convito*: 'Nothing sensible in all the world is fitter to be made an image of God than the Sun, which first illumines itself, then all the celestial and elemental bodies; so God illumines Himself first with intellectual light, then the celestial and other intelligencies.'

The opening stanza contains the first among many references in these cantos to the ultimate mystery of the divine nature, the Holy Trinity, the infinite fulness and eternal self-fellowship of the Godhead. In creation, in providence, in redemption, in the operations of the circling heavens and in the life of men, the Father is conceived as the operative Power, the Son as the guiding Wisdom, 'the Word', the Spirit as the Love which is 'breathed forth'—in the traditional language 'proceeds'—from the Father and the Son; so these souls of the wise rejoice in their knowledge of the infinite Power working with infinite Wisdom for the ends of infinite Love, and it is revealed to them as matter for eternal revelation 'how He breathes forth and how begets.'

It belongs to Dante's spiritual realism that he finds the heavens declaring the glory of God, not merely in their general splendour, but specifically in the device of the ecliptic and the 'spiral' course of the Sun by which it brings the changing seasons to the earth, imprinting on it the goodness of heaven and 'measuring time for us', so that the ultimate mysteries of the

Godhead are in one context with the common order of the world, the daily sounding of the hours of prayer and the coming of the spring. At the time, probably, when he was occupied with the *Paradiso* a proposal had come to him for his return to Florence on terms so humiliating that he refused them with indignation: 'On such conditions I shall never enter Florence more. What then? Shall I not everywhere look on the mirror of the sun and the stars? Can I not meditate the sweetest truths everywhere under heaven unless I first make myself inglorious, nay abject, to the people and the state of Florence?' Here, in Paradise, looking on the mirror of the Sun and the stars and considering what they mean for men, he tells of the consolation of his exile.

But he was conscious of his readers all the time, for whom, against all precedent, he wrote of these high matters in the vernacular, and it is not surprising if some of them found his astronomical expansions fatiguing and if he felt it necessary to bid them have patience with this 'foretaste' of a subject in which they will find much pleasure if they continue in it, before they are weary. 'Such a constant dragging in of astronomical lore may seem to us puerile or pedantic; but for Dante the astronomical situation had the charm of a landscape, literally full of the most wonderful lights and shadows; and it had also the charm of a hard-won discovery that unveiled the secrets of nature. To think straight, to see things as they are or as they might naturally be, interested him more than to fancy things impossible; and in this he shows, not want of imagination, but true imaginative power and imaginative maturity. . . . In Dante the fancy is not empty or arbitrary; it is serious, fed on the study of real things' (*G. Santayana*).

In the deepening assurance of God to which he has been brought by Beatrice, Dante is so rapt that he forgets Beatrice herself, and she smiles on him with pleasure; for a true theology delights to be forgotten in worship. But revelation has lessons for him still. 'The splendour of her smiling eyes broke up the absorption of my mind and set it on many objects', and he found himself with her surrounded by the company of those who had been his chief teachers. Her smiling eyes are the demonstration of the truth, and that demonstration was, in fact, mediated to Dante by the succession of those that are wise in the things of God. Thus Dante, the learned pupil of Aquinas and the rest, makes his acknowledgement to Beatrice—like Wordsworth's to Dorothy:

'She gave me eyes, she gave me ears;

.   .   .   .   .

A heart, the fountain of sweet tears;
And love and thought and joy.'

What other poet besides these two would have put *thought* among such gifts? But Dante put thought before heart and love and joy.

We are told repeatedly of the sweetness of the song of the souls here and they are compared to flowers in a garland and to ladies in a dance—images that we do not readily associate with theological teaching and in particular with the dialectical subtleties of the Schoolmen; for the whole language of the canto has its significance in the idea that the knowledge of God which is all the aim and worth of theology is not mere learning but spiritual assurance, and that such assurance can be told only in song.

The twelve spirits 'surround' Beatrice 'with looks of love'; they are intent, that is, on divine truth, on all sides of it. Yet their writings cover much that we should not think of so describing,—ecclesiastical and civil law (Gratian), the doctrine of angels (Dionysius), natural science (Isidore), church history (Bede), royal wisdom (Solomon). The saints are chosen, as if deliberately, for their diversity, to demonstrate that the truth of God is the truth not only in itself but also in its operation, in human history and institutions, in the whole natural order, and that the glory of these twelve lies in their knowledge of whatever most concerns God's being and His works and ways with men.

The eighth in the list is given exceptional space, as one to whom Dante wished to give exceptional honour. He 'makes plain'—still, in his book—the 'world's deceitfulness', and now he 'rejoices in the vision of all good', having 'come from martyrdom and exile to this peace.' *The Consolation of Philosophy* by

Boethius, the great statesman and philosopher of the beginning of the sixth century, was much read in the Middle Ages, and its calm and elevated wisdom had brought to Dante in his years of spiritual despondency new direction and hope, as he more than once acknowledges in the *Convito*. These lines are a further expression of that indebtedness. Boethius was a Christian, and, though his book is written in pagan terms—a conversation with the Lady Philosophy—, it is well described by Mr. Christopher Dawson as 'a perfect expression of the union of the Christian spirit with the classical tradition.'

All the saints in the circle are named by Aquinas, who more than any other summed up for Dante the Christian doctrine of God. Siger, the last-named and the next to Aquinas on the other side from the great Albert of Cologne, was Aquinas's contemporary as a teacher in the University of Paris, where his bold speculations had brought upon him grave charges of heresy. In the earthly life Aquinas was among Siger's stoutest opponents; in the reconciling light of Paradise they join their voices to make its harmonies. Dante's experience might well make him sympathetic with one who, to his cost, 'demonstrated invidious truths',—truths that rouse not only opposition but enmity. The incidental reference to the Street of Straw where Siger had lectured not only adds a characteristic touch of objectivity, but may be taken to suggest Dante's claim to have had first-hand reports in Paris of Siger's teaching from those who had heard him, and to be speaking with knowledge when he said, through Aquinas, that Siger *sillogizzò*—reasoned out by syllogism—*invidiosi veri*.

The closing lines of the canto, lines of 'harmony and sweetness' like the sounds they tell of, come on the reader with an unexpectedness which adds much to their felicity, and they combine, in a manner which is only Dante's, homely imagery and spiritual elevation. The song of these devotees of the truth is like the early chime that wakes the monastery, calling 'the well-ordered spirit' to prayer—a familiar sound to Dante—, and their various testimony acts and reacts between one and another in their perfect fellowship, like the wheels and levers of the clock. The ultimate utterance of the truth of God must be a song, 'such harmony is in immortal souls'.

PARADISO

O INSENSATA cura de' mortali,
    quanto son difettivi sillogismi
    quei che ti fanno in basso batter l'ali!
Chi dietro a iura, e chi ad aforismi
    sen giva, e chi seguendo sacerdozio,
    e chi regnar per forza o per sofismi,
e chi rubare, e chi civil negozio;
    chi nel diletto della carne involto
    s'affaticava, e chi si dava all'ozio,
quando, da tutte queste cose sciolto,   10
    con Beatrice m'era suso in cielo
    cotanto glorïosamente accolto.
Poi che ciascuno fu tornato ne lo
    punto del cerchio in che avanti s'era,
    fermossi, come a candellier candelo.
E io senti' dentro a quella lumera
    che pria m'avea parlato, sorridendo
    incominciar, faccendosi più mera:
'Così com' io del suo raggio resplendo,
    sì, riguardando nella luce etterna,   20
    li tuoi pensieri onde cagioni apprendo.
Tu dubbi, e hai voler che si ricerna
    in sì aperta e 'n sì distesa lingua
    lo dicer mio, ch'al tuo sentir si sterna,
ove dinanzi dissi "U' ben s' impingua,"
    e là u' dissi "Non surse il secondo";
    e qui è uopo che ben si distingua.

CANTO XI

The story of St Francis; the decadence of the Dominicans

O INSENSATE care of mortals, how vain are the reasonings that make thee beat thy wings in downward flight! One was going after law, another after the *Aphorisms*,[1] one following the priesthood and another seeking to rule by force or craft, one set on robbery and another on affairs of state, one labouring in the toils of fleshly delights and another given up to idleness; while I, set free from all these things, was high in heaven with Beatrice, received thus gloriously.

When each had come back to the point of the circle where it was before, it stopped, like a candle on its stand, and within that radiance that had already spoken to me I heard begin, while it smiled and turned brighter: 'Even as I reflect its beams, so, gazing into the Eternal Light, I perceive thy thoughts and the cause of them. Thou art perplexed and wouldst have my words made clearer, in plain and explicit terms on the level of thy understanding, when I said before "Where there is good fattening", and again where I said "There never arose a second"; and here it is necessary to make a clear distinction.

La provedenza, che governa il mondo
  con quel consiglio nel quale ogni aspetto
  creato è vinto pria che vada al fondo,   30
però che andasse ver lo suo diletto
  la sposa di colui ch'ad alte grida,
  disposò lei col sangue benedetto,
in sè sicura e anche a lui più fida,
  due principi ordinò in suo favore,
  che quinci e quindi le fosser per guida.
L'un fu tutto serafico in ardore;
  l'altro per sapïenza in terra fue
  di cherubica luce uno splendore.
Dell' un dirò, però che d'amendue   40
  si dice l'un pregiando, quale uom prende,
  perch'ad un fine fuor l'opere sue.
Intra Tupino e l'acqua che discende
  del colle eletto dal beato Ubaldo,
  fertile costa d'alto monte pende,
onde Perugia sente freddo e caldo
  da Porta Sole; e di retro le piange
  per grave giogo Nocera con Gualdo.
Di questa costa, là dov'ella frange
  più sua rattezza, nacque al mondo un sole, 50
  come fa questo tal volta di Gange.
Però chi d'esso loco fa parole,
  non dica Ascesi, chè direbbe corto,
  ma Orïente, se proprio dir vole.
Non era ancor molto lontan dall'orto,
  ch'el cominciò a far sentir la terra
  della sua gran virtute alcun conforto;
chè per tal donna, giovinetto, in guerra
  del padre corse, a cui, come alla morte,
  la porta del piacer nessun diserra;   60
e dinanzi alla sua spirital corte
  et coram patre le si fece unito;
  poscia di dì in dì l'amò più forte.
Questa, privata del primo marito,
  millecent'anni e più dispetta e scura
  fino a costui si stette sanza invito;

'The Providence that rules the world with that counsel in which every created sight is vanquished before it reaches the bottom—in order that the bride of Him who, with loud cries,[2] wedded her with His sacred blood should go to her Beloved secure in herself and faithfuller to Him—ordained for her behoof two princes to be her guides on this side and on that. The one was all seraphic in ardour; the other, for wisdom, was on earth a splendour of cherubic light.[3] I shall tell of the one, since to praise one, whichever we take, is to speak of both; for their labours were to one end.

'Between the Topino and the water that falls from the hill chosen by the blessed Ubaldo hangs a fertile slope of the lofty mountain from which Perugia feels cold and heat at Porta Cole, and behind it Nocera and Gualdo grieve under a heavy yoke.[4] From this slope, where it most breaks its steepness, a sun rose on the world, as this does sometimes from the Ganges; therefore let him who makes mention of that place not say *Ascesi*, for he would say too little, but *Orient*, if he would name it rightly.[5] He was not yet far from his rising when he began to make the earth feel some strengthening from his mighty influence; for, still a youth, he ran into strife with his father for a lady to whom, as to death, none willingly unlocks the door, and before his spiritual court *et coram patre* he was joined to her, and thenceforth loved her better every day.[6] She, bereft of her first husband,[7] despised and obscure eleven hundred years and more, remained without a suitor till he came; nor

nè valse udir che la trovò sicura
  con Amiclate, al suon della sua voce,
  colui ch'a tutto 'l mondo fè paura;
nè valse esser costante nè feroce,   70
  sì che, dove Maria rimase giuso,
  ella con Cristo salse in su la croce.
Ma perch' io non proceda troppo chiuso,
  Francesco e Povertà per questi amanti
  prendi oramai nel mio parlar diffuso.
La lor concordia e i lor lieti sembianti,
  amore e maraviglia e dolce sguardo
  facìeno esser cagion di pensier santi;
tanto che 'l venerabile Bernardo
  si scalzò prima, e dietro a tanta pace   80
  corse e, correndo, li parve esser tardo.
Oh ignota ricchezza! oh ben ferace!
  Scalzasi Egidio, scalzasi Silvestro
  dietro allo sposo, sì la sposa piace.
Indi sen va quel padre e quel maestro
  con la sua donna e con quella famiglia
  che già legava l'umile capestro.
Nè li gravò viltà di cor le ciglia
  per esser fi' di Pietro Bernardone,
  nè per parer dispetto a maraviglia;   90
ma regalmente sua dura intenzione
  ad Innocenzio aperse, e da lui ebbe
  primo sigillo a sua religïone.
Poi che la gente poverella crebbe
  dietro a costui, la cui mirabil vita
  meglio in gloria del ciel si canterebbe,
di seconda corona redimita
  fu per Onorio dall'Etterno Spiro
  la santa voglia d'esto archimandrita.
E poi che, per la sete del martiro,   100
  nella presenza del Soldan superba
  predicò Cristo e li altri che 'l seguiro,
e per trovare a conversione acerba
  troppo la gente, per non stare indarno,
  reddissi al frutto dell'italica erba,

did it avail when men heard that he who put all the
world in fear found her unmoved, with Amyclas,
at the sound of his voice;[8] nor did it avail her to
have such courage and constancy that, where Mary
stayed below, she mounted on the cross with Christ.
But, lest I proceed too darkly, take now Francis
and Poverty for these lovers in all I have said. Their
harmony and happy looks moved men to love and
wonder and sweet contemplation and led them to
holy thoughts, so that the venerable Bernard first
went barefoot and ran after that great peace and,
running, thought himself too slow. O wealth un-
known and fruitful good! Barefoot goes Giles,
barefoot goes Sylvester, after the bridegroom,
so greatly does the bride delight them. Then that
father and master went on his way with his lady
and with that family which now was bound with
the lowly cord; nor did cowardice of heart weigh
down his brow for being Pietro Bernardone's son
nor for appearing an object of wonder and contempt,
but royally he opened his stern resolve to Innocent
and had from him the first seal upon his order.[9]
When the company of Poor Brothers increased
behind him whose wondrous life were better sung
in heaven's glory, the holy purpose of this chief
shepherd was encircled with a second crown by the
Eternal Spirit through Honorius.[10] And when,
in thirst for martyrdom, he had preached Christ
and them that followed Him in the proud presence
of the Sultan, and, finding the people unripe for
conversion and not being willing to remain for no
purpose, he had returned to the harvest of the

167

nel crudo sasso intra Tevero e Arno
   da Cristo prese l'ultimo sigillo,
   che le sue membra due anni portarno.
Quando a colui ch'a tanto ben sortillo
   piacque di trarlo suso alla mercede   110
   ch'el meritò nel suo farsi pusillo,
a' frati suoi, sì com'a giuste rede,
   raccomandò la donna sua più cara,
   e comandò che l'amassero a fede;
e del suo grembo l'anima preclara
   mover si volse, tornando al suo regno,
   e al suo corpo non volse altra bara.
Pensa oramai qual fu colui che degno
   collega fu a mantener la barca
   di Pietro in alto mar per dritto segno;   120
e questo fu il nostro patrïarca;
   per che, qual segue lui com'el comanda,
   discerner puoi che buone merce carca.
Ma 'l suo peculio di nova vivanda
   è fatto ghiotto, sì ch'esser non puote
   che per diversi salti non si spanda;
e quanto le sue pecore remote
   e vagabunde più da esso vanno,
   più tornano all'ovil di latte vote.
Ben son di quelle che temono 'l danno   130
   e stringonsi al pastor; ma son sì poche,
   che le cappe fornisce poco panno.
Or se le mie parole non son fioche
   e se la tua audienza è stata attenta,
   se ciò ch'è detto alla mente rivoche,
in parte fia la tua voglia contenta,
   perchè vedrai la pianta onde si scheggia,
   e vedra' il corregger che argomenta
"U' ben s' impingua, se non si vaneggia".'

Italian fields, then, on the rough crag between Tiber and Arno, he received from Christ the last seal, which his members bore for two years.[11] When He that had destined him to so much good was pleased to take him up to the reward he had won by making himself lowly, to his brothers, as to the rightful heirs, he commended his most dear lady and bade them love her faithfully; and from her bosom the glorious soul chose to set forth, returning to its kingdom, and for its body would have no other bier.[12]

'Consider now what he was that was his fit colleague to keep Peter's bark on the right course in the high sea, and such was our Patriarch;[13] from which thou mayst perceive that he who follows him as he commands carries good merchandise. But his flock has grown so greedy of new fare that it must needs scatter through wild pastures, and the farther his sheep go wandering from him the emptier of milk they return to the fold. Some there are, indeed, that for fear of harm keep close to the shepherd, but they are so few that little stuff serves for their cowls.

'If now my words are not obscure and if thy listening has been intent, if thou recall to mind what I said, thy desire shall in part be satisfied and thou shalt see how the plant is wasted and what is meant by the rebuke, "Where there is good fattening if they do not stray".'

1. The *Aphorisms* of Hippocrates was much used as a medical text-book.

2. 'Jesus cried with a loud voice and gave up the ghost' (*Mk.* xv. 37).

3. St Francis, 'seraphic' because the Seraphim are the spirits of love, and St Dominic, 'cherubic' because the Cherubim are the spirits of knowledge.

4. Assisi lies on the lower slope of Monte Subasio, which faces Perugia from the east; farther east, Nocera and Gualdo, small Umbrian towns, were oppressed by Guelf Perugia, then in the hands of the Angevins.

5. *Ascesi*, the old name of Assisi, is identical with the Italian for 'I rose'; *Orient*, the east or the sunrise, recalls the Vulgate of *Lu.* i. 78, '*Visitavit nos oriens ex alto*'—'the dayspring from on high hath visited us.' At the vernal equinox 'this' sun rises directly east, 'from the Ganges', when it was supposed to have peculiar splendour.

6. In his 24th year, 1206, Francis, for love of poverty, stripped himself naked and formally renounced all claim on his father's wealth before the bishop *et coram patre*—'and in his father's presence'.

7. Christ.

8. Amyclas, a fisherman secure in his poverty, was unmoved when Caesar addressed him.

9. The Franciscan Rule was approved by Pope Innocent III in 1210.

10. The Order was confirmed by Pope Honorius III in 1223.

11. Francis preached before the Sultan of Egypt in 1219. He received the stigmata on Monte La Verna in the Casentino in 1224, 2 years before his death.

12. When he was dying Francis had himself laid naked on the bare ground.

13. St Dominic.

NOTE

'He should not be called a true philosopher who is the friend of wisdom for gain, as are lawyers, physicians, and almost all in the religious orders, who do not study for the sake of knowledge but for the gaining of money or dignities.' So Dante wrote in the *Convito*, and now, among the 'true philosophers', he makes appeal from the secondary ends of the earthly life to the absolute standards of Paradise, and confirms it with the love-story of Francis and Poverty.

The canto is almost wholly occupied with the speech of Aquinas, and in the curious pedantry of his first lines, about Dante's mental questions, Dante seems deliberately to adopt the scholastic manner. 'To make a clear distinction' is in the common academic technique and, from Aquinas, it is in character.

In its main matter, too, the canto is full of the language and ideas of the times. We have the two contemporary saints whose figures dominated the religious temper of the generations between them and Dante, the saints respectively of love and knowledge, not rival, as their orders had largely become, but complementary. We have the glowing imagery, partly taken from the language of Francis himself, in which his legend was preserved in the thirteenth and fourteenth centuries—his rising on the world like the sun, his choice of the Lady Poverty and his lifelong devotion to her expressed in his 'happy looks', his family of Poor Brothers growing to great numbers, his death on the bare ground, and his last charge to his 'heirs' to care for his dear lady. For Dante's first readers the story, as he tells it, had the intimacy of pictures long familiar, belonging to the cult of Francis as the new embodiment of the spirit of Christ on earth. He is content to add hardly a single image to those found in the existing Franciscan literature, and his account of Francis is largely a transcript in verse of passages from St Bonaventura's *Legend of the Blessed Francis*.

But it is not only as an artist telling the romantic story that Dante centres our interest on the Saint's love of poverty. 'Of the Saint's other virtues—humility, chastity, patience, love of peace, etc.—he gives no indication. He would see only the heroic love of poverty, demonstrated by his example and preached by Francis in times when all men, even the Church, had no other thought but the making of gain by whatever means and the possession and enjoyment of it. He judged, and not wrongly, that the most outstanding and efficacious feature in the Saint was that love. Practising poverty and rendering it lovable, he had made the hard reality, which they had borne with hatred and cursing, appear to the wretched as a state of ideal perfection; and because "his family" did not follow in his steps, the most severe and just reproach that could be brought against them was to recall and glorify the example and teaching of their father and master' (*F. Torraca*). This is broadly true, but it is too much to say that Dante gives no indication of the humbleness of Francis; and indeed the beauty of his portraiture lies partly in its combination of personal humbleness with personal daring and authority and these qualities blended in an elation and gay assurance that are proper to a love-story and that gained for the Saint the name of 'Christ's minstrel'.

It had become the custom in the churches of the two orders that on St Francis's Day the preacher should be a Dominican and on St Dominic's Day a Franciscan, and here it is the Dominican Aquinas who praises Francis and in the following canto the Franciscan Bonaventura who praises Dominic. The device is not only an obvious rebuke of the jealousies and disputes which often estranged the orders; it is also Dante's lesson that love and knowledge, 'seraphic ardour' and 'cherubic light', are alike of God, so that 'to praise one' of the saints 'is to speak of both'. (*Ardore* and *splendore* are, significantly, in the rhyme.) Having spoken of Francis, Aquinas is content to claim for his own 'patriarch' that he was a 'fit colleague', and then, having set the standard, he rebukes his own Dominican Order for sinning against it. The 'wild pastures' for which, he says, the flock is greedy are the high places of the Church, the honours and profits and comforts that beguile the friars to wander from their shepherd.

The summary account of the three successive 'seals' put on the work of Francis is significant. By the authority of the two popes, the authority, that is, of the Eternal Spirit through them, his order became an integral part of the Church Militant, of the ideal religious order of humanity; but on the rough crags of La Verna, the world at its barest with its least hold on the soul, Francis had 'the last seal' directly from Christ Himself, an immediate fellowship in His sufferings, the marks of the nails and the spear; and of the many miracles attributed to St Francis this miracle of the stigmata is the only one of which Dante makes use. Dante's line echoes the words of St Paul: 'I bear in my body the marks of the Lord Jesus'. At the first Francis chose his Lady Poverty 'before his spiritual court *et coram patre*', as it were with all the legal formalities, and later he twice acknowledged and accepted the Church's authority in his life-work; but before the end he passed beyond every outward authority and found his warrant in a purely personal and individual experience. He was both the obedient child of the Church and the mystic who went beyond it.

At the end of the canto Dante reverts to the wordy mannerism of the Dominican lecturer—'If now my words have not been obscure', etc.—, mannerisms which he can hardly have taken seriously, and we can imagine him smiling as he wrote them. By the time Dante studied in Paris, probably in the earlier years of his exile, more than thirty years had passed since Aquinas had lectured there; but there would still be many from whom Dante could gather, and would be eager to gather, reminiscences of 'the Ox of Knowledge' who, in his books, was Dante's greatest teacher and had in Dante his greatest pupil. It may well be such a reminiscence that Dante gives us here.

Sì tosto come l'ultima parola
   la benedetta fiamma per dir tolse,
   a rotar cominciò la santa mola;
e nel suo giro tutta non si volse
   prima ch'un'altra di cerchio la chiuse,
   e moto a moto e canto a canto colse;
canto che tanto vince nostre muse,
   nostre serene in quelle dolci tube,
   quanto primo splendor quel ch'e' refuse.
Come si volgon per tenera nube   10
   due archi paralleli e concolori,
   quando Iunone a sua ancella iube,
nascendo di quel d'entro quel di fori,
   a guisa del parlar di quella vaga
   ch'amor consunse come sol vapori;
e fanno qui la gente esser presaga,
   per lo patto che Dio con Noè pose,
   del mondo che già mai più non s'allaga;
così di quelle sempiterne rose
   volgìensi circa noi le due ghirlande,   20
   e sì l'estrema all' intima rispose.
Poi che 'l tripudio e l'altra festa grande
   sì del cantare e sì del fiammeggiarsi
   luce con luce gaudïose e blande
insieme a punto e a voler quetarsi,
   pur come li occhi ch'al piacer che i move
   conviene insieme chiudere e levarsi;
del cor dell' una delle luci nove
   si mosse voce, che l'ago alla stella
   parer mi fece in volgermi al suo dove;   30

CANTO XII

*The Second Circle; St Bonaventura; the story
of St Dominic; the decadence of the Franciscans*

As soon as the blessed flame took up the last word
the holy millstone began to turn, and it had not
made a full circle before another enclosed it round
and matched motion with motion and song with
song, song which as far surpassed our Muses and our
Sirens in those sweet pipes as a first splendour its
reflection. As two bows parallel and of like colours
bend through thin cloud when Juno commands
her handmaid,[1] the outer born of the inner—like
the voice of that wandering nymph whom love
consumed as the sun does vapours[2]—, and make the
people here presage, because of the covenant God
made with Noah, that the world will never again
be flooded; thus the two wreaths of those eternal
roses circled round us and thus the farther answered
to the nearer.

When the dance and all the great festival of both
song and flames, light with light joyful and gracious,
stopped together at one moment and with one
consent, just as eyes moved with one impulse must
needs close and open together, from the heart of
one of the new lights came a voice which made
me seem the needle to the star as I turned to its
place;[3] and it began: 'The love that makes me fair

e cominciò: 'L'amor che mi fa bella
   mi tragge a ragionar dell'altro duca
   per cui del mio sì ben ci si favella.
Degno è che, dov'è l'un, l'altro s'induca;
   sì che, com'elli ad una militaro,
   così la gloria loro insieme luca.
L'essercito di Cristo, che sì caro
   costò a rïarmar, dietro alla 'nsegna
   si movea tardo, sospeccioso e raro,
quando lo 'mperador che sempre regna   40
   provide alla milizia, ch'era in forse,
   per sola grazia, non per esser degna;
e come è detto, a sua sposa soccorse
   con due campioni, al cui fare, al cui dire
   lo popol disvïato si raccorse.
In quella parte ove surge ad aprire
   Zefiro dolce le novelle fronde
   di che si vede Europa rivestire,
non molto lungi al percuoter dell'onde
   dietro alle quali, per la lunga foga,   50
   lo sol tal volta ad ogni uom si nasconde,
siede la fortunata Calaroga
   sotto la protezion del grande scudo
   in che soggiace il leone e soggioga.
Dentro vi nacque l'amoroso drudo
   della fede cristiana, il santo atleta
   benigno a' suoi ed a' nemici crudo.
E come fu creata, fu repleta
   sì la sua mente di viva virtute,
   che, nella madre, lei fece profeta.   60
Poi che le sponsalizie fuor compiute
   al sacro fonte intra lui e la fede,
   u' si dotar di mutüa salute,
la donna che per lui l'assenso diede,
   vide nel sonno il mirabile frutto
   ch' uscir dovea di lui e delle rede.
E perchè fosse qual era in costrutto,
   quinci si mosse spirito a nomarlo
   del possessivo di cui era tutto.

draws me to speak of the other leader, on whose behalf so much good is spoken here of mine; it is fitting that where the one is the other should be brought in, so that, as they fought for one end, their glory should shine together.

'Christ's army, which cost so dear to rearm, was moving, slow, doubtful and few, behind the standard, when the Emperor who reigns eternally took thought for His soldiers in their peril—only of His grace, not for their deserving—and, as was said, succoured His bride by two champions at whose deeds and words the scattered people rallied.

'In that part where sweet Zephyr rises to open the new leaves in which Europe sees herself reclad, not far from the beating of the waves behind which the sun, after his long flight, sometimes hides himself from all men, lies favoured Calahorra under protection of the great shield in which the lion is subject and sovereign.⁴ In it was born the loving liegeman of the Christian faith, the holy athlete, gracious to his own and pitiless to enemies; and his mind, as soon as it was created, was so full of living power that in his mother's womb it made her prophetic.⁵ When the espousals between him and the faith were completed at the holy font where they dowered each other with mutual salvation, the lady who gave the assent for him saw in her sleep the marvellous fruit that should spring from him and from his heirs;⁶ and, that he might be expressly that which he was indeed, there went forth hence a spirit to name him by the possessive of Him whose he was completely.⁷

Domenico fu detto; e io ne parlo 70
   sì come dell'agricola che Cristo
   elesse all'orto suo per aiutarlo.
Ben parve messo e famigliar di Cristo;
   che 'l primo amor che 'n lui fu manifesto,
   fu al primo consiglio che diè Cristo.
Spesse fïate fu tacito e desto
   trovato in terra dalla sua nutrice,
   come dicesse: "Io son venuto a questo."
Oh padre suo veramente Felice!
   oh madre sua veramente Giovanna, 80
   se, interpretata, val come si dice!
Non per lo mondo, per cui mo s'affanna
   di retro ad Ostïense e a Taddeo,
   ma per amor della verace manna
in picciol tempo gran dottor si feo;
   tal che si mise a circuir la vigna
   che tosto imbianca, se 'l vignaio è reo.
E alla sedia che fu già benigna
   più a' poveri giusti, non per lei,
   ma per colui che siede, che traligna, 90
non dispensare o due o tre per sei,
   non la fortuna di prima vacante,
   non decimas, quae sunt pauperum Dei,
addimandò, ma contro al mondo errante
   licenza di combatter per lo seme
   del qual ti fascian ventiquattro piante.
Poi con dottrina e con volere inseme
   con l'officio apostolico si mosse
   quasi torrente ch'alta vena preme;
e nelli sterpi eretici percosse 100
   l' impeto suo, più vivamente quivi
   dove le resistenze eran più grosse.
Di lui si fecer poi diversi rivi
   onde l'orto cattolico si riga,
   sì che i suoi arbuscelli stan più vivi.
Se tal fu l'una rota della biga
   in che la Santa Chiesa si difese
   e vinse in campo la sua civil briga,

He was called Dominic, and I speak of him as of the labourer whom Christ chose to help Him in His garden. He seemed indeed a messenger and of the household of Christ; for the first love that was manifest in him was for the first counsel given by Christ.[8] Many a time his nurse found him silent and awake on the ground, as if he said "For this am I come".[9] O father of him, Felice indeed! O mother of him, Giovanna indeed, if, interpreted, it means what they say![10] Not for the world, for which men now toil after the Ostian and Taddeo,[11] but for love of the true manna, he became in a short time so great a teacher that he began to go round the vineyard, which soon withers if the keeper is at fault; and to the seat which is now less kind to the upright poor than once it was—not in itself, but in him who sits there degenerate[12]—he appealed, not that he might dispense two or three for six,[13] not for the chance of the first vacancy, *non decimas, quae sunt pauperum Dei*,[14] but for leave to fight with the erring world for the seed of which twenty-four plants encircle thee.[15] Then, with both learning and zeal and with the apostolic office, he went forth like a torrent driven from a high spring, and on the heretic thickets his force struck with most vigour where the resistance was stubbornest.[16] From him there sprang then various streams by which the Catholic garden is watered, so that its saplings have new life.

'If such was the one wheel of the chariot in which Holy Church defended herself and overcame in the field her civil strife, surely the excellence of the

ben ti dovrebbe assai esser palese
   l'eccellenza dell'altra, di cui Tomma   110
   dinanzi al mio venir fu sì cortese.
Ma l'orbita che fè la parte somma
   di sua circunferenza, è derelitta,
   sì ch' è la muffa dov'era la gromma.
La sua famiglia, che si mosse dritta
   coi piedi alle sue orme, è tanto volta,
   che quel dinanzi a quel di retro gitta.
E tosto si vedrà della ricolta
   della mala coltura, quando il loglio
   si lagnerà che l'arca li sia tolta.   120
Ben dico, chi cercasse a foglio a foglio
   nostro volume, ancor troverìa carta
   u' leggerebbe "I' mi son quel ch' i' soglio";
ma non fia da Casal nè d'Acquasparta,
   là onde vegnon tali alla scrittura,
   ch' uno la fugge, e altro la coarta.
Io son la vita di Bonaventura
   da Bagnoregio, che ne' grandi offici
   sempre pospuosi la sinistra cura.
Illuminato ed Augustin son quici,   130
   che fuor de' primi scalzi poverelli
   che nel capestro a Dio si fero amici.
Ugo da San Vittore è qui con elli,
   e Pietro Mangiadore e Pietro Ispano,
   lo qual giù luce in dodici libelli;
Natàn profeta e 'l metropolitano
   Crisostomo e Anselmo e quel Donato
   ch'alla prim'arte degnò porre mano.
Rabano è qui, e lucemi da lato
   il calavrese abate Giovacchino,   140
   di spirito profetico dotato.
Ad inveggiar cotanto paladino
   mi mosse l' infiammata cortesia
   di fra Tommaso e 'l discreto latino;
e mosse meco questa compagnia.'

other must be very plain to thee, about which, before I came, Thomas was so courteous. But the track made by the topmost part of its rim is abandoned, so that there is mould where there was crust.[17] His family, which started out straight forward with their feet in his footprints, is so turned about that it throws back him in front on him behind; and soon will be seen some harvest of the bad tillage, when the tares shall complain that the bin is refused to them.[18] I admit, indeed, that he that should search our volume leaf by leaf would still find a page where he might read, "I am what I always was",[19] but it will not be from Casale or from Acquasparta, where such readers come to the Rule that the one shirks and the other narrows it.[20]

'I am the living soul of Bonaventura of Bagnorea, who in great offices ever put last the left-hand care.[21] Here are Illuminato and Augustine, who were among the first barefoot Poor Brothers that in the cord made themselves God's friends; Hugh of St Victor is here with them, and Peter the Bookworm, and Peter the Spaniard who shines below in twelve books; Nathan the prophet, and Chrysostom the Metropolitan, and Anselm, and that Donatus who deigned to set his hand to the first art; Rabanus is here, and beside me shines the Calabrian Abbot Joachim, who was endowed with a spirit of prophecy.[22]

'The glowing courtesy and well-judged language of Brother Thomas have moved me to celebrate so great a paladin,[23] and with me have moved this company.'

1. Iris, the rainbow.

2. The nymph Echo, who wasted away for love of Narcissus.

3. St Bonaventura, General of the Franciscans (1256–74) and biographer of St Francis.

4. Calahorra in Castile, the birthplace of St Dominic (1170–1221), 'not far' from the Atlantic shore; the arms of the Kingdom of Leon and Castile showed two lions and two castles quartered, one lion below, another above.

5. The soul was regarded as a direct creation in the foetus (*Purg.* xxv). St Dominic's mother dreamt she was to give birth to a dog with a burning torch in its mouth, and the Dominicans were sometimes called *Domini canes*, the dogs of the Lord.

6. His godmother dreamt of him with a bright star in his brow which illumined the world.

7. *Domenico*, 'the Lord's'.

8. Perhaps a reference to *Matt.* vi. 33: 'Seek ye first the kingdom of God.'

9. An echo, perhaps, of *Mk.* i. 38 in the Vulgate: '*Ad hoc enim veni*', 'for to this end am I come'.

10. *Felice*, happy; *Giovanna*, the grace of God.

11. 13th century writers on canon law and on medicine.

12. Pope Boniface VIII.

13. Not to keep back part of the money given for pious uses.

14. 'Not for tithes, which belong to God's poor.'

15. The faith is the 'seed' of the saints.

16. Dominic got authorization for his Order from Pope Honorius III in 1216 and preached against the Albigensian heresies.

17. The Fransiscans had left the ways of the first friars. Good wine in the cask makes a crust, bad makes a mould.

18. There was strife among the Franciscans between the 'Spirituals', the strict party, and the 'Conventuals', the moderate or lax party, and some of the Spirituals seceded and were excommunicated. 'In the time of harvest I will say to the reapers, Gather ye together first the tares and bind them in bundles to burn them, but gather the wheat into my barn' (*Matt.* xii. 30).

19. Words spoken by the Rule,—there are some Franciscans in whom the Rule may be read in its original integrity.

20. Ubertine of Casale and Matteo of Acquasparta were leaders of the two parties that differed in their reading of the Franciscan Rule.

21. 'In her'—wisdom's—'left hand riches and honour' (*Prov.* iii. 16).

22. Illuminato and Augustine, early followers of Francis not otherwise noteworthy; Hugh of St Victor (a famous abbey near Paris), master of Richard of St Victor and Peter Lombard (*Par.* x); Peter the Bookworm, a commentator, also of St Victor; Peter the Spaniard, writer on logic who became Pope John XXI, the only contemporary pope in Dante's Paradise; Nathan, the prophet who charged David with his sin (2 *Sam.* xii.); Chrysostom, Patriarch of Constantinople in the 4th century, who denounced the evils of the court; Anselm, Archbishop of Canterbury and scholastic in the 11th century; Donatus, whose school grammar was long in use (grammar was the first of the seven 'arts' in the regular course of medieval education); Rabanus, German commentator and historian; Abbot Joachim, who wrote a commentary on the Apocalypse and whose prophetic teaching had much influence among the Franciscan Spirituals.

23. St Dominic.

NOTE

In eager confirmation of Aquinas's 'last word' about the 'good fattening' in the Dominican way, the Dominican circle, as we may call it, breaks in with its song and circling, and soon there is seen and heard another circle beyond it. It is the circle of the Franciscans and of those who were regarded as representing their ideals of love and service. The two circles, of knowledge and of love, of learning and of service, move and sing in harmony together—'the outer born of the inner', 'the farther answered to the nearer', matching 'motion with motion and song with song'—and by that various and united testimony of the saints, like a voice and its echo, like the two arches 'parallel and of like colours' of a double rainbow, the world is assured with Noah of God's covenant with men. The whole complex of imagery, involved and insistent even for Dante, is significant and coherent.

Their song, we are told, surpassed 'the song, itself super-human, of the Muses and Sirens, who, being creatures of fancy, are *ours*, belong to our world. This song, that is to say, surpassed the sublimest not only to be heard but to be imagined on earth' (*C. Grabher*). Dante consistently maintains that the heights of pagan utterance are hints, and no more than hints, of the truth of God in Christ. His readers will recall the 'corollary' of *Purgatorio* xxviii: 'Those who in old times sang of the age of gold'.

There is much obvious correspondence between the accounts of the two great saints in the eleventh and twelfth cantos; and there is also this broad contrast, that Aquinas's account of Francis is, from first to last, a love-story, a romance of the spirit, and Bonaventura's of Dominic is the story of a soldier, a 'holy athlete', a 'liegeman of the Christian faith' who 'fights with the erring world' for 'Christ s army' in peril. The story of

Francis sets forth the compulsion of a great love, that of Dominic the imperatives of the truth, both belonging to the soul's wisdom which is the note of this heaven. Dominic was not, either in Dante's representation of him or in historical fact, primarily a persecutor of heretics; according to the traditions he was a man of loving and generous temper and humble piety. His attack on the heresies of the Albigenses was in the first place purely spiritual, by his writings and by his own and his followers' preaching; but in the ferment of ideas which distracted the Church in the thirteenth century and with the convictions which he shared with the whole Christian world of his day, he could not but become a persecutor. He was 'gracious to his own and pitiless to enemies' and he supported his friend Bishop Folco of Marseilles (*Par.* ix) in the cruel 'crusade' against the Albigenses. For Dominic as for Dante, heretics persistent in their heresy were deserters from the field in the most imperative of all wars. Dominic, in Dante's account, was like a zephyr from the west that comes to open the young leaves over Europe, and like a torrent bursting on the heretic thickets, and—this is the final word—the source of streams that still water the garden of the Church.

Dominic is here a far less human figure than Francis and much more a sheer spiritual force. There is much more of miracle in his story, as Dante tells it, than in that of Francis. In the womb 'his mind' made his mother prophetic; he is the subject of strange dreams; from the font he is the pledged bridegroom of the faith; named by special inspiration 'the Lord's', he makes a straight course in his calling to his predestined end. The power of the truth in Dominic is not so much that of personal conviction as a kind of spiritual possession which uses him as it will.

By a device that is used again three times with different applications later in the *Paradiso*, Dominic is wholly identified with the cause of Christ. Bonaventura tells that Christ chose him, that he was Christ's messenger and servant, and that his first love was for Christ's first counsel, and the name *Cristo*, occurring here three times, is made to rhyme only with itself.

Then in the involved symbolism that was traditional in prophetic speech and with much mixture of metaphor—as if to suggest the moral confusion of which he speaks—Bonaventura deplores the corruptions and dissensions in the Order whose General he was thirty years before, and through him Dante rebukes both the narrowness of the Spirituals and the laxity of the Conventuals in some of their leaders.

The accounts of Francis and Dominic both begin with a careful geographical statement of their places of birth, Assisi and Calahorra, and that leads naturally and at once to the cosmic significance of the sunrise and of the west wind that reclothes Europe with new leaves. The master-saints come of the unfathomable 'Providence that rules the world', and of 'the Emperor who reigns eternally'. There is a curious correspondence between the two cantos in the fifty-first line of each. Francis, we are told, was 'a sun' that 'rose on the world, as this does sometimes' (in the spring equinox) 'from the Ganges'; and Dominic was born 'not far from the beating of the waves behind which the sun, after his long flight, sometimes' (in the summer solstice) 'hides himself from all men'. The Ganges and the Atlantic coast were, for Dante, the extreme limits of the inhabited world, and the carefully corresponding expressions in the two cantos, in which there is so much correspondence, may well be meant to suggest the ideally world-wide scope of the mission of the two saints and the possible fulfilment of the prophecy: 'From the rising of the sun even unto the going down of the same my name shall be great among the Gentiles' (*Mal.* i. 11).

The choice of the souls in the Franciscan circle is even less obvious than that in the Dominican in the tenth canto. Illuminato and Augustine are named first, as men of no other distinction but their early loyalty to Francis, and 'with them' are three men of learning and of public note. Nathan, whose place in history is due only to his rebuke of David's sin, is grouped with the great names of Chrysostom, who also defied the great in his time, of Anselm, and of Donatus, the teacher of St Jerome, who 'deigned' to write a school-book. It would seem to be Dante's enforcement of the lesson of Francis's own example, that the essential wisdom of the spirit is as truly and effectively expressed in life as in doctrine.

The list ends with two commentators on Scripture, and the

latter of these is of peculiar significance here. The Abbot Joachim, of the generation before Francis, was a visionary, a preacher, a commentator on prophecy, and for a great part of his life a hermit in the wild hill-country of Calabria. By his advocacy and example of evangelical poverty, his outlook on a new age for the world, and the ardour and power of his preaching, he was the immediate forerunner of Francis, who was twenty years old when Joachim died, and he may well have been a decisive factor in Francis' life. His distinctive doctrine was known later as the Everlasting Gospel, from the words of *Rev.* xiv. 6; 'I saw another angel fly in the midst of heaven, having the everlasting gospel to preach unto them that dwell on the earth'. It was a doctrine of the three great ages of history,— that of the Father, the age of law, the times of the Old Testament,—that of the Son, the age of faith, the times of the New Testament and the Church,—and that of the Spirit, the age of a new inward enlightenment and spiritual freedom, which was soon to come, with no more need—so, at least, some of Joachim's followers taught—for the institutions of religion. This teaching had wide influence in thirteenth century Italy, especially among the Franciscan Spirituals, and it was later condemned by the Church and strongly opposed by Bonaventura as Franciscan General. Here in Paradise Joachim 'shines' by the side of Bonaventura, who says of him that he was 'dowered with a spirit of prophecy',—words which are 'the echo, or perhaps the source, of the anthem which pilgrims sing still in Calabria on the day of the Blessed Joachim' (*G. G. Coulton*). The fact that his teaching was condemned in particular by Pope Boniface would not prejudice Joachim with Dante. The judgement here on Joachim is Dante's rather than Bonaventura's, and Dante would show that these two saints, divided in their thoughts on earth, are now, like Siger and Aquinas in the first circle, reconciled in the light of the Sun. In connection with Joachism Mr Coulton speaks of 'that comparative freedom of thought which makes the thirteenth century, especially in Italy, so living a period in the history of the pre-reformation Church. . . . There was too much life and growth to be easily repressed.'

'Never had the prospects of Christendom seemed more hopeful

or its spiritual ideals nearer to their realisation than in the thirteenth century. Men believed that they were on the threshold of great events and they saw in St Francis the herald of a new age. The extreme form of this apocalyptic tendency is represented by the followers of Joachim of Flora, who announced the coming of the third kingdom and the Eternal Gospel. It finds expression in most of the great minds of the age, in St Bonaventura and Mechtild of Magdeburg, in Roger Bacon and Ramon Lull and Dante. Thus St Bonaventura, who was no Joachist but rather the representative of the opposite tendency in the Order, regards St Francis as the type of the new seraphic order of spiritual men, and as the herald of the time when the City of God will be built up and restored as it was in the beginning in the likeness of the Heavenly City and when the reign of peace will come' (*C. Dawson*). Whatever Dante may have thought of the apocalyptic expectations of his time, he knew and deeply shared 'that passionate longing for a new world which was the real soul of Joachism' (*G. G. Coulton*).

PARADISO

IMAGINI chi bene intender cupe
　　quel ch' i' or vidi—e ritegna l' image,
　　mentre ch' io dico, come ferma rupe—
quindici stelle che 'n diverse plage
　　lo cielo avvivan di tanto sereno,
　　che soperchia dell'aere ogne compage;
imagini quel carro a cu' il seno
　　basta del nostro cielo e notte e giorno,
　　sì ch'al volger del temo non vien meno;
imagini la bocca di quel corno　　　　　　　　　　　10
　　che si comincia in punta dello stelo
　　a cui la prima rota va dintorno,
aver fatto di sè due segni in cielo,
　　qual fece la figliuola di Minoi
　　allora che sentì di morte il gelo;
e l'un nell'altro aver li raggi suoi,
　　e amendue girarsi per maniera,
　　che l'uno andasse al prima e l'altro al poi;
e avrà quasi l'ombra della vera
　　costellazione e della doppia danza　　　　　　　　20
　　che circulava il punto dov' io era;
poi ch'è tanto di là da nostra usanza,
　　quanto di là dal mover della Chiana
　　si move il ciel che tutti li altri avanza.
Lì si cantò non Bacco, non Peana,
　　ma tre persone in divina natura,
　　ed in una persona essa e l'umana.

CANTO XIII

Creation perfect in Adam and in Christ; Solomon's gift of kingly understanding; warning against hasty judgements

LET him imagine, who would rightly understand what I saw now—and let him hold the image, while I speak, firm as a rock—, fifteen stars that quicken various regions of the sky with such brightness as overcomes every obstruction in the air; let him imagine that Wain for which the bosom of our sky suffices night and day so that in the turning of its pole it is not diminished; let him imagine the mouth of the Horn that begins at the end of the axle on which the first wheel revolves,[1]—and all these to have made of themselves two constellations in heaven such as the daughter of Minos made when she felt the chill of death,[2] and the one to have its beams within the other, and both to revolve in such a manner that the one goes first and the other after. Then he will have as it were a shadow of the real constellation and of the double dance that circled round the point where I was; for it is as far beyond our experience as the motion of the heaven that outstrips all the rest is beyond the motion of the Chiana.[3] There they sang, not Bacchus and no Paean,[4] but three Persons in the divine nature, and in one Person that nature and the human.

Compiè il cantare e volger sua misura;
   e attesersi a noi quei santi lumi,
   felicitando sè di cura in cura.   30
Ruppe il silenzio ne' concordi numi
   poscia la luce in che mirabil vita
   del poverel di Dio narrata fumi,
e disse: 'Quando l'una paglia è trita,
   quando la sua semenza è già riposta,
   a batter l'altra dolce amor m' invita.
Tu credi che nel petto onde la costa
   si trasse per formar la bella guancia
   il cui palato a tutto 'l mondo costa,
ed in quel che, forato dalla lancia,   40
   e poscia e prima tanto sodisfece,
   che d'ogni colpa vince la bilancia,
quantunque alla natura umana lece
   aver di lume, tutto fosse infuso
   da quel valor che l'uno e l'altro fece;
e però miri a ciò ch' io dissi suso,
   quando narrai che non ebbe 'l secondo
   lo ben che nella quinta luce è chiuso.
Or apri li occhi a quel ch' io ti rispondo,
   e vedrai il tuo credere e 'l mio dire   50
   nel vero farsi come centro in tondo.
Ciò che non more e ciò che può morire
   non è se non splendor di quella idea
   che partorisce, amando, il nostro sire:
chè quella viva luce che sì mea
   dal suo lucente, che non si disuna
   da lui nè dall'amor ch'a lor s' intrea,
per sua bontate il suo raggiare aduna,
   quasi specchiato, in nove sussistenze,
   etternalmente rimanendosi una.   60
Quindi discende all'ultime potenze
   giù d'atto in atto, tanto divenendo,
   che più non fa che brevi contingenze;
e queste contingenze essere intendo
   le cose generate, che produce
   con seme e sanza seme il ciel movendo.

When the singing and the circling had completed their measure these holy lights gave heed to us, rejoicing to pass from care to care. Then the light within which the wondrous life of the Poor Man of God was told me broke the silence among the divine concordant souls, and he said: 'Since the one sheaf is threshed and its grain now garnered, sweet charity bids me beat out the other.[5] Thou believest that into the breast from which the rib was taken to form her fair face whose palate cost all the world dear,—and into that, pierced by the spear, which gave satisfaction for both past and future such as outweighs in the balance every fault, all the light that is allowed to human nature was infused by the Power which made the one and the other; and therefore thou marvellest at what I said before when I told thee that the excellence which is enclosed in the fifth light never had a second.[6] Open now thine eyes to the answer I give thee and thou shalt see that thy belief and my words meet in the truth as the centre of the circle.

'That which dies not and that which can die are nothing but the splendour of that Idea which our Sire, in Loving, begets; for that living Light which so streams from its shining Source that it is not parted from it nor from the Love which with them makes the Three, of its own goodness gathers its beams, as it were mirrored, in nine subsistences, remaining forever one.[7] Thence it descends to the last potencies, passing down from act to act and becoming such that it makes nothing more than brief contingencies; and by these contingencies I mean things generated with or without seed, which the heavens by their motions produce. The

La cera di costoro e chi la duce
   non sta d'un modo; e però sotto 'l segno
   ideale poi più e men traluce.
Ond'elli avvien ch'un medesimo legno,   70
   secondo specie, meglio e peggio frutta;
   e voi nascete con diverso ingegno.
Se fosse a punto la cera dedutta
   e fosse il cielo in sua virtù suprema,
   la luce del suggel parrebbe tutta;
ma la natura la dà sempre scema,
   similemente operando all'artista
   c' ha l'abito dell'arte e man che trema.
Però se 'l caldo amor la chiara vista
   della prima virtù dispone e segna,   80
   tutta la perfezion quivi s'acquista.
Così fu fatta già la terra degna
   di tutta l'animal perfezïone;
   così fu fatta la Vergine pregna:
sì ch' io commendo tua oppinïone,
   che l' umana natura mai non fue
   nè fia qual fu in quelle due persone.
Or s' i' non procedesse avanti piue,
   "Dunque, come costui fu sanza pare?"
   comincerebber le parole tue.   90
Ma perchè paia ben ciò che non pare,
   pensa chi era, e la cagion che 'l mosse,
   quando fu detto "Chiedi", a dimandare.
Non ho parlato sì, che tu non posse
   ben veder ch'el fu re che chiese senno
   acciò che re sufficïente fosse;
non per sapere il numero in che enno
   li motor di qua su, o se necesse
   con contingente mai necesse fenno;
non *si est dare primum motum esse*,   100
   o se del mezzo cerchio far si pote
   triangol sì ch' un retto non avesse.
Onde, se ciò ch' io dissi e questo note,
   regal prudenza è quel vedere impari
   in che lo stral di mia intenzion percote;

wax of these things and that which moulds it are
not always in the same state, and therefore beneath
the stamp of the idea the light then shines through
more and less; hence it comes that trees of one and
the same species bear better and worse fruit and
you are born with different talents.[8] If the wax were
moulded perfectly and the heavens were at the height
of their power, all the brightness of the seal would
be seen; but nature always gives it defectively,
working like the artist who has the skill of his art
and a hand that trembles. But if the burning Love
moves the clear Vision of the primal Power and
makes of that its seal, all perfection is attained there.
Thus, once, was the dust made fit for all the per-
fection of a living creature, and thus was the Virgin
made to be with child; so that I approve thy judge-
ment that nature never was nor shall be what it
was in these two persons.[9] Now, if I went no farther,
"How, then, was that other without an equal?"
would be thy first words. But, to make quite clear
what is obscure to thee, think who he was and what
moved him to his petition when he was bidden
"Ask". I have not spoken so darkly but that thou
canst see that he was a king, who asked for wisdom
that he might be fit to be a king,[10] not to know the
number of the movers here above, nor if *necesse* with
a contingent ever made *necesse*,[11] nor *si est dare
primum motum esse*,[12] nor if a triangle can be made
in the semicircle so that it has no right angle.[13]
Therefore, if thou note this along with what I said,
royal wisdom is that unmatched vision on which
the arrow of my intention strikes; and if thou have

e se al "surse" drizzi li occhi chiari,
   vedrai aver solamente rispetto
   ai regi, che son molti, e i buon son rari.
Con questa distinzion prendi 'l mio detto;
   e così puote star con quel che credi   110
   del primo padre e del nostro Diletto.
E questo ti sia sempre piombo a' piedi,
   per farti mover lento com' uom lasso
   e al sì e al no che tu non vedi:
chè quelli è tra li stolti bene a basso,
   che sanza distinzione afferma e nega
   così nell'un come nell'altro passo;
perch'elli 'ncontra che più volte piega
   l'oppinïon corrente in falsa parte,
   e poi l'affetto l' intelletto lega.   120
Vie più che 'ndarno da riva si parte,
   perchè non torna tal qual e' si move,
   chi pesca per lo vero e non ha l'arte.
E di ciò sono al mondo aperte prove
   Parmènide, Melisso, e Brisso, e molti,
   li quali andavano e non sapean dove:
sì fè Sabellio e Arrio e quelli stolti
   che furon come spade alle Scritture
   in render torti li diritti volti.
Non sien le genti, ancor, troppo sicure   130
   a giudicar, sì come quei che stima
   le biade in campo pria che sien mature:
ch' i' ho veduto tutto il verno prima
   lo prun mostrarsi rigido e feroce,
   poscia portar la rosa in su la cima;
e legno vidi già dritto e veloce
   correr lo mar per tutto suo cammino,
   perire al fine all' intrar de la foce.
Non creda donna Berta e ser Martino,
   per vedere un furare, altro offerere,   140
   vederli dentro al consiglio divino;
chè quel può surgere, e quel può cadere.'

careful regard to "arose" thou wilt see it to have sole reference to kings,—who are many, and the good ones rare. Take my words with this distinction, and they can stand then with what thou believest of the first father and of our Beloved.[14]

'And let this always be lead on thy feet to make thee slow, like a weary man, in moving either to the yea or the nay where thou dost not see clearly; for he ranks very low among the fools, in the one case as in the other, who affirms or denies without distinguishing, since it often happens that a hasty opinion inclines to the wrong side and then the feelings bind the intellect. Far worse than in vain he casts off from the shore, for he does not return the same as he sets out, who fishes for the truth without the art. And of this manifest proofs to the world are Parmenides, Melissus, Bryson,[15] and many who knew not whither they went; so were Sabellius and Arius[16] and these fools who were to the Scriptures like swords that give back the natural face distorted.

'So also let not the people be too sure in judging, like those that reckon the corn in the field before it is ripe. For I have seen the briar first show harsh and rigid all through the winter and later bear the rose upon its top, and once I saw a ship that ran straight and swift over the sea through all its course perish at the last entering the harbour. Let not Dame Bertha and Master Martin, when they see one rob and another make an offering, think they see them within the divine counsel; for the one may rise and the other fall.'

1. The 15 stars of first magnitude in medieval astronomy, the 7 stars of the Great Bear, and the 2 brightest of the Little Bear ('the Horn', of which the point is the Pole Star); 24 stars altogether, which are arranged in 2 circles of 12. 'The first wheel', the daily motion of the heavens from east to west.

2. Ariadne, taken to heaven by Bacchus, her lover; her wreath became the Corona Borealis.

3. The Chiana, a sluggish stream in Tuscany, here contrasted with the Primum Mobile, the swiftest of the spheres.

4. A hymn to Apollo.

5. Aquinas has explained the line, 'Where there is good fattening if they do not stray', and he is now to explain the other, 'There never arose a second of such vision' (*Par.* xi).

6. If Adam and Christ had perfect understanding, how can it be said that 'there never arose a second' like Solomon?

7. The divine creative light operates on primal matter through the angelic orders—'subsistences', creations not dependent on any other creatures—and the spheres which they control, and produces earthly creatures.

8. 'The imprinting influences of heaven and the imprinted matter of earth are not always in equally propitious habit, and hence individual diversities of excellence' (*P. H. Wicksteed*).

9. In the creation of Adam and the conception of Christ, God—in three Persons as Love, Wisdom and Power—and Nature wrought perfectly.

10. 'God said, Ask what I shall give thee. And Solomon said, . . . Give thy servant an understanding heart to judge thy people' (1 *Kgs.* iii. 5–9); cp. *Par.* x.

11. ' "If a necessary and a contingent premise can ever give a necessary conclusion." No limitation that occurs in either of the premises can be escaped in the conclusion' (*P. H. Wicksteed*).

12. 'If primal motion is admissible',—motion not caused by other motion.

13. Such questions in angelology, logic, physics and geometry would have been idle for Solomon.

14. 'Arose' being taken to mean 'rose to be king', Solomon is compared, not with Adam or with Christ, but with other kings.

15. Greek philosophers disparaged by Aristotle.

16. Third and fourth century heretics.

NOTE

'Let him imagine'—the bidding is given three times—twenty-four bright stars chosen from the whole sky and re-arranged in a new constellation of two concentric circles. Let us do our best, all our imagining of heavenly things is like a child's game —playing with stars—and comes as far short of the realities of the spirit as earth of heaven. These living constellations of the wise do not sing of the old imagined gods, but of the mysteries of the God they know, of the Trinity and the Incarnation, and their knowledge continually prompts their love,—of the two circles 'the one goes first and the other after'. Here again, as at the beginning of the eighth and twelfth cantos, the realities of Christianity are compared and contrasted with the shadows of paganism.

It is Aquinas, the eulogist of Francis in the eleventh canto, the thinker who spoke of the lover and speaks now at love's bidding, that is the voice of wisdom here, meeting Dante's unspoken question as he has done many a time through his pages.

From a question about the Scripture story of Solomon's gift of wisdom arises a discourse on the whole range of creation, with its starting-point in the Holy Trinity, and the Trinity is three times defined in the theological language of the time: 'that Idea which our Sire, in Loving, begets',—'that living Light, its shining Source, the Love which with them makes the Three', —'the burning Love, the clear Vision, the primal Power'. It is the same language as that which introduced the subject of the heaven of the Sun at the beginning of the tenth canto. 'The creation of things eternal and of things temporal alike is the resplendent manifestation of the idea which the triune God, in His love, generates. The living light in the Son, emanating from its lucent source in the Father, in union with the love of the Holy Spirit, the three remaining always one, pours out its radiance through the nine orders of the Angelic Hierarchy, who distribute it by means of the heavens of which they are the Intelligences. Through the various movements and conjunctions of the heavens the creative light descends to the lowest elements, producing all the varieties of contingent things' (*C. E. Norton*). Aquinas (quoted by Vernon) explains that '*idea* in Greek is in Latin called *form*'. *Idea, word, form,* the divine creative force and principle by which the whole creation and each created thing has its own specific being and significance,—that conception, derived from Plato and Aristotle and turned to Christian use in the Fourth Gospel, dominates all scholastic thinking, especially in its more orthodox and traditional examples. Men have their specific congenital qualities and defects from the varying dispositions and influences of the heavens at their birth and the imperfect primal stuff of which they partake, and only in man according to God's original idea, in Adam and in Christ, the Word made flesh, is man free of all human faultiness and out of comparison with Solomon or any other.

The defective working of 'nature', the moving heavens, on 'the wax of things', primal undifferentiated matter, illustrates 'the veiled dualism which may constantly be traced in Dante's conception of the universe. The *prima materia,* though explicitly declared to be the direct creation of God (Cantos vii and xxix), is here and elsewhere treated as something external, on which His power acts and which answers only imperfectly to it' (*P. H. Wicksteed*). How nature and primal matter, both direct creations of God, should produce an imperfect world is a problem which Dante does not face, much less solve, and which he might have met with his own words from *Purgatorio* iii, 'Be content, race of men, with the *quia*'. In other terms it is our problem still.

The divine creative power operating through the angels and the stars is repeatedly spoken of, here and elsewhere, as light. 'Light, according to Dante's conception, belongs intimately to divine things and is inherent in them; it is, so to speak, the outward nature of divinity itself; God is light. True light belongs to the blessedness of Paradise as the smile to human happiness; more than the expression or manifestation of divinity, it is divinity *in act*, in its sensible form. Only in that way can we understand . . . what he says here when he calls the totality of created things "the splendour" of the idea which God, of Himself, begets in loving' (*S. de Chiara, L.D.*). It is Dante's version of the language of *Hebrews*, 'His Son, by whom he made the worlds, being the brightness of his glory, and the express image of his person'—in the Vulgate, *splendor gloriae, et figura substantiae eius*—'and upholding all things by the word of his power'. In Aquinas's account here of creation—'That which dies not and that which can die'—'the conceptions are not abstractions but living forces, the agents in creation: light, the heavens, nature. We do not have a piece of reasoning but an animated history, with a clarity and vigour of representation which make God and Nature to be real poetic personalities' (*F. de Sanctis*).

From no one as from Aquinas had Dante learned the lesson of intellectual integrity as a high essential of the life of the spirit, the need for deliberation and for 'distinctions' in judgement and in speech, and the mental offence of undefined and ambiguous terms and of unreasoned and hasty assurance. It is very Dantesque, and very Thomist, to warn against the feelings binding the intellect; and it is in character both for Aquinas and for Dante that the lesson is applied not only to the supreme matters of creation and providence but also to practical human affairs, that Solomon is commended for making his own kingly business his first care, and that philosophers and theologians are made to share their lesson and their reproach with Dame Bertha and Master Martin who pass their easy judgements on their neighbours. Wisdom 'was set up from everlasting, from the beginning, or ever the earth was'; and also 'she crieth at the gates, at the entry of the city, at the coming in at the doors'.

PARADISO

DAL centro al cerchio, e sì dal cerchio al centro,
  movesi l'acqua in un ritondo vaso,
  secondo ch'è percossa fuori o dentro:
nella mia mente fè subito caso
  questo ch' io dico, sì come si tacque
  la glorïosa vita di Tommaso,
per la similitudine che nacque
  del suo parlare e di quel di Beatrice,
  a cui sì cominciar, dopo lui, piacque:
'A costui fa mestieri, e nol vi dice   10
  nè con la voce nè pensando ancora,
  d'un altro vero andare alla radice.
Diteli se la luce onde s' infiora
  vostra sustanza, rimarrà con voi
  etternalmente sì com'ell'è ora;
e se rimane, dite come, poi
  che sarete visibili rifatti,
  esser potrà ch'al veder non vi noi.'
Come, da più letizia pinti e tratti,
  alla fïata quei che vanno a rota   20
  levan la voce e rallegrano li atti,
così, all'orazion pronta e divota,
  li santi cerchi mostrar nova gioia
  nel torneare e nella mira nota.
Qual si lamenta perchè qui si moia
  per viver colà su, non vide quive
  lo rifrigerio dell'etterna ploia.

CANTO XIV

The resurrection of the body; the Third Circle;
the Sphere of Mars; the courageous; the cross
of souls

FROM centre to rim, and again from rim to centre, the water in a round vessel moves, according as it is struck from without or within; this, as I tell it, dropped suddenly into my mind as soon as the glorious living soul of Thomas was silent, by the likeness that sprang from his speech and that of Beatrice, who was pleased to begin thus after him: 'This man has need, and does not tell you of it either by word or as yet in thought, to search into another truth. Tell him if the light with which your substance blooms will remain with you in eternity as it is now, and, if it remains, tell him how it is possible after you are made visible again that it should not be painful to your sight.'[1]

As, impelled and drawn by increase of happiness, dancers in a round raise their voices all together and quicken their steps, so at the eager and devout petition the holy circles showed new joy in their wheeling and in their wondrous song. Whoso laments that we die here to live above has not seen there the refreshment from the eternal showers. That

Quell'uno e due e tre che sempre vive
 e regna sempre in tre e 'n due e 'n uno,
 non circunscritto, e tutto circunscrive, 30
tre volte era cantato da ciascuno
 di quelli spirti con tal melodia,
 ch'ad ogni merto sarìa giusto muno.
E io udi' nella luce più dia
 del minor cerchio una voce modesta,
 forse qual fu dall'angelo a Maria,
risponder: 'Quanto fia lunga la festa
 di paradiso, tanto il nostro amore
 si raggerà dintorno cotal vesta.
La sua chiarezza seguita l'ardore; 40
 l'ardor la visïone, e quella è tanta,
 quant' ha di grazia sovra suo valore.
Come la carne glorïosa e santa
 fia rivestita, la nostra persona
 più grata fia per esser tutta quanta;
per che s'accrescerà ciò che ne dona
 di gratuito lume il sommo bene,
 lume ch'a lui veder ne condiziona;
onde la visïon crescer convene,
 crescer l'ardor che di quella s'accende, 50
 crescer lo raggio che da esso vene.
Ma sì come carbon che fiamma rende,
 e per vivo candor quella soverchia,
 sì che la sua parvenza si difende;
così questo fulgor che già ne cerchia
 fia vinto in apparenza dalla carne
 che tutto dì la terra ricoperchia;
nè potrà tanta luce affaticarne;
 chè li organi del corpo saran forti
 a tutto ciò che potrà dilettarne.' 60
Tanto mi parver subiti e accorti
 e l'uno e l'altro coro a dicer 'Amme!'
 che ben mostrar disio de' corpi morti;
forse non pur per lor, ma per le mamme,
 per li padri e per li altri che fuor cari
 anzi che fosser sempiterne fiamme.

One and Two and Three who ever lives and ever reigns in Three and in Two and in One[2] and uncircumscribed circumscribes all, was sung three times by every one of these spirits in such a strain as would be fit reward for every merit. And I heard in the divinest light of the lesser circle[3] a gentle voice, such perhaps as the angel's to Mary, reply: 'As long as the feast of Paradise shall last, so long our love shall radiate this vesture about us. Its brightness answers to our ardour, the ardour to our vision, and that is in the measure each has of grace beyond his merit. When the flesh, glorified and holy, shall be put on again, our person shall be more acceptable for being all complete, so that the light freely granted to us by the Supreme Goodness shall increase, light which fits us to see Him; from that must vision increase, the ardour increase that is kindled by it, the radiance increase which comes from that. But like a coal that gives flame and with its white glow outshines it so that its own appearance is preserved, so this effulgence that now surrounds us will be surpassed in brightness by the flesh which the earth still covers. Nor will such light have power to trouble us, for the organs of the body shall be strong for all that can delight us.'[4]

So quick and eager seemed to me both the one and the other choir to say *Amen* that they plainly showed their desire for their dead bodies,—not perhaps for themselves alone, but for their mothers, for their fathers, and for the others who were dear before they became eternal flames.

Ed ecco intorno, di chiarezza pari,
    nascere un lustro sopra quel che v'era,
    per guisa d'orizzonte che rischiari.
E sì come al salir di prima sera   70
    comincian per lo ciel nove parvenze,
    sì che la vista pare e non par vera,
parvemi lì novelle sussistenze
    cominciare a vedere, e fare un giro
    di fuor dall'altre due circunferenze.
Oh vero sfavillar del Santo Spiro!
    come si fece subito e candente
    alli occhi miei che, vinti, non soffriro!
Ma Beatrice sì bella e ridente
    mi si mostrò, che tra quelle vedute   80
    si vuol lasciar che non seguir la mente.
Quindi ripreser li occhi miei virtute
    a rilevarsi; e vidimi translato
    sol con mia donna in più alta salute.
Ben m'accors' io ch' io era più levato,
    per l'affocato riso della stella,
    che mi parea più roggio che l' usato.
Con tutto il core e con quella favella
    ch'è una in tutti a Dio feci olocausto,
    qual convenìesi alla grazia novella.   90
E non er'anco del mio petto esausto
    l'ardor del sacrificio, ch' io conobbi
    esso litare stato accetto e fausto;
chè con tanto lucore e tanto robbi
    m'apparvero splendor dentro a due raggi,
    ch' io dissi: 'O Eliòs che sì li addobbi!'
Come distinta da minori e maggi
    lumi biancheggia tra' poli del mondo
    Galassia sì, che fa dubbiar ben saggi;
sì costellati facean nel profondo   100
    Marte quei raggi il venerabil segno
    che fan giunture di quadranti in tondo.
Qui vince la memoria mia lo 'ngegno;
    chè quella croce lampeggiava Cristo,
    sì ch' io non so trovare essemplo degno;

And lo, all round and all of equal brightness, rose a lustre surpassing what was there, like a brightening horizon. And just as on the approach of evening new lights begin to show through the sky so that the sight seems and seems not real, it seemed to me that I began to see there new spirits making a ring beyond the other two circles. Ah, very sparkling of the Holy Ghost! How suddenly glowing it became to my eyes, which were overcome and could not bear it! But Beatrice showed herself to me so fair and smiling, it must be left among those sights that did not follow my memory. From this my eyes recovered strength to raise themselves again, and I saw myself translated, alone with my Lady, to higher blessedness.

I was well assured that I had risen higher by the enkindled smile of the star, which seemed to me more ruddy than its wont.[5] With all my heart and in that tongue which is one for all I made such a whole burnt-offering to God as befitted the new grace; and the burning of the sacrifice was not yet completed in my breast when I knew that offering to be accepted and propitious, for splendours of such brightness and so ruddy appeared to me within two beams that I said: 'O Divine Sun that dost so glorify them!' As the Galaxy, pricked out with greater and lesser lights, whitens between the poles of the universe so that it perplexes the wisest,[6] these beams, thus constellated, made in the depth of Mars the venerable sign which the meeting of the quadrants makes in a circle.[7] Here my memory defeats my skill, for that cross so flamed forth Christ that I can find for it no fit comparison;

ma chi prende sua croce e segue Cristo,
 ancor mi scuserà di quel ch' io lasso,
 vedendo in quell'albor balenar Cristo.
Di corno in corno e tra la cima e 'l basso
 si movìen lumi, scintillando forte   110
 nel congiugnersi insieme e nel trapasso:
così si veggion qui diritte e torte,
 veloci e tarde, rinovando vista,
 le minuzie de' corpi, lunghe e corte,
moversi per lo raggio onde si lista
 tal volta l'ombra che, per sua difesa,
 la gente con ingegno e arte acquista.
E come giga e arpa, in tempra tesa
 di molte corde, fa dolce tintinno
 a tal da cui la nota non è intesa,   120
così da' lumi che lì m'apparinno
 s'accogliea per la croce una melode
 che mi rapiva, sanza intender l' inno.
Ben m'accors' io ch'elli era d'alte lode,
 però ch'a me venìa 'Resurgi' e 'Vinci'
 come a colui che non intende e ode.
Io m' innamorava tanto quinci,
 che 'nfino a lì non fu alcuna cosa
 che mi legasse con sì dolci vinci.
Forse la mia parola par troppo osa,   130
 posponendo il piacer delli occhi belli
 ne' quai mirando, mio disio ha posa;
ma chi s'avvede che i vivi suggelli
 d'ogni bellezza più fanno più suso,
 e ch' io non m'era lì rivolto a quelli,
escusar puommi di quel ch' io m'accuso
 per escusarmi, e vedermi dir vero;
 chè 'l piacer santo non è qui dischiuso,
perchè si fa, montando, più sincero.

but he that takes up his cross and follows Christ shall yet forgive me for what I leave untold, when he sees Christ flash in that dawn. From horn to horn and between the summit and the base lights were moving that sparkled brightly as they met and passed; so we see here, direct and aslant, swift and slow, changing appearance, the particles of matter, long and short, move through the beam which sometimes streaks the shade that men devise for their protection with cunning and skill. And as viol and harp strung with many chords in harmony chime sweetly for one who does not catch the tune, so from the lights that appeared to me there a melody gathered through the cross which held me rapt though I did not follow the hymn. I perceived, indeed, that it was of high praises, for there came to me 'Arise' and 'Conquer', as one hears without understanding; by which I was so moved to love that till then nothing had bound me with so sweet a chain.

My words, perhaps, seem too bold, making less of my delight in the fair eyes looking into which my desire finds rest; but he who takes note that these living seals of all beauty have more power with each ascent and that I had not there turned to them again may excuse me in that for which I accuse to excuse myself and may see that I speak truth; for that holy delight is not here excluded, since it becomes purer as we rise.

PARADISO

1. If the souls retain their brightness when they recover their bodies at the general resurrection, how will they bear to look at each other with their bodily sight?

2. One God, two natures in Christ, three Persons in the Godhead.

3. Solomon, 'the fifth light, the most beautiful among us' (*Par.* x).

4. 'It is sown in weakness; it is raised in power: it is sown a natural body; it is raised a spiritual body' (1 *Cor.* xv. 43–44).

5. The planet Mars.

6. The nature of the Milky Way was much debated.

7. The Greek cross, familiar from the crossed halo of Christ.

NOTE

Dante has given a great place in the heaven of the Sun to Aquinas, and now that Aquinas is silent the homely image of the water in a bowl rippling between the centre and the rim at once recalls the reader to the scene of the great shining circles of the wise and Beatrice with Dante in the centre, and suggests the correspondence and rapport between Beatrice, for Dante the spirit of revelation, and the great theologian.

Dante's question to the spirits about the radiance that surrounds each of them is the occasion for an outburst of praise to the source of all that light. Their song is, in effect, a continuation of that in the thirteenth canto: 'There they sang, not Bacchus and no Paean, but three Persons in the divine nature, and in one Person that nature and the human.' Here we have a bolder attempt to find expression for the inexpressible, in which the 'chiastic' formality of the terms suggests the eternal oneness and with that the eternal diversity of God in His being and working, with an outgoing and return between unity and trinity which *seem* to alternate and *are* simultaneous and unchanging: 'That One and Two and Three who ever lives and ever reigns in Three and in Two and in One, and uncircumscribed circumscribes all, was sung three times by every one of these spirits.'

The doctrine of bodily resurrection was much discussed by medieval theologians, and it was cherished as carrying with it the idea of the soul's perfecting as an individual, a recognizable personality, eager to renew and confirm in eternity the old human ties; for the soul in its perfection becomes not less but more personal and individual. The process, so to call it, by which the spirits are made to shine and are to shine still more brightly when their bodies make them 'all complete', is through the sequence, twice noted, of vision, love, light. The whole process is of grace, and this is emphasized, in Dante's manner, by the succession of cognate words: *grazia*, grace,—*grato*, acceptable,—*di gratuito*, freely. All this account of things is put into the mouth of Solomon, doubtless as the supposed author of the *Song*, which was taken to celebrate the nuptials of Christ and the Church and the joys of heaven, 'the feast of Paradise'; and that is why his voice was 'such perhaps as the angel's to Mary', which first told of the Word made flesh.

It is in this immediate context, of the perfected heavenly life—'and lo, all round'—, that the Third Circle in this sphere of the knowledge of God, embracing the other two circles, appears. The description of it is brief, twelve lines, and it is vague, as of something that is hardly definable. It is 'a lustre surpassing what was there, like a brightening horizon'; like the first stars at dusk it 'seems and seems not real' and 'it seemed to me that I began to see'; none of its 'new spirits' are identified; Dante asks no questions about them and Beatrice has nothing to say. But the words 'Ah, very sparkling of the Holy Ghost!', words of Dante as narrator, would surely connect this Third Circle of the wise, in the minds of his first readers, with the prophecy of the coming age of the Spirit, 'the Everlasting Gospel', made by the Abbot Joachim, the last-named of the saints in the Second Circle (*Par.* xii). That hope of a new age in which the orders and institutions of the Church would be fulfilled in a deeper, more inward and direct apprehension of divine things—an age

> 'When love is an unerring light,
> And joy its own security'—

had been the occasion of long and strenuous controversy, and was very familiar to Dante's contemporaries, so that a hint would suggest it to them. Whether or not with specific reference to Joachim's teaching, this strange and fleeting vision, reaching indefinitely into the far spaces of the Sun, 'beyond the other two circles' of the wise, and flaming, as he looks at it, into sudden splendour, is Dante's declaration that it belongs to the knowledge of God and the illumination of the Spirit to know that the truth is greater, infinitely and always, than all men's knowledge of it. It is at that moment that Beatrice shows him the wonder of her smile,—'and I saw myself translated, along with my Lady, to higher blessedness.'

Is it possible that this fleeting glimpse of the Third Circle, in its relation to the other two, may explain, by contrast, the curious language, with its apparently excessive emphasis, at the beginning of the thirteenth canto, where we are bidden keep before us the image of the two star-circles, 'while I speak, firm as a rock'? For his spiritual assurance Dante relies, and bids us rely, not, primarily, on our human hopes and longings, but on a revelation which is history,—a revelation of which the two circles of the saints are not only a testimony but themselves a part. By holding such testimony 'firm as a rock', by our settled assurance, on evidence, that the Divine Power and Wisdom and Love are the ultimate meaning of history and of our life, we may attain, if only in a life beyond life, to a greater vision and a deeper inspiration, the 'very sparkling of the Holy Ghost'.

The sphere of Mars into which they pass is described as 'higher blessedness'. For greater than all knowledge of God in itself is spiritual fortitude, the daring and bearing of pain or death for the love of God and the service of men. Mars, the planet of war, glows redder at their coming, and in its depths, white against its redness, is 'the venerable sign' of sacrificial love, the mark of the crusader. The spirits there are God's soldier-martyrs who have contended for the faith and whose life and death have been a costly sacrifice. Dante is true to his own character and temper when he represents himself as deeply moved and as making of himself a whole burnt-offering when he enters the sphere and, at the sight of that fellowship, says: 'O Divine Sun that dost so glorify them!' The line is an example of Dante's extreme pregnancy of expression, which is sometimes hardly translatable. *Eliòs* is his own coinage and is apparently meant to combine the Hebrew *El*, God,—expressly referred to in the twenty-sixth canto—or *Eli*, my God,—familiar from the cry of Jesus in the story of the crucifixion—and the Greek *Helios*, the Sun. The verb *addobbare* has meanings varying from *adorn* to *furnish* and *equip*, and is cognate with the English *dub*, for the act of a sovereign in granting a knighthood. These souls are called 'splendours'; that is to say, in Dante's use of the word, their brightness is not their own, it is derived, a reflection of the light of God, as the stars, in the science of the time, shine by reflection of the sun. In its whole context the line—a thought and devout acknowledgement rather than an exclamation (it is only *said*)—cannot mean less than this: that it is so, and only so, while they are held within the light of the cross, 'within two beams', identified with its supreme sacrifice, that these souls in the sphere of Mars are adorned and equipped and appointed for their calling as fighters in God's cause. That is the warfare of the saints and the only warfare that is ever justified for men in the light of heaven.

It is an instance of Dante's habitual relevancy that the Galaxy is described as 'perplexing the wisest', like the unfathomable meaning of the cross. From its whiteness, pricked out with ruddy splendours each containing a redeemed soul, there flashes on him a momentary, incommunicable vision of Christ, whose name is again, as in the twelfth canto, set apart from every other name by its triple rhyming with itself. It is unnecessary, and hardly possible, to imagine an actual visible presence of Christ here, especially as in the medieval iconography of the cross the cross itself is constantly used as the symbol of Christ. 'Iconographically considered, the Son of God is in the cross' (*M. Didron*). Here, it is in His soldiers and martyrs themselves, such as those named in the eighteenth canto, that Christ flames forth and is rightly known. The whole scene is one of Dante's richest and most imposing complexes of imagery, and it is illustrated and made more convincing by a comparison deliberately commonplace, with the motes dancing in a sunbeam from a shutter. It is as real as that.

Dante saw that cross of fighting saints 'flame forth Christ', and the cross was itself Christ's 'sign of victory' crowned with which Virgil has seen Him in Hell (*Inf.* iv); and then he heard snatches of their praise of Christ, catching the words 'Arise' and 'Conquer'. When Dante imagined this scene and wrote it down he was a man of fifty or more and older than his years, worn with labour and strife, with poverty and humiliating dependence, with estrangement and defeat, watching from his last refuge in Ravenna a disorded world in which now he could take no part. These scenes in Mars are, of course, reported as belonging to his experience 'in the middle of the journey of our life', in his last year in Florence. But it was Dante in Ravenna to whom this vision was given, and most of all in the *Paradiso* it is the later, much-experienced man that matters for our interpretation of his poem. There is less in the *Paradiso* than in the earlier parts of the *Comedy* of confident forecasting of events, but there is more of 'the glory of Him who moves all things'; and when Dante heard that melody gather through the cross it is not strange that it held him rapt though he did not follow the hymn, or that, when he caught the great sounds of praise addressed to the victorious Christ—even only 'as one hears without understanding'—he, who had fought and failed in the world, was so moved to love that till then nothing had bound him with so sweet a chain. All of Dante must be read in the context of himself, and, so read, this passage is a poignant and moving confession of faith from one who 'against hope believed in hope'.

This scene excels in glory as in significance all that Dante had yet seen in Paradise. It is a vision of daring and sacrifice for a divine end, and nothing in the lower heavens compares with that even in Beatrice's eyes, 'the living seals of all beauty'. For he has not yet turned to look at her here; he has not yet known the soul's sacrificial fortitude in its relation to the whole truth of God, as he is to know it in this cross of souls.

PARADISO

BENIGNA volontade in che si liqua
   sempre l'amor che drittamente spira,
   come cupidità fa nella iniqua,
silenzio puose a quella dolce lira,
   e fece quïetar le sante corde
   che la destra del cielo allenta e tira.
Come saranno a' giusti preghi sorde
   quelle sustanze che, per darmi voglia
   ch' io le pregassi, a tacer fur concorde?
Bene è che sanza termine si doglia   10
   chi, per amor di cosa che non duri,
   etternalmente quello amor si spoglia.
Quale per li seren tranquilli e puri
   discorre ad ora ad or subito foco,
   movendo li occhi che stavan sicuri,
e pare stella che tramuti loco,
   se non che dalla parte ond'el s'accende
   nulla sen perde, ed esso dura poco;
tale dal corno che 'n destro si stende
   a piè di quella croce corse un astro   20
   della costellazion che lì resplende;
nè si partì la gemma dal suo nastro,
   ma per la lista radïal trascorse,
   che parve foco dietro ad alabastro:
sì pia l'ombra d'Anchise si porse,
   se fede merta nostra maggior musa,
   quando in Eliso del figlio s'accorse.

CANTO XV

Cacciaguida; ancient Florence

GRACIOUS will, into which rightly-breathing love always resolves itself, as does cupidity into ill-will, imposed silence on that sweet lyre and stilled the sacred strings which the right hand of heaven tightens and relaxes. How shall these spirits be deaf to righteous prayers who, to prompt me to beg of them, became silent with one consent? Well may he grieve without end who robs himself eternally of that love for love of what does not endure.

As through the still and cloudless evening sky runs at times a sudden fire, catching the eyes that were unheeding, and seems a star changing its place but that from the part where it kindles none is missing and it lasts but a moment; so from the horn that extends on the right ran to the foot of that cross a star of the resplendent constellation that is there. And the gem did not leave its ribbon, but ran across by the radial strip and seemed fire behind alabaster. With such affection did Anchises' shade reach out, if we may trust our greatest muse, when in Elysium he knew his son.[1]

'O sanguis meus, o superinfusa
 gratïa Deï, sicut tibi cui
 bis unquam coeli ianüa reclusa?'   30
Così quel lume: ond' io m'attesi a lui;
 poscia rivolsi alla mia donna il viso,
 e quinci e quindi stupefatto fui;
chè dentro alli occhi suoi ardea un riso
 tal, ch' io pensai co' miei toccar lo fondo
 della mia grazia e del mio paradiso.
Indi, a udire ed a veder giocondo,
 giunse lo spirto al suo principio cose
 ch' io non lo 'ntesi, sì parlò profondo;
nè per elezïon mi si nascose,   40
 ma per necessità, chè 'l suo concetto
 al segno de' mortal si soprapose.
E quando l'arco dell'ardente affetto
 fu sì sfogato, che 'l parlar discese
 inver lo segno del nostro intelletto,
la prima cosa che per me s' intese,
 'Benedetto sia tu' fu 'trino e uno,
 che nel mio seme se' tanto cortese!'
E seguì: 'Grato e lontano digiuno,
 tratto leggendo del magno volume   50
 du' non si muta mai bianco nè bruno,
soluto hai, figlio, dentro a questo lume
 in ch' io ti parlo, mercè di colei
 ch' all'alto volo ti vestì le piume.
Tu credi che a me tuo pensier mei
 da quel ch'è primo, così come raia
 dall' un, se si conosce, il cinque e 'l sei;
e però chi mi sia e perch' io paia
 più gaudïoso a te, non mi domandi,
 che alcun altro in questa turba gaia.   60
Tu credi 'l vero; chè i minori e' grandi
 di questa vita miran nello speglio
 in che, prima che pensi, il pensier pandi;
ma perchè 'l sacro amore in che io veglio
 con perpetüa vista e che m'asseta
 di dolce disïar, s'adempia meglio,

'O *sanguis meus, o superinfusa gratia Dei, sicut tibi bis unquam coeli janua reclusa?*'[2] That light spoke thus; therefore I gave heed to it, then turned my eyes again to my Lady; and on the one hand and on the other I was amazed, for within her eyes glowed such a smile that I thought I touched with mine the depth of my grace and of my paradise.

Then, a joy to hearing and to sight, the spirit added to his first words things I did not comprehend, so deep was his speech; nor did he conceal himself from me by choice but by necessity, for his conceiving was set above the mark of mortals. And when the bow of burning love was so relaxed that his speech came down towards the mark of our intellect, the first thing I understood was: 'Blessed be Thou, three-fold and one, who showest such favour to my seed!' And he continued: 'Happy and long craving, drawn from the reading of the great volume where there is never change of black or white,[3] thou hast satisfied, my son, within this light in which I speak to thee, thanks to her who clad thee with wings for the lofty flight. Thou believest that thy thought flows forth to me from Him who is the First, even as from the unit, when it is known, radiate the five and six,[4] and therefore thou dost not ask me who I am and why I appear to thee more joyful than any other in this happy throng. Thou believest rightly, for small and great in this life gaze into the mirror in which, before thou thinkest, thou makest plain the thought.[5] But, that the holy love in which I keep watch with constant vision and which makes me thirst with sweet desire may be better satisfied, let thy voice, confident, bold and

la voce tua sicura, balda e lieta
   suoni la volontà, suoni 'l disio,
   a che la mia risposta è già decreta!'
Io mi volsi a Beatrice, e quella udìo   70
   pria ch' io parlassi, e arrisemi un cenno
   che fece crescer l'ali al voler mio.
Poi cominciai così: 'L'affetto e 'l senno,
   come la prima equalità v'apparse,
   d'un peso per ciascun di voi si fenno,
però che 'l sol che v'allumò e arse
   col caldo e con la luce, è sì iguali,
   che tutte simiglianze sono scarse.
Ma voglia ed argomento ne' mortali,
   per la cagion ch'a voi è manifesta,   80
   diversamente son pennuti in ali;
ond' io, che son mortal, mi sento in questa
   disagguaglianza, e però non ringrazio
   se non col core alla paterna festa.
Ben supplico io a te, vivo topazio
   che questa gioia preziosa ingemmi,
   perchè mi facci del tuo nome sazio.'
'O fronda mia in che io compiacemmi
   pur aspettando, io fui la tua radice':
   cotal principio, rispondendo, femmi.   90
Poscia mi disse: 'Quel da cui si dice
   tua cognazione e che cent'anni e piùe
   girato ha il monte in la prima cornice,
mio figlio fu e tuo bisavol fue:
   ben si convien che la lunga fatica
   tu li raccorci con l'opere tue.
Fiorenza dentro dalla cerchia antica,
   ond'ella toglie ancora e terza e nona,
   si stava in pace, sobria e pudica.
Non avea catenella, non corona,   100
   non gonne contigiate, non cintura
   che fosse a veder più che la persona.
Non faceva, nascendo, ancor paura
   la figlia al padre; chè 'l tempo e la dote
   non fuggìen quinci e quindi la misura.

joyful, sound forth the will and the longing to which already my answer is decreed.'

I turned to Beatrice, and she heard before I spoke and smiled to me a sign that made the wings grow on my will; then I began: 'Love and intelligence, as soon as the Primal Equality was plain to you, became equally poised in each of you, since the Sun that illumined and warmed you with its heat and light has such equality that all comparisons came short of it. But will and faculty in mortals, for the reason that is plain to you, are not equally feathered in their wings, so that I, who am mortal, feel in myself this inequality and therefore can only give thanks with the heart for thy paternal greeting.[6] But I beseech thee, living topaz who art a gem in this rich jewel, that thou satisfy me with thy name.'

'O my branch, in whom I rejoiced only expecting thee, I was thy root.'[7] Thus he began his answer to me, then said: 'He from whom thy house is named and who for a hundred years and more has gone round the mountain on the first terrace was my son and thy great-grandfather; it is most fitting that thou shouldst shorten his long labour with thy good offices.[8]

'Florence, within her ancient circle from which she still takes tierce and nones[9], abode in peace, sober and chaste. She had no bracelet, no tiara, no embroidered gowns, no girdle that should be seen more than the wearer. Not yet did the daughter at her birth put the father in fear, for age and dowry did not part from the due measure on the one side and the other.[10] She had no houses empty of

219

Non avea case di famiglia vote;
   non v'era giunto ancor Sardanapalo
   a mostrar ciò che 'n camera si pote.
Non era vinto ancora Montemalo
   dal vostro Uccellatoio, che, com'è vinto   110
   nel montar su, così sarà nel calo.
Bellincion Berti vid' io andar cinto
   di cuoio e d'osso, e venir dallo specchio
   la donna sua sanza il viso dipinto;
e vidi quel de' Nerli e quel del Vecchio
   esser contenti alla pelle scoperta,
   e le sue donne al fuso e al pennecchio.
Oh fortunate! ciascuna era certa
   della sua sepultura, ed ancor nulla
   era per Francia nel letto diserta.   120
L'una vegghiava a studio della culla,
   e, consolando, usava l' idïoma
   che prima i padri e le madri trastulla;
l'altra, traendo alla rocca la chioma,
   favoleggiava con la sua famiglia
   de' Troiani, di Fiesole e di Roma.
Sarìa tenuta allor tal maraviglia
   una Cianghella, un Lapo Salterello,
   qual or sarìa Cincinnato e Corniglia.
A così riposato, a così bello   130
   viver di cittadini, a così fida
   cittadinanza, a così dolce ostello,
Maria mi diè, chiamata in alte grida;
   e nell'antico vostro Batisteo
   insieme fui cristiano e Cacciaguida.
Moronto fu mio frate ed Eliseo:
   mia donna venne a me di val di Pado;
   e quindi il sopranome tuo si feo.
Poi seguitai lo 'mperador Currado;
   ed el mi cinse della sua milizia,   140
   tanto per bene ovrar li venni in grado.
Dietro li andai incontro alla nequizia
   di quella legge il cui popolo usurpa,
   per colpa de' pastor, vostra giustizia.

family, nor had Sardanapalus yet come there to show what could be done in the chamber.[11] Not yet did your Uccellatoio surpass Montemario, which, surpassed in its rise, shall be too in its fall.[12] Bellincion Berti[13] I saw go girt with leather and bone, and his lady come from the mirror with unpainted face, and I saw dei Nerli and del Vecchio content in plain buff and their ladies at the spindle and flax. O favoured women! Each was sure of her burial-place and was not yet deserted in her bed for France.[14] One kept watch, tending the cradle, and, soothing her child, would use the tongue that first delights fathers and mothers; another, drawing the tresses from the distaff, would tell among her family tales of the Trojans, of Fiesole and Rome. A Cianghella, a Lapo Salterello, would have been held as great a wonder then as now would Cincinnatus and Cornelia.[15] To a citizen's life so peaceful and so fair, to a community so loyal, to so sweet a dwelling-place, Mary gave me when called on with loud cries, and in your ancient Baptistery I became at once Christian and Cacciaguida. Moronto was my brother, and Eliseo. My wife came to me from the valley of the Po, and from her was taken thy surname. Later, I followed the Emperor Conrad, and he girded me of his knighthood, so greatly did I win his favour by good service; I went after him against the iniquity of that law whose people, by fault of the shepherds, usurp

Quivi fu' io da quella gente turpa
disviluppato dal mondo fallace,
lo cui amor molt'anime deturpa;
venni dal martiro a questa pace.'

your right.[16] There I was set free by that foul race
from the entanglements of the deceitful world the
love of which corrupts many souls, and came from
martyrdom to this peace.'

1. A reference to Virgil's account in the *Aeneid* of Aeneas's visit to the world of the dead, where he met his father Anchises.

2. 'O my own blood! O grace of God poured forth above measure! To whom as to thee was heaven's gate ever opened twice?'

3. The book of the divine foreknowledge.

4. Dante's thought is as inevitably derived by the redeemed from God's knowledge of it as all numbers are derived from unity.

5. 'Thou understandest my thought afar off' (*Ps.* cxxxix. 2).

6. God's attributes are all in equal perfection, and that equal balance of will and faculty is given to the redeemed,—'We shall be like him, for we shall see him as he is' (1 *John* iii. 2); but in mortals feeling is disproportioned to utterance, so Dante cannot speak his thanks.

7. Of Cacciaguida, Dante's great-great-grandfather, who lived in the first half of the 12th century, practically nothing is known except from these cantos.

8. His purgation of pride may be hastened by Dante's good works and prayers. 'Well may we help them to wash away the stains they carried hence' (*Purg.* xi).

9. The bells of the Abbey Church, the Badia, close to the old walls of Florence, rang for the daily services at 9 a.m. and noon.

10. The age of marriage for women was not too low, nor the dowry too high.

11. No mansions were large beyond the needs of the household. The wantonness of Sardanapalus of Assyria was proverbial.

12. Montemario, a height giving the first sight of Rome to a traveller from the north, as Uccellatoio does of Florence; the view of Florence should surpass that of Rome, first in splendour, then in decay.

13. The ancestor of the great Conti Guidi through his daughter 'the good Gualdrada' (*Inf.* xvi).

14. Many ambitious Florentines went to France for trading in Dante's time.

15. Cianghella and Salterello, Florentine contemporaries of Dante of bad repute, contrasted with the hero and heroine of ancient Rome.

16. Cacciaguida fought in the Second Crusade (1147–9) under the Emperor Conrad III; 'that law', Islam, whose adherents, by the negligence of the popes, keep possession of Holy Land.

NOTE

The rapture of the hero-saints of Mars does not detach them from common human kindness, their 'rightly-breathing love resolves itself into gracious will', and 'to prompt me to beg of them', the whole chorus is 'silent with one consent'. The sense of strangeness and splendour is maintained in the opening of the canto,—the sudden silence, the swift red flash of the one light along the white lines of the cross, Cacciaguida's outburst of affection in the language of the Church and of heaven, and the new beauty in Beatrice's eyes that leaves Dante in amazement. The surpassing quality of his experience here is further marked by his inability to understand Cacciaguida's next words to him and by his own response in a formal and elaborate diction suited to the occasion of their meeting and to that height of Paradise.

Cacciaguida addresses Dante as 'my blood', 'my seed', 'my son', 'my branch'. The knight of the Empire who has fought in its battles for the cause of Christ—as Dante and his age conceived it—, taking up his cross and giving his life, insistently claims Dante as one of his stock, and this language is a forecast of the whole interview that follows, in which Dante is commissioned anew, called to be worthy of his heritage and to serve his generation at his personal cost. The mention of Anchises is a reference not merely to a classical paternal greeting, but also to a like prophecy of his son's calling in a mighty cause—'that glorious Rome that shall extend her empire to the world and her genius to heaven' (*Aeneid* vi); and Virgil, 'our greatest muse', was the spokesman and prophet of Rome, Rome in its noblest meaning, the civilizer of the world and the fulfilment of a divine destiny, the Rome of Dante's dream.

This canto and the two following are the most personal and intimate in the *Paradiso*, telling of Dante's greatest ancestor,

of Florence, dear to them both, and, in that context, of Dante's
own life and calling. This, in particular, is a consecration of
family affection and pure patriotism, the Roman *pietas*. Caccia-
guida greets his descendant of the fourth generation with a
passionate tenderness and begs Dante's prayers for his son,
who is still purging the sin of pride which he shared with his
own great-grandson. The old crusader pours out his heart
in recollections of their native city and its ancient ways, recalling
the tales his mother told him of Troy—traditionally the mother-
city of Rome—and of Fiesole and Rome—traditionally the
mother-cities of Florence. Such tales—'the epic of ancient
virtue, civil and domestic,' (*C. Grabher*)—were very familiar
in Florence, where they were handled with a free inventiveness
by the early chroniclers; the mother 'would tell tales' (*favoleg-
giava*, fabled) 'among her family'. 'The Florentines reported
the origins of their city thus. After the division of tongues
through the attempt to build the Tower of Babel, Atalanta
built the first city, which then *fu sola* and was therefore called
Fiesole. Dardanus, one of her sons, went to the east and there
built Troy. From Troy Aeneas came to Italy; a descendant of
Aeneas founded Rome; the Romans destroyed Fiesole; Romans
and Fiesolans founded Florence. All this, with many ornaments,
some of them very strange, may be read in the earliest compila-
tions of Florentine chronicles' (*F. Torraca*).

Cacciaguida's early memories and affections are not lost or
weakened in the glory of the heavenly life. When he rushed
meteor-like to meet his descendant he still kept within the lines
of the cross, and it is in his vision of God itself that he has
known, with 'happy and long craving', that Dante would come
to him. His love of home and kin is a part of his state of re-
demption and the old life of Florence is linked with the life of
Paradise.

When Dante asks his ancestor for his name Cacciaguida
begins his reply by speaking, not of himself, but of his son,
who is in need of Dante's devout help in Purgatory, and of
Florence as he knew it two hundred years before, naming the
one thing that is common to its older, nobler state and its
present, the daily calls to prayer, the familiar bell for tierce and
nones. All the rest of the comparison is contrast, the imagined

brightness of the old city casting proportionately dark shadows on the new. 'Not yet . . . not yet' was that Florence of Caccia-guida's memory—abiding 'in peace, sober and chaste,'—the Florence Dante has known, turbulent, ostentatious, wanton. Then, at the end and in a few lines, Cacciaguida, the fine flower of that life so fair and peaceful, tells of his own career: how he went forth to die for God's cause, now neglected by the popes themselves, and in the strife 'was set free from the entanglements of the deceitful world, and came from martyrdom to this peace'. The words inevitably recall those of the account of Boethius in the tenth canto, where it is said that he 'makes plain the deceitful world' and that he 'came from martyrdom and exile to this peace'; and in both these passages *il mondo fallace* is made to rhyme, and to contrast, with *questa pace,*— 'the deceitful world' and 'this peace'. So marked a correspon-dence must, in Dante, be intentional and significant. Boethius exposed the world's deceitfulness to the world, and he served God well; Cacciaguida fought and gave his life against it, and he served God better,—that was his 'higher blessedness'.

We are not here concerned with the justice and measure of Dante's judgements of the old and the new Florence, but with his imagination of a city whose common habits and intimate domestic ways were in accord with the glories of Paradise, so that while Cacciaguida talks of them the saintly hosts of Mars stay silent from their song. Meredith says that 'men are known by their way of loving', and this was Dante's way of loving Florence; he loved it for what he believed it had been and for what it might be still, and the thought of it fills his lines with lyric passion.

PARADISO

O POCA nostra nobiltà di sangue,
   se glorïar di te la gente fai
   qua giù dove l'affetto nostro langue,
mirabil cosa non mi sarà mai;
   chè là dove appetito non si torce,
   dico nel cielo, io me ne gloriai.
Ben se' tu manto che tosto raccorce;
   sì che, se non s'appon di dì in dìe,
   lo tempo va dintorno con le force.
Dal 'voi' che prima Roma sofferìe,   10
   in che la sua famiglia men persevra,
   ricominciaron le parole mie;
onde Beatrice, ch'era un poco scevra,
   ridendo, parve quella che tossìo
   al primo fallo scritto di Ginevra.
Io cominciai: 'Voi siete il padre mio;
   voi mi date a parlar tutta baldezza;
   voi mi levate sì, ch' i' son più ch' io.
Per tanti rivi s'empie d'allegrezza
   la mente mia, che di sè fa letizia   20
   perchè può sostener che non si spezza.
Ditemi dunque, cara mia primizia,
   quai fuor li vostri antichi, e quai fuor li anni
   che si segnaro in vostra puerizia:
ditemi dell'ovil di San Giovanni
   quanto era allora, e chi eran le genti
   tra esso degne di più alti scanni.'

CANTO XVI

Family pride; the decline of great Florentine families

O OUR poor nobility of blood, if thou makest men glory in thee here below, where our affections languish, it will never be a thing for me to wonder at; for there, where appetite is not warped, in Heaven itself, I gloried in thee. Truly thou art a mantle that quickly shrinks, so that if we do not add to it day by day time goes round it with the shears.

With the *you* which Rome was the first to allow and in which her children least persevere[1] I began again to speak; at which Beatrice, who stood a little apart, seemed by her smile like her who coughed at the first fault written of Guinevere.[2] I began: 'You are my father, you give me all boldness to speak, you uplift me so that I am more than myself; by so many streams my mind is filled with happiness that it rejoices in itself that it can bear it without bursting. Tell me then, dear stock from which I spring, what were your ancestors and what years were chronicled in your boyhood; tell me of the sheepfold of Saint John,[3] how large it was then and what families in it were worthy of its chief seats.'

Come s'avviva allo spirar di venti
   carbone in fiamma, così vid' io quella
   luce risplendere a' miei blandimenti;   30
e come alli occhi miei si fè più bella,
   così con voce più dolce e soave,
   ma non con questa moderna favella,
dissemi: 'Da quel dì che fu detto "Ave"
   al parto in che mia madre, ch'è or santa,
   s'alleviò di me ond'era grave,
al suo Leon cinquecento cinquanta
   e tre fïate venne questo foco
   a rinfiammarsi sotto la sua pianta.
Li antichi miei e io nacqui nel loco   40
   dove si truova pria l'ultimo sesto
   da quei che corre il vostro annüal gioco.
Basti de' miei maggiori udirne questo:
   chi ei si fosser e ónde venner quivi,
   più è tacer che ragionare onesto.
Tutti color ch'a quel tempo eran ivi
   da poter arme tra Marte e 'l Batista,
   erano il quinto di quei ch'or son vivi.
Ma la cittadinanza, ch'è or mista
   di Campi, di Certaldo e di Fegghine,   50
   pura vedìesi nell'ultimo artista.
Oh quanto fora meglio esser vicine
   quelle genti ch' io dico, e al Galluzzo
   e a Trespiano aver vostro confine,
che averle dentro e sostener lo puzzo
   del villan d'Aguglion, di quel da Signa,
   che già per barattare ha l'occhio aguzzo!
Se la gente ch'al mondo più traligna
   non fosse stata a Cesare noverca,
   ma come madre a suo figlio benigna,   60
tal fatto è fiorentino e cambia e merca,
   che si sarebbe volto a Simifonti,
   là dove andava l'avolo alla cerca;
sarìesi Montemurlo ancor de' Conti;
   sarìeno i Cerchi nel piovier d'Acone,
   e forse in Valdigrieve i Buondelmonti.

As coal quickens to flame in a breath of wind,
so I saw that light kindle at my words of affection;
and as it became more fair in my sight, so with
a voice sweeter and gentler, but not in this modern
speech, he said to me: 'From that day when *Ave*
was spoken till the birth by which my mother, who
is now blest, was lightened of her burden of me,
this fire came to its Lion five hundred and fifty-
three times to be re-kindled under its paw.[4] My
ancestors and I were born at the place where the
furthest ward is reached by the runner in your
yearly games. Let it suffice thee to hear thus much
of my forebears; as to who they were and whence
they came it is more fitting to be silent than to
speak. All who were there at that time between
Mars and the Baptist[5] able to bear arms were a fifth
of the number now living, but the citizenship,
which is now mixed with Campi and Certaldo and
Figline,[6] was seen pure in the humblest artisan.
Ah, how much better would it be to have these
people I name for neighbours, with your bounds
at Galluzzo and Trespiano, than to have them inside
and to endure the stench of the boor from Aguglion
and of him from Signa who already has a sharp
eye for jobbery![7] If the people that of all the world
are most degenerate had not been a stepmother to
Caesar, but kind like a mother to her son, there is
one turned Florentine that trucks and trades who
would be sent back to Semifonte, where his grand-
father went a-begging, Montemurlo would still
belong to the Counts, the Cerchi would be in Acone
Parish and the Buondelmonti perhaps in Valdi-

Sempre la confusion delle persone
  principio fu del mal della cittade,
  come del corpo il cibo che s'appone;
e cieco toro più avaccio cade   70
  che 'l cieco agnello; e molte volte taglia
  più e meglio una che le cinque spade.
Se tu riguardi Luni e Urbisaglia
  come sono ite, e come se ne vanno
  di retro ad esse Chiusi e Sinigaglia,
udir come le schiatte si disfanno
  non ti parrà nova cosa nè forte,
  poscia che le cittadi termine hanno.
Le vostre cose tutte hanno lor morte,
  sì come voi; ma celasi in alcuna   80
  che dura molto; e le vite son corte.
E come 'l volger del ciel della luna
  cuopre e discuopre i liti sanza posa,
  così fa di Fiorenza la Fortuna:
per che non dee parer mirabil cosa
  ciò ch' io dirò delli alti Fiorentini
  onde è la fama nel tempo nascosa.
Io vidi li Ughi, e vidi i Catellini,
  Filippi, Greci, Ormanni e Alberichi,
  già nel calare, illustri cittadini;   90
e vidi così grandi come antichi,
  con quel della Sannella, quel dell'Arca,
  e Soldanieri e Ardinghi e Bostichi.
Sovra la porta ch'al presente è carca
  di nova fellonia di tanto peso
  che tosto fia iattura della barca,
erano i Ravignani, ond'è disceso
  il conte Guido e qualunque del nome
  dell'alto Bellincione ha poscia preso.
Quel della Pressa sapeva già come   100
  regger si vuole, ed avea Galigaio
  dorata in casa sua già l'elsa e 'l pome.
Grand'era già la colonna del Vaio,
  Sacchetti, Giuochi, Fifanti e Barucci
  e Galli e quei ch'arrossan per lo staio.

greve.[8] The mixture of peoples was ever the beginning of the city's ills, as food in excess is of the body's, and a blind bull falls more headlong than a blind lamb, and often one sword cuts more and better than five. If thou consider Luni and Urbisaglia, how they are gone, and how Chiusi and Senigallia are going after them,[9] then to hear how families come to naught will not seem to thee a thing new or strange, since the cities have an end. All your affairs are mortal, even as yourselves, but in some things that last long this is concealed, and lives are short; and as the turning of the moon's heaven covers and lays bare the shores unceasingly, so fortune does with Florence. It should not therefore seem a marvellous thing that I have to tell of the great Florentines whose fame is hid by time. I saw the Ughi, I saw the Catellini, Filippi, Greci, Ormanni and Alberichi, illustrious citizens already in decline, and I saw, as great as they were ancient, dell' Arca with della Sannella, and Soldanieri and Ardinghi and Bostichi. Over the gate which today is loaded with such a weight of unheard-of perfidy that there will soon be shipwreck of the bark were the Ravignani, of whose line is Count Guido and all that have since taken their name from the great Bellincion.[10] Della Pressa knew already how to rule, and Galigaio already had in his house the gilded hilt and pommel.[11] Great already was the pale of vair,[12] the Sacchetti, Giuochi, Fifanti and Barucci and Galli, and those that blush for the

Lo ceppo di che nacquero i Calfucci
   era già grande, e già eran tratti
   alle curule Sizii e Arrigucci.
Oh quali io vidi quei che son disfatti
   per lor superbia! e le palle dell'oro   110
   fiorìan Fiorenza in tutti suoi gran fatti.
Così facìeno i padri di coloro
   che, sempre che la vostra chiesa vaca,
   si fanno grassi stando a consistoro.
L'oltracotata schiatta che s' indraca
   dietro a chi fugge, e a chi mostra 'l dente
   o ver la borsa, com'agnel si placa,
già venìa su, ma di picciola gente;
   sì che non piacque ad Ubertin Donato
   che poi il suocero il fè lor parente.   120
Già era il Caponsacco nel mercato
   disceso giù da Fiesole, e già era
   buon cittadino Giuda ed Infangato.
Io dirò cosa incredibile e vera:
   nel picciol cerchio s'entrava per porta
   che si nomava da quei della Pera.
Ciascun che della bella insegna porta
   del gran barone il cui nome e 'l cui pregio
   la festa di Tommaso riconforta,
da esso ebbe milizia e privilegio;   130
   avvegna che con popol si rauni
   oggi colui che la fascia col fregio.
Già eran Gualterotti ed Importuni;
   e ancor sarìa Borgo più quïeto,
   se di novi vicin fosser digiuni.
La casa di che nacque il vostro fleto,
   per lo giusto disdegno che v' ha morti,
   e puose fine al vostro viver lieto,
era onorata, essa e suoi consorti:
   o Buondelmonte, quanto mal fuggisti   140
   le nozze sue per li altrui conforti!
Molti sarebber lieti, che son tristi,
   se Dio t'avesse conceduto ad Ema
   la prima volta ch'a città venisti.

bushel.[13] The stock from which the Calfucci sprang was already great, and already were brought to the seats of office Sizii and Arrigucci. Ah, how great I saw those who now are undone by their pride;[14] and the golden balls flowered Florence in all her great doings.[15] So did the fathers of those who, whenever your church is vacant, fatten themselves by sitting in council.[16] The insolent breed that plays the dragon behind him that flees and is mild as a lamb to him that shows his teeth—or else his purse—was already on the rise, but of mean stock, so that it did not please Ubertino Donato when his father-in-law made him their kinsman.[17] Already Caponsacco had come down from Fiesole to the market-place, and already Giuda and Infangato were citizens of repute. One thing I will tell incredible and true: the inner circle used to be entered by a gate that was named from the della Pera.[18] Everyone bearing the noble arms of the great Baron whose name and praise the feast of Thomas renews had from him knighthood and privilege, though he that decks it with a border sides today with the people.[19] Already there were Gualterotti and Importuni, and the Borgo would still be quieter if they had been spared new neighbours.[20] The house from which your tears have sprung, through the just resentment that has brought death among you and made an end of your happy life, was honoured, it and its associates.[21] O Buondelmonte, how ill for thee that thou didst fly from its nuptials at another's bidding! Many would be happy that are sorrowful if God had given thee up to the Ema the first time thou camest to the city;[22] but it was

Ma convenìesi a quella pietra scema
   che guarda 'l ponte che Fiorenza fesse
   vittima nella sua pace postrema.
Con queste genti e con altre con esse,
   vid' io Fiorenza in sì fatto riposo,
   che non avea cagione onde piangesse: 150
con queste genti vid' io glorïoso
   e giusto il popol suo, tanto che 'l giglio
   non era ad asta mai posto a ritroso,
nè per divisïon fatto vermiglio.'

fitting that to that wasted stone which guards the bridge Florence should offer a victim in her last days of peace.

'With these families, and with others besides, I saw Florence in such tranquillity that she had nothing to cause her grief; with these I saw her people so glorious and so just that the lily had never been reversed on the spear, nor by dissension changed to red.'[23]

1. The honorific plural was supposed (mistakenly) to have been first used at Rome in address to Julius Caesar and later to have been disused there. By this reference Dante taunts Rome for its disloyalty to the Empire.

2. One of Guinevere's ladies, overhearing her amorous words to Lancelot, coughed to warn her.

3. Florence, described from its patron-saint the Baptist.

4. From the time of the Annunciation to Cacciaguida's birth Mars had made 553 revolutions, returning always to its conjunction with the constellation Leo. Allowing two years for a revolution, his birth falls in 1106.

5. From the old statue of Mars at the Ponte Vecchio (*Inf.* xiii) to the Baptistery; all Florence, south to north.

6. Villages near Florence.

7. Two intriguing political lawyers of Dante's time.

8. Papal hostility to the Empire under Frederick II—the Church was 'a stepmother to Caesar'—caused great political disorder in north Italy; cp. *Purg.* vi, 'Ah, ye that should be devout', etc. 'The Counts', the powerful Conti Guidi, sold their castle of Montemurlo to Florence in 1254.

9. Ancient cities of north Italy.

10. The Cerchi, leaders of the White Guelfs—'the party of the rustics' (*Inf.* vi)—now lived over the Gate of St Peter; many of them were exiled in 1302. Gualdrada, daughter of Bellincion Berti (*Par.* xv), was married to Count Guido.

11. The signs of knighthood.

12. A stripe of miniver, part of the arms of the Pigli.

13. A family disgraced by one of its members, who falsified the salt measure in 1299; cp. 'an age when the records and measures were safe' (*Purg.* xii).

14. The Uberti, the family of Farinata (*Inf.* x).

15. The arms of the Lamberti, the family of Mosca (*Inf.* xxviii).

16. Two families were the patrons of the see of Florence and shared the revenues during a vacancy, which they could prolong.

17. The Adimari—Filippo Argenti (*Inf.* viii) belonged to a branch of them—, one of whom married a daughter of Bellincion Berti, another daughter being already married to Ubertino Donato.

18. The della Pera family had become unimportant by Dante's time.

19. 'The great Baron' was Hugh, Marquis of Tuscany (10th century), who was commemorated in the Badia on St Thomas's Day, the day of his death. Giano della Bella, who bore the arms of the Baron, became the popular leader in Florence at the end of the 13th century.

20. The Buondelmonti.

21. The Amidei, offended by the jilting of a daughter of their house by Buondelmonte, murdered him near the ancient statue of Mars—'that wasted stone'—in 1215; the crime was regarded as the beginning of the strife of Guelfs and Ghibellines in Florence. Cp. *Inf.* xiii, Note 7, and xxviii, Note 10.

22. The Ema is a stream near Florence which would be crossed by the first of the Buondelmonti to come to the city.

23. The lily of Florence had never been disgraced by defeat. In 1251 the Guelfs, having expelled the Ghibellines, changed the white lily to red.

NOTE

The subject of the canto is 'our poor nobility of blood', and
Dante confessed to his pride in his noble ancestor. He addressed
him with the usual *thou*—in the previous canto—until he
heard, as if for the first time, of Cacciaguida's knighthood
under the Emperor Conrad; and when he adopted the honorific
you—three times in three lines—Beatrice, 'who stood a little
apart', smiled at his foible. It was a foible, indeed, that could
run, like Queen Guinevere's greeting to Lancelot, to deadly
consequences, 'red ruin and the breaking-up of laws'. Years
before, in the *Convito*, Dante had discussed the true nature
of nobility and had condemned 'the opinion of the vulgar'
about it as 'so persistent that without any other consideration
and with no enquiry after any other reason everyone is called
gentle who is a son or grandson of a man of worth, though he
himself may be of no account. . . . Let not him of the Uberti
of Florence or him of the Visconti of Milan say: "Because I
am of such a family I am noble"; for the divine seed does not
fall on a family, that is on a stock, but on the several persons,
and the stock does not make the several persons noble but the
several persons ennoble the stock.' Nowhere was it plainer than
in Florence to what disastrous extremes family pride and
ambition could go, and here we have a part of Dante's own
confession of his sin of pride, already recorded in the *Pur-
gatorio*. But in Cacciaguida the stock itself is ennobled and
Dante rejoices to honour him.

On the family tree Cacciaguida is deliberately restrained.
'Replying to Dante's question, "Who were your ancestors?",
Cacciaguida told him merely where they lived. . . . The question
itself showed that it would have gratified the Poet, in that
glorying of his in the nobility of his blood, to hear authoritative
confirmation of the belief, received from domestic tradition or

239

taking shape in his mind by induction, according to which there lived again in him "the holy seed of the Romans" (*Inf.* xv). But how could a saint in heaven, "where appetite is not warped", second that motive of vainglory?' (*F. Torraca*). 'Of my elders I will say no more. Let it suffice to know that they did not come from the country, but were born and had their dwelling within the limits of the first circle. It is more fitting to be silent than to talk about my stock and its origin' (*Casini-Barbi*). It is the pride of a great gentleman. Probably what is told us here is all that Dante himself knew of his forebears, that they were not of the newcomers but of the older Florentine stock, and he thought it worth his while to record that Cacciaguida's ancestors, who were his own, were born, as far back as memory could reach, within the walls of Florence.

Cacciaguida glows at the appeal of his descendant for news of the Florence of the fourth generation before his own, and he falls back into the Florentine dialect of his day, talking to Dante 'not in this modern speech' in which Dante must report him. The canto is full of family and place names and local allusions, unfamiliar to a modern reader but in the same degree full of memories for its first readers in Florence. During the years between Cacciaguida and Dante, a century and a half, Florence had been transformed. Many more of the feudal barons of German blood had been brought in from the surrounding country and their towers had risen to dominate the city, and many of the men of the smaller towns and villages had become —themselves or their children—rich Florentine merchants and financiers and lawyers. New interests and problems and conflicts had arisen within the walls, and these were complicated and embittered by the intermittent strife of Church and Empire in north Italy which issued in the confused and disastrous struggle of Guelf and Ghibelline and later of Black Guelf and White, and in Dante's own exile and the defeat of all his hopes. For one of his austere and intolerant temper and proud domestic and civic tradition it was inevitable that 'the mixture of peoples' should appear to be 'ever the beginning of the city's ills', and most fitting that he should pass this judgement on Florence through the lips of his great ancestor. So it is that Cacciaguida tells him of the ebbing like a tide of the once-great

Florentine families, of the city's corruption by the admission of robber-lords and baser stocks with their own standards, and of the family feuds and ambitions which led to the madness of civil strife and the disgrace of the republic. There is in Cacciaguida's speech much of his own, and Dante's, contempt for the fool-fury of these turbulent clans and greedy traders which wasted the city they both loved. Cacciaguida had fought in God's cause, as he conceived it; they offered heathen sacrifice to a 'wasted stone', to Mars, the city's 'first patron', who still holds it as by a spell and 'afflicts it with his art' (*Inf.* xiii). In contrast with the earthly Mars is the heavenly, in whose sphere Cacciaguida now talks with Dante, the contrast between men's mean and brutal strife for place and power and the struggle of the martyrs for the crown-rights of Christ. 'Mars becomes here, as in the *Inferno*, a vivid symbol of the fatality that weighs on Florence, contrasting, in its dark craving for hatred and slaughter, with the christianized Mars from whom this heaven is named and whose influence moves the soldiers of Christ' (*C. Grabher*).

QUAL venne a Climenè, per accertarsi
  di ciò ch'avea incontro a sè udito,
  quei ch'ancor fa li padri ai figli scarsi;
tal era io, e tal era sentito
  e da Beatrice e dalla santa lampa
  che pria per me avea mutato sito.
Per che mia donna 'Manda fuor la vampa
  del tuo disio' mi disse, 'sì ch'ella esca
  segnata bene della interna stampa;
non perchè nostra conoscenza cresca   10
  per tuo parlare, ma perchè t'ausi
  a dir la sete, sì che l'uom ti mesca.'
'O cara piota mia che sì t' insusi,
  che come veggion le terrene menti
  non capere in trïangol due ottusi,
così vedi le cose contingenti
  anzi che sieno in sè, mirando il punto
  a cui tutti li tempi son presenti;
mentre ch' io era a Virgilio congiunto
  su per lo monte che l'anime cura   20
  e discendendo nel mondo defunto,
dette mi fuor di mia vita futura
  parole gravi, avvegna ch' io mi senta
  ben tetragono ai colpi di ventura.
Per che la voglia mia sarìa contenta
  d' intender qual fortuna mi s'appressa;
  chè saetta previsa vien più lenta.'
Così diss' io a quella luce stessa
  che pria m'avea parlato; e come volle
  Beatrice, fu la mia voglia confessa.   30

CANTO XVII

*Dante's future; Can Grande; Cacciaguida's
charge to Dante*

LIKE him who came to Clymene to be reassured
about that which he had heard against himself,
him who still makes fathers wary with their sons,[1]
such was I and such I was perceived to be both by
Beatrice and by the holy lamp that had changed
its place for me before. Therefore my Lady said
to me: 'Put forth the flame of thy desire, so that it
may issue marked clearly with the internal stamp,
not to add to our knowledge by thy words, but to
practise the telling of thy thirst, so that the draught
may be poured out for thee.'

'O my dear seed-plot, who art raised so high
that, even as earthly minds see that there cannot be
two obtuse angles in a triangle, so thou, gazing
on the point to which all times are present,[2] seest
contingent things before they are in themselves,—
while I was in Virgil's company upon the mountain
that heals the souls, and descending into the dead
world, grave words were spoken to me of my future
life, though I feel myself set foursquare against the
blows of chance; so that my desire would be met
if I knew what fortune approaches me, for an arrow
foreseen comes more gently.' I said this to that same
light that had talked with me before, and as Beatrice
bade my wish was declared.

Nè per ambage, in che la gente folle
 già s' inviscava pria che fosse anciso
 l'Agnel di Dio che le peccata tolle,
ma per chiare parole e con preciso
 latin rispuose quello amor paterno,
 chiuso e parvente del suo proprio riso:
'La contingenza, che fuor del quaderno
 della vostra matera non si stende,
 tutta è dipinta nel cospetto etterno:
necessità però quindi non prende   40
 se non come dal viso in che si specchia
 nave che per corrente giù discende.
Da indi sì come viene ad orecchia
 dolce armonia da organo, mi vene
 a vista il tempo che ti s'apparecchia.
Qual si partìo Ippolito d'Atene
 per la spietata e perfida noverca,
 tal di Fiorenza partir ti convene.
Questo si vuole e questo già si cerca,
 e tosto verrà fatto a chi ciò pensa   50
 là dove Cristo tutto dì si merca.
La colpa seguirà la parte offensa
 in grido, come suol; ma la vendetta
 fia testimonio al ver che la dispensa.
Tu lascerai ogni cosa diletta
 più caramente; e questo è quello strale
 che l'arco dello essilio pria saetta.
Tu proverai sì come sa di sale
 lo pane altrui, e come è duro calle
 lo scendere e 'l salir per l'altrui scale. 60
E quel che più ti graverà le spalle,
 sarà la compagnia malvagia e scempia
 con la qual tu cadrai in questa valle;
che tutta ingrata, tutta matta ed empia
 si farà contra te; ma, poco appresso,
 ella, non tu, n'avrà rossa la tempia.
Di sua bestialità il suo processo
 farà la prova; sì ch'a te fia bello
 averti fatta parte per te stesso.

Not with dark sayings, with which the foolish
people were once ensnared before the Lamb of
God who takes away sins was slain,[3] but in plain
words and express terms, that fatherly love replied,
hidden and revealed by his own smile: 'Contin-
gency, which does not extend beyond the volume of
your material world, is all depicted in the Eternal
Vision, yet does not thence derive necessity, any
more than does a ship that drops down stream from
the eyes in which it is mirrored; from thence, as
sweet harmony comes from an organ to the ear,
comes to my sight the time that is in store for thee.[4]
As Hippolytus was driven from Athens on account
of his cruel and perfidious stepmother,[5] so must
thou be driven from Florence. This is determined,
nay is already contrived and will soon be accom-
plished, by him who meditates it in the place where
Christ is bought and sold all day.[6] The blame, in
the common cry, shall follow the injured side, as
always, but the vengeance shall be testimony to
the truth that dispenses it. Thou shalt leave every-
thing loved most dearly, and this is the shaft which
the bow of exile shoots first. Thou shalt prove how
salt is the taste of another man's bread and how
hard is the way up and down another man's stairs.
And that which shall weigh heaviest on thy shoul-
ders is the wicked and senseless company with
which thou shalt fall into that valley, which shall
become wholly ungrateful, quite mad and furious
against thee; but before long they, not thou, shall
have the brows red for this. Of their brutish folly
their doings shall give proof, so that it shall be to
thine honour to have made a party by thyself.

Lo primo tuo refugio, il primo ostello   70
   sarà la cortesia del gran Lombardo
   che 'n su la scala porta il santo uccello;
ch' in te avrà sì benigno riguardo,
   che del fare e del chieder, tra voi due,
   fia primo quel che, tra gli altri, è più tardo.
Con lui vedrai colui che 'mpresso fue,
   nascendo, sì da questa stella forte,
   che notabili fien l'opere sue.
Non se ne son le genti ancora accorte
   per la novella età, chè pur nove anni   80
   son queste rote intorno di lui torte;
ma pria che 'l Guasco l'alto Arrigo inganni,
   parran faville della sua virtute
   in non curar d'argento nè d'affanni.
Le sue magnificenze conosciute
   saranno ancora, sì che' suoi nemici
   non ne potran tener le lingue mute.
A lui t'aspetta ed a' suoi benefici;
   per lui fia trasmutata molta gente,
   cambiando condizion ricchi e mendici.   90
E portera'ne scritto nella mente
   di lui, e nol dirai;' e disse cose
   incredibili a quei che fien presente.
Poi giunse: 'Figlio, queste son le chiose
   di quel che ti fu detto; ecco le 'nsidie
   che dietro a pochi giri son nascose.
Non vo' però ch'a' tuoi vicini invidie,
   poscia che s' infutura la tua vita
   vie più là che 'l punir di lor perfidie.'
Poi che, tacendo, si mostrò spedita   100
   l'anima santa di metter la trama
   in quella tela ch' io le porsi ordita,
io cominciai, come colui che brama,
   dubitando, consiglio da persona
   che vede e vuol dirittamente e ama:
'Ben veggio, padre mio, sì come sprona
   lo tempo verso me, per colpo darmi
   tal, ch'è più grave a chi più s'abbandona;

'Thy first refuge and inn thou shalt find in the courtesy of the great Lombard who bears on the ladder the sacred bird,[7] and he will hold thee in so gracious regard that, of doing and asking between you two, that shall be first which with others comes after. With him thou shalt see one who at his birth so took the impress of this mighty star that his deeds will be renowned.[8] The people have not yet taken note of him, because of his youth, for these wheels have circled about him only nine years; but before the Gascon deceives the noble Henry[9] sparks of his heroism shall appear in his disregard both of wealth and toil, and his munificence shall yet be known so that his enemies cannot keep silence about it. Look to him and to his benefits. Through him there shall be altered fortune for many, rich changing state with beggars. And thou shalt bear this written in thy mind about him and shalt not tell it'—and he told things which shall be incredible to those that witness them. Then he added: 'Son, these are the glosses on what was told thee, these are the snares that are hid behind a few revolving years; yet I would not have thee envious of thy fellow-citizens, for thy life shall far outlast the punishment of their perfidies.'

After the holy soul, falling silent, showed that he had finished putting the woof into the web of which I had set the warp for him, I began, as one in doubt that craves counsel of him who sees and rightly wills and loves: 'I see well, my father, how time spurs towards me to deal me such a blow as falls most heavily on him that is most heedless;

per che di provedenza è buon ch' io m'armi,
   sì che, se 'l loco m'è tolto più caro,   110
   io non perdessi li altri per miei carmi.
Giù per lo mondo sanza fine amaro,
   e per lo monte del cui bel cacume
   li occhi della mia donna mi levaro,
e poscia per lo ciel di lume in lume,
   ho io appreso quel che s' io ridico,
   a molti fia sapor di forte agrume;
e s' io al vero son timido amico,
   temo di perder viver tra coloro
   che questo tempo chiameranno antico.'   120
La luce in che rideva il mio tesoro
   ch' io trovai lì, si fè prima corusca,
   quale a raggio di sole specchio d'oro;
indi rispuose: 'Coscïenza fusca
   o della propria o dell'altrui vergogna
   pur sentirà la tua parola brusca.
Ma nondimen, rimossa ogni menzogna,
   tutta tua visïon fa manifesta;
   e lascia pur grattar dov'è la rogna.
Chè se la voce tua sarà molesta   130
   nel primo gusto, vital nutrimento
   lascerà poi, quando sarà digesta.
Questo tuo grido farà come vento,
   che le più alte cime più percuote;
   e ciò non fa d'onor poco argomento.
Però ti son mostrate in queste rote,
   nel monte e nella valle dolorosa
   pur l'anime che son di fama note,
che l'animo di quel ch'ode, non posa
   nè ferma fede per essemplo ch'aia   140
   la sua radice incognita ed ascosa,
nè per altro argomento che non paia.'

it is well, therefore, that I arm me with foresight, so that, if the dearest place is taken from me, I may not lose the others by my songs. Down through the world of endless bitterness, and on the mountain from whose fair summit the eyes of my Lady lifted me, and after, through the heavens from light to light, I have learned that which, if I tell again, will taste for many of bitter herbs; and if I am a timid friend to truth I fear to lose my life among those who will call these times ancient.'

The light within which was smiling the treasure I had found there first became ablaze like a golden mirror in the sun, then replied: 'Conscience dark with its own or another's shame will indeed feel thy words to be harsh; but none the less put away every falsehood and make plain all thy vision,—and then let them scratch where is the itch. For if thy voice is grievous at first taste, it will afterwards leave vital nourishment when it is digested. This cry of thine shall do as does the wind, which strikes most on the highest summits; and that is no small ground of honour. For that reason have been shown to thee, in these wheels, on the mountain, and in the woeful valley, only souls that are known to fame; because the mind of one who hears will not pause or fix its faith for an example that has its roots unknown or hidden or for other proof that is not manifest.'

1. Phaeton, the son of Apollo and Clymene, when his paternity was questioned came to his mother for assurance that he was Apollo's child, then demanded of his father the charge of the chariot of the sun for a day and misguided it.

2. In the 9th sphere God is represented by a radiant point of light (*Par.* xxviii).

3. 'Not with riddles such as the oracles gave out before they fell silent at the coming of Christ' (*C. E. Norton*).

4. Past and future events are all present to God, and they are seen by the redeemed in their vision of God; yet that 'Eternal Vision' of the future does not interfere with human freewill.

5. Hippolytus, son of Theseus Duke of Athens, when Phaedra his stepmother failed to seduce him, was slandered by her and driven from Athens.

6. By Pope Boniface VIII, who in the spring of 1300 was believed to be scheming against the Whites in Florence.

7. Bartolommeo della Scala, Lord of Verona, whose family arms were a ladder surmounted by the imperial eagle.

8. Bartolommeo's younger brother, Can Grande della Scala (1291–1329), who became Lord of Verona, Imperial Vicar, and the foremost soldier in Italy.

9. Clement V (*Inf.* xix) of Gascony was the first of the French Popes at Avignon and the creature of Philip IV of France; he first favoured the Emperor Henry VII, then secretly opposed him; he died in 1314, within a year after the Emperor.

NOTE

Cacciaguida, representing for Dante all that was finest and most heroic in the old life of Florence, had welcomed his descendant, and Dante had 'gloried' in his own 'nobility of blood'. But that nobility was but a shrinking mantle; it was a high privilege only as it was a high calling. Dante had fallen on evil days and evil tongues and in the course of his journey had had obscure warnings of disaster; now he sought assurance, like Phaeton, Apollo's child. Was he, in spirit, of Cacciaguida's lineage? Should not the crusader be 'wary with his son'? Was Dante's own enterprise and apostolate something better than Phaeton's misguiding of the sun? He must 'practise the telling of his thirst' for the opening of his mind to the assurance of his calling. His questions here are surely a true report of Dante's recollection, in the peace of his last years, of his own mind as it was in the troubled and uncertain earlier years of his exile.

Cacciaguida's reply to Dante is prefaced by six lines in which the 'dark sayings' of pagan oracles are contrasted with the 'express terms' of the Christian spokesman,—a contrast determined by the death of the Lamb of God. For it is in the Divine Martyr that His martyrs, Cacciaguida and Dante among them, find their confidence.

The 'grave words' that had been spoken to him of his future life were chiefly those of Farinata (*Inf*. x) and of Brunetto Latini (*Inf*. xv), and in neither case had they been explicit. But by Cacciaguida in Paradise all 'contingency', all the incalculableness and perversity of earthly happenings and human wills, are seen in God, and the story of exile and bitterness which he tells to Dante 'in plain words and express terms' comes to his own sight in his vision of God with its earthly discords resolved, 'as comes to our ear sweet harmony from an organ'. 'With a bold but fitting metaphor the Poet calls the realities of the world "the volume of your matter"; they follow one another like the pages of a book, but in God succession has no place' (*G. Vandelli*). Contingency, depicted in the Eternal Vision, does not take the character of necessity, of a pre-determined fate, any more than a moving ship reflected in the eyes of an observer. 'We might say that Dante thinks with the imagination. . . . The consistency of fore-knowledge with freewill is one of the most difficult and abstract conceptions; but here it is not a conception, it is a vision, a spectacle' (*F. de Sanctis*). It is thus that Dante declares his faith in grace and providence as he looks back on a time which might seem a mere contradiction of them. It is in that setting, in the heaven of Mars, by the voice of Cacciaguida and in the form of prophecy, that he tells of his own life, by way of making his claim that he too, in his wrongs and griefs, is of the kindred of the prophets and martyrs, and from 'our poor nobility of blood' he rises to this loftier pride. His conscience speaks through his great ancestor, 'in whose celestial light conscience itself is personified' (*L. del Lungo, L.D.*). The interview with Brunetto is in some respects repeated in this with Cacciaguida. Both are vindications of Dante's integrity, but this with a deeper resonance. The other, in Hell, has its outcome in the defiance of fortune: 'Turn Fortune her wheel then as she list—and the clown his mattock!'; this, in Paradise, ends in a high charge laid on him with its risks and cost: 'This cry of thine shall do as does the wind, which strikes most on the highest summits; and that is no small point of honour.' In no other of the heavens does Dante so identify himself, morally, with its souls. If he ever aspired to appear one day to a pilgrim like himself in one of the spheres of Paradise, it was surely here, in the sphere of Mars, among the soldier-saints.

He recalls, when he writes, the years from the assumed date of his vision to the writing of the *Paradiso*, looking back, as Cacciaguida looked forward; from the time, that is, of his public life in Florence, through the strife and intrigue that led to the exile of the White Guelfs and of Dante among them in 1302, and the slanders, as false as Phaedra's against Hippolytus, that blackened his name when his stepmother-city failed to seduce him and then cast him out,—his wandering years in Italy, with his stay at Verona in the court of the great Ghibelline

Scaligers, first in the reign of Can Grande's older brother, then in that of Can Grande himself,—his share in the first attempts of the exiled Ghibellines and White Guelfs to force their return to Florence, in which they learned for themselves, as Farinata warned him, 'how hard is that art' (*Inf.* x),—to his quarrel with the other exiles and separation from all their parties. Cacciaguida's last line on Dante's relations with his companions —'to have made a party by thyself'—has in the original an untranslatable quality of decision and finality which is given chiefly by the accumulation of sharp dentals, six t's in six words: '*averti fatta parte per te stesso*'. That door is closed.

It is both unnecessary and impossible for us either to accept or to correct Dante's fierce and sweeping judgements of his companions in exile, and we may suppose that he was not an easy colleague and counsellor and that there was sometimes another side to the story. In the words he puts into the mouth of Cacciaguida we do not have a measured and historical estimate of Dante's contemporaries, we do not have the work of a historian; but we have a true report of Dante himself, of his lofty standards for civic life, his scorn for the treacheries and turbulence of Church and commune, his flaming sense of his wrongs, and the call that came to him in his griefs to prophesy to his generation. It is one 'who sees and rightly wills and loves', the spokesman of a nobler age, that bids him make plain all his vision, 'and then let them scratch where is the itch'. Nowhere in the *Comedy* does Dante more plainly demonstrate his proud, dedicated, impassioned spirit.

In the course of the canto Dante pays splendid tribute to his greatest patron, Can Grande of Verona. He was a boy of nine at the supposed date of the vision, and in his early manhood when the canto was written, and at that time the head of the imperial cause in Italy. Can Grande is believed by many students to be 'the hound' of the first canto of the *Inferno*, who 'shall not feed on land or pelf, but on wisdom and love and valour', and who is to hunt down the wolf of covetousness; and the description agrees well with that here. In a long letter addressed to 'the magnificent and victorious lord, Lord Can Grande della Scala, . . . his most devoted Dante Alighieri, Florentine by birth, not in character,' dedicated the *Paradiso* to

253

him: 'To you I inscribe it, to you make offer of it, to you, in a word, commend it.' Here, in the centre of its central canto, through the lips of one who is for Dante the type of heroic manhood and in the light of 'this mighty star' under which Can Grande was born, he sets his praise of the man he had come to know and love as a youth in the palace at Verona for 'the sparks of his heroism'. When this was written 'the noble Henry' was dead and the cause of the Empire in Italy was in fact a lost cause; but Dante still looked to Can Grande for 'incredible things' in the service of the greatest of earthly interests, the world's reconciliation and order and peace.

Along with this canto should be read a passage, written years before, from the *Convito*: 'Since it was the pleasure of the citizens of Florence, the most beautiful and famous daughter of Rome, to cast me forth from her sweet bosom in which I was born and nourished up to the summit of my life and in which, with their good leave, I desire with all my heart to rest my weary spirit and to finish the time that is given me, I have gone through almost all the parts to which this tongue extends, a pilgrim, almost a beggar, showing against my will the wound of fortune, which is wont too often to be imputed to the wounded. I have been, in truth, a ship without sail or rudder, borne to diverse ports and narrows and shores by the dry wind that rises from wretched poverty, and I have appeared vile in the eyes of many who, perhaps on account of a certain fame, have imagined me in another guise, in whose view not only was my person despised, but all my work was made of less account, both that already done and that which was yet to do.' 'He was only a poor outcast, loaded with a charge of infamy which the light of his amorous verse did not yet serve to dissipate; but in his breast was a fire that burned with such heat as in no other,—the consciousness of a mission which God had given him as a poet to sustain him in his sorrows, his craving for justice, his faith in the triumph of the ideal' (*U. Cosmo*).

Three times in the course of the canto there occurs a reference to the stages of Dante's imagined journey, which is all brought into the context of his life and of the ruling motive of his poem: the prophetic purpose of testimony and challenge and appeal to his generation and to 'those who will call these times ancient', on behalf of the eternal providence of God. Here he is blood-brother to Bunyan's Mr Valiant-for-truth, who said, at the end of his journey: 'I am going to my Fathers, and tho' with great difficulty I am got hither, yet now I do not repent me of all the trouble I have been at to arrive where I am. My sword I give to him that shall succeed me in my Pilgrimage, and my Courage and Skill to him that can get it. My Marks and Scars I carry with me, to be a witness for me that I have fought his Battles who now will be my Rewarder.'

Già si godea solo del suo verbo
   quello specchio beato, e io gustava
   lo mio, temprando col dolce l'acerbo;
e quella donna ch'a Dio mi menava
   disse: 'Muta pensier: pensa ch' i' sono
   presso a colui ch'ogni torto disgrava.'
Io mi rivolsi all'amoroso sono
   del mio conforto; e qual io allor vidi
   nelli occhi santi amor, qui l'abbandono;
non perch' io pur del mio parlar diffidi,   10
   ma per la mente che non può reddire
   sovra sè tanto, s'altri non la guidi.
Tanto poss' io di quel punto ridire,
   che, rimirando lei, lo mio affetto
   libero fu da ogni altro disire,
fin che il piacere etterno, che diretto
   raggiava in Beatrice, dal bel viso
   mi contentava col secondo aspetto.
Vincendo me col lume d'un sorriso,
   ella mi disse: 'Volgiti ed ascolta;   20
   chè non pur ne' miei occhi è paradiso.'
Come si vede qui alcuna volta
   l'affetto nella vista, s'elli è tanto,
   che da lui sia tutta l'anima tolta,
così nel fiammeggiar del fulgor santo,
   a ch' io mi volsi, conobbi la voglia
   in lui di ragionarmi ancora alquanto.

CANTO XVIII

The fighting saints; the Sphere of Jupiter;
just rulers; the Eagle of souls

ALREADY that blessed mirror was rejoicing by
himself in his own thoughts and I was tasting mine,
tempering the bitter with the sweet, when the Lady
who was leading me to God said: 'Change thy
thought; consider that I am in His presence who
lifts the burden of every wrong.'

I turned at the loving voice of my comfort and
what I saw then of love in the holy eyes I leave
here untold, not only because I distrust my speech
but because memory cannot return on itself so
far unless One guide it. So much I can tell again
of that moment, that, as I gazed at her, my heart
was freed from every other desire so long as the
Eternal Joy that shone direct on Beatrice satisfied
me from the fair eyes with its second aspect.[1]
Overcoming me with the light of a smile, she said
to me: 'Turn and listen, for not only in my eyes
is Paradise.'

As here sometimes emotion is seen in the face to
be such that the whole soul is seized with it, so
in the flaming of the holy effulgence to which I
turned I recognized his wish to have some further

257

El cominciò: 'In questa quinta soglia
   dell'albero che vive della cima
   e frutta sempre e mai non perde foglia,   30
spiriti son beati, che giù, prima
   che venissero al ciel, fuor di gran voce,
   sì ch'ogni musa ne sarebbe opima.
Però mira ne' corni della croce:
   quello ch' io nomerò, lì farà l'atto
   che fa in nube il suo foco veloce.'
Io vidi per la croce un lume tratto
   dal nomar Iosuè com'el si feo;
   nè mi fu noto il dir prima che 'l fatto.
E al nome dell'alto Maccabeo   40
   vidi moversi un altro roteando,
   e letizia era ferza del paleo.
Così per Carlo Magno e per Orlando
   due ne seguì lo mio attento sguardo,
   com'occhio segue suo falcon volando.
Poscia trasse Guiglielmo, e Renoardo,
   e 'l duca Gottifredi la mia vista
   per quella croce, e Ruberto Guiscardo.
Indi, tra l'altre luci mota e mista,
   mostrommi l'alma che m'avea parlato   50
   qual era tra i cantor del cielo artista.
Io mi rivolsi dal mio destro lato
   per vedere in Beatrice il mio dovere
   o per parlare o per atto segnato;
e vidi le sue luci tanto mere,
   tanto gioconde, che la sua sembianza
   vinceva li altri e l'ultimo solere.
E come, per sentir più dilettanza
   bene operando, l'uom di giorno in giorno
   s'accorge che la sua virtute avanza,   60
sì m'accors' io che 'l mio girar dintorno
   col cielo insieme avea cresciuto l'arco,
   veggendo quel miracol più adorno.
E qual è 'l trasmutare in picciol varco
   di tempo in bianca donna, quando il volto
   suo si discarchi di vergogna il carco,

speech with me, and he began: 'In this fifth lodge-
ment of the tree which lives from the top and is
always in fruit and never sheds its leaves[2] are blessed
spirits which below, before they came to heaven,
were of so great fame that every muse would be
enriched by them; look, therefore, at the horns of
the cross, and each one I name will do there as
does its swift fire in a cloud.'[3]

I saw a light drawn through the cross at the name
of Joshua as soon as it was spoken, nor did I note
the speech before the fact; and at the name of the
great Maccabaeus[4] I saw another move wheeling,
and joy was the whip to the top; so for Charlemagne
and Roland[5] my intent gaze followed two of them
as the eye follows its falcon in flight; next William
and Renouard and the Duke Godfrey drew my
sight through that cross, and Robert Guiscard too.[6]
Then, having left me and mingled with the other
lights, the soul that had talked with me showed me
what was his skill among the singers of that heaven.

I turned on my right to see in Beatrice my duty
signified by word or gesture, and I saw her eyes so
clear, so joyful, that her aspect surpassed all it
had been at other times, even the last. And as from
feeling more delight in well-doing a man is conscious
day by day of his advance in virtue, so I was con-
scious, when I saw that miracle more fair, that my
circling along with the heavens had increased its
arc; and such a change as passes in a moment over
the face of a pale woman when she is freed from
a burden of shame there was for my eyes when

al fu nelli occhi miei, quando fui volto,
   per lo candor della temprata stella
   sesta, che dentro a sè m'avea ricolto.
Io vidi in quella giovïal facella   70
   lo sfavillar dell'amor che lì era,
   segnare alli occhi miei nostra favella.
E come augelli surti di rivera
   quasi congratulando a lor pasture,
   fanno di sè or tonda or altra schiera,
sì dentro ai lumi sante creature
   volitando cantavano, e faciensi
   or *D,* or *I,* or *L* in sue figure.
Prima, cantando, a sua nota moviensi;
   poi, diventando l'un di questi segni,   80
   un poco s'arrestavano e taciensi.
O diva Pegasea che li 'ngegni
   fai glorïosi e rendili longevi,
   ed essi teco le cittadi e' regni,
illustrami di te, sì ch' io rilevi
   le lor figure com' io l' ho concette:
   paia tua possa in questi versi brevi!
Mostrarsi dunque in cinque volte sette
   vocali e consonanti; ed io notai
   le parti sì, come mi parver dette.   90
'*DILIGITE IUSTITIAM*' primai
   fur verbo e nome di tutto 'l dipinto;
   '*QUI IUDICATIS TERRAM*' fur sezzai.
Poscia nell'emme del vocabol quinto
   rimasero ordinate; sì che Giove
   pareva argento lì d'oro distinto.
E vidi scendere altre luci dove
   era il colmo dell'emme, e lì quetarsi
   cantando, credo, il ben ch'a sè le move.
Poi come nel percuoter de' ciocchi arsi   100
   surgono innumerabili faville,
   onde li stolti sogliono augurarsi;
resurger parver quindi più di mille
   luci, e salir, qual assai e qual poco
   sì come il sol che l'accende sortille;

I had turned, on account of the whiteness of the temperate sixth star, which had received me into itself.[7]

I saw in that torch of Jove the sparkling of the love that was there trace out our speech to my eyes; and as birds risen from a river-bank, as if rejoicing together over their pasture, make of themselves, now a round flock, now another shape, so within the lights holy creatures were singing as they flew and made themselves, in the figures they formed, now *D*, now *I*, now *L*. First, singing, they moved to their own notes; then, becoming one of these shapes, they paused for a little and were silent.

O divine Pegasean that givest glory and long life to genius, as it does through thee to cities and kingdoms,[8] illumine me with thyself that I may set forth their shapes as I deciphered them. Let thy power appear in these brief lines.

They showed themselves, then, in five times seven vowels and consonants, and I noted them severally, and what they seemed to me to mean. *DILIGITE IUSTITIAM*—these were the first verb and noun of the whole design; *QUI IUDI-CATIS TERRAM*,[9] the last. Then in the *M* of the fifth word they kept their order, so that Jupiter seemed there silver pricked out with gold; and I saw other lights descend on the very summit of the *M* and settle there, singing, I think, of the good that draws them to itself. Then, as when burning logs are struck rise innumerable sparks, from which the foolish are accustomed to make auguries, so more than a thousand lights appeared to rise again from there and to mount, some much, some little, as the Sun that kindles them appointed;

e quïetata ciascuna in suo loco,
    la testa e 'l collo d'un'aguglia vidi
    rappresentare a quel distinto foco.
Quei che dipinge lì, non ha chi 'l guidi;
    ma esso guida, e da lui si rammenta   110
    quella virtù ch'è forma per li nidi.
L'altra beatitudo, che contenta
    pareva prima d' ingigliarsi all'emme,
    con poco moto seguitò la 'mprenta.
O dolce stella, quali e quante gemme
    mi dimostraron che nostra giustizia
    effetto sia del ciel che tu ingemme!
Per ch' io prego la mente in che s' inizia
    tuo moto e tua virtute, che rimiri
    ond'esce il fummo che 'l tuo raggio vizia;   120
sì ch' un' altra fïata omai s'adiri
    del comperare e vender dentro al templo
    che si murò di segni e di martiri.
O milizia del ciel cu' io contemplo,
    adora per color che sono in terra
    tutti svïati dietro al malo essemplo!
Già si solea con le spade far guerra;
    ma or si fa togliendo or qui or quivi
    lo pan che 'l pio Padre a nessun serra.
Ma tu che sol per cancellare scrivi,   130
    pensa che Pietro e Paulo, che moriro
    per la vigna che guasti, ancor son vivi.
Ben puoi tu dire: 'I' ho fermo 'l disiro
    sì a colui che volle viver solo
    e che per salti fu tratto al martiro,
ch' io non conosco il pescator nè Polo.'

and when each had settled in its place I saw the
head and neck of an eagle represented in that
pricked-out fire. He that designs there has none
to guide Him. He Himself guides, even as we
recognize to be from Him that power which is form
for the nests.[10] The rest of the blessed spirits, which
seemed at first content to form a lily on the *M*, with
a little movement followed out the design.

O sweet star, how many and how bright were
the gems which made it plain to me that our
justice is the effect of the heaven thou dost
gem![11] I pray, therefore, the Mind in which thy
motion and thy power begin that it look on the
place whence comes the smoke that dims thy
beam,[12] so that once again it may be wroth at the
buying and selling in the temple whose walls were
built with miracles and martyrdoms. O hosts of
heaven whom I contemplate, pray for those that
are on earth, all led astray by ill example. Once it
was the custom to make war with swords, but now
it is made with refusing, now here, now there, the
bread which the merciful Father bars from none.[13]
But thou that writest only to cancel, take thought
that Peter and Paul, who died for the vineyard
thou layest waste, are yet alive. Well mayst thou
say: 'I have so set my heart on him who chose
to live solitary and was dragged by dances to martyr-
dom[14] that I know neither the Fisherman nor Paul.

1. The reflection of the divine joy.

2. The fifth sphere of Paradise, the heaven of Mars.

3. Like lightning.

4. Joshua, who led the first conquests of Israel in Canaan, and Judas Maccabaeus, who delivered the Jews from Syrian oppression in the 2nd century B.C.

5. Charlemagne, who defended the Church and restored the Empire (*Par.* vi), and Roland, his nephew and paladin in fighting the Saracens in Spain (*Inf.* xxxi).

6. Count William of Orange and Renouard, a legendary Saracen convert, fought together against the Saracens in the 9th century; Duke Godfrey, leader of the First Crusade and King of Jerusalem, and Robert Guiscard, founder of the Norman dynasty in S. Italy, where he fought the Greeks and Saracens,—both in the 11th century.

7. The planet Jupiter, 'temperate' because it is 'between the cold of Saturn and the heat of Mars' (*Convito*).

8. Probably Calliope, the Muse of Epic Poetry (*Purg.* i), called a Pegasean from Pegasus, the winged horse whose hoof opened the spring Helicon from which the Muses drank.

9. 'Love justice, ye that judge the earth' (*Book of Wisdom* i. 1).

10. The divine creative force in natural instinct, which is the formative principle of the birds' nests,—*form* in the scholastic sense (*Par.* i).

11. All earthly justice is inspired by heavenly justice.

12. The Papal court.

13. Popes punished their enemies with refusal of the sacraments by interdict. John XXII, Pope when Dante was writing, imposed interdicts and then remitted them for cash; he excommunicated Can Grande in 1317.

14. The Baptist, whose figure was on the gold florin of Florence. Pope John XXII copied it in his mint at Avignon.

NOTE

While Cacciaguida, seeing the events of time in their eternal aspect, is rejoicing in his thought, Dante, still within the limits of mortality, is tasting his, 'tempering the bitter with the sweet'; then, turning at the voice of Beatrice, he finds such comfort in her eyes as 'freed him from every other desire', and here he dwells on the experience with a unique expansion and emphasis. It is 'the eternal joy' of God in that which is done and borne for His service that is reflected on Dante by Beatrice, and the final persuasion of it comes to him in the light of her smile. And yet it is Beatrice herself that bids him 'Turn and listen, for not only in my eyes is Paradise'. His absorption in Beatrice, in his sense of heavenly truth in her, must not detach his mind from the actual cause of God on earth and those that have served it best. Even in Paradise his faith must still be held in the context of the earthly struggle. He sees flashing through the cross with the swift energy which is their quality eight of the great fighting saints of Scripture and of Christian history whose names were for him and for his first readers a summary of that age-long, costly contention; and when Cacciaguida joins them, he 'showed me what was his skill among the singers of that heaven'. 'There is gathered here in the person of Cacciaguida the epic spirit of the Middle Ages which mingles history and legend and invokes personages each of whom represents a struggle and a cycle, actual or virtual, of songs; and in their choice and order is the spirit of the Poet, practised in binding together remote facts and those nearer with the bond of a single great idea, the struggle for the faith' (*V. Capetti, L.D.*).

In no other instance of his passage with Beatrice from one planetary sphere to the next does Dante give so much space and significance to the fact as here. When he was brought from the red glow of Mars into the white serenity of Jupiter, from the virtues that belong to war to those of peace, 'I saw her eyes so clear, so joyous, that her aspect surpassed all it had been at other times, even the last'; 'I was conscious, when I saw that miracle more fair, that my circling with the heaven had increased its arc'; and this experience is compared to a man's 'advance in virtue' and to the clearing of a flush of shame from a pale woman's face. So much pains does he take to show that public justice in peace—itself the cause for which the saints in Mars have striven in war—is a greater achievement than any victory; it demands a larger view of the world and a more disciplined mind and will; reaching it, the soul must move in a greater arc; its symbol is 'the temperate sixth star', 'the torch of Jove'. No lesson could be more deeply characteristic of Dante.

The text from the Vulgate that appears letter by letter must be conceived of in Gothic capitals, to provide the *M* with a central upright—𝕸—which can be developed to form, first a lily, then the Eagle's head and neck, and with the right and left uprights to form, 'with a little movement', the wings. The following seems the natural interpretation of the whole curious scene. The text that was spelled out to Dante's eyes— 'five times seven vowels and consonants' which he 'noted severally'—offers a kind of succession and summary of men's best approaches to just civil government in the history of the world. Human government must, by its nature, be *spelled out*, with trial and imperfection and correction, and every just government, in the measure of its justice, is a forecast of the divine idea and a step towards its realization. The final *M*, which is named three times and which is gradually built up into the heraldic Eagle—the last letter of the last word, *TERRAM*, the earth, as it were the goal of all earthly order—stands for *Monarchia*, Empire, the consummated unity of all peoples in a just world-order and common obedience.

It is in an elaborate and hesitating way that Dante describes his gradual apprehension of his vision, beginning with a mere succession of letters, each seen by itself and meaningless; and it is only after his appeal to the divine power that gives glory and long life to genius and, through it, to cities and kingdoms that he tells how he 'noted them severally and what they seemed to him to mean': first, words, 'the first noun and verb, and the last', then, a familiar sentence from Scripture, a part of the Word of God itself, and in that text the love of justice 'first', the office of judge 'last'. Was it possible for Dante to describe more definitely and deliberately his own gradual discovery of a divine meaning in history and his final assurance, as it is described in the *De Monarchia*, that the ancient supremacy of Rome in the world derived, not merely from its force of arms and the strife of nations, but from the prevailing and beneficent divine purpose in the affairs of men? 'Considering it merely superficially, I judged that Rome gained it, not by any just right, but only by force of arms; but afterwards, my mind having pierced to the marrow of it, I recognized by most conclusive signs that divine providence had brought it about.'

It is on the final *M* that he saw 'other lights'—the world's rulers who have learned to accept the high imperial tradition—descend, and it is they, 'more than a thousand' of them, that rise and, 'when each had settled in its place', form the head and neck of the Roman Eagle, the divine augury and promise—in contrast with the foolish auguries trusted by men—of the world's final order and peace. The rest of the *M* completes the Eagle's form, and even the French-Guelf-Florentine lily yields and passes as all men find their place in the earthly providence of God. In the heaven of Mercury—still within range of the earth's shadow—Justinian has already told of the Empire's small beginnings, its great course of conquest, its strange and essential part in the scheme of man's redemption (*Par.* vi). That is the flight of the Eagle on earth, its history among men, hindered and betrayed by men's factions and ambitions, yet, in its idea, 'the bird of God', 'the most holy standard', and invincible. Here we have the Eagle in heaven, all that Empire so conceived can mean for men, the pure white glory of public justice and civil peace, the blessedness of those who have hungered and thirsted after righteousness and are filled; and Dante's appeal to the 'divine Pegasean' shows how urgent and how hard a task it is to tell of it.

Nothing could be more artificial or less imaginative in itself than this device of the lights spelling out a text of Scripture, and it is the more notable that the whole account of it is so vitalized by Dante's own wonder and intentness, by his vivid similes—

the gay flocks of birds 'risen from a river bank', the sparks from burning logs—and by the constant impression of life's motives in the souls that make these shapes. It is 'the sparkling of the love that was there' that 'represented our speech to my eyes'; the judges of the earth are adjured not primarily to do justice, but to love it, for to love justice is to *be* just; the souls sing, as they mount, 'of the good that draws them to itself', and, at the beginning of the next canto, 'the congregated souls' are said to be 'happy in their sweet fruition'. The Sun kindles these lights and appoints each to its place. For the whole design of Empire on earth and the very conception of civil authority and order among men is not merely a human device or an accident of history. This is a 'divine image'; it comes from the Designer whose creative work is the order of the universe to its last created thing, 'form for the nests'; 'He that designs there has none to guide Him. He Himself guides', and 'all our justice is the effect of the heaven' of this 'sweet star'. Once Dante had looked for the speedy fulfilment of his hope to the Empire of Henry VII; now he knows that the true Empire is a pattern showed to him in the mount, an end to which all the best the just have striven for and the world has known of human order is but a distant approach and prophecy. The letters of the text and the Eagle are formed of the just rulers themselves, of the very being and shining quality of their souls. For justice is a spiritual thing, an attribute of the soul; it exists so, or not at all, and it is thus that Dante sets forth that dominating passion of his life.

This canto and the next are a more splendid statement of the main contention of the *De Monarchia*: that civil authority derives, not from the Church, as the Church then claimed, but directly from God, from Justice itself. 'It is plain, therefore', he says at the end of the pamphlet, 'that the authority of temporal monarchy descends on the Empire without any intermediary, from the fount of universal authority.'

In lines 113–117 there is an interesting example of Dante's device of significant rhyme: *l'emme*, 'the *M*', Monarchia, world-order through the world Empire,—*gemme*, 'gems', the historical succession of just rulers, severally serving the one end through the ages,—*ingemme*, the sweet star that 'gems' this heaven, that heavenly justice which is the source and measure and end of all approximate earthly justice. The three words sum up the vision.

'Politically speaking, Dante, when he wrote the *Paradiso* (like Milton when he wrote *Paradise Lost*), was a disillusioned man. On the other hand, the poem it completes was entitled by himself a Comedy, a story that ends happily. After Henry of Luxemburg's death Dante had given up all hope of seeing his political ideal *realized* in his lifetime or at any period he could himself foresee. But surely it is clear from the whole spirit pervading cantos xviii and xix that he continued to hope that it would continue to be effective, under the providence of God, as a "regulative" idea in the future history of his country and the world. And this hope reconciled him to his own immediate and personal disappointment. He finds himself, at the end of the poem, in harmony with the universe and the love that moves it' (*G. L. Bickersteth*).

At the end of the canto he turns from his contemplation of the righteous rulers to the world in which he writes, a world darkened by the smoke that dims the beam of this star. That smoke is the Church's present contribution to the world's life, and it comes from the court of Pope John XXII at Avignon, the court which is the exemplar to all men of wantonness and corruption and political intrigue, the chief place of traffic in sacred things, where the names of the Forerunner and the Apostles of Christ are known only as a jest. The Baptist—he who, in his folly, 'chose to live solitary and was dragged by dances to martyrdom' —is only a profitable figure on a coin; Peter is 'the Fisherman'; and the usual *Paolo* becomes the familiar, and here contemptuous, *Polo*. 'This function of judgement thus assumed by a Catholic layman was something wholly new in the world' (*J. H. Bridges*).

PARADISO

PAREA dinanzi a me con l'ali aperte
  la bella image che nel dolce frui
  liete facevan l'anime conserte:
parea ciascuna rubinetto in cui
  raggio di sole ardesse sì acceso,
  che ne' miei occhi rifrangesse lui.
E quel che mi convien ritrar testeso,
  non portò voce mai, nè scrisse incostro,
  nè fu per fantasia già mai compreso;
ch' io vidi e anche udi' parlar lo rostro,   10
  e sonar nella voce e 'io' e 'mio',
  quand'era nel concetto 'noi' e 'nostro'.
E cominciò: 'Per esser giusto e pio
  son io qui essaltato a quella gloria
  che non si lascia vincere a disio;
ed in terra lasciai la mia memoria
  sì fatta, che le genti lì malvage
  commendan lei, ma non seguon la storia.'
Così un sol calor di molte brage
  si fa sentir, come di molti amori   20
  usciva solo un suon di quella image.
Ond' io appresso: 'O perpetüi fiori
  dell'etterna letizia, che pur uno
  parer mi fate tutti vostri odori,
solvetemi, spirando, il gran digiuno
  che lungamente m' ha tenuto in fame,
  non trovandoli in terra cibo alcuno.

CANTO XIX

The speech of the Eagle; the question of the virtuous heathen; the mystery of Divine Justice; the wickedness of Christian kings

BEFORE me appeared with open wings the beautiful image made by the congregated souls, happy in their sweet fruition; each seemed a little ruby in which the sun's ray burned with such a flame that it was thrown back into my eyes. And that of which I have now to tell never tongue conveyed, nor ink wrote, nor ever was conceived by fancy. For I saw and I heard the beak talk and utter with its voice *I* and *mine* when its meaning was *we* and *ours*; and it began: 'For being just and merciful I am here exalted to that glory which desire cannot surpass, and on earth I left such a memory that the wicked people there commend it but do not continue its story.' Thus is felt a single glow from many brands, as from that image came forth a single sound of many loves.

And I then: 'O perpetual flowers of the eternal bliss who make all your odours seem to me but one, breathe forth and deliver me from the great fast that has long kept me hungry, finding no food for it on

Ben so io che se 'n cielo altro reame
    la divina giustizia fa suo specchio,
    che 'l vostro non l'apprende con velame.   30
Sapete come attento io m'apparecchio
    ad ascoltar; sapete qual è quello
    dubbio che m'è digiun cotanto vecchio.'
Quasi falcone ch'esce del cappello,
    move la testa e con l'ali si plaude,
    voglia mostrando e faccendosi bello,
vid' io farsi quel segno, che di laude
    della divina grazia era contesto,
    con canti quai si sa chi là su gaude.
Poi cominciò: 'Colui che volse il sesto   40
    allo stremo del mondo, e dentro ad esso
    distinse tanto occulto e manifesto,
non potè suo valor sì fare impresso
    in tutto l' universo, che 'l suo verbo
    non rimanesse in infinito eccesso.
E ciò fa certo che 'l primo superbo,
    che fu la somma d'ogni creatura,
    per non aspettar lume, cadde acerbo;
e quinci appar ch'ogni minor natura
    è corto recettacolo a quel bene   50
    che non ha fine e sè con sè misura.
Dunque nostra veduta, che convene
    essere alcun de' raggi della mente
    di che tutte le cose son ripiene,
non pò da sua natura esser possente
    tanto, che suo principio non discerna
    molto di là da quel che l'è parvente.
Però nella giustizia sempiterna
    la vista che riceve il vostro mondo,
    com'occhio per lo mare, entro s' interna;   60
che, ben che dalla proda veggia il fondo,
    in pelago nol vede; e nondimeno
    èli, ma cela lui l'esser profondo.
Lume non è, se non vien dal sereno
    che non si turba mai; anzi è tenebra,
    od ombra della carne, o suo veleno.

earth. I know well that though the Divine Justice is mirrored in another realm of heaven yours apprehends it without a veil. You know with what intentness I am prepared to listen, you know what is that doubt which is so old a fast in me.'

As the falcon released from the hood moves its head and flaps its wings, showing its eagerness and preening its feathers, so I saw that sign, woven of praises of the Divine Grace, bear itself, with songs such as he knows who rejoices there above. Then it began: 'He that turned His compass about the bounds of the world[1] and within it devised so variously things hidden and manifest, could not make His Power to be so impressed on the whole universe that His Word should not remain in infinite excess; and, in proof of this, the first proud spirit, who was the highest of all creatures, fell unripe through not waiting for light, from which it is plain that every lesser nature is too scant a vessel for that good which has no limit and measures itself by itself.[2] Thus our vision, which must needs be one of the rays of the Mind of which all things are full, cannot by its nature be of such power that it should not perceive its origin to be far beyond all that appears to it.[3] Therefore the sight that is granted to your world penetrates within the Eternal Justice as the eye into the sea; for though from the shore it sees the bottom, in the open sea it does not, and yet the bottom is there but the depth conceals it.[4] There is no light but that which comes from the clear sky that is never clouded; else it is darkness, either the shadow of the flesh or

Assai t'è mo aperta la latebra
 che t'ascondeva la giustizia viva,
 di che facei question cotanto crebra;
chè tu dicevi: "Un uom nasce alla riva   70
 dell' Indo, e quivi non è chi ragioni
 di Cristo nè chi legga nè chi scriva;
e tutti suoi voleri e atti boni
 sono, quanto ragione umana vede,
 sanza peccato in vita od in sermoni.
Muore non battezzato e sanza fede:
 ov'è questa giustizia che 'l condanna?
 ov'è la colpa sua, se ei non crede?"
Or tu chi se' che vuo' sedere a scranna,
 per giudicar di lungi mille miglia   80
 con la veduta corta d'una spanna?
Certo a colui che meco s'assottiglia,
 se la Scrittura sovra voi non fosse,
 da dubitar sarebbe a maraviglia.
Oh terreni animali! oh menti grosse!
 La prima volontà, ch'è da sè bona,
 da sè, ch'è sommo ben, mai non si mosse.
Cotanto è giusto quanto a lei consona:
 nullo creato bene a sè la tira,
 ma essa, radïando, lui cagiona.'   90
Quale sovresso il nido si rigira
 poi c' ha pasciuti la cicogna i figli,
 e come quel ch'è pasto la rimira;
cotal si fece, e sì levai i cigli,
 la benedetta imagine, che l'ali
 movea sospinte da tanti consigli.
Roteando cantava, e dicea: 'Quali
 son le mie note a te, che non le 'ntendi,
 tal è il giudicio etterno a voi mortali.'
Poi si quetaron quei lucenti incendi   100
 dello Spirito Santo ancor nel segno
 che fè i Romani al mondo reverendi,
esso ricominciò: 'A questo regno
 non salì mai chi non credette 'n Cristo,
 vel pria vel poi ch'el si chiavasse al legno.

its poison.[5] Now is laid well open to thee the hiding-place that concealed from thee the living Justice of which thou hast so often made question. For thou saidst: "A man is born on the bank of the Indus, and none is there to speak, or read, or write of Christ, and all his desires and doings are good, so far as human reason sees, without sin in life or speech. He dies unbaptized and without faith. Where is this justice that condemns him? Where is his fault if he does not believe?" Now, who art thou[6] that wouldst sit upon the bench and judge a thousand miles away with sight short of a span? Assuredly, for him that would reason it out with me, if the Scriptures were not set over you there would be abundant room for question. O earthly creatures, gross minds! The Primal Will, which in itself is good, from itself, the Supreme Good, never was moved; whatever accords with it is in that measure just; no created good draws it to itself, but it, raying forth, creates that good.'[7]

As the stork circles over the nest when she has fed her young and as the one that is fed looks up to her, so did the blessed image and so I lifted up my brow and it moved the wings that were impelled by so many counsels. Wheeling, it sang, then spoke: 'As are my notes to thee who canst not follow them, such is the Eternal Judgement to you mortals.'

When these shining fires of the Holy Ghost had paused, still in the sign that made the Romans reverend to the world, it began again: 'To this kingdom none ever rose who did not believe in Christ, either before or after He was nailed to the

Ma vedi: molti gridan "Cristo, Cristo!"
 che saranno in giudicio assai men prope
 a lui, che tal che non conosce Cristo;
e tai Cristiani dannerà l'Etiope,
 quando si partiranno i due collegi,   110
 l'uno in etterno ricco, e l'altro inope.
Che potran dir li Perse a' vostri regi,
 come vedranno quel volume aperto
 nel qual si scrivon tutti suoi dispregi?
Lì si vedrà, tra l'opere d'Alberto,
 quella che tosto moverà la penna,
 per che 'l regno di Praga fia diserto.
Lì si vedrà il duol che sovra Senna
 induce, falseggiando la moneta,
 quel che morrà di colpo di cotenna.   120
Lì si vedrà la superbia ch'asseta,
 che fa lo Scotto e l' Inghilese folle,
 sì che non può soffrir dentro a sua meta.
Vedrassi la lussuria e 'l viver molle
 di quel di Spagna e di quel di Boemme,
 che mai valor non conobbe nè volle.
Vedrassi al Ciotto di Ierusalemme
 segnata con un' I la sua bontate,
 quando 'l contrario segnerà un'emme.
Vedrassi l'avarizia e la viltate   130
 di quei che guarda l' isola del foco,
 ove Anchise finì la lunga etate;
e a dare ad intender quanto è poco,
 la sua scrittura fian lettere mozze,
 che noteranno molto in parvo loco.
E parranno a ciascun l'opere sozze
 del barba e del fratel, che tanto egregia
 nazione e due corone han fatte bozze.
E quel di Portogallo e di Norvegia
 lì si conosceranno, e quel di Rascia   140
 che male ha visto il conio di Vinegia.
Oh beata Ungheria se non si lascia
 più malmenare! e beata Navarra
 se s'armasse del monte che la fascia!

tree. But note, many cry *Christ, Christ*! who shall
be far less near to Him at the Judgement than
such as know not Christ, and such Christians the
Ethiopian shall condemn when the two companies
are parted, the one forever rich, the other poor.
What can the Persians say to your kings when they
see that volume opened in which are written all
their infamies?[8] There shall be seen, among the
deeds of Albert, that one, soon to move the pen,
by which the Kingdom of Prague shall be made
desolate. There shall be seen the misery brought
on the Seine from the debasement of the currency
by him that shall die from the charge of a boar.
There shall be seen the pride that makes men thirst
and so maddens the Scot and the Englishman that
neither can keep within his bounds. It will show
the wantonness and soft living of him of Spain, and
of him of Bohemia who never knew worth nor
sought it. It will show for the Cripple of Jerusalem
his goodness marked with an *I*, while an *M* will
mark the opposite. It will show the avarice and
cowardice of him that holds the island of fire where
Anchises ended his long life; and to make plain
his insignificance his record shall be in contractions
that will note much in little space; and manifest
to all shall be the foul deeds of his uncle and his
brother, by whom a lineage so illustrious and two
crowns have been dishonoured; and he of Portugal
and he of Norway shall be known there, and he of
Rascia, who to his own hurt has seen the coin of
Venice.[9]

'O happy Hungary, if she no longer let herself
be wronged! And happy Navarre, if she arm herself

E creder de' ciascun che già, per arra
di questo, Nicosia e Famagosta
per la lor bestia si lamenti e garra,
che dal fianco dell'altre non si scosta.

with the mountains that surround her! And, for earnest of this, all men should know that Nicosia and Famagosta lament and complain of their own beast, which keeps its place beside the rest.'[10]

1. 'He set a compass upon the face of the depth' (*Prov.* viii. 27).

2 The divine creative thought, 'the Word', being infinite, surpasses creation itself and the comprehension of every created intelligence, even that of Lucifer before his fall.

3. Our vision, the further it reaches, is the more aware of its limit.

4. 'Thy judgements are a great deep' (*Ps.* xxxvi. 6).

5. Ignorance or sin.

6. 'Nay but, O man, who art thou that repliest against God?' (*Rom.* ix. 20).

7. The Divine Goodness is the only source, and the only measure, of justice, and it cannot itself be judged except by itself.

8. 'The books were opened: . . . and the dead were judged out of those things which were written in the books, according to their works' (*Rev.* xx. 12).

9. Emperor Albert (*Purg.* vi), who invaded Bohemia in 1304; Philip IV of France, killed by a boar in 1314; Edward I and Wallace in the war of Scottish independence; Ferdinand of Castile; Wenceslaus of Bohemia, 'who battens on wantonness and ease' (*Purg.* vii); Charles II of Naples, titular King of Jerusalem, father of Charles Martel (*Par.* viii),—his virtue, liberality, is one ('*I*'), his vices a thousand ('*M*'); Frederick II of Sicily, who deserted the imperial cause in 1313; his uncle and his brother, Kings of the Balearic Isles and of Aragon; Dionysius of Portugal and Hakon of Norway, both probably little known to Dante; Stephen of Rascia (old Servia), who copied the Venetian ducat in baser metal.

10. Hungary was delivered from misrule by the accession in 1301 of the son of Charles Martel, Dante's friend (*Par.* viii). Navarre too would be 'happy' were she not falling to the French crown by marriage. Nicosia and Famagosta, towns in Cyprus, are a warning, since Cyprus is in the hands of the dissolute French ruler, Henry of Lusignano, and her experience shows what Navarre may expect.

NOTE

In describing the 'beautiful image' of Divine Justice Dante multiplies the terms by which to indicate at once its manifoldness and its unity. 'The congregated souls' are each like a little ruby reflecting singly the sun's rays; but—here alone among the spheres—no one of the souls speaks individually, but all speak collectively in a voice which is 'a single sound of many loves', like 'a single glow from many brands'; they are flowers whose 'odours seem to me but one'; and the movements of 'the blessed image' are 'impelled by many counsels'. All the imperfect attainments of just men in the course of history to establish a just order in the world contribute and combine to form the image of that perfect justice at which they aim and which is one in heaven and earth. There is no other justice but the Divine Justice; there is no justice for any that is not justice for all; and that identity of interest is the ultimate, only justice for men and nations. Dante's amazement here is no naïve wonder at a talking constellation; it is amazement at the moral miracle which he sees in his dream. The kings of the earth— now such as are described at the end of the canto, warring, treacherous, oppressive—are here ranked in harmony and peace as the fulfilment of the divine thought of a perfected human order such as 'never tongue conveyed, nor ink wrote, nor ever was conceived by fancy; for I saw and I heard the beak talk and utter with its voice *I* and *mine* when its meaning was *we* and *ours*'. (This is surely an echo of Paul's language in I Cor. ii. 9, and of its context.) The kings of Dante's vision find all their authority and guidance in the Eagle, Divine Justice itself, and in this aspect of it the *Comedy* is a cry out of the depths of an unjust and disordered world for the fulfilment of all that is best in human history and in human hope.

The language here stresses also the idea that the Divine

Justice, in itself and in its historical operations, is at the same time Grace. The Eagle is exalted 'for being just and merciful', it is 'woven of the praises of the Divine Grace'; it is like the mother stork that feeds its young and hovers over them; the just souls are 'shining fires of the Holy Ghost', and the Holy Ghost is the love of God.

The heraldic Eagle is compared first to a falcon and then to a stork, and it is impossible to suppose that Dante made these comparisons as mere picturesque variants of his original image. In the contexts in which they stand, the falcon pluming itself for flight seems to suggest earthly justice as a continual aspiration after the infinite, unfathomable heavenly justice—that aspiration which *is* earthly justice; and the stork, the accepted symbol of parental piety, hovering over its young in the nest—these the symbol of filial obedience—suggests justice actual, vigilant, beneficent in human experience, a work of God for which to give thanks; and both of these aspects are present in Dante's thought. 'After the legal principle of the Imperium and the rule of Divine Justice have been set forth by Justinian and Beatrice in the second heaven (*Par.* vi and vii), we find ourselves on a level where Imperium and righteousness appear no longer harsh and relentless, but wise, gentle and infinite, as a mystery. Therefore the imperial eagle must, above all, show how Divine Justice lies beyond the reach of human knowledge, and how, therefore, it cannot be understood, but must be accepted, revered, loved, trusted. To doubters it appears something arbitrary, to the pious as gracious choice, to the sinner as unexpected punishment' (*K. Vossler*). The comparison of the Eagle to the falcon and the stork seems to embody what was, in fact, Dante's meaning in this canto and the next,—that, for our human thought, the Divine Justice must, because it is divine, be at once unfathomable and infinitely gracious.

It is to the image of Justice that Dante appeals for solution of the doubt that is 'so old a fast' in him, and his words have an eagerness which recalls the scene in the fourth canto of the *Inferno*. There, when he was told by Virgil of the virtuous heathen confined in Limbo only for their lack of baptism and of right worship, 'great grief seized me at the heart, for I knew people of much worth who were suspended in that Limbo'. And then, as if with a cry, he broke forth: 'Tell me, my Master, tell me, sir, did ever anyone, either by his own merit or another's, go out hence and go afterwards to bliss?' Both passages are true autobiography.

The question was a real one for Dante and the Christian thinkers of his time, whose problem it was to answer it consistently with the established forensic doctrines of justice and grace. It is not answered here, but, after St Paul's example, declared unanswerable. The infinite creative Will is not only just, it is the only justice, and by its nature it is, and must remain, unfathomable; 'yet the bottom is there, but the depth conceals it'. Even 'our vision', says the Eagle that consists of souls in bliss, comes short. 'Our very demand for justice is but a ray of light from God Himself. It is some imperfect apprehension, some derived sense, of justice, outflowing from the inmost being of God, that makes us demand justice in the universe. And for that demand to turn back on its own source in protest is for the derivative ray to challenge the source from which it flows' (*P. H. Wicksteed*).

In response to his question Dante is assured that no calling on the name of Christ, no profession of Christian faith, can of itself set men near to Christ in the Judgement. And here again the name of Christ is in the triple rhyme for greater emphasis, bringing into comparison sincere faith in Christ, sham profession of Christ, and mere ignorance of Christ. On that follows a fierce indictment of 'your kings', the chief ruling sovereigns of the time, baptized and orthodox Christians every one of them and the worse on that account. The actual kings are judged by the ideal Empire—'still in the sign that made the Romans reverend to the world'—and the doings of rulers are judged by the only end that can ever justify their rule.

In this passage, as in the description of the fall of the proud in *Purgatorio* xii, Dante enforces his meaning with an acrostic. The initial letters of the nine stanzas of the royal black list, each letter occurring three times, spell the old Italian word *LUE*—*V* being taken as equivalent to *U*—, meaning pestilence; for the device means that, or else it means nothing, and Dante never means nothing. It is the expression of his contempt

283

for 'such Christians', and it is the more characteristic and the more scathing because the foul word occurs as if not by his choice but inevitably, in the mere account of them; they are a plague on the world and it is impossible to speak of them in decent terms. They are the precise opposite of the souls that form the Eagle, and in naming them so Dante is obedient to the charge laid on him by Cacciaguida to 'make plain all his vision' and 'like the wind strike most on the highest summits'.

In the list of royalties the first is an Emperor whom Dante regarded as no Emperor, but a usurper, 'German Albert' (*Purg.* vi); Frederick of Sicily was, in Dante's eyes, a traitor to the Imperial cause, the worse because he ruled in the place sacred to the memory of Anchises, father of Aeneas and of the royal line of Rome and foreteller of the Empire; and Philip IV of France, who a few years before this was written, was the chief enemy of the Empire in Europe. Philip is referred to four times elsewhere in the *Divine Comedy*: as 'he that rules France' (*Inf.* xix), 'the pest of France' (*Purg.* vii), 'the new Pilate' (*Purg.* xx), the 'savage lover' of the wanton Church (*Purg.* xxxii), never once by his name; and he is here dismissed from our attention as 'he that shall die from the charge of a boar', as if that was his fitting epitaph. The list is followed by a warning of the spread of the French contagion.

A curious point is raised in Dante's words to the Eagle: 'I know well that though the Divine Justice is mirrored in another realm of heaven yours apprehends it without a veil.' This is his passing acknowledgment of the traditional order of the angelic hierarchy, which is detailed in the twenty-eighth canto and according to which the 'Thrones', the rank of angels who deliver the Divine Judgements, are associated, not with the sphere of Jupiter, but with that of Saturn. It seems as if Dante was embarrassed by the old tradition, which did not really suit his purposes in the *Paradiso* but to which he felt bound to give formal deference. Plumptre gives the sense of the stanza: 'If elsewhere in Heaven the Divine Justice finds a mirror, how much more in Jupiter.'

PARADISO

QUANDO colui che tutto 'l mondo alluma
 dell'emisperio nostro sì discende,
 che 'l giorno d'ogne parte si consuma,
lo ciel, che sol di lui prima s'accende,
 subitamente si rifà parvente
 per molte luci, in che una risplende;
e questo atto del ciel mi venne a mente,
 come 'l segno del mondo e de' suoi duci
 nel benedetto rostro fu tacente;
però che tutte quelle vive luci,   10
 vie più lucendo, cominciaron canti
 da mia memoria labili e caduci.
O dolce amor che di riso t'ammanti,
 quanto parevi ardente in que' flailli,
 ch'avìeno spirto sol di pensier santi!
Poscia che i cari e lucidi lapilli
 ond' io vidi ingemmato il sesto lume
 puoser silenzio alli angelici squilli,
udir mi parve un mormorar di fiume
 che scende chiaro giù di pietra in pietra, 20
 mostrando l' ubertà del suo cacume.
E come suono al collo della cetra
 prende sua forma, e sì com'al pertugio
 della sampogna vento che penetra,
così, rimosso d'aspettare indugio,
 quel mormorar dell'aguglia salissi
 su per lo collo, come fosse bugio.

CANTO XX

Just rulers in the eye of the Eagle; Trajan and Ripheus; the salvation of pagans; predestination

WHEN he that lightens all the world sinks from our hemisphere so far that day is spent on every side, the sky, which before was kindled by him alone, suddenly shows itself again with many lights in which one shines;[1] and this change in the sky came to my mind when the standard of the world and of its chiefs was silent in the blessed beak. For all those living lights, shining still more brightly, began songs that slip and fall from my memory. O sweet Love that mantlest thyself in a smile, how glowing didst thou show in those flutes that were filled only with the breath of holy thoughts!

After the bright and precious jewels with which I saw the sixth light gemmed had made silence in their angelic chimes, I seemed to hear the murmur of a stream that fell limpid from rock to rock, showing the abundance of its mountain source; and as the sound takes its form at the neck of the lute and the wind at the vent of the pipe it fills, so, keeping me waiting no longer, that murmur of the Eagle rose up through the neck as if it were

287

Fecesi voce quivi, e quindi uscissi
   per lo suo becco in forma di parole,
   quali aspettava il core, ov' io le scrissi.   30
'La parte in me che vede, e pate il sole
   nell'aguglie mortali' incominciommi,
   'or fisamente riguardar si vole,
perchè de' fuochi ond' io figura fommi,
   quelli onde l'occhio in testa mi scintilla,
   e' di tutti lor gradi son li sommi.
Colui che luce in mezzo per pupilla,
   fu il cantor dello Spirito Santo,
   che l'arca traslatò di villa in villa:
ora conosce il merto del suo canto,   40
   in quanto effetto fu del suo consiglio,
   per lo remunerar ch'è altrettanto.
Dei cinque che mi fan cerchio per ciglio,
   colui che più al becco mi s'accosta,
   la vedovella consolò del figlio:
ora conosce quanto caro costa
   non seguir Cristo, per l'esperïenza
   di questa dolce vita e dell'opposta.
E quel che segue in la circunferenza
   di che ragiono, per l'arco superno,   50
   morte indugiò per vera penitenza:
ora conosce che 'l giudicio etterno
   non si trasmuta, quando degno preco
   fa crastino là giù dell'odïerno.
L'altro che segue, con le leggi e meco,
   sotto buona intenzion che fè mal frutto,
   per cedere al pastor si fece greco:
ora conosce come il mal dedutto
   dal suo bene operar non li è nocivo,
   avvegna che sia 'l mondo indi distrutto.   60
E quel che vedi nell'arco declivo,
   Guiglielmo fu, cui quella terra plora
   che piagne Carlo e Federigo vivo:
ora conosce come s' innamora
   lo ciel del giusto rege, ed al sembiante
   del suo fulgor lo fa vedere ancora.

hollow. There it became a voice that came forth thence by the beak in the form of words such as my heart, where I wrote them down, awaited.

'That part in me which in mortal eagles sees and endures the sun thou must now watch intently,' it began to me 'for, of the fires of which I make my form, those with which the eye sparkles in my head are the highest in all their ranks. He that shines in the middle for pupil was the singer of the Holy Ghost, who carried the ark from house to house;[2] now he knows the merit of his song so far as it was the fruit of his own counsel,[3] by the reward that is proportioned to it. Of the five who make an arch for my eyebrow, he that is nearest to my beak consoled the poor widow for her son;[4] now he knows how dear it costs not to follow Christ, by experience of this sweet life and of its opposite. And he that follows on the same curve on the upward arc delayed his death by a true repentance;[5] now he knows that the eternal decree is not changed when fitting prayer below makes today's event tomorrow's. The next following, with good intention that had bad fruit, made himself Greek, with the laws and me, so as to give place to the Shepherd;[6] now he knows that the evil derived from his good deed does not harm him though the world is brought to ruin by it. And he thou seest on the downward arc was William, for whom that land mourns that weeps on account of the living Charles and Frederick;[7] now he knows how heaven is moved with love for the just king, as by the effulgence of his aspect he still makes plain.

289

Chi crederebbe giù nel mondo errante,
   che Rifeo Troiano in questo tondo
   fosse la quinta delle luci sante?
Ora conosce assai di quel che 'l mondo   70
   veder non può della divina grazia,
   ben che sua vista non discerna il fondo.'
Quale allodetta che 'n aere si spazia
   prima cantando, e poi tace contenta
   dell' ultima dolcezza che la sazia,
tal mi sembiò l' imago della 'mprenta
   dell'etterno piacere, al cui disio
   ciascuna cosa qual ell'è diventa.
E avvegna ch' io fossi al dubbiar mio
   lì quasi vetro allo color ch' el veste,   80
   tempo aspettar tacendo non patìo,
ma della bocca 'Che cose son queste?'
   mi pinse con la forza del suo peso;
   per ch' io di coruscar vidi gran feste.
Poi appresso, con l'occhio più acceso,
   lo benedetto segno mi rispose
   per non tenermi in ammirar sospeso:
'Io veggio che tu credi queste cose
   perch' io le dico, ma non vedi come;
   sì che, se son credute, sono ascose.   90
Fai come quei che la cosa per nome
   apprende ben, ma la sua quiditate
   veder non può se altri non la prome.
Regnum coelorum vïolenza pate
   da caldo amore e da viva speranza,
   che vince la divina volontate;
non a guisa che l'omo a l'om sobranza,
   ma vince lei perchè vuole esser vinta,
   e, vinta, vince con sua beninanza.
La prima vita del ciglio e la quinta   100
   ti fa maravigliar, perchè ne vedi
   la regïon delli angeli dipinta.
De' corpi suoi non uscir, come credi,
   gentili, ma cristiani, in ferma fede
   quel de' passuri e quel de' passi piedi.

Who in the erring world below would believe that Trojan Ripheus[8] was the fifth of the holy lights in this round? Now he knows much that the world cannot see of the Divine Grace, although his sight does not discern the bottom.'

Like the lark that soars in the air, first singing, then silent, content with the last sweetness that satiates it, such seemed to me that image, the imprint of the Eternal Pleasure by whose will all things come to have their being.[9] And although I was to my perplexity there as glass to the colour that coats it, my question did not bear to wait its time in silence, but by its weight and pressure forced from my lips: 'How can these things be?'; at which I saw a great revelry of flashing lights. And then, its eye kindling yet more, the blessed sign replied, not to keep me in suspense and amazement: 'I see that thou believest these things because I tell them, but seest not how they can be, so that, though they are believed, they are hidden; thou art like one that knows a thing well by name but cannot perceive the quiddity of it unless some one set it forth. *Regnum coelorum* suffereth violence[10] from fervent love and lively hope, which conquer the Divine Will, not as man masters man, but conquer it because it would be conquered, and, being conquered, conquers with its own goodness. The first living soul and the fifth of the eyebrow make thee marvel to see the region of the angels decked with them. They came forth from their bodies not, as thou thinkest, gentile,[11] but Christian, with firm faith, the one in the Feet that were to suffer, the other in these Feet having suffered. For

Chè l'una dello 'nferno, u' non si riede
   già mai a buon voler, tornò all'ossa;
   e ciò di viva spene fu mercede;
di viva spene, che mise la possa
   ne' prieghi fatti a Dio per suscitarla,   110
   sì che potesse sua voglia esser mossa.
L'anima glorïosa onde si parla,
   tornata nella carne, in che fu poco,
   credette in lui che potea aiutarla;
e credendo s'accese in tanto foco
   di vero amor, ch'alla morte seconda
   fu degna di venire a questo gioco.
L'altra, per grazia che da sì profonda
   fontana stilla, che mai creatura
   non pinse l'occhio infino alla prima onda,   120
tutto suo amor là giù pose a drittura;
   per che, di grazia in grazia, Dio li aperse
   l'occhio alla nostra redenzion futura:
ond'ei credette in quella, e non sofferse
   da indi il puzzo più del paganesmo;
   e riprendìene le genti perverse.
Quelle tre donne li fur per battesmo
   che tu vedesti dalla destra rota,
   dinanzi al battezzar più d'un millesmo.
O predestinazion, quanto remota   130
   è la radice tua da quelli aspetti
   che la prima cagion non veggion tota!
E voi, mortali, tenetevi stretti
   a giudicar; chè noi, che Dio vedemo,
   non conosciamo ancor tutti li eletti;
ed ènne dolce così fatto scemo,
   perchè il ben nostro in questo ben s'affina,
   che quel che vole Dio, e noi volemo.'
Così da quella imagine divina,
   per farmi chiara la mia corta vista,   140
   data mi fu soave medicina.
E come a buon cantor buon citarista
   fa seguitar lo guizzo della corda,
   in che più di piacer lo canto acquista,

from Hell, where there is no returning to right will, the one came again to his bones; and this was the reward of a lively hope, the lively hope that gave power to the prayers made to God to raise him up so that it should be possible for his will to be moved. The glorious soul I tell of, having returned to the flesh for a short time, believed in Him that was able to help him, and, believing, was kindled to such a fire of true love that on his second death he was worthy to come to this festival. The other, through grace which wells from so deep a fountain that no creature ever thrust his eye to its primal spring, set all his love below on righteousness; therefore from grace to grace God opened his eyes to our coming redemption, so that he believed in it and from that time endured no longer the stench of paganism but rebuked the perverse peoples for it. Those three ladies whom thou sawest by the right wheel[12] stood for baptism to him more than a thousand years before baptizing. O predestination, how far removed is thy root from their gaze who see not the First Cause whole! And you mortals, keep yourselves restrained in judging, for we, who see God, do not yet know all the elect; and this very lack is sweet to us, because in this good our good is perfected, that that which God wills we will too.'

Thus by that divine image was given sweet medicine to clear the shortness of my sight. And as a good lutanist makes the trembling string accompany a good singer, by which the song gains

sì, mentre che parlò, sì mi ricorda
 ch' io vidi le due luci benedette,
 pur come batter d'occhi si concorda,
con le parole mover le fiammette.

more sweetness, so, while it spoke, I remember to have seen the two blessed lights, just as winking eyes keep time together, move with the words their little flames.

1. 'As the stars in Dante's astronomy reflect the light of the sun, so does the power of minor kings and princes proceed from that of the Emperor' (*E. G. Gardner*).

2. King David, who brought the ark from the house of Abinadab to Jerusalem (2 *Sam.* vi. 1–9).

3. The line 'contains by implication Dante's doctrine of inspiration. The human instrument of the Divine Spirit has a genuine part to play' (*P. H. Wicksteed*).

4. The Emperor Trajan, who was recalled to life by the prayer of Pope Gregory I and converted to Christianity; for 'the poor widow' see *Purg.* x.

5. King Hezekiah, who was warned by the prophet of his approaching death; in answer to his prayer his life was prolonged for 15 years (2 *Kgs.* xx. 1–7).

6. The Emperor Constantine, who transferred the Roman government to the East, and by whose 'Donation' (a fabrication of the 9th century) the Pope claimed temporal sovereignty in Rome; cp. *Inf.* xix.

7. King William the Good of Naples and Sicily in the 12th century; in 1300 these parts were ruled by Charles, 'the Cripple of Jerusalem', and Frederick II; cp. *Par.* xix.

8. Ripheus is known only in the *Aeneid*, where he is called 'the most just among the Trojans and the most zealous for the right'.

9. 'The imprint of the divine pleasure is the Imperial eagle, which, as the symbol of the divinely appointed Monarchy, was stamped by God's providence on the face of the world' (*H. F. Tozer*).

10. *Matt.* xi. 12: '*Regnum coelorum vim patitur*'; as if to say there is Scripture for it.

11. Not unbelievers.

12. The three ladies representing faith, hope and love, on the right of the gospel car in the Earthly Paradise (*Purg.* xxix).

NOTE

The single voice of the Eagle breaks up into many voices, and as the stars sparkle each with its own reflection of the one light of the sun, so the world's just rulers, each in his own station, welcome the Eagle's declaration of the depth of Divine Justice and the breadth of Divine Grace, and its reprobation of the kings named at the end of the last canto. Then, by a process described with a curious elaboration, the Eagle regains its single voice, 'keeping me waiting no longer'. Three times in the canto Dante uses the same word, *aspettare*, as an expression of his eagerness for the demonstration of the Divine Justice in the order of the world. How long had Dante—how long have we all—been kept waiting for a just Empire of humanity!

The unity of the ideal Empire, as Dante conceives it, is not an abstract unity of blind obedience, but a concord of just minds in a commonwealth of the world maintaining the liberty of its peoples and accepting one authority because it is of divine appointment and because it is the guardian of all men's peace and freedom. 'When it is said that the human race can be ruled by one sovereign prince it is not to be understood that every small decision of each municipality can come directly from him. . . . For nations, kingdoms and cities have their own special features and must be regulated by laws differing for one and another' (*De Monarchia*). It is noted by Wicksteed that 'the systems of law annually issued, by which justice was administered in the Italian commonwealths, were avowedly based on Roman law, with such modifications or supplements as were judged necessary under the special conditions. What Dante has in mind when he speaks of the Empire is the enforcing of the general principles embodied in the Roman law'. In the *Convito* he describes Roman law as *scritta ragione*, 'written reason'.

The identification of earthly justice with the authority of a German-elected Emperor ruling the nations was indeed a fantastic dream; but all the more it demonstrates the depth and compelling force of Dante's conviction that justice, and one justice for all, is the one principle of world-unity and peace; and it was only on these terms, based on history and providence, that it was possible for him then to conceive it.

The imagery of music—the songs of the living lights, the lute, the pipe, the lark, the singer and his accompaniment—is especially prominent in this canto, the last of the three on the sphere of Jupiter, as if for Dante, in a world ruled by such kings as have been named in the black list, nothing but music could express the consummation of earthly justice which 'his heart awaited'.

The head of the Eagle, like a heraldic sign and perhaps conceived as a great mosaic seen against the white sheen of the planet, appears in profile, and the eye is shown in full circle. The six lights that form the pupil and the eyebrow are, in idea, the greatest representatives of justice on earth, and are recognized as such by the whole body of just rulers, that is, the whole form of the Eagle. As the eye of a mortal eagle 'endures the sun'—like Milton's eagle 'kindling her undazzled eyes at the full midday beam'—so these have the clearest vision of the divine purpose for the world; and the repeated formula, 'now he knows', tells of them comprehending the Divine Justice now as they never did on earth, though even now 'not discerning the bottom'. These types of just rule stand in obvious contrast with the kings of Europe named before.

The first four—David, Trajan, Hezekiah and Constantine— are, alternately, rulers of Israel and Judah and of the Empire, and David is the pupil of the Eagle's eye. 'It was in the very same age that David was born and Rome was born, that is, that Aeneas came from Troy to Italy, which was the origin of the most noble city of Rome, as the records testify; so that the divine choice of the Roman Empire is manifest from the birth of the holy city being contemporaneous with the root of Mary's race' (*Convito*). The first true king of the elect people represents uniquely, as it were, the combination of spiritual and temporal authority among men. He is at once 'the singer of the Holy

Ghost' and the bringer of the ark, the sign of the divine presence, to his new capital; his kingdom is founded on worship. In the case of the other three of these there is some wonder of grace recognized: Trajan's restoration to life and his conversion, Hezekiah's lengthened life in response to his penitence, Constantine's great error condoned. The fifth, 'the just king' in contrast with his successors, is the only modern among them, as if to mark his singularity among modern rulers; and the last, an almost unknown figure from pagan antiquity, is witness to the reach of Divine Grace quite beyond the Christian world's conception.

The presence of Trajan and Ripheus high among the saints is really the answer of the Eagle to Dante's question in the last canto, and he stresses his wonder and his eagerness to know of them; his perplexity 'did not bear to wait its time in silence', and 'the blessed sign, not to keep me in suspense and amazement', replied to him. Both represent the imperial race, Ripheus before and Trajan after Christ. Dante has already honoured Trajan for his clemency and humbleness in the tenth canto of the *Purgatorio*, and here he recalls the story, universally accepted, of his restoration to life and of St Gregory's hope working along with Trajan's own faith and love for his salvation.

The salvation of Ripheus, on the other hand, seems to be entirely Dante's own invention and is the more significant. The words of St Peter in *Acts* x. 35: 'In every nation he that feareth him, and worketh righteousness',—*justitiam*, in the Vulgate—'is accepted with him', taken along with the description of Ripheus in the *Aeneid* as 'the most just'—*justissimus*— 'among the Trojans', the imperial race, would be conclusive for Dante; and it was impossible for him to believe that the saving gifts of faith and hope and love—the three 'theological' virtues are repeatedly referred to in the canto—would be withheld from Ripheus by the Grace which, being divine, is infinite. 'The ordinary place of these "three ladies" is where he saw them in the Earthly Paradise, at the right wheel of the Chariot of the Church. But they are not bound to the Chariot. Divine grace is not the slave of the ordinary means by which it works' (*J. S. Carroll*). Predestination is itself a mystery of grace, and grace, by its nature and necessity, is deeper even than the vision of the saints who see God's face. The 'violence' suffered by the kingdom of heaven, the prevailing force of intercession and of the spirit of righteousness in a man, is not a victory *over* the Divine Will, but a victory *of* the Divine Will; it is the prevailing of grace itself and the fulfilment, in ways past our reckoning, of the mystery of predestination. It has been noted by Butler that in the passage of the *Aeneid* where it is told that Ripheus fell in the defence of Troy, the words that follow are *Dis aliter visum*, 'to the gods it seemed otherwise', words which may have contributed to Dante's treatment of Ripheus here. It is an instance of his refusal, in the name both of justice and of grace, to regard Christian truth as a closed system bounded by our understanding, and for his larger faith he found warrant both in Scripture and in Aquinas. It is his attempt 'to account scholastically for the impulse of the poet's heart' (*K. Vossler*), and this is not the only passage in the *Paradiso* which seems to show, by comparison with the *Inferno* and the *Purgatorio*, that Dante's faith broadened and deepened during his last years in Ravenna.

It is in connection with the lines about Ripheus that Dante makes his third comparison of the heavenly Eagle with an earthly bird, this time the soaring, singing, then silent, lark, 'content with the last sweetness that satiates it'; and the last sweetness of the Eagle's song was of the unfathomableness of grace. Grace and justice, in their divine perfection, are functions the one of the other, and the Eagle is like the lark in its rapture; for to love justice, with joy in its gracious working, that only is to be just.

The Eagle is a vast, formal, heraldic figure, as must be the representation in symbol of the institution of world government; and its impersonal character is emphasized when we are told that the 'murmur of the Eagle rose up through the neck, as if it were hollow'. The three living birds with which the Eagle, in its actions and functions, is compared—the falcon, the stork and the skylark—are all real, convincing, portrayed from life. Their actions are described in a kind of crescendo: the falcon slipping from the hood, preening its feathers and preparing for flight; the mother-stork hovering in the air over its young; the lark, soaring, jubilating, then suddenly silent, watched and listened to with as rapt attention as was Wordsworth's or Shelley's. The imagined creatures *live*, most of all the lark, as lived in the heart of the Poet God's thought of justice for the world of men and, in that, the unmeasured working of His grace. So such answer as was possible was made to Dante's question, and 'by the divine image' of Eternal Justice 'was given sweet medicine to clear the shortness of his sight'.

'There is an expanding progress in Dante's gradual apprehension of the true nature and rightness of Divine Justice, under tuition of the Eagle. "Thy statutes have been my songs in the house of my pilgrimage"; the fixed statute became the unfettered soaring song, the mosaic Eagle the living bird. Such is Dante's comment on Virgil's *Dis aliter visum*. It is simultaneously true that the Eagle (the law of the universe, that which makes everything what it is) is a perfectly rigid (or mechanical) design, and yet is also a thing alive and pulsating with love: a paradox and a mystery only to be apprehended by the poetic imagination, which finds expression for it by the bird-symbols here employed. Dante, being a Thomist, has to get at Love through Justice, at God's Heart through His Reason, not the other way round. If a Franciscan had been writing these cantos, the bird would have been a Dove, not an Eagle; and he would have reversed the order of the comparisons, have begun with the lark and ended with the falcon. He would have *first* heard the lark's song, *then* seen it as a statute. To Dante it is first a statute, then a song. But to Dante and St Francis alike, *qua* poets, it is both simultaneously, an inseparable unity as actually experienced' (*G. L. Bickersteth*).

PARADISO

GIÀ eran li occhi miei rifissi al volto
    della mia donna, e l'animo con essi,
    e da ogni altro intento s'era tolto.
E quella non ridea; ma 'S' io ridessi'
    mi cominciò 'tu ti faresti quale
    fu Semelè quando di cener fessi;
chè la bellezza mia, che per le scale
    dell'etterno palazzo più s'accende,
    com' hai veduto, quanto più si sale,
se non si temperasse, tanto splende,   10
    che 'l tuo mortal podere, al suo fulgore,
    sarebbe fronda che trono scoscende.
Noi sem levati al settimo splendore,
    che sotto il petto del Leone ardente
    raggia mo misto giù del suo valore.
Ficca di retro alli occhi tuoi la mente,
    e fa di quelli specchi alla figura
    che 'n questo specchio ti sarà parvente.'
Qual savesse qual era la pastura
    del viso mio nell'aspetto beato   20
    quand' io mi trasmutai ad altra cura,
conoscerebbe quanto m'era a grato
    ubidire alla mia celeste scorta,
    contrapesando l'un con l'altro lato.
Dentro al cristallo che 'l vocabol porta,
    cerchiando il mondo, del suo chiaro duce
    sotto cui giacque ogni malizia morta,

CANTO XXI

The Sphere of Saturn; the contemplatives; the ladder; St Peter Damian; monastic degeneracy

ALREADY my eyes were fixed again on the face of my Lady, and with them my mind, which was withdrawn from every other thought; and she did not smile, but 'Were I to smile' she began to me 'thou wouldst become like Semele when she was turned to ashes;[1] for my beauty, which thou hast seen kindle more the higher we climb by the stairs of the eternal palace, is so shining that if it were not tempered thy mortal powers in its blaze would be as a branch split by a thunderbolt. We have risen to the seventh splendour, which beneath the breast of the burning Lion rays down now mingled with its power.[2] Set thy mind behind thine eyes and make of them mirrors to the shape which in this mirror will appear to thee.'

One that knew what was the pasture of my sight in that blessed aspect might recognize, when I directed my mind elsewhere, what joy it was to me to be obedient to my heavenly guide, balancing the one scale with the other.

Within the crystal which, circling about the world, bears the name of the world's famous chief under whom all wickedness lay dead,[3] I saw, of the colour

di color d'oro in che raggio traluce
  vid' io uno scaleo eretto in suso
  tanto, che nol seguiva la mia luce.   30
Vidi anche per li gradi scender giuso
  tanti splendor, ch' io pensai ch'ogni lume
  che par nel ciel quindi fosse diffuso.
E come, per lo natural costume,
  le pole insieme, al cominciar del giorno,
  si movono a scaldar le fredde piume;
poi altre vanno via sanza ritorno,
  altre rivolgon sè onde son mosse,
  e altre roteando fan soggiorno;
tal modo parve me che quivi fosse   40
  in quello sfavillar che 'nsieme venne,
  sì come in certo grado si percosse.
E quel che presso più ci si ritenne,
  si fè sì chiaro, ch' io dicea pensando:
  'Io veggio ben l'amor che tu m'accenne.'
Ma quella ond' io aspetto il come e 'l quando
  del dire e del tacer, si sta; ond' io,
  contra il disio, fo ben ch' io non dimando.
Per ch'ella, che vedea il tacer mio
  nel veder di colui che tutto vede,   50
  mi disse: 'Solvi il tuo caldo disio.'
E io incominciai: 'La mia mercede
  non mi fa degno della tua risposta;
  ma per colei che 'l chieder mi concede,
vita beata che ti stai nascosta
  dentro alla tua letizia, fammi nota
  la cagion che sì presso mi t' ha posta;
e dì perchè si tace in questa rota
  la dolce sinfonia di paradiso,
  che giù per l'altre suona sì divota.'   60
'Tu hai l'udir mortal sì come il viso;'
  rispuose a me 'onde qui non si canta
  per quel che Beatrice non ha riso.
Giù per li gradi della scala santa
  discesi tanto sol per farti festa
  col dire e con la luce che mi ammanta;

of gold that flashes in the sun, a ladder which rose to such a height that my sight could not follow it. I saw, too, descending by the steps, so many splendours that I thought every light that shows in heaven had been poured out there; and as by natural habit the daws rise together at daybreak to warm their cold feathers, then some fly off not to return, some turn back to where they set out, and some stay wheeling about, such movements appeared to me in that sparkling throng that drew together, as soon as it lighted on a certain step.

And the one that stopped nearest us became so bright that I said in my mind: 'I see well the love thou signallest to me.' But she on whom I wait to know how and when to speak and when to be silent keeps still, so that I do well, against my desire, to ask no question. She, therefore, who saw my silence in seeing Him who sees all said to me: 'Satisfy thy eager desire.' And I began: 'My merit does not make me worthy of thy answer, but for her sake who gives me leave to ask, blest living soul that remainest hid within thy happiness, let me know the cause that has brought thee so near me; and say why in this wheel the sweet symphony of Paradise is silent which through the others below sounds so devoutly.'

'Thy hearing is mortal even as thy sight,' he answered me 'therefore there is no singing here for the same reason that Beatrice has no smile. I have come down the steps of the sacred stairway so far only to give thee welcome with speech and with the light that mantles me; nor was it greater love that

305

nè più amor mi fece esser più presta;
   chè più e tanto amor quinci su ferve,
   sì come il fiammeggiar ti manifesta.
Ma l'alta carità, che ci fa serve   70
   pronte al consiglio che 'l mondo governa,
   sorteggia qui sì come tu osserve.'
'Io veggio ben,' diss' io 'sacra lucerna,
   come libero amore in questa corte
   basta a seguir la provedenza etterna;
ma questo è quel ch'a cerner mi par forte,
   perchè predestinata fosti sola
   a questo officio tra le tue consorte.'
Nè venni prima all' ultima parola,
   che del suo mezzo fece il lume centro,   80
   girando sè come veloce mola;
poi rispuose l'amor che v'era dentro:
   'Luce divina sopra me s'appunta,
   penetrando per questa in ch' io m' inventro,
la cui virtù, col mio veder congiunta,
   mi leva sopra me tanto, ch' i' veggio
   la somma essenza della quale è munta.
Quinci vien l'allegrezza ond' io fiammeggio;
   perch'alla vista mia quant'ella è chiara
   la chiarità della fiamma pareggio.   90
Ma quell'alma nel ciel che più si schiara,
   quel serafin che 'n Dio più l'occhio ha fisso,
   alla dimanda tua non satisfara;
però che sì s' innoltra nello abisso
   dell'etterno statuto quel che chiedi,
   che da ogni creata vista è scisso.
E al mondo mortal, quando tu riedi,
   questo rapporta, sì che non presumma
   a tanto segno più mover li piedi.
La mente, che qui luce, in terra fumma;   100
   onde riguarda come può là giùe
   quel che non pote perchè 'l ciel l'assumma.'
Sì mi prescrisser le parole sue,
   ch' io lasciai la quistione, e mi ritrassi
   a dimandarla umilmente chi fue.

made me swifter, for love as much and more burns up there, as the flaming shows thee, but the deep charity which makes us prompt in service of the Counsel that rules the world allots here as thou perceivest.'

'I see indeed, holy lamp,' I said 'how free love serves in this court for fulfilment of the Eternal Providence; but this I find it hard to understand, why thou alone among thy fellows wast predestined to this charge.'

And I had not reached the last word when the light made of its middle a centre and spun round like a rapid millstone. Then the love that was within it replied: 'A divine light is focused upon me, piercing through this in which I am embosomed, whose virtue, joined with my own vision, raises me so far above myself that I see the Supreme Essence from which it is drawn. From this comes the gladness with which I am aflame; for to my sight, in the measure of its clearness, I match the clearness of my flame.[4] But that soul in heaven that is most illumined, that seraph whose eye is most fixed on God, will not satisfy thy question; for what thou askest is so far removed in the abyss of the Eternal Ordinance that it is cut off from every created vision. And to the mortal world, when thou returnest, bear this report, so that it may no more presume to set its steps to such a goal. The mind, which shines here, on earth smokes; consider then how it could do down there what it cannot though heaven raise it to itself.'

His words so restrained me that I gave up the question and checked myself, only asking him humbly who he was.

'Tra' due liti d'Italia surgon sassi,
   e non molto distanti alla tua patria,
   tanto, che' troni assai suonan più bassi,
e fanno un gibbo che si chiama Catria,
   di sotto al quale è consecrato un ermo,   110
   che suole esser disposto a sola latria.'
Così ricominciommi il terzo sermo;
   e poi, continüando, disse: 'Quivi
   al servigio di Dio mi fe' sì fermo,
che pur con cibi di liquor d'ulivi
   lievemente passava caldi e geli,
   contento ne' pensier contemplativi.
Render solea quel chiostro a questi cieli
   fertilemente; e ora è fatto vano,
   sì che tosto convien che si riveli.   120
In quel loco fu' io Pietro Damiano,
   e Pietro Peccator fu' nella casa
   di Nostra Donna in sul lito adriano.
Poca vita mortal m'era rimasa,
   quando fui chiesto e tratto a quel cappello
   che pur di male in peggio si travasa.
Venne Cefàs e venne il gran vasello
   dello Spirito Santo, magri e scalzi,
   prendendo il cibo da qualunque ostello.
Or voglion quinci e quindi chi i rincalzi   130
   li moderni pastori e chi li meni,
   tanto son gravi! e chi di retro li alzi.
Cuopron de' manti loro i palafreni,
   sì che due bestie van sott'una pelle:
   oh pazïenza che tanto sostieni!'
A questa voce vid' io più fiammelle
   di grado in grado scendere e girarsi,
   e ogni giro le facea più belle.
Dintorno a questa vennero e fermarsi,
   e fero un grido di sì alto suono,   140
   che non potrebbe qui assomigliarsi:
nè io lo 'ntesi; sì mi vinse il tuono.

'Between the two shores of Italy and not far
distant from thy native place rise crags so high
that the thunder sounds far below them; and
they make a ridge that is called Catria, beneath
which is consecrated a hermitage which once was
wholly given to worship.' Thus he began again,
addressing me the third time; then continued:
'There I became so constant in God's service that
with food seasoned only with olive-juice I passed
easily through heats and frosts, content in contem-
plative thoughts.[5] That cloister used to yield
abundant harvest to these heavens, and now it is
become barren so that it must soon be exposed.
In that place I was Peter Damian, and I was Peter
the Sinner in the House of Our Lady on the
Adriatic shore. Little of mortal life remained to me
when I was sought out and dragged to that hat which
is passed on only from bad to worse. Cephas came,
and the great vessel of the Holy Ghost came,
lean and barefoot, taking their food at any inn.[6]
Now the modern shepherds want one on this side
and one on that to prop them up and one to lead
them—so portly are they—and one behind to lift
their train. They cover their palfreys with their
cloaks, so that two beasts go under one skin.
O Patience, that endurest so much!'

At his voice I saw more little flames descend
from step to step, wheeling, and every turn made
them more beautiful. They came about him and
stopped and raised a cry of such volume that nothing
here could be likened to it; nor did I understand
it, its thunder so overcame me.

1. Semele, Princess of Thebes, loved by Jupiter, persuaded him to appear to her in his undisguised godhead and was consumed in his splendour.

2. Saturn, then in conjunction with Leo.

3. Saturn, the father of Jupiter and mythical King of Crete, whose reign was the Golden Age; cp. *Inf.* xiv.

4. 'As long as the feast of Paradise shall last, so long our love shall radiate this vesture about us', etc. (*Par.* xiv).

5. St Peter Damian, a famous Benedictine monk of the 11th century who became Abbot of his monastery in the Apennines, then Bishop and Cardinal—'that hat'; he often signed himself 'Peter the Sinner'.

6. Sts Peter and Paul. 'Go your ways. . . . Carry neither purse, nor scrip, nor shoes. . . . And in the same house remain, eating and drinking such things as they give' (*Luke* x. 3, 4, 7).

NOTE

The sphere of Saturn, the farthest and coldest of the planets in Dante's astronomy, is the sphere of temperance, the fourth of the cardinal virtues, conceived by medieval Christendom as ascetic abstraction from material things and absorption in the things of the spirit. It is well defined by Sir Herbert Grierson as 'the impassioned vision of the worth of things.' The souls in Saturn are the great contemplatives, and we have seen, especially in some of the later cantos of the *Purgatorio*—the dream of Leah and Rachel and the relations of Matilda and Beatrice in the Earthly Paradise—, that the medieval Church regarded the life of contemplation as essentially a higher life, in closer relation with the ultimate truth of things, than the life of action. Beatrice and Dante have 'risen' from Jupiter to Saturn. In contemplation —so it was conceived—the soul passes from active endeavour to spiritual attainment, a nearer approach to the ultimate vision.

Here 'Dante encounters an atmosphere of monastic discipline' (*C. H. Grandgent*). He hesitates, more than elsewhere, to break the silence with his questions. 'Silence, ecstasy, sublime absorption in God,—these are the fundamental motives that inform the vision of the seventh heaven' (*F. P. Luiso, L.D.*). Dante has nothing to say of the ascent from Jupiter, his eyes and mind are set on Beatrice, he is 'withdrawn from every other thought', and it is from her he learns that they 'have risen to the seventh splendour'. If she had smiled or the souls had sung there, the smile or the song would have expressed the truth of God as God is known to these contemplatives, and that is still beyond his capacity. The most that is yet given to him is to mirror in his eyes the stairway crowded with the souls from the Empyrean, the stair itself a mirror of the life that is beyond his sight; 'for now we see in a mirror, darkly, but then face to face'. With the habitual consistency of Dante's imagery, Damian's words about the illumination of the souls of the redeemed—'A divine light is focused upon me', etc.,—are a kind of summary and forecast of Dante's own experience as it is recorded in the last canto of the *Comedy*; there as here the imagery is chiefly of light.

The account of the singing of the souls in the successive planetary spheres is another example of Dante's consistent inventiveness. In the four lower spheres, of the Moon, Mercury, Venus and the Sun, the subjects of the songs are named and the singing in each is described with ever fuller expressions of his delight in it. Then, in the heaven of Mars, 'a melody gathered through the cross which held me rapt, though I did not follow the hymn', and 'there came to me "Arise" and "Conquer"', as one hears without understanding'. In the heaven of Jupiter, which is full of music, he heard 'songs such as he knows who rejoices there above, . . . songs that slip and fall from my memory', and of their words nothing remained with him. And here, in the last planetary sphere, there is silence, as of 'melodies unheard' by mortal ears. 'Here is no festival, no pageant, only an ascent and descent, a silent, luminous breathing of the spirits in God' (*K. Vossler*).

This planet of divine contemplation, like the planet of love (*Par.* viii), takes from the pagan divinity merely *il vocabol*; it bears the mere name of the world's famous chief under whom all wickedness lay dead. The passage recalls the language of Matilda in the Earthly Paradise (*Purg.* xxviii): 'Those who in old times sang of the age of gold and of its happy state perhaps dreamed on Parnassus of this place.' This golden ladder, 'which rose to such a height that my sight did not follow it', is beyond the reach of all the ancient poets' dreams.

Like the Cross in Mars and the Eagle in Jupiter, the stairway in Saturn was an image very familiar to Dante's first readers, conveying its sense without explanation. 'In these three emblems—Cross, Eagle, Ladder,—is summed up all that the Middle Ages held dearest' (*C. H. Grandgent*). They meant, respectively, human redemption, earthly order, and spiritual vision. Jacob's dream—'Behold a ladder set up on the earth, and the top of it reached to heaven, and behold the angels of God ascending and descending on it' (*Gen.* xxviii. 12)—was widely used by preachers, with much play of devout fancy, as a picture of the monastic life, in which the contemplatives 'climb by contemplation up to God Himself and descend by compassion among men' (*St Bernard, quoted by E. G. Gardner*); and in line with that is the probable explanation of the elaborate comparison of the souls there with 'the daws at daybreak'. ' "Some stay wheeling about", and are those that never cease from contemplation nor ever leave the hermitage or monastery for any cause. "Some turn back to where they set out", and are those moved with charitable zeal who return to the active life among men to sow by word and good example the seeds of virtue, and then turn back to where they set out, that is, to contemplative solitude. "Some fly off not to return", being those who by fervent zeal for their neighbour are kept far from the hermitage, unwearied labourers in the Lord's vineyard' (*F. P. Luiso, L.D.*). Gardner notes that the mystics spoke of contemplation as 'the science of love'.

St Peter Damian was one of those who turned back to where they set out. Born in a poor family of Ravenna, he became a monk and Abbot of his monastery and was widely known for his learning, his religious devotion, and his ascetic severities. His name and story would be cherished and familiar in Ravenna where, probably, Dante wrote these cantos. On the Pope's insistence he became Bishop and Cardinal, but after eight years of this publicity he returned to his mountain cloister, where his last years were spent. 'He constituted himself a kind of universal censor; popes, prelates, clergy, monks, all fell under the lash of his tongue', and 'one main reason for Dante's choice of Peter Damian as the soul who could come nearest him upon the ladder was their common indignation against prelates whose unbridled avarice and luxury were the ruin of the Church' (*J. S. Carroll*). 'The passions of the great monks of earlier centuries were reflected intensely in the spirit of Dante. There was the same ardour of strife, the same violence of language, the same craving to hold the infinite in his own breast. More than all else the long hospitality of the Benedictine monasteries had made him feel the harmony of his soul with the soul and the destiny of Peter Damian' (*U. Cosmo*). According to an old and likely tradition Dante lodged for a time in

Damian's old monastery on the high slopes of Monte Catria, where he would have ready access to the writings of the saint. There is, at any rate, a clear echo of some of them in the outburst put into his lips here against the clerical dignitaries of this later time. Of the picture, at the end of the canto, of the modern shepherds on their palfreys, an early commentator says simply: 'Everyone has seen it.'

In the sphere of justice below Dante has been told of the mystery of the predestination of the soul to Paradise; here, in the sphere of contemplation, he asks about the soul's predestination *in* Paradise. Why was Damian chosen to speak to him? He has come down, Damian says, simply to make Dante welcome, moved by 'the deep charity'—it is the more general word, more inclusive than 'love', that he uses—which makes them all willing servants of the Divine Counsel; and Dante accepts and confirms the idea that it is this 'free love', the immediate, intuitive, unconstrained response to grace, that qualifies the redeemed soul to know and to fulfil its predestination in the divine purpose. Why is Damian, alone among his fellows, predestined to this charge? Dante has asked. But that is to ask why Damian is Damian, the man for his task, why a soul is itself and not another, a separate creation of God with its own function. The whole passage accumulates expressions for the same conception—'the Counsel that rules the world', 'the eternal Providence', 'the eternal Ordinance'—and the Poet, even here among the contemplatives in Paradise, will not try to go behind it. In the twentieth canto the Eagle of justice exclaimed: 'O predestination, how far removed is thy root from their gaze who see not the First Cause whole!' Here, Dante has asked about Damian's predestination to his function, and 'he is not told; he cannot be. But if the poetry cannot do that it can make the helpless answer an answer of such a kind that the helplessness opens into the depth of that Whole. The lines do what so much theology does not do; they cause us almost to experience the reason that we cannot know' (*C. Williams*).

Saturn, the cold star, was, as Dante then saw it and as in fact it was in the spring of 1300, 'beneath the breast of the burning Lion', and its beams mingled with the Lion's force. Purged of earthly passions, these heavenly visionaries, so far from passionless, are aflame with a devotion to God and to His purposes which turns to wrath at the evils that shame His Church, and their cry as they crowd round Damian, still on the ladder of contemplation, resounds in the silence of their sphere.

Oppresso di stupore, alla mia guida
   mi volsi, come parvol che ricorre
   sempre colà dove più si confida;
e quella, come madre che soccorre
   subito al figlio palido e anelo
   con la sua voce, che 'l suol ben disporre,
mi disse: 'Non sai tu che tu se' in cielo?
   e non sai tu che 'l cielo è tutto santo,
   e ciò che ci si fa vien da buon zelo?
Come t'avrebbe trasmutato il canto,   10
   e io ridendo, mo pensar lo puoi,
   poscia che 'l grido t' ha mosso cotanto;
nel qual, se 'nteso avessi i prieghi suoi,
   già ti sarebbe nota la vendetta
   che tu vedrai innanzi che tu muoi.
La spada di qua su non taglia in fretta
   nè tardo, ma' ch'al parer di colui
   che disïando o temendo l'aspetta.
Ma rivolgiti omai inverso altrui;
   ch'assai illustri spiriti vedrai,   20
   se com' io dico l'aspetto redui.'
Come a lei piacque, li occhi ritornai,
   e vidi cento sperule che 'nseme
   più s'abbellivan con mutüi rai.
Io stava come quei che 'n sè repreme
   la punta del disio, e non s'attenta
   di domandar, sì del troppo si teme;

CANTO XXII

*St Benedict; the degeneracy of the Benedictines;
the ascent to the Starry Sphere; the sight of the
earth*

OVERWHELMED with amazement, I turned to my
guide, like a child that runs back always to the
place where it has most confidence; and she,
like a mother who quickly comforts her pale and
breathless boy with the voice that has often re-
assured him, said to me: 'Knowest thou not thou
art in heaven? Knowest thou not that heaven is
all holy and that whatever is done here comes of
righteous zeal? How the song, and I by smiling,
would have confounded thee thou canst now con-
ceive since this cry has so much moved thee;
and in it, if thou hadst understood their prayers,
the vengeance would have been known to thee
already which thou shalt see before thy death.
The sword here above does not strike in haste
or tardily, except as it seems to him that awaits
it with desire or with fear. But turn now to the
others, for thou shalt see many illustrious spirits
if thou direct thy sight as I say.'

I turned my eyes as she bade and I saw a hundred
little spheres which beautified each other with
their mutual beams. I stood as one who restrains
in himself the prick of desire and for fear of pre-
sumption dare not ask a question; and the largest

e la maggiore e la più luculenta
  di quelle margherite innanzi fessi,
  per far di sè la mia voglia contenta.   30
Poi dentro a lei udi': 'Se tu vedessi
  com' io la carità che tra noi arde,
  li tuoi concetti sarebbero espressi.
Ma perchè tu, aspettando, non tarde
  all'alto fine, io ti farò risposta
  pur al pensier da che sì ti riguarde.
Quel monte a cui Cassino è nella costa
  fu frequentato già in su la cima
  dalla gente ingannata e mal disposta;
e quel son io che su vi portai prima   40
  lo nome di colui che 'n terra addusse
  la verità che tanto ci sublima;
e tanta grazia sopra me relusse,
  ch' io ritrassi le ville circunstanti
  dall'empio colto che 'l mondo sedusse.
Questi altri fuochi tutti contemplanti
  uomini fuoro, accesi di quel caldo
  che fa nascere i fiori e' frutti santi.
Qui è Maccario, qui è Romoaldo,
  qui son li frati miei che dentro ai chiostri   50
  fermar li piedi e tennero il cor saldo.'
E io a lui: 'L'affetto che dimostri
  meco parlando, e la buona sembianza
  ch' io veggio e noto in tutti li ardor vostri,
così m' ha dilatata mia fidanza,
  come 'l sol fa la rosa quando aperta
  tanto divien quant'ell' ha di possanza.
Però ti priego, e tu, padre, m'accerta
  s' io posso prender tanta grazia, ch' io
  ti veggia con imagine scoverta.'   60
Ond'elli: 'Frate, il tuo alto disio
  s'adempierà in su l'ultima spera,
  ove s'adempion tutti li altri e 'l mio.
Ivi è perfetta, matura ed intera
  ciascuna disïanza; in quella sola
  è ogni parte là ove sempr'era,

and most lustrous of these pearls came forward
to satisfy my desire regarding itself. Then within
it I heard: 'If thou sawest as I do the charity that
burns among us thou wouldst have uttered thy
thoughts; but lest thou be delayed in thy lofty
aim by waiting I shall answer the thought itself
about which thou art so guarded.

'That mountain on whose slope Cassino lies
was once frequented on its summit by the deluded
and perverse people, and it was I who first carried
up there His name who brought to earth the truth
that so exalts us; and such grace shone down on
me that I drew away the neighbouring towns from
the impious worship that led the world astray.[1]
These other fires were all men of contemplation,
kindled by that heat which brings holy flowers
and fruits to birth. Here is Macarius; here is
Romualdus;[2] here are my brothers who stayed
their feet within the cloisters and kept steadfast
hearts.'

And I said to him: 'The affection thou showest
in talking with me and the marks of kindness which
I see and note in all your fires have expanded my
confidence as the sun does the rose when it opens
to its fullest bloom; therefore I pray thee—and tell
me, father, if I may gain so great a favour—that
I may see thee with thy face unveiled.'

And he: 'Brother, thy high desire shall be fulfilled
above in the last sphere, where is fulfilment of all
the others, and my own.[3] There all we long for is
perfect, ripe and whole. In it alone each part is

perchè non è in loco, e non s' impola;
 e nostra scala infino ad essa varca,
 onde così dal viso ti s' invola.
Infin là su la vide il patrïarca   70
 Iacob porgere la superna parte,
 quando li apparve d'angeli sì carca.
Ma, per salirla, mo nessun diparte
 da terra i piedi, e la regola mia
 rimasa è per danno delle carte.
Le mura che solìeno esser badia
 fatte sono spelonche, e le cocolle
 sacca son piene di farina ria.
Ma grave usura tanto non si tolle
 contra 'l piacer di Dio, quanto quel frutto 80
 che fa il cor de' monaci sì folle;
chè quantunque la Chiesa guarda, tutto
 è della gente che per Dio dimanda;
 non di parenti nè d'altro più brutto.
La carne de' mortali è tanto blanda,
 che giù non basta buon cominciamento
 dal nascer della quercia al far la ghianda.
Pier cominciò sanz'oro e sanz'argento,
 e io con orazione e con digiuno,
 e Francesco umilmente il suo convento. 90
E se guardi il principio di ciascuno,
 poscia riguardi là dov' è trascorso,
 tu vederai del bianco fatto bruno.
Veramente Iordan volto retrorso
 più fu, e 'l mar fuggir, quando Dio volse,
 mirabile a veder che qui 'l soccorso.'
Così mi disse, e indi si raccolse
 al suo collegio, e 'l collegio si strinse;
 poi, come turbo, in su tutto s'avvolse.
La dolce donna dietro a lor mi pinse 100
 con un sol cenno su per quella scala,
 sì sua virtù la mia natura vinse;
nè mai qua giù dove si monta e cala
 naturalmente, fu sì ratto moto,
 ch'agguagliar si potesse alla mia ala.

where it always was, for it is not in space and does not turn on poles; and our ladder goes up to it and therefore steals thus from thy sight. The patriarch Jacob saw the top of it reach that height, when it appeared to him so laden with angels. But now none lifts his foot from the earth to climb it, and my Rule is left to waste the paper; the walls that were once an abbey have become dens and the cowls are sacks full of rotten meal. But heavy usury is not exacted so contrary to God's pleasure as is that fruit which so turns the hearts of the monks to folly; for all that is in the Church's keeping is for them that ask in God's name, not for kinsfolk or others more vile.[4] So soft is mortal flesh that a good beginning below does not last from the springing of the oak to the bearing of the acorn. Peter began his fellowship without gold or silver,[5] and I mine with prayer and fasting, and Francis his with humility; and if thou look at the starting-point of each, then look again whither it has strayed, thou shalt see it become dark from white. Nevertheless, Jordan driven back and the sea that fled at God's will[6] were sights more marvellous than succour here.'

He spoke thus to me, and drew back to his company, and the company pressed close together; then, like a whirlwind, all were swept above. The sweet Lady, with only a sign, impelled me after them up that stairway, so did her power overcome my nature; and never here below, where we mount and descend by natural law, was motion so swift as might match my flight. So may I sometime

S' io torni mai, lettore, a quel divoto
   triunfo per lo quale io piango spesso
   le mie peccata e 'l petto mi percuoto,
tu non avresti in tanto tratto e messo
   nel foco il dito, in quant' io vidi 'l segno   110
   che segue il Tauro e fui dentro da esso.
O glorïose stelle, o lume pregno
   di gran virtù, dal quale io riconosco
   tutto, qual che si sia, il mio ingegno,
con voi nasceva e s'ascondeva vosco
   quelli ch'è padre d'ogni mortal vita,
   quand' io senti' di prima l'aere tosco;
e poi, quando mi fu grazia largita
   d'entrar nell'alta rota che vi gira,
   la vostra regïon mi fu sortita.   120
A voi divotamente ora sospira
   l'anima mia, per acquistar virtute
   al passo forte che a sè la tira.
'Tu se' sì presso all' ultima salute'
   cominciò Beatrice, 'che tu dei
   aver le luci tue chiare ed acute;
e però, prima che tu più t' inlei,
   rimira in giù, e vedi quanto mondo
   sotto li piedi già esser ti fei;
sì che 'l tuo cor, quantunque può, giocondo   130
   s'appresenti alla turba triunfante
   che lieta vien per questo etera tondo.'
Col viso ritornai per tutte quante
   le sette spere, e vidi questo globo
   tal, ch' io sorrisi del suo vil sembiante;
e quel consiglio per migliore approbo
   che l' ha per meno; e chi ad altro pensa
   chiamar si puote veramente probo.
Vidi la figlia di Latona incensa
   sanza quell'ombra che mi fu cagione   140
   per che già la credetti rara e densa.
L'aspetto del tuo nato, Iperïone,
   quivi sostenni, e vidi com si move
   circa e vicino a lui, Maia e Dïone.

return, reader, to that devout triumph for which
I often bewail my sins and beat my breast, thou
hadst not drawn out and thrust in thy finger in
the fire[7] before I saw the sign that follows the Bull
and was within it.[8]

O glorious stars, O light pregnant with mighty
power from which I acknowledge all my genius,
whatever it be, with you was born and with you
hidden he that is the father of each mortal life when
I first tasted the Tuscan air; and after, when grace
was granted me to enter into the high wheel that
bears you round, your region was assigned to me.
To you my soul now sighs devoutly that it may
gain strength for the hard task that draws it to
itself.

'Thou art so near to the final blessedness'
Beatrice began 'that thou must have thine eyes
clear and keen; and therefore, before thou go
farther into it, look down and see how much of the
universe I have already put beneath thy feet, so
that with all fulness of joy thy heart may present
itself to the triumphal host that comes rejoicing
through this rounded ether.'

With my sight I returned through every one of
the seven spheres, and I saw this globe such that
I smiled at its paltry semblance; and that judgement
which holds it for least I approve as best, and he
whose thought is on other things may rightly be
called just. I saw Latona's daughter glowing,
without that shadow for which I once believed her
to be rare and dense;[9] thy son's aspect, Hyperion,
I endured there, and I saw how Maia and Dione
move in their circles near him;[10] from thence

323

Quindi m'apparve il temperar di Giove
   tra 'l padre e 'l figlio; e quindi mi fu chiaro
   il varïar che fanno di lor dove.
E tutti e sette mi si dimostraro
   quanto son grandi, e quanto son veloci,
   e come sono in distante riparo.   150
L'aiuola che ci fa tanto feroci,
   volgendom' io con li etterni Gemelli,
   tutta m'apparve da' colli alle foci.
Poscia rivolsi li occhi alli occhi belli.

appeared to me the tempering of Jove between his
father and his son,[11] and from thence the changes
were clear to me which they make in their positions;
and all seven showed me what is their magnitude
and what their speed and at what distances their
stations. The little threshing-floor that makes us
so fierce all appeared to me from hills to river-
mouths, while I was wheeling with the eternal
Twins. Then to the fair eyes I turned my eyes again.

1. St Benedict, founder of western monasticism in the 6th century, built the monastery of Monte Cassino, between Rome and Naples, on the site of an ancient temple of Apollo.

2. St Macarius of Alexandria (4th century), the chief promoter of eastern monasticism. St Romualdus (11th century), founder of the reformed Benedictines, the Camaldoli.

3. The Empyrean, beyond time and space.

4. 'The fruit', the Church's revenues, belongs to the poor, not to the relatives or the concubines of the clergy.

5. 'Peter said, Silver and gold have I none' (*Acts* iii. 6).

6. The miracles by which the children of Israel crossed the Red Sea and the Jordan. 'The sea saw it and fled; Jordan was driven back' (*Ps.* cxiv. 3).

7. 'Drawn out and thrust in'; the order reversed to give the impression of instantaneous action.

8. In the Starry Heaven the Bull is followed by the Twins, with which the Sun was in conjunction at Dante's birth, between 21st May and 21st June. The influence of the Twins favoured intellect and learning.

9. Latona's daughter by Jupiter is Diana, the Moon. Dante now sees the Moon's further side, supposed to be free from spots (*Par.* ii).

10. The Titan Hyperion was the father of Helios, the Sun. Maia and Dione were the mothers, respectively, of Mercury and Venus by Jupiter.

11. Jupiter's father was Saturn and his son Mars; he 'tempers' the cold of his father with the heat of his son (*Par.* xviii).

NOTE

The great cry of the contemplatives breaking the silence of
Saturn startles Dante and he turns back from the horror of the
Church's corruptions and the rage which they provoke in the
saints to his refuge in Beatrice. From her he learns that he knows
little of the life of contemplation, with its deeper sense of the
mind of God, if he supposes it to detach the soul's interest
from the present life of the Church on earth, and that 'righteous
zeal' is itself a mark of true spiritual contemplation. It was a
lesson very congenial to Dante.

It is the corruptions, not of the world at large, but of the
Church in its shepherds, that peculiarly enrage the saints.
'While in the *Inferno* and the *Purgatorio* the interest is turned
on men in general, in the *Paradiso* the moral digressions, the
invectives, those unexpected glances of wrath cast from the
heavens on the distant earth, are directed on ecclesiastics of
every class, at the men of the Church who ought to be a pathway
between earth and heaven. . . . The first person with whom
Dante talks in Paradise is a nun; the first moral question on
which he digresses concerns the vow of chastity; the last
political invective is against the pontiffs; Beatrice's last digression
is against wicked preachers and traffickers in indulgences; the
question of monasticism is dealt with many times' (*M. Bon-
tempelli, L.D.*).

Once more, as when he shrank from addressing Damian,
Dante is hushed by the spirit of the sphere, and, 'for fear of
presumption' he 'dare not ask a question'. A part of the Rule
of St Benedict reads: 'The ninth degree of humility is that a
monk restrain his tongue from speaking, and, keeping silence,
do not speak until he is spoken to' (*quoted by Carroll*), and
Dante, as if by instinct, keeps that rule here. On the threshold
of the highest heavens he is himself schooled in contemplation.

It was proper that St Benedict, the father of monasticism in the Western Church, should be described as 'the largest and most lustrous of these pearls', and that the soft radiance of the pearl should be the image chosen for the special quality of contemplative holiness. After St Benedict, Sts Macarius and Romualdus are representative, respectively, of eastern and western monasticism, the latter, like St Damian, a native of Ravenna.

Benedict's reference to the final blessedness in the Empyrean —which 'is not in space and does not turn on poles', where there is no past or future and all time is present, where desire is one with fulfilment—and his words about 'our ladder', identifying it with the ladder of Jacob's dream whose top 'reached to heaven', are Dante's way of declaring that the true monastic life has nothing beyond it but that final blessedness of which it is a continual foretaste. It is in that context and in relation to that life of aspiration that St Benedict pronounces judgement on the monastic corruptions of the time,—*corruptio optimi pessima*. And yet he ends with 'Nevertheless' and the hope of a miracle of deliverance.

In immediate response to Dante's naming of him 'father', Benedict calls Dante 'brother', ranking him by anticipation of their company; and now, at a sign from Beatrice, he is swept up in a moment of rapture after the saints of that heaven— literally, she '*thrust* me up that stairway'—and, for the higher visions, he becomes himself a contemplative.

He finds himself in the sphere of the Fixed Stars, and in that part of it which is, so to speak, native to him, the constellation of the Twins under which he was born and which, in the astrology of the time, has an influence favourable to intellectual and literary power. Its 'glorious stars'—that is to say, the Cherubim, the spirits of knowledge who control and operate the Starry Sphere—have made Dante, in the way of providence, the man he was and is, Dante Alighieri of Florence, where he 'first tasted the Tuscan air'; and now, as he enters this 'high wheel', their region is allotted to him, and in them he seeks his fitness for his present task, to see and tell of the last heavens. No man could be more conscious than Dante that he was himself and not another, and it is his consistent teaching that the soul loses nothing of its distinctive identity in salvation, but gains and perfects it. His part was to 'follow his star', as he was bidden by his old Florentine master, Brunetto Latino (*Inf.* xv), to be himself as God has made him and can make him. The influence of 'the eternal Twins' belongs to God's providence for him, and by the grace given him he is brought more effectually under the seal of the divine purpose, God's peculiar stamp on his soul when He called him by his name. Still, at this height above the world, Dante's imagination works in the concrete of personality and experience.

And to know the height to which he has risen, to have his eyes clear and keen for heavenly and earthly things in their true relations, he must know the depth from which he has come, and, looking down through the seven planetary spheres, he sees 'this globe' in 'its paltry semblance' and takes the measure, 'from hills to river-mouths', of 'the little threshing-floor that makes us so fierce'. Besides the visions, in some respects similar to this, of Cicero and Boethius, Dante may well have had in mind the language of St Benedict, quoted by Gardner: 'All creatures are, as it were, nothing to that soul which beholdeth the Creator; for though it see but a glimpse of that light which is in the Creator, yet very small do all things seem that be created; for by means of that supernatural light the capacity of the inward soul is enlarged and is in God so extended that it is far above the world.'

From that height Dante sees all the planets moving in their spheres as members of one great providential system, with their interrelations oddly indicated by their mythological consanguinities, encompassing with their heavenly influences the world that is unworthy of them.

Then Dante turns his eyes on hers where he finds the demonstration of all the truth and worth of things.

PARADISO

Come l'augello, intra l'amate fronde,
    posato al nido de' suoi dolci nati
    la notte che le cose ci nasconde,
che, per veder li aspetti disïati
    e per trovar lo cibo onde li pasca,
    in che gravi labor li sono aggrati,
previene il tempo in su aperta frasca,
    e con ardente affetto il sole aspetta,
    fiso guardando pur che l'alba nasca;
così la donna mia stava eretta   10
    e attenta, rivolta inver la plaga
    sotto la quale il sol mostra men fretta:
sì che, veggendola io sospesa e vaga,
    fecimi qual è quei che disïando
    altro vorrìa, e sperando s'appaga.
Ma poco fu tra uno e altro quando,
    del mio attender, dico, e del vedere
    lo ciel venir più e più rischiarando.
E Beatrice disse: 'Ecco le schiere
    del triunfo di Cristo e tutto il frutto   20
    ricolto del girar di queste spere!'
Parìemi che 'l suo viso ardesse tutto,
    e li occhi avea di letizia sì pieni,
    che passar men convien sanza costrutto.
Quale ne' plenilunii sereni
    Trivïa ride tra le ninfe etterne
    che dipingon lo ciel per tutti i seni,

CANTO XXIII

*The Church Triumphant; Christ, Mary and
Gabriel; their ascent*

As the bird among the loved branches, having
sat on the nest of her sweet brood through the night
that hides things from us, anticipates the time on
the open spray that she may see their longed-for
looks and find the food to nourish them for which
her heavy toils are welcome to her, and with ardent
longing awaits the sun, watching with fixed gaze
for the dawn to break; so my Lady stood erect
and intent, turned towards the part beneath which
the sun shows less haste.[1] I, therefore, seeing her
in suspense and longing, became as one that is
moved with desire and satisfied with hope. But the
time was short between the one moment and the
next, my expectancy, I mean, and my seeing the
sky turn more and more resplendent; and Beatrice
said: 'Lo the hosts of Christ's triumph and all the
fruit garnered from the wheeling of these spheres!'[2]
It seemed to me that her face was all aflame, and
her eyes were so full of gladness that I must pass
on without words for it. As in clear nights of full
moon Trivia[3] smiles among the eternal nymphs
that deck the sky through all its depths, I saw,

vidi sopra migliaia di lucerne
   un sol che tutte quante l'accendea,
   come fa il nostro le viste superne;   30
e per la viva luce trasparea
   la lucente sustanza tanto chiara
   nel viso mio, che non la sostenea.
Oh Beatrice dolce guida e cara!
   Ella mi disse: 'Quel che ti sobranza
   è virtù da cui nulla si ripara.
Quivi è la sapïenza e la possanza
   ch'aprì le strade tra 'l cielo e la terra,
   onde fu già sì lunga disïanza.'
Come foco di nube si diserra   40
   per dilatarsi sì che non vi cape,
   e fuor di sua natura in giù s'atterra,
la mente mia così, tra quelle dape
   fatta più grande, di sè stessa usciò,
   e che si fesse rimembrar non sape.
'Apri li occhi e riguarda qual son io:
   tu hai vedute cose, che possente
   se' fatto a sostener lo riso mio.'
Io era come quei che si risente
   di visïone oblita e che s'ingegna   50
   indarno di ridurlasi alla mente,
quand' io udì' questa proferta, degna
   di tanto grato, che mai non si stingue
   del libro che 'l preterito rassegna.
Se mo sonasser tutte quelle lingue
   che Polimnìa con le suore fero
   del latte lor dolcissimo più pingue,
per aiutarmi, al millesmo del vero
   non si verrìa, cantando il santo riso
   e quanto il santo aspetto facea mero;   60
e così, figurando il paradiso,
   convien saltar lo sacrato poema,
   come chi trova suo cammin riciso.
Ma chi pensasse il ponderoso tema
   e l'omero mortal che se ne carca,
   nol biasmerebbe se sott'esso trema:

above thousands of lamps, a Sun which kindled each one of them as ours does the sights we see above, and through the living light the shining substance[4] showed so bright in my eyes that they could not bear it.

O Beatrice, sweet guide and dear! She said to me: 'That which overcomes thee is power from which there is no defence. Here is the wisdom and the might[5] that opened the ways between heaven and earth and for which of old there was such long desire.'

As fire breaks from a cloud, swelling till it has not room there, and against its nature falls to the earth,[6] so my mind, grown greater at that feast, was transported from itself and of what it became has no remembrance.

'Open thine eyes and look at me as I am; thou hast seen such things that thou hast gained strength to bear my smile.' I was like one that wakes from a forgotten dream and strives in vain to bring it again to mind when I heard this invitation, worthy of such gratitude that it can never be blotted from the book that records the past. Though all those tongues which Polyhymnia and her sisters[7] have nourished with their sweetest milk should sound now to aid me, it would not come to a thousandth part of the truth, in singing the holy smile and how it lit up the holy aspect; and so, picturing Paradise, the sacred poem must make a leap like one that finds his path cut off. But he that considers the weighty theme and the mortal shoulder that is burdened with it will not blame it if it tremble

333

non è pileggio da picciola barca
   quel che fendendo va l'ardita prora,
   nè da nocchier ch'a sè medesmo parca.
'Perchè la faccia mia sì t' innamora,   70
   che tu non ti rivolgi al bel giardino
   che sotto i raggi di Cristo s' infiora?
Quivi è la rosa in che il verbo divino
   carne si fece; quivi son li gigli
   al cui odor si prese il buon cammino.'
Così Beatrice; e io, che a' suoi consigli
   tutto era pronto, ancora mi rendei
   alla battaglia de' debili cigli.
Come a raggio di sol che puro mei
   per fratta nube già prato di fiori   80
   vider, coverti d'ombra, li occhi miei;
vid' io così più turbe di splendori,
   fulgorate di su da raggi ardenti,
   sanza veder principio di fulgori.
O benigna virtù che sì li 'mprenti,
   su t'essaltasti, per largirmi loco
   alli occhi lì che non t'eran possenti.
Il nome del bel fior ch' io sempre invoco
   e mane e sera, tutto mi ristrinse
   l'animo ad avvisar lo maggior foco.   90
E come ambo le luci mi dipinse
   il quale e il quanto della viva stella
   che là su vince, come qua giù vinse,
per entro il cielo scese una facella,
   formata in cerchio a guisa di corona,
   e cinsela e girossi intorno ad ella.
Qualunque melodia più dolce sona
   qua giù e più a sè l'anima tira,
   parrebbe nube che squarciata tona,
comparata al sonar di quella lira   100
   onde si coronava il bel zaffiro
   del quale il ciel più chiaro s' inzaffira.
'Io sono amore angelico, che giro
   l'alta letizia che spira del ventre
   che fu albergo del nostro disiro;

beneath the load. It is no passage for a little bark, this which the daring prow goes cleaving, nor for a pilot that would spare himself.

'Why does my face so enamour thee that thou dost not turn to the fair garden that flowers under the rays of Christ? There is the rose[8] in which the divine Word was made flesh. There are the lilies for whose fragrance the good way was taken.'[9] Beatrice said this; and I, who was all eager for her counsels, gave myself again to the struggle of my feeble eyelids.

As in the sun's rays streaming clear through a broken cloud my eyes, sheltered by shade, once saw a field of flowers, so I saw many hosts of splendours flashed upon from above by burning rays, without seeing the source of the brightness. O gracious Power who thus settest Thy stamp on them, Thou didst ascend so as to grant scope to the eyes there that had not strength for Thee. The name of the fair flower which I always invoke morning and evening absorbed all my mind as I gazed on the greatest of the fires;[10] and when the quality and magnitude of the living star who surpasses there above as she surpassed here below were pictured in both my eyes, there descended through the sky a torch which, circling, took the likeness of a crown that encircled her and wheeled about her.[11] Whatever melody sounds sweetest here below and most draws the soul to itself would seem thunder bursting from a cloud compared with the sound of that lyre that crowned the fair sapphire by which the sky is so brightly ensapphired.

'I am angelic love who encircle the supreme joy which breathes from the womb that was the inn

335

e girerommi, donna del ciel, mentre
   che seguirai tuo figlio, e farai dia
   più la spera suprema perchè li entre.'
Così la circulata melodia
   si sigillava, e tutti li altri lumi   110
   facean sonare lo nome di Maria.
Lo real manto di tutti i volumi
   del mondo, che più ferve e più s'avviva
   nell'alito di Dio e nei costumi,
avea sopra di noi l' interna riva
   tanto distante, che la sua parvenza,
   là dov' io era, ancor non appariva:
però non ebber li occhi miei potenza
   di seguitar la coronata fiamma
   che si levò appresso sua semenza.   120
E come fantolin che 'nver la mamma
   tende le braccia, poi che 'l latte prese,
   per l'animo che 'nfin di fuor s' infiamma;
ciascun di quei candori in su si stese
   con la sua fiamma, sì che l'alto affetto
   ch'elli avìeno a Maria mi fu palese.
Indi rimaser lì nel mio cospetto,
   '*Regina coeli*' cantando sì dolce,
   che mai da me non si partì 'l diletto.
Oh quanta è l' ubertà che si soffolce   130
   in quelle arche ricchissime che foro
   a seminar qua giù buone bobolce!
Quivi si vive e gode del tesoro
   che s'acquistò piangendo nello essilio
   di Babilon, ove si lasciò l'oro.
Quivi triunfa, sotto l'alto filio
   di Dio e di Maria, di sua vittoria,
   e con l'antico e col novo concilio,
colui che tien le chiavi di tal gloria.

of our desire, and I shall circle thee, Lady of Heaven, until thou follow thy Son and make more divine by entering it the highest sphere.' So that circling melody reached its close, and all the other lights made Mary's name resound.

The royal mantle of all the world's revolving spheres, which most burns and is most quickened in the breath of God and in His working,[12] had its inner bound so distant that it was still out of sight where I was, so that my eyes were not able to follow the crowned flame that rose after her seed. And like an infant that stretches out its arms to its mother after it has taken the milk, its impulse kindling into outward flame, each of these white radiances reached upward with its flame, so that the deep affection they had for Mary was made plain to me; then they remained there in my sight, singing *Regina coeli*[13] so sweetly that the delight has never left me. O how great is the abundance that is stored in these so rich garners that were good sowers here below![14] Here they live and rejoice in the treasure which they gained with tears in the exile of Babylon, where they spurned its gold. Here triumphs in his victory, under the exalted Son of God and of Mary and with both the old and the new assembly, he that holds the keys of such glory.[15]

1. The zenith.

2. 'The blessed who have turned to good the natural inclinations given them by the influences of the heavens' (*Casini-Barbi*).

3. An alternative name for Diana used by Virgil and other Latin poets; the Moon.

4. The glorified person of Christ.

5. 'Christ the power of God and the wisdom of God' (1 *Cor*. i. 24).

6. Lightning.

7. The Muse of sacred poetry and the other Muses.

8. In the Roman Litany Mary is called 'the Mystic Rose'.

9. The Apostles. 'We are unto God a sweet savour of Christ' (2 *Cor*. ii. 15); in the Vulgate '*Christi bonus odor*'.

10. The Virgin Mary.

11. The Archangel Gabriel.

12. The outermost of the material heavens, the Primum Mobile.

13. A hymn to the Virgin sung in Easter week: 'O Queen of Heaven, rejoice, for He whom thou wast worthy to bear rose as He said. Pray to God for us. Hallelujah.'

14. 'They are now filled with the good which they sowed on earth' (*C. H. Grandgent*). 'He that soweth to the Spirit shall of the Spirit reap life everlasting' (*Gal*. vi. 8).

15. St Peter, with the saints before and after Christ. 'I will give unto thee the keys of the kingdom of heaven' (*Matt*. xvi. 19).

NOTE

The twenty-third canto begins with the loveliest of Dante's bird-similes—like the others, both observed and imagined—representing Beatrice 'erect and intent', 'in suspense and longing', waiting, on his behalf, for the vision of the Church Triumphant. 'As the ecstatic dreamer approaches the confines of the material universe he begins to catch a glimpse of reality, of the true life of the world of spirit' (*C. H. Grandgent*).

The sphere of the Fixed Stars has two closely-related functions in the scheme of Dante's Paradise. On the one hand, it receives from above and disperses to the spheres below through the diversity of its stars the vital powers which are dispensed by its own rank of angels, the Cherubim; so that ultimately it is concerned with the varieties of human personality for the various needs and uses of society. It 'is the individuating principle of all life; from it we receive the peculiarities of our body, spirit and character, the germ and kernel of our personality' (*K. Vossler*). It has been already described by Beatrice in the second canto: 'The heaven that so many lights make fair takes its impress from the profound mind that turns it, and of that stamp becomes itself the seal; and as the soul within your dust is diffused through different members which are adapted to various faculties, so the Intelligence unfolds its bounty, multiplied through the stars, itself wheeling on its own unity.' On the other hand, 'the Starry Sphere is a traditional symbol of the Church' (*C. H. Grandgent*), and here we find the sum and spiritual unity of the saints in all their kinds and with all their individual qualities, all kindled by the one light of Christ, as, in Dante's astronomy, all the stars are kindled by the sun. It is the fulfilment of the manifold providence of God in all the revolving heavens below it, 'Christ's triumph and all the fruit garnered from the wheeling of these spheres'. In the pageantry of the twenty-ninth and thirtieth cantos of the *Purgatorio* the Church Militant is set forth in symbols which are definitely and elaborately invented and disposed,—the seven streaming lights in front, the twenty-four elders preceding and the seven following the car of the Church, which is occupied by Beatrice, and the virtues on either side of it, with Matilda in attendance. The Church Triumphant is shown with no such detailed and elaborated symbolism, but in a spectacle of splendours best reported of by earthly comparisons; and nowhere are Dante's similes more beautiful in themselves or more suggestive of things beyond themselves,—the mother-bird on the open spray waiting for the dawn, the full moon in a starry sky, the flowery meadow in sunshine seen from shade, the baby, suckled, reaching out to its mother. It is by that language of familiar and exquisite imagery that the unspeakable things of the eighth sphere are made credible and real. 'The heaven that appears to his fancy is all in his heart, from which comes a succession of images in which light, song, motion, form and feeling melt into a whole in which, by a divine miracle, the unspeakable has found the most definite expression, and an atmosphere of paradise is created which enraptures the eyes and the soul' (*G. Grabher*).

Christ appears here for a moment as the Head of the Church Triumphant, and even that momentary glimpse of the unbearable brightness of 'the shining substance' of His person—perhaps suggested by the story of the Transfiguration: 'His face did shine as the sun, and his raiment was white as the light' —enabled Dante to bear the wonder, but the lesser wonder, of Beatrice's smile. It is as if he meant that to see Christ, at all, is to gain a new capacity for all the persuasions of the truth of God.

The Church Militant centres in Beatrice, the Church Triumphant in the Virgin, 'the rose in which the divine Word was made flesh', 'the inn of our desire'; and Beatrice is here but an observer, first expectant and eager, then directing Dante's attention. For we are passing from the reflection to the light itself, from the doctrine to the realities of which the doctrine tells.

The cult of the Virgin, which was so greatly stimulated by St Francis and his followers in the thirteenth century, was really the cult of the Incarnation, and Mary, for the worshipper, the peculiar channel and embodiment of grace. Here she is described as 'the fair sapphire by which the sky is so brightly ensapphired', and the words come on the reader with something of the thrill of surprise as the sole reference in the *Paradiso* to the blue sky, a reference emphasized, in Dante's manner, by the echo of *zaffiro* in *s'inzaffira* and confirmed by the *Regina coeli* that follows. When Dante says that the sky is 'ensapphired' by the Virgin, can he mean less than that 'the sweet hue of the oriental sapphire' which he saw gather in the serene face of the heavens from the foot of Purgatory, the blue vault which he was approaching in his ascent through all the spheres of Paradise, is a prevailing effluence from Mary's presence, an image of the encompassing Grace that came to men through her? The language may have been suggested by *Ex*. xxiv. 10: 'And they saw the God of Israel; and there was under his feet as it were a paved work of a sapphire stone, and as it were the sky when it is clear'—*et quasi caelum, cum serenum est*.

It is just when he is able to bear the smile of Beatrice that Dante is bidden not to look only at her but also at the rose and the lilies in the garden, and this is only one of various incidents of the kind that occur in the course of his journey. In the Earthly Paradise, when he is absorbed in Beatrice, the evangelical virtues, by their exclamation 'Too fixed!', require him to give his mind to the earthly history of the Church and the disasters that fall on it (*Purg*. xxxii); in the sphere of Mars Beatrice says to Dante: 'Turn, listen; for not only in my eyes is Paradise', and he is directed to the heroes of the cross who have fought for the Church and the faith (*Par*. xviii); on his arrival in the sphere of Saturn he has to leave 'the pasture of his sight in that blessed aspect' and 'direct his mind elsewhere' and look at the great contemplatives on the heavenly stairway (*Par*. xxi); and there is a similar conception in the description of the approach of the pageant of revelation in the Earthly Paradise, where Dante says that Matilda 'chid him' for his absorption in the 'living lights' of the Spirit and his neglect of the actual movement of revelation 'which comes behind them' (*Purg*. xxix). This is an instance, one of many, of the insistent and significant recurrence of an idea in Dante's scheme, the idea

341

in this case that the truth of God is not truth only, but also fact, in its defeat, or its struggle, or its victory,—that the divine purpose for men is not ideal and aspiration only, but also effectual motive and attainment,—and that human life, for all its shames and through all its strivings, is directed to an actual fulfilment greater than men's thoughts and dreams. It was, indeed, a chief function of Dante, by his very grasp and exposition of scholastic thinking and by the energy and concreteness of his mind, to rescue it—rescuing himself, too—from its abstractness and to bring it to the test and proof of life, to relate it in all its meaning to that which God and man are and do. In this spiritual and moral realism which marks *The Divine Comedy* from beginning to end Dante was a true follower of the saint whom he held, among all the saints, in a peculiar reverence and affection, Francis of Assisi, and still more of the Master of them both.

In this eighth heaven we do not have the final vision of the redeemed, which is yet to come in the Empyrean, and Dante is still within the bounds of time and space and under the schooling of Beatrice, the discipline of ordered truth. It is the process and the means of redemption that are represented here, not yet its final issue,—Christ seen in a flash, His glorified human person gleaming through the glory of His soul,—Mary, the chosen instrument of the Incarnation, with Gabriel to recall the familiar scene in Nazareth,—the Apostles who first won men to Christ's way,—the ascension of Christ beyond men's sight, and then, 'after her seed', of Mary,—and the song to her of the redeemed as they reach after her with their flames. And just as Dante's purgation was completed by the challenge of Beatrice in the Earthly Paradise, so the main business of this sphere for him, told in the cantos following, is his examination by the Church's greatest representatives in the specific virtues of the Christian life.

'O SODALIZIO eletto alla gran cena
   del benedetto Agnello, il qual vi ciba
   sì, che la vostra voglia è sempre piena,
se per grazia di Dio questi preliba
   di quel che cade della vostra mensa,
   prima che morte tempo li prescriba,
ponete mente all'affezione immensa,
   e roratelo alquanto: voi bevete
   sempre del fonte onde vien quel ch'ei pensa.'
Così Beatrice; e quelle anime liete   10
   si fero spere sopra fissi poli,
   fiammando forte, a guisa di comete.
E come cerchi in tempra d'orïoli
   si giran sì, che 'l primo a chi pon mente
   quïeto pare, e l'ultimo che voli;
così quelle carole, differente-
   mente danzando, della sua ricchezza
   mi facìeno stimar, veloci e lente.
Di quella ch' io notai di più carezza
   vid' io uscire un foco sì felice,   20
   che nullo vi lasciò di più chiarezza;
e tre fïate intorno di Beatrice
   .si volse con un canto tanto divo,
   che la mia fantasia nol mi ridice.
Però salta la penna e non lo scrivo;
   chè l'imagine nostra a cotai pieghe,
   non che 'l parlare, è troppo color vivo.

CANTO XXIV

St Peter; his examination of Dante on faith

'O FELLOWSHIP elect to the great supper of the blessed Lamb, who feeds you so that your desire is ever satisfied,[1] since by God's grace this man has foretaste of that which falls from your table, before death appoints his time, give heed to his measureless craving and bedew him with some drops; you drink always from the fountain whence comes that on which his mind is set.' Beatrice said this; and those happy spirits formed themselves in circles on fixed poles, flaming brightly like comets. And as wheels in the structure of a clock revolve so that, to one watching them, the first seems at rest and the last to fly, so those choirs, dancing severally fast and slow, made me gauge their wealth.

From the one I noted as the richest I saw come forth a fire so joyful that it left none there of greater brightness, and it wheeled three times round Beatrice with so divine a song that my fancy does not repeat it to me, therefore my pen leaps and I do not write of it; for our imagination, much more our speech, has colours too bright for such folds.[2]

'O santa suora mia che sì ne preghe
  divota, per lo tuo ardente affetto
  da quella bella spera mi disleghe.'   30
Poscia, fermato il foco benedetto
  alla mia donna dirizzò lo spiro,
  che favellò così com' i' ho detto.
Ed ella: 'O luce etterna del gran viro
  a cui Nostro Signor lasciò le chiavi
  ch' ei portò giù di questo gaudio miro,
tenta costui di punti lievi e gravi,
  come ti piace, intorno della fede,
  per la qual tu su per lo mare andavi.
S'elli ama bene e bene spera e crede,   40
  non t'è occulto perchè 'l viso hai quivi
  dov'ogni cosa dipinta si vede;
ma perchè questo regno ha fatto civi
  per la verace fede, a glorïarla
  di lei parlare è ben ch'a lui arrivi.'
Sì come il baccellier s'arma e non parla
  fin che 'l maestro la question propone,
  per approvarla, non per terminarla,
così m'armava io d'ogni ragione
  mentre ch'ella dicea, per esser presto   50
  a tal querente ed a tal professione.
'Dì, buon cristiano, fatti manifesto:
  fede che è?' Ond' io levai la fronte
  in quella luce onde spirava questo;
poi mi volsi a Beatrice, ed essa pronte
  sembianze femmi perch' ïo spandessi
  l'acqua di fuor del mio interno fonte.
'La Grazia che mi dà ch' io mi confessi'
  comincia' io 'dall'alto primopilo,
  faccia li miei concetti bene espressi.'   60
E seguitai: 'Come 'l verace stilo
  ne scrisse, padre, del tuo caro frate
  che mise teco Roma nel buon filo,
fede è sustanza di cose sperate,
  ed argomento delle non parventi;
  e questa pare a me sua quiditate.'

346

'O my holy sister who prayest to us thus devoutly, by thy glowing affection thou dost loose me from that fair circle.' When it was still the blessed fire breathed forth these words to my Lady as I have told them.

And she: 'O eternal light of the great soul with whom our Lord left the keys which He brought down of this wondrous joy, test this man on points light and grave as thou seest good regarding the faith by which thou walkedst on the sea.[3] Whether he loves rightly and rightly hopes and believes is not hid from thee, since thou hast seen it there where all things are seen depicted; but since this kingdom has made its citizens by the true faith, it rightly falls to him to speak of it, that he may glorify it.'

Just as the bachelor arms himself and does not speak till the master submits the question—for argument, not for settlement[4]—, so I armed myself with all my reasons while she was speaking, to be ready for such a questioner and for such a profession.

'Speak, good Christian, declare thyself. What is faith?' At which I lifted up my brow to that light from which this breathed; then I turned to Beatrice, who quickly signed to me with a glance that I should pour forth the waters of my inward spring.

'May the grace which grants it to me to make my confession to the Chief Centurion' I began 'give me right utterance for my thoughts.' And I went on: 'As the truthful pen of thy dear brother wrote of it who with thee, father, put Rome on the good path, faith is the substance of things hoped for and the evidence of things not seen;[5] and this I take to be its quiddity.'

Allora udi': 'Dirittamente senti,
  se bene intendi perchè la ripose
  tra le sustanze, e poi tra li argomenti.'
E io appresso: 'Le profonde cose   70
  che mi largiscon qui la lor parvenza,
  alli occhi di là giù son sì ascose,
che l'esser loro v'è in sola credenza,
  sopra la qual si fonda l'alta spene;
  e però di sustanza prende intenza.
E da questa credenza ci convene
  sillogizzar, sanz'avere altra vista;
  però intenza d'argomento tene.'
Allora udi': 'Se quantunque s'acquista
  giù per dottrina, fosse così 'nteso,   80
  non li avrìa loco ingegno di sofista.'
Così spirò di quello amore acceso;
  indi soggiunse: 'Assai bene è trascorsa
  d'esta moneta già la lega e 'l peso:
ma dimmi se tu l' hai nella tua borsa.'
  Ond' io: 'Sì, ho, sì lucida e sì tonda,
  che nel suo conio nulla mi s' inforsa.'
Appresso uscì della luce profonda
  che lì splendeva: 'Questa cara gioia
  sopra la quale ogni virtù si fonda,   90
onde ti venne?' E io: 'La larga ploia
  dello Spirito Santo ch'è diffusa
  in su le vecchie e 'n su le nuove cuoia,
è sillogismo che la m' ha conchiusa
  acutamente sì, che 'nverso d'ella
  ogni dimostrazion mi pare ottusa.'
Io udi' poi: 'L'antica e la novella
  proposizion che così ti conchiude
  perchè l'hai tu per divina favella?'
E io: 'La prova che 'l ver mi dischiude   100
  son l'opere seguite, a che natura
  non scaldò ferro mai nè battè ancude.'
Risposto fummi: 'Dì, chi t'assicura
  che quell'opere fosser? Quel medesmo
  che vuol provarsi, non altri, il ti giura.'

Then I heard: 'Thou thinkest rightly if thou understandest well why he placed it among the substances and after among the evidences.'

And I then: 'The deep things which so richly manifest themselves to me here are so hidden from men's eyes below that there their existence lies in belief alone, on which is based the lofty hope; and therefore it takes the character of substance.[6] And from this belief we must reason, without seeing more; therefore it holds the character of evidence.'

Then I heard: 'If all that is acquired below for doctrine were thus understood, there would be no room left for sophist's wit.'

This breathed from that kindled love; and it continued: 'Now the alloy and the weight of this money have been well examined; but tell me if thou hast it in thy purse.'

I therefore: 'I have indeed, so bright and round that of its mintage I am in no doubt.'

Then there came from the depth of the light that was shining there: 'This precious jewel on which every virtue rests, whence did it come to thee?'

And I: 'The plenteous rain of the Holy Spirit that is poured out on the old and new parchments[7] is a syllogism which has established it for me with such acuteness that every other demonstration, compared with that, seems to me futile.'

I heard then: 'The old premiss and the new which are so conclusive for thee, why dost thou hold them for divine utterance?'

And I: 'The proof which declares the truth to me is the works that followed, for which nature never heated iron nor smote anvil.'[8]

'Tell me,' came the reply 'who assures thee that these works ever were? The very thing that must be proved, nothing else, attests them to thee.'

'Se 'l mondo si rivolse al cristianesmo'
  diss' io 'sanza miracoli, quest' uno
  è tal, che li altri non sono il centesmo;
chè tu intrasti povero e digiuno
  in campo, a seminar la buona pianta   110
  che fu già vite e ora è fatta pruno.'
Finito questo, l'alta corte santa
  risonò per le spere un 'Dio laudamo'
  nella melode che là su si canta.
E quel baron che sì di ramo in ramo,
  essaminando, già tratto m'avea,
  che all'ultime fronde appressavamo,
ricominciò: 'La Grazia, che donnea
  con la tua mente, la bocca t'aperse
  infino a qui come aprir si dovea,   120
sì ch' io approvo ciò che fuori emerse:
  ma or convene spremer quel che credi,
  e onde alla credenza tua s'offerse.'
'O santo padre, spirito che vedi
  ciò che credesti sì che tu vincesti
  ver lo sepulcro più giovani piedi,'
comincia' io 'tu vuo' ch' io manifesti
  la forma qui del pronto creder mio,
  e anche la cagion di lui chiedesti.
E io rispondo: Io credo in uno Dio   130
  solo ed etterno, che tutto il ciel move,
  non moto, con amore e con disio.
E a tal creder non ho io pur prove
  fisice e metafisice, ma dalmi
  anche la verità che quinci piove
per Moïsè, per profeti e per salmi,
  per l'Evangelio e per voi che scriveste
  poi che l'ardente Spirto vi fè almi.
E credo in tre persone etterne, e queste
  credo una essenza sì una e sì trina,   140
  che soffera congiunto "sono" ed "este."
Della profonda condizion divina
  ch' io tocco mo, la mente mi sigilla
  più volte l'evangelica dottrina.

'If the world was converted to Christianity without miracles,' I said 'that one is such that the rest are not a hundredth part of it;[9] for thou didst enter the field poor and fasting to sow the good plant that was once a vine and is now become a thorn.'

This ended, the high and holy court resounded through its circles with a *Te Deum laudamus* in the strains that are sung there above.

And that Baron,[10] who had brought me thus from branch to branch in his examination so that we approached the farthest boughs, began again: 'The grace that wooes thy mind has till now opened thy lips aright, so that I approve what has come from them; but now thou must declare what thou believest and whence it was offered to thy belief.'

'O holy father, spirit who seest that which thou believedst so that thou didst outstrip younger feet to the sepulchre,'[11] I began 'thou wouldst have me make plain here the form[12] of my willing faith and askest too the source of it. And I reply: I believe in one God, sole and eternal, who, unmoved, moves all heaven with love and desire; and for this belief I have not only proofs physical and metaphysical, but it is given me also in the truth that rains down hence through Moses and the Prophets and the Psalms,[13] through the Gospel and through you who wrote after the burning Spirit made you holy.[14] And I believe in three eternal Persons; and these I believe to be one Essence, so one and so three-fold that it admits agreement both with *are* and *is*. With the profound divine state of being of which I speak the Gospel teaching many times stamps my mind. This is the beginning, this is

351

Quest' è il principio, quest' è la favilla
   che si dilata in fiamma poi vivace,
   e come stella in cielo in me scintilla.'
Come 'l segnor ch'ascolta quel che i piace,
   da indi abbraccia il servo, gratulando
   per la novella, tosto ch'el si tace;   150
così, benedicendomi cantando,
   tre volte cinse me, sì com' io tacqui
   l'apostolico lume al cui comando
io avea detto; sì nel dir li piacqui!

the spark which then broadens to a living flame and
shines within me like a star in heaven.'

As the master who listens to that which pleases
him then embraces his servant, rejoicing in his
news, as soon as he is silent; so, singing benedictions
on me, the apostolic light at whose bidding I had
spoken encircled me three times when I was silent,
I so pleased him with my words.

1. 'Blessed are they which are called unto the marriage supper of the Lamb' (*Rev.* xix. 9). 'The Lamb which is in the midst of the throne shall feed them' (*Rev.* vii. 17).

2. The illuminating pigments of the time were too bright for the shaded folds of drapery; so, human imagination and language could not deal with the involutions of St Peter's rendering of plain-song. The addition of *fioriture* was regarded as the accomplishment of a virtuoso. Cp. Cacciaguida's 'skill among the singers' (*Par.* xviii).

3. 'Peter walked on the water, to go to Jesus' (*Matt.* xiv. 29).

4. In the university's oral examination for the doctorate.

5. *Heb.* xi. 1. The epistle was ascribed to St Paul.

6. *Sub-stance*, that which stands below, or gives support.

7. The Old and New Testaments.

8. The miracles of Scripture, which could not be fabricated by nature.

9. The argument is taken from St Augustine.

10. Secular titles were often applied to sacred personages in the Middle Ages.

11. Though John reached the sepulchre before Peter, Peter—traditionally the older—entered it first; cp. *John* xx. 3–8.

12. Scholastic *forma*, the essence.

13. 'All things must be fulfilled, which were written in the law of Moses, and in the prophets, and in the psalms, concerning me' (*Luke* xxiv. 44).

14. At Pentecost. 'There appeared unto them eleven tongues, like as of fire, and it sat upon each of them. And they were all filled with the Holy Ghost' (*Acts* ii. 3–4).

NOTE

At the beginning of the second canto Dante spoke of 'the angels' bread by which men here'—on earth—'live, but never come from it satisfied'; here he speaks of 'the great supper of the blessed Lamb' by which 'desire is ever satisfied'. The language marks the difference between the Militant and the Triumphant Church. Beatrice appeals on Dante's behalf to the whole fellowship, and from the circle that was 'the richest' in the possession of divine truth—the glorious company of the Apostles—comes St Peter, the first and chief representative of the Church Militant, now the spokesman of the Church Triumphant, of whom we are told at the end of the previous canto that here he 'triumphs in his victory'. He is elect from that 'elect fellowship' as Dante's fittest examiner in the faith.

The three gospel virtues, according to Aquinas, are the essential qualifications of the soul for the final vision which Dante is approaching, and Beatrice, in her theological character, brings him as a university bachelor before the master for oral examination on them, and in the first place before Peter for examination on faith—not merely on *the* faith, but on *his* faith. The incident with its technicalities of proof by question and reply, premises and conclusion, substance and evidence, recalls scenes familiar in Dante's old memories of university life in Bologna and Paris,—'the practice, well-known to Dante, of the medieval schools of philosophy and theology, in which the Master would propose from his chair the questions, which would then be discussed between the doctors, bachelors and scholars present, and after the discussion of each question the Master, on another day, would set it forth again, with the arguments pro and con, and end by pronouncing his own judgement' (*Casini-Barbi*). The formal, official character of the interview is marked, not only by the curt exchange of question and answer, but also by the fact that in it Peter is not once called by his name; he is called by nine descriptive phrases —'the blessed fire', 'the eternal light of the great soul', etc.,

355

never simply Saint Peter, until, in the opening of the next canto, all the Apostle's greatness is, as it were, gathered up in his personal name: 'Peter thus encircled my brow.' There is something, too, of an impersonal quality given to the whole scene by the various terms used for Peter's utterance: 'the fire breathed forth these words', 'this was breathed from that kindled love', 'then I heard', 'then came forth from the depth of the light', never the customary 'he said'. This is no personal conversation like most of the interviews of the poem. It is a measuring of the soul's integrity and a giving of glory to the faith; and as it begins with the joyful fire wheeling three times round Beatrice with its divine song, it ends with the apostolic light encircling Dante three times and singing benedictions on him. He is thus ceremonially acknowledged and approved by the Master as the pupil of Beatrice, the true learner of the truth of God, and the formalities of theology are absorbed and sublimated in the glories of his great experience.

There is an early and credible tradition that Dante was at one time brought under suspicion and enquiry by the Inquisition for heresy, and if this was the fact the canto takes the character in part of an apologia. This would be consistent with the challenging tone of Peter's questions and with the detailed and repeated emphasis and warmth of Dante's confession of faith and declaration of his orthodoxy, features which are much more marked here than in the corresponding passages in the following cantos where he is examined in hope and love. The money in his purse is 'so bright and round that of its mintage [he is] in no doubt'; and he declares 'the form of [his] willing'—ready, unhesitating—'belief', and says that the doctrine of the Holy Trinity 'is the spark which broadens to a lively flame and shines within [him] like a star in heaven'. His language could not be more explicit if it was meant as a vindication of himself in face of a charge which he regarded as a grave one, and this quality is strongly confirmed by the opening lines of the next canto.

The whole discussion is a notable illustration of the attitude of the medieval Church, in its best representatives, to its own faith. For Aquinas as for Dante, faith is primarily an intellectual conviction, a reasoned conformity of the mind with the revealed nature of the universe. The analysis of this conviction—its nature, its ground, its possession of the soul, its content, the prescribed channels through which that content flows, and its consummation in the doctrine of God—is in strange contrast with the lyric raptures and splendours of the previous canto. It is a deliberate contrast, and it is characteristic both of Dante and of his age. The faith of the saints, of which this canto treats, is not primarily raptures and splendours; it is a sober certainty of waking bliss, an established and assured conviction of an infinite encompassing power and wisdom and love, which three are one. That is the faith of which he says that it shines within him like a star in heaven, and for which the apostolic light three times encircles his brow. Here, as always in Dante, the assurance of the truth precedes the hope and love which that assurance prompts and justifies. To Aquinas, 'the active intelligence is the very essence of the soul and the root of human responsibility and liberty. . . . This insistence on the rationality and freedom of the individual personality is a new note in medieval thought. It marks the end of the oriental and Byzantine absorption of the human mind in the Absolute and the Transcendent, and the beginning of the distinctively western ideal of a philosophy of man and of the human mind, a philosophy which recognizes the dependence of human knowledge on sensible experience without excluding it from the world of spiritual reality and religious truth' (*C. Dawson*). No words occur more constantly throughout the *Paradiso* than *vedere*, to see, with its synonyms and derivatives, and the aim and consummation of the whole story is the Beatific Vision,—'my sight gaining strength as I looked',—'my sight was wholly given to it' (*Par.* xxxiii).

When Dante spoke of the world's conversion to Christianity and of St Peter's part in it, all the circles together broke into the *Te Deum*, the Church's song of salvation, which not long before, entering the gate of Purgatory, he had 'seemed to hear'. There it was sung by the weeping penitents on the mountain, 'the words now distinguished, now lost' (*Purg.* ix); here it is sung by the perfected saints 'in the strains that are sung there above', and it resounds through their circles. The Church Militant and the Church Triumphant unite in the same praise, for they are one fellowship still.

357

PARADISO

SE mai continga che 'l poema sacro
   al quale ha posto mano e cielo e terra,
   sì che m' ha fatto per più anni macro,
vinca la crudeltà che fuor mi serra
   del bello ovile ov' io dormi' agnello,
   nimico ai lupi che li danno guerra;
con altra voce omai, con altro vello
   ritornerò poeta, ed in sul fonte
   del mio battesmo prenderò 'l cappello;
però che nella fede, che fa conte   10
   l'anime a Dio, quivi intra' io, e poi
   Pietro per lei sì mi girò la fronte.
Indi si mosse un lume verso noi
   di quella spera ond' uscì la primizia
   che lasciò Cristo de' vicari suoi;
e la mia donna, piena di letizia,
   mi disse: 'Mira, mira: ecco il barone
   per cui là giù si visita Galizia.'
Sì come quando il colombo si pone
   presso al compagno, l'uno all'altro pande,   20
   girando e mormorando, l'affezione;
così vid' io l'uno dall'altro grande
   principe glorïoso essere accolto,
   laudando il cibo che là su li prande.
Ma poi che 'l gratular si fu assolto,
   tacito *coram me* ciascun s'affisse,
   ignito sì che vincea il mio volto.

CANTO XXV

*St James; his examination of Dante on hope;
St John*

IF it ever come to pass that the sacred poem to
which both heaven and earth have set their hand
so that it has made me lean for many years should
overcome the cruelty that bars me from the fair
sheepfold where I slept as a lamb, an enemy to the
wolves that make war on it, with another voice now
and other fleece I shall return a poet and at the
font of my baptism take the laurel crown; for there
I entered into the faith that makes souls known to
God,[1] and after, because of it, Peter thus encircled
my brow.

On that a light moved towards us from that
circle from which had come the first-fruit that
Christ left of His vicars,[2] and my Lady, full of
gladness, said to me: 'See, see, that is the Baron for
whom below they visit Galicia.'[3]

Just as, when the dove alights beside its mate,
the one displays its fondness for the other, circling
it and cooing, so I saw the one great and glorious
prince received by the other, both giving praise
for the feast they share above. But, when the joyful
greeting was finished, they both stopped silent
coram me,[4] so aflame that they overcame my sight.

359

Ridendo allora Beatrice disse:
  'Inclita vita per cui la larghezza
  della nostra basilica si scrisse, 30
fa risonar la spene in questa altezza:
  tu sai, che tante fiate la figuri,
  quante Iesù ai tre fè più carezza.'
'Leva la testa e fa che t'assicuri;
  che ciò che vien qua su dal mortal mondo,
  convien ch'ai nostri raggi si maturi.'
Questo conforto del foco secondo
  mi venne; ond' io levai li occhi a' monti
  che li 'ncurvaron pria col troppo pondo.
'Poi che par grazia vuol che tu t'affronti 40
  lo nostro imperadore, anzi la morte,
  nell'aula più secreta co' suoi conti,
sì che, veduto il ver di questa corte,
  la spene che là giù bene innamora
  in te ed in altrui di ciò conforte,
dì quel ch'ell'è, e come se ne 'nfiora
  la mente tua, e dì onde a te venne.'
  Così seguì 'l secondo lume ancora.
E quella pia che guidò le penne
  delle mie ali a così alto volo, 50
  alla risposta così mi prevenne:
'La Chiesa militante alcun figliuolo
  non ha con più speranza, com'è scritto
  nel sol che raggia tutto nostro stuolo:
però li è conceduto che d'Egitto
  vegna in Ierusalemme, per vedere,
  anzi che 'l militar li sia prescritto.
Li altri due punti, che non per sapere
  son dimandati, ma perch'ei rapporti
  quanto questa virtù t'è in piacere, 60
a lui lasc' io, chè non li saran forti
  ne di iattanzia; ed elli a ciò risponda,
  e la grazia di Dio ciò li comporti.'
Come discente ch'a dottor seconda
  pronto e libente in quel ch'elli è esperto,
  perchè la sua bontà si disasconda,

Smiling, Beatrice said then: 'Illustrious living soul who didst write of the bounty of our royal court,[5] make hope resound in this height; thou canst, who wast the type of it all those times when Jesus showed most favour to the three.'[6]

'Lift up thy head and take confidence, for all that comes up here from the mortal world must be ripened in our beams.' This assurance came to me from the second fire; therefore I lifted up my eyes to the hills whose greatness weighed them down before. 'Since our Emperor, of His grace, wills that thou shouldst come before thy death face to face with His nobles in the inner chamber, so that, having seen the truth of this court, thou mayst with that strengthen in thyself and others the hope that begets true love below, say what it is and how it blossoms in thy mind, and say whence it came to thee.' Thus the second light continued.

And that compassionate one who directed the feathers of my wings to so high a flight anticipated my reply: 'The Church Militant has not a child more full of hope, as is written in the Sun that irradiates all our host; therefore is it granted him to come from Egypt to Jerusalem that he may see it before his warfare is accomplished. The other two points about which thou didst ask—not for enlightenment, but for him to report how dear this virtue is to thee—I leave to himself; for they will not be hard for him, nor occasion for boasting. So let him answer them, and for this God's grace be his help!'

Like a pupil who answers his master, ready and eager in his subject that he may show his parts,

'Spene' diss' io 'è uno attender certo
   della gloria futura, il qual produce
   grazia divina e precedente merto.
Da molte stelle mi vien questa luce;   70
   ma quei la distillò nel mio cor pria
   che fu sommo cantor del sommo duce.
"Sperino in te" nella sua teodìa
   dice "color che sanno il nome tuo":
   e chi nol sa, s'elli ha la fede mia?
Tu mi stillasti, con lo stillar suo,
   nella pistola poi; sì ch' io son pieno,
   ed in altrui vostra pioggia repluo.'
Mentr' io diceva, dentro al vivo seno
   di quello incendio tremolava un lampo   80
   subito e spesso a guisa di baleno.
Indi spirò: 'L'amore ond' io avvampo
   ancor ver la virtù che mi seguette
   infin la palma ed all'uscir del campo,
vuol ch' io rispiri a te che ti dilette
   di lei; ed èmmi a grato che tu diche
   quello che la speranza ti promette.'
E io: 'Le nove e le scritture antiche
   pongono il segno, ed esso lo mi addita,
   dell'anime che Dio s' ha fatte amiche.   90
Dice Isaia che ciascuna vestita
   nella sua terra fia di doppia vesta;
   e la sua terra è questa dolce vita.
E 'l tuo fratello assai vie più digesta,
   là dove tratta delle bianche stole,
   questa revelazion ci manifesta.'
E prima, appresso al fin d'este parole,
   'Sperent in te' di sopr' a noi s' udì;
   a che rispuoser tutte le carole.
Poscia tra esse un lume si schiarì   100
   sì che se 'l Cancro avesse un tal cristallo,
   l'inverno avrebbe un mese d'un sol dì.
E come surge e va ed entra in ballo
   vergine lieta, sol per fare onore
   alla novizia, non per alcun fallo,

'Hope' I said 'is a sure expectation of future glory, and it springs from divine grace and precedent merit. This light comes to me from many stars, but he first distilled it in my heart who was the sovereign singer of the Sovereign Lord.[7] In his divine song he says: "Let them hope in thee that know thy name"; and who does not know it that holds my faith? Besides his showers, thou didst shower on me in thy epistle, so that I am full and in turn rain your rain on others.'

While I spoke, within the living heart of that fire quivered a flash, sudden and repeated like lightning; then it breathed forth: 'The love with which I still burn for the virtue that followed me even to the palm and the departure from the field bids me breathe again to thee who delightest in it; and I would fain hear thee tell what is hope's promise to thee.'

And I: 'The new and the ancient Scriptures set forth the goal for the souls that God has made His friends, and this directs me to it. Isaiah says that each in his own land shall be clothed with double vesture,[8] and their own land is this sweet life; and thy brother, where he tells of the white robes,[9] declares this revelation to us far more expressly.'

And first, immediately I had finished speaking, *Sperent in te*[10] was heard above us, to which all the choirs responded; then one light among them shone out so that if the Crab held such a gem winter would have a month of unbroken day.[11] And as a happy maiden rises and comes forward and enters the dance, only to do honour to the bride, not for

così vid' io lo schiarato splendore
   venire a' due che si volgìeno a nota
   qual convenìesi al loro ardente amore.
Misesi lì nel canto e nella rota;
   e la mia donna in lor tenea l'aspetto,   110
   pur come sposa tacita ed immota.
'Questi è colui che giacque sopra 'l petto
   del nostro pellicano, e questi fue
   di su la croce al grande officio eletto.'
La donna mia così; nè però piùe
   mosser la vista sua di stare attenta
   poscia che prima le parole sue.
Qual è colui ch'adocchia e s'argomenta
   di vedere eclissar lo sole un poco,
   che, per veder, non vedente diventa;   120
tal mi fec' io a quell'ultimo foco
   mentre che detto fu: 'Perchè t'abbagli
   per veder cosa che qui non ha loco?
In terra terra è 'l mio corpo, e saràgli
   tanto con li altri, che 'l numero nostro
   con l'etterno proposito s'agguagli.
Con le due stole nel beato chiostro
   son le due luci sole che saliro;
   e questo apporterai nel mondo vostro.'
A questa voce l'infiammato giro   130
   si quïetò con esso il dolce mischio
   che si facea nel suon del trino spiro,
sì come, per cessar fatica o rischio,
   li remi, pria nell'acqua ripercossi,
   tutti si posano al sonar d'un fischio.
Ahi quanto nella mente mi commossi,
   quando mi volsi per veder Beatrice,
   per non poter veder, ben che io fossi
presso di lei, e nel mondo felice!

any lightness, so I saw the splendour that had brightened approach the two who were wheeling to the song as befitted their burning love. He joined there in the singing and the dance, and my Lady held her looks on them, just like a bride silent and motionless.

'This is he that lay on the breast of our Pelican,[12] he that was chosen from the cross for the great charge.'[13] My Lady said this; but no more after than before her speech was her gaze moved from its intentness.

As one that strains his eyes, trying to see the sun in partial eclipse, and by seeing becomes sightless, such I became before that last fire, while it spoke: 'Why dost thou dazzle thyself to see that which has no place here?[14] My body is earth in the earth, and it will be there with the rest till our number tallies with the eternal purpose. With the two robes in the blessed cloister are only the two lights that have ascended,[15] and this report thou shalt take back to your world.'

At these words the flaming circle fell silent, together with the sweet mingled sound that was made by the three-fold breath, just as, to avoid fatigue or danger, oars till then struck through the water stop all at once at the sound of a whistle.

Ah, how troubled in mind I was when I turned to see Beatrice, not to be able to see her, though I was by her side and in the happy world!

1. 'The Lord knoweth them that are his' (2 *Tim.* ii. 19).

2. St Peter, regarded as the first of the popes.

3. St James, St John's brother, identified by Dante with the martyr under Herod Agrippa, with the author of the Epistle, and with the 'pillar' of the Church mentioned in *Gal.* ii. 9; his supposed burial-place in the Spanish Province of Galicia was long a famous place of pilgrimage.

4. Before me.

5. 'Every good gift and every perfect gift is from above, and cometh down from the Father of lights' (*Jas.* i. 17), etc., etc.

6. The raising of Jairus's daughter (*Mark* v. 37), the Transfiguration (*Mark* ix. 2), and Gethsemane (*Mark* xiv. 33).

7. David, 'the singer of the Holy Ghost' (*Par.* xx).

8. 'In their land they shall possess the double. . . . He hath clothed me with the garments of salvation' (*Isa.* lxi. 7, 10). 'The double' was taken to mean soul and body, as double clothing.

9. 'Lo, a great multitude, . . . clothed with white robes' (*Rev.* vii. 9), etc.

10. 'Let them hope in thee' (*Ps.* ix. 10).

11. From 21st December to 21st January the Crab rises at sunset and sets at sunrise.

12. The pelican, supposed to nourish its young with blood from its own breast, was a familiar symbol of Christ. 'There was leaning on Jesus' bosom one of his disciples, whom Jesus loved' (*John* xiii. 23).

13. Jesus 'saith unto his mother, Woman, behold thy son! Then saith he to the disciple, Behold thy mother!' (*John* xix. 26–27).

14. John's body,—a reference to the legend that John did not die but was transported bodily to heaven; cp. *John* xxi. 20–23.

15. Only Christ and the Virgin have ascended with 'the two robes', soul and body (*Par.* xxiii).

NOTE

In 1319, two years before his death, Dante received in Ravenna a letter in Latin hexameters from a young friend, Giovanni del Virgilio, a lecturer in the University of Bologna, who was known by that name for his devotion to the ancient poet. Virgilio reproaches him respectfully for writing his great poem in the vernacular and promises that if Dante will produce a Latin poem on a heroic theme, for which he suggests a choice of some recent public events in Italy, Virgilio will put Dante's name before the university—Dante's own university—for the honour of the laurel crown. It was an honour which had never yet been given to a writer in the vernacular. In his reply, written also in Latin hexameters and in playful pastoral terms, Dante says it will be more fitting, when he has completed the *Paradiso*, that he should hide his grey hairs under the laurel leaves in his native place on the Arno, 'if ever I return there'. In the character of a shepherd tending his flock in the hills he tells of his 'best-loved ewe' that 'chews the grass under a great rock' and is 'full of milk', and he promises to send to his friend 'ten measures' of its milk—which, in the whole context, is generally understood to mean the last ten cantos, not yet completed, of the *Paradiso*. The language is playful, but it declares in fact Dante's grave claim for his work in the vernacular to the high name of poetry and his assurance that it was his warrant for the laurel crown.

The opening lines here are obviously in the context of Dante's exchange of verses with Virgilio and may have been suggested by it. But here Dante's claim for 'the sacred poem'—so described also in the twenty-third canto—and his appeal to Florence are joined with the declaration of his Christian faith. It is to his 'beautiful Saint John', where he was received at the font into the Church Militant, that he hopes to return, having been received by St Peter himself in the Church Triumphant.

In the sentence of condemnation passed upon him by the authorities of Florence 'he had been described as a foe of the Church's party—*fidelium devotorum Sanctae Romanae Ecclesiae*; and nevertheless his faith is triumphantly accepted in heaven by that Church's first supreme Pontiff' (*E. G. Gardner*). Such a charge, with that of heresy, would very readily be brought against one regarded as a renegade from his original Guelf-Papal tradition who had become the most fervid spokesman, on his own terms, of the Ghibelline-Imperialist cause. In this and the previous canto Dante repudiates the charge and vindicates himself at once as citizen, as poet, and as believing Christian.

'St James is the only Apostle whose death is recorded in the Bible. The "certain expectation" led him to martyrdom and made him a suitable exponent of hope. So says Chrysostom' (*C. H. Grandgent*). For hope, as a man of Dante's temper and experience conceives of it, is not a soft and easy virtue, it is not mere hopefulness; its type is the martyr's hope, an endurance and mastery in the soul, the virtue that followed the Apostle 'even to the palm and the departure from the field'.

In these cantos there is an illustration of the pains taken by Dante in the working out of his imagery for his purpose. The three Apostles representing the three Gospel virtues stand in a close and significant relation and sequence; faith, coming first, is immediately followed by hope and both by love, 'the greatest of these'. When Peter, at the end of the twenty-fourth canto, gives his ardent welcome to Dante's faith, immediately, at the beginning of the twenty-fifth canto, the hope springs up in him of his vindication and return to Florence, and at that point—'On that a light moved towards us'—Peter is joined by James, 'as a dove alights beside its mate and the one displays its fondness for the other'. When his declaration of hope was completed, 'immediately I had finished speaking, *Sperent in te* was heard above us' and 'one light shone out', the light of John, a light to make the darkest nights of winter as day, and it joined the other two, while 'my Lady held her looks on them, just like a bride, silent and motionless'. Each of the three virtues has its being in their unity. The absorption of Beatrice is stressed by repetition in the two stanzas, and it surely represents, in the language of Dante, the still rapture of the Church, the bride of Christ, in contemplating that consummation of grace, love the fulfilling of the law.

We have already noted a significant correspondence and difference between the pageant of the Church Militant in the *Purgatorio* and the vision here of the Church Triumphant, and we find both correspondence and difference again. There, in the pageant, the gospel virtues are represented by three symbolic ladies 'dancing to their angelic roundelay' (*Purg.* xxix and xxxi); here, these virtues are embodied in the three scriptural figures who were, for Dante, their historical protagonists. The Apostles are identified by their New Testament records. They are more than symbols; for we are now in the higher region of 'the truth of this court', higher than that of the shadowy figures of the Earthly Paradise.

Again, in the account of the pageant much of the language is military, the 'army' with its 'banners' is a fighting force; here, the chosen terms signify an imperial court at peace. Peter and James are called 'barons'; Beatrice bids Dante see 'the hosts of Christ's triumph' and speaks of 'the bounty of our royal court'; James speaks of 'our Emperor' and of 'His nobles in the inner chamber'; and Dante tells us that he 'saw the one great and glorious prince received by the other, both giving praise for the feast they share above'. Something Dante may have seen of an imperial court when he was present at the coronation of Henry VII at Milan in 1311, and in some of the petty and ceremonious courts of Italy he had been from time to time a guest and an intimate observer during his years of exile,—with the Scaligers at Verona, with the Malaspini in Lunigiana, and now with the Polentani at Ravenna. The comparisons, strange enough to us, of the greetings of Peter and James with the meeting of two doves, 'circling and cooing', and of John joining the other two with a happy maiden entering the dance at a wedding-party, may be taken as bright—and amused—glimpses of court life as he had seen it. The mutual greetings of the two Apostles had first to be 'finished', and Dante uses here the formal Latin *coram me* for the dignified courtesy of the two 'nobles'. Dante's hope for the early triumph of an earthly Empire, an established and secure order of justice and peace for all men, was, when he wrote the *Paradiso* in his last years, dim, and his refuge now was in the thought of 'Jerusalem', the city of the soul, the eternal realm of 'our Emperor', 'that Rome of which Christ is Roman'.

It is not Dante himself, but Beatrice, that replies to St James's first question, when she declares Dante to be the child of the Church Militant and one full of hope. This may well be Dante's way of recalling the scene in the Earthly Paradise (*Purg.* xxx) in which Beatrice will not let him be comforted by the song of the angels, 'In thee, Lord, have I hoped', till he has paid 'some scot of penitence and shedding of tears'. Here, with the Church Triumphant, his soul is free and his hope is winged and Beatrice herself justifies him in it and praises him for it. In his last words to her (*Par.* xxxi) Dante calls Beatrice 'Lady in whom my hope finds its strength'.

His definition here of Christian hope is an almost exact quotation of the words of Peter the Lombard, the great twelfth century scholastic whom Dante had seen in the heaven of the Sun (*Par.* x). That sure expectation of future glory 'springs from divine grace and precedent merit'. God's grace moves a man to hope in God, and through that hope grace moves him to such a life as has by grace its reward in the fulfilment of his hope; so that all is of grace.

The passage following, about the 'double vesture' and 'the two robes', with its medieval interpretation of Scripture, rests on the current view that the redeemed still await the recovery of their bodies from their graves at the general resurrection. The doctrine is an expression in the theological language of the time of the idea of the redeemed life as containing in its final perfection all that belongs to the good of the earthly life, of soul and body, with

> 'Relations dear, and all the charities
> Of father, son and brother.'

In that respect the redeemed still live in hope of their full redemption, and they sing their responses to the chant of the angels in the heaven above them, 'Let them hope in thee'.

Dante's temporary blindness will be considered in the Note to Canto XXVI.

PARADISO

MENTR' io dubbiava per lo viso spento,
  della fulgida fiamma che lo spense
  uscì un spiro che mi fece attento,
dicendo: 'Intanto che tu ti risense
  della vista che hai in me consunta,
  ben è che ragionando la compense.
Comincia dunque; e dì ove s'appunta
  l'anima tua, e fa ragion che sia
  la vista in te smarrita e non defunta;
perchè la donna che per questa dia   10
  region ti conduce, ha nello sguardo
  la virtù ch'ebbe la man d'Anania.'
Io dissi: 'Al suo piacere e tosto e tardo
  vegna rimedio alli occhi che fuor porte
  quand'ella entrò col foco ond' io sempr'ardo.
Lo ben che fa contenta questa corte,
  Alfa ed O è di quanta scrittura
  mi legge amore o lievemente o forte.'
Quella medesma voce che paura
  tolta m'avea del subito abbarbaglio,   20
  di ragionare ancor mi mise in cura;
e disse: 'Certo a più angusto vaglio
  ti conviene schiarar: dicer convienti
  chi drizzò l'arco tuo a tal berzaglio.'
E io: 'Per filosofici argomenti
  e per autorità che quinci scende
  cotale amor convien che in me s' imprenti.

CANTO XXVI

St John's examination of Dante on love; Adam;
Dante's questions

WHILE I was in fear for my lost sight there came forth from the resplendent flame that had quenched it a breathing which held me intent, and it said: 'Till thou recover the sight thou hast consumed in me thou shalt do well to make up for it with speech. Begin then, and say on what aim thy soul is set. And be assured that thy sight is but confounded, not destroyed; for the Lady who guides thee through this divine region has in her look the same virtue as had the hand of Ananias.'[1]

And I said: 'May healing come soon or late as she will to eyes that were the doors when she entered with the fire with which I always burn. The good that satisfies this court is alpha and omega of all the scripture that love reads to me in tones loud or low.'

The same voice that had delivered me from my fear at the sudden dazzling made me eager to speak again, when it said: 'Assuredly thou must sift with a finer sieve, thou must tell who directed thy bow on that target.'

And I: 'By philosophic arguments and by authority that descends from here,[2] such love must

373

Chè 'l bene, in quanto ben, come s' intende,
    così accende amore, e tanto maggio
    quanto più di bontate in sè comprende.   30
Dunque all'essenza ov'è tanto avvantaggio,
    che ciascun ben che fuor di lei si trova
    altro non è ch'un lume di suo raggio,
più che in altra convien che si mova
    la mente, amando, di ciascun che cerne
    il vero in che si fonda questa prova.
Tal vero all'intelletto mio sterne
    colui che mi dimostra il primo amore
    di tutte le sustanze sempiterne.
Sternel la voce del verace autore,   40
    che dice a Moïsè, di sè parlando:
    "Io ti farò vedere ogni valore."
Sternilmi tu ancora, incominciando
    l'alto preconio che grida l'arcano
    di qui là giù sovra ogni altro bando.'
E io udi': 'Per intelletto umano
    e per autoritadi a lui concorde
    de' tuoi amori a Dio guarda il sovrano.
Ma dì ancor se tu senti altre corde
    tirarti verso lui, sì che tu suone   50
    con quanti denti questo amor ti morde.'
Non fu latente la santa intenzione
    dell'aguglia di Cristo, anzi m'accorsi
    dove volea menar mia professione.
Però ricominciai: 'Tutti quei morsi
    che posson far lo cor volgere a Dio,
    alla mia caritate son concorsi;
chè l'essere del mondo e l'esser mio,
    la morte ch'el sostenne perch' io viva,
    e quel che spera ogni fedel com' io,   60
con la predetta conoscenza viva,
    tratto m' hanno del mar dell'amor torto,
    e del diritto m' han posto alla riva.
Le fronde onde s' infronda tutto l'orto
    dell'ortolano etterno, am' io cotanto
    quanto da lui a lor di bene è porto.'

needs imprint itself on me; for the good, by virtue of its goodness, kindles love as soon as it is known, and so much the more the more of good it contains in itself. To that Essence, then, in which is such pre-eminence that every good found outside of it is nothing but a light from its radiance,[3] must be moved with love, more than to aught else, the mind of everyone who discerns the truth on which this reasoning rests. This truth he sets forth to my understanding who established for me the primal love of all the eternal beings;[4] the voice of the truthful Author sets it forth where, speaking of Himself, He says to Moses: "I will make thee see all goodness";[5] thou too settest it forth to me in the beginning of thy sublime announcement, which, more than any other heralding, proclaims below the mystery of this place above.'[6]

And I heard: 'On the ground of human reason and of the authorities in harmony with it, the highest of all thy loves looks to God; but say further if thou feelest other cords draw thee to Him, so that thou mayst name all the teeth by which this love bites thee.'

The holy purpose of Christ's Eagle[7] was not hidden; it was, indeed, plain to me where he would direct my profession. Therefore I began again: 'All those things whose bite can make the heart turn to God have wrought together in my charity; for the world's existence and my own, the death He bore that I might live, and that which every believer hopes for as I do, with the living assurance of which I spoke, have drawn me from the sea of perverse love and have brought me to the shore of the love that is just. The leaves with which all the garden of the eternal Gardener is embowered I love in the measure of the good He has bestowed on them.'

Sì com''io tacqui, un dolcissimo canto
   risonò per lo cielo, e la mia donna
   dicea con gli altri: 'Santo, santo, santo!'
E come a lume acuto si disonna   70
   per lo spirto visivo che ricorre
   allo splendor che va di gonna in gonna,
e lo svegliato ciò che vede aborre,
   sì nescia è la subita vigilia
   fin che la stimativa non soccorre;
così delli occhi miei ogni quisquilia
   fugò Beatrice col raggio de' suoi,
   che rifulgea da più di mille milia:
onde mei che dinanzi vidi poi;
   e quasi stupefatto domandai   80
   d'un quarto lume ch' io vidi con noi.
E la mia donna: 'Dentro da quei rai
   vagheggia il suo fattor l'anima prima
   che la prima virtù creasse mai.'
Come la fronda che flette la cima
   nel transito del vento, e poi si leva
   per la propria virtù che la sublima,
fec' io in tanto in quant'ella diceva,
   stupendo, e poi mi rifece sicuro
   un disio di parlare ond' io ardeva.   90
E cominciai: 'O pomo che maturo
   solo prodotto fosti, o padre antico
   a cui ciascuna sposa è figlia e nuro,
divoto quanto posso a te supplico
   perchè mi parli: tu vedi mia voglia,
   e per udirti tosto non la dico.'
Tal volta un animal coverto broglia,
   sì che l'affetto convien che si paia
   per lo seguir che face a lui la 'nvoglia;
e similmente l'anima primaia   100
   mi facea trasparer per la coverta
   quant'ella a compiacermi venìa gaia.
Indi spirò: 'Sanz'essermi proferta
   da te, la voglia tua discerno meglio
   che tu qualunque cosa t'è più certa;

As soon as I was silent, a strain of sweetest song resounded through the heaven, and my Lady sang with the rest 'Holy, holy, holy!' And as sleep is broken by a piercing light when the visual spirit runs to meet the brightness that passes through film after film,[8] and the awakened man shrinks from what he sees, so unaware is his sudden waking till judgement comes to his help,—thus Beatrice chased every mote from my eyes with the radiance of her own which shone more than a thousand miles, so that I saw then better than before. And I asked in amazement about a fourth light which I saw beside us.

And my Lady answered: 'Within these rays looks with love on his Maker the first soul the First Power ever created.'

As the branch that bends its top in a gust of wind and then springs up, raised by its own force, so did I while she was speaking,—amazed, then restored to confidence by the desire to speak with which I burned; and I began: 'O fruit that alone wast brought forth ripe, O ancient father of whom every bride is daughter and daughter-in-law, as humbly as I may I beseech thee to speak with me. Thou seest my wish, and to hear thee sooner I do not tell it.'

Sometimes an animal that is covered up stirs so that its impulse is made to appear by the wrappings that follow its movement; and in like manner the primal soul showed me through its covering how gladly it came to do me pleasure. Then it breathed forth: 'Without thy telling of it I discern thy wish better than thou whatever is most certain

377

perch' io la veggio nel verace speglio
  che fa di sè pareglio all'altre cose,
  e nulla face lui di sè pareglio.
Tu vuogli udir quant'è che Dio mi pose
  nell'eccelso giardino ove costei   110
  a così lunga scala ti dispose,
e quanto fu diletto alli occhi miei,
  e la propria cagion del gran disdegno,
  e l' idïoma ch' usai e ch' io fei.
Or, figliuol mio, non il gustar del legno
  fu per sè la cagion di tanto essilio,
  ma solamente il trapassar del segno.
Quindi onde mosse tua donna Virgilio,
  quattromilia trecento e due volumi
  di sol desiderai questo concilio;   120
e vidi lui tornare a tutt' i lumi
  della sua strada novecento trenta
  fïate, mentre ch' io in terra fu'mi.
La lingua ch' io parlai fu tutta spenta
  innanzi che all'ovra inconsummabile
  fosse la gente di Nembròt attenta;
chè nullo effetto mai razïonabile,
  per lo piacere uman che rinovella
  seguendo il cielo, sempre fu durabile.
Opera naturale è ch' uom favella;   130
  ma così o così, natura lascia
  poi fare a voi secondo che v'abbella.
Pria ch' i' scendessi all' infernale ambascia,
  I s'appellava in terra il sommo bene
  onde vien la letizia che mi fascia;
e *EL* si chiamò poi: e ciò convene,
  chè l'uso de' mortali è come fronda
  in ramo, che sen va e altra vene.
Nel monte che si leva più dall'onda,
  fu' io, con vita pura e disonesta,   140
  dalla prim'ora a quella che seconda,
come 'l sol muta quadra, l'ora sesta.'

to thee; for I see it in the truthful mirror which makes of itself a reflection of all else and of which nothing makes of itself the reflection.[9] Thou wouldst hear how long it is since God put me in the lofty garden where this Lady prepared thee for so long a stair,—and how long it was a delight to my eyes,—and the real cause of the great wrath,—and the language that I used and shaped. Know then, my son, that not the tasting of the tree in itself was the cause of so long exile, but solely the trespass beyond the mark.[10] In the place from which thy Lady sent Virgil I longed for this assembly during four thousand, three hundred and two revolutions of the sun, and I saw it return to all the lights on its track nine hundred and thirty times while I lived on earth.[11] The tongue I spoke was all extinct before Nimrod's race gave their mind to the unaccomplishable task;[12] for no product whatever of reason—since human choice is renewed with the course of heaven—can last forever. It is a work of nature that man should speak, but whether in this way or that nature then leaves you to follow your own pleasure. Before I descended to the anguish of Hell the Supreme Good from whom comes the joy that swathes me was named *I* on earth, and later He was called *El*;[13] and that is fitting, for the usage of mortals is like a leaf on a branch, which goes and another comes. On the mountain that rises highest from the sea I lived, pure, then guilty, from the first hour to that following the sixth, when the sun changes quadrant.'[14]

1. 'Ananias . . . putting his hands on him said, Brother Saul, the Lord, even Jesus, . . . hath sent me, that thou mightest receive thy sight, and be filled with the Holy Ghost. . . . And he received sight forthwith, and arose, and was baptized' (*Acts* ix. 17–18).

2. By reason and revelation.

3. 'That which dies not and that which can die are nothing but the splendour of that Idea which our Sire, in Loving, begets' (*Par.* xiii).

4. Aristotle taught that the heavens—understood by Dante to include the angelic 'Intelligences' which control the heavens—are moved by desire for the unmoved First Cause. 'I believe in one God, who, unmoved, moves all heaven with love and desire' (*Par.* xxiv).

5. 'The Lord said unto Moses, . . . I will make all my goodness pass before thee' (*Ex.* xxxiii. 17–19),—in the Vulgate, '*Ego ostendam omne bonum tibi*'.

6. A reference, perhaps, to *John* i. 1–18: 'In the beginning was the word', etc. There are also other interpretations.

7. The eagle was the symbol of St John the Evangelist in medieval art.

8. Each sensory organ was supposed to be provided with a 'spirit' by whose operation external impacts cause sensations.

9. All created things are perfectly reflected in God, but no created thing is sufficient to reflect Him as He is. 'It is evident that every lesser nature is too scant a vessel for that good which has no limit and measures itself by itself' (*Par.* xix).

10. 'The serpent said unto the woman, . . . In the day ye eat thereof, then your eyes shall be opened, and ye shall be as gods, knowing good and evil. And . . . she took of the fruit thereof, and did eat, and gave also unto her husband with her, and he did eat' (*Gen.* iii. 4–6). The first sin was pride.

11. The following is Dante's chronology:

The creation of Adam	5198 B.C.
Adam's death and descent into Limbo (*Inf.* iv)	4268 B.C.
Christ's descent into Hell and deliverance of the Old Testament saints	34 A.D.

12. It was supposed that Nimrod designed the Tower of Babel; cp. *Inf.* xxxi and *Purg.* xii.

13. In medieval Jewish writings the letter *I* or *J*—equivalent to the Hebrew initial *yod*—was used in place of *Jah* or *Jehovah* out of reverence for the sacred name, and this practice, along with a mistaken interpretation of *Ex.* vi. 3, may have led Dante to the view in the text.

14. 6 a.m. to 1 p.m. The length of Adam's stay in Eden was variously estimated by medieval theologians.

NOTE

At the end of the twenty-fifth canto St John—described just
before by Beatrice as 'he that lay on the breast of our Pelican,
he that was chosen from the cross for the great charge'—rebuked
Dante for dazzling himself 'to see that which has no place here',
the Apostle's body; and the statement that Dante 'strains his
eyes' on John stands in immediate context and contrast with
the absorbed gaze of Beatrice on the Apostle. The passage
seems to be a reminiscence of *John* xxi. 23: 'Then went this
saying abroad among the brethren, that that disciple should
not die: yet Jesus said not unto him, He shall not die; but, If I
will that he tarry till I come, what is that to thee?' The matter
is left, so to speak, an open question, and in popular legend
'this saying' later took the meaning that John, without death,
was taken bodily to heaven. In Dante's narrative here it seems
plain that his irrelevant curiosity and preoccupation with a
supposed physical fact, as of one staring at a solar eclipse, blind
him for the time to Beatrice, the truth of God, and to the real
significance of John as the beloved disciple and the paladin
and teacher of love. Then, suddenly, 'the flaming circle' of the
three Apostles 'stopped and was silent'. Dante's sight was
'but confounded, not destroyed', and the virtue of Beatrice's
look would restore it, as Paul's sight was restored by the hand
of Ananias and he was 'filled with the Holy Ghost',—the context
is relevant. Meantime he is to 'make up for' his loss of sight
with speech; and he is led by John's questions to declare the
warrant which he finds for love in reason and in Scripture and
to make his profession that in all good he finds the Divine
Goodness which is the only good. John urges him further to
declare 'by how many teeth this love bites' him; *con quanti
denti questo amor ti morde,*—the number of *t*'s and *d*'s gives
the line a singular emphasis. Dante understands and is

obedient to 'the holy purpose of Christ's Eagle'—the eagle
is traditionally the farthest-sighted of earthly creatures—;
and he makes his declaration of all that has wrought together
in his charity and of his full committal to the love that rests
on faith and hope and includes them in itself, the love that
is more than affection—'my charity'—and that contemplates
the whole of life and redemption and creation, love in the
compass and completeness of its meaning: 'The leaves with
which the garden of the eternal Gardener is embowered I love
in the measure of the good He has bestowed on them.' It was
then—'as soon as I was silent'—that Dante heard the song of
the saints and that Beatrice chased away every mote from his
eyes with the radiance of her own and he saw better than before.
'To love beings in and for God is not to treat them as a mere
means or a mere occasion for loving God, but to love and cherish
their being as an end, because it *merits* love, in the degree to
which that merit and their dignity spring from the sovereign
love and the sovereign loving-kindness of God. So we under-
stand the paradox whereby in the end the saint includes in a
universal love of kinship and of piety . . . all that passes in
time, all the weakness and the beauty of things, all he had left
behind him on his journey' (*J. Maritain*). The whole incident,
as Dante tells it, belongs to the setting of love in order
in him.

The legend of John's bodily assumption originated in the
Eastern Church and was never fully accepted in the West.
Aquinas admitted it merely as 'a pious belief'. A very few
illustrations of it have survived from earlier centuries of Eastern
iconography, and the only known example in the West is the
well-known painting by Giotto in the great Franciscan Church
of Santa Croce in Florence. It dates, probably, from only a
few years after Dante's death and the publication of the *Paradiso*,
and it is fair to say that Giotto, or his employer, went quite out
of his way in the choice of the subject. The person of the
Apostle is represented in its full weight and bulk, drawn
upwards by the light that streams from the face of Christ in the
sky; and by the character of the figure and the visible amaze-
ment of John's disciples the miracle is made as convincing
as no one but Giotto could make it. In all the circumstances,

is it an unlikely conjecture that the picture was commissioned as a papal and Franciscan defence of the legend against Dante's rationalism? 'This report', which Dante was charged to 'take back to your world', that the spirit of John had said to him in Paradise: 'My body is earth in the earth', might well give offence to some of the clergy and devout laity in Florence as a gratuitous addition to the impieties of the notorious enemy of the Church. To us it is an evidence, one among many, of Dante's concern to clear the mind of the people of the superstitions that cumbered and materialized their faith,—in this case a fancy all but repudiated in Scripture.

The place given to Adam in Dante's poem and in medieval thinking is peculiar. On the one hand, Adam and Eve are the first of human sinners, who have left to mankind a heritage of guilt; on the other hand, in the poem as in Christian tradition, they are the first of all the souls in Limbo to be delivered in the Harrowing of Hell. In *Inferno* iv Virgil tells of 'a mighty one, crowned with a sign of victory,' who 'took from among us our first parent'. Adam is named there first among the Old Testament saints, and in *Paradiso* xxxii he is seen seated in the Empyrean beside the Virgin, who has Eve at her feet. Here, in the Church Triumphant, Adam appears as the first and farthest-reaching evidence of human redemption. Humanity fell in him as its representative, so the work of redemption is tested and proved in him, and he is here the one human figure to join the fellowship of the three Apostles who stand for the virtues of the Christian life. Traditionally, Adam was created with all natural perfections—the dust was 'made fit for all the perfections of a living creature' (*Par.* xiii)—and the place given him here means the redemption of the natural man in the life of the spirit. He fell by his 'trespass beyond the mark', just as Eve 'did not bear to stay under any veil' (*Purg.* xxix); now he finds his freedom and fulfilment in the obedience which consists of faith and hope and love.

The surprising comparison of Adam's movements showing through his enveloping light with those of an animal that stirs under a covering cloth is an instance of what has been noted as a marked feature of the *Paradiso*, the use of homely, sometimes even vulgar, imagery, like some of the Gothic figures in the stone and wood of the cathedrals. Dante deliberately breaks through the limits of classical poetic propriety in order to preserve the vigour of reality in the ethereal heights. Among many examples are: the description of the Franciscan Order in its decadence as a cask of mouldy wine (*Par.* xii), and of the Benedictine cowls as sacks full of rotten meal (*Par.* xxii), the comparison of the soldier-saints in the cross of Mars with the motes in a sunbeam that comes through the chink in a shutter (*Par.* xiv), the charge given to Dante by Cacciaguida: 'Make plain all thy vision, and then let them scratch where is the itch' (*Par.* xvii). It is a mark of the convincing objectivity of Dante's whole narrative; he could never have put it so, we think, unless he had seen and heard it. The 'ancient father', appearing out of the furthest depths of humanity, talking of his life in Eden in the beginning of time, is real and present with him and we accept the interview without question.

Dante's query, meaningless for us, about Adam's language was perfectly natural for him. Not only was Adam a solid historical personage for him, but Dante was a student of language and its history, and he had written, some fifteen or sixteen years before, part of a Latin treatise, never finished, on the vernaculars of Italy. A comparison of his statements on these subjects shows that in the years between he had changed his mind and had reached what we may fairly call a more scientific view of the conditions of human speech. In the *De Vulgari Eloquentia* he wrote: 'A certain form of speech was created by God along with the first soul. . . . In this form of speech Adam spoke; in this form of speech all his posterity spoke, down to the building of the Tower of Babel, by interpretation the Tower of Confusion; this form of speech the sons of Heber, who are called Hebrews, inherited. After the confusion it continued with them alone, in order that our Redeemer, who in His humanity sprang from them, should use, not the language of confusion, but that of grace.' And as to the question of 'the first word uttered by the first speaker' he had said in the same context that it is only reasonable to hold that 'it was the equivalent of *God*, that is, *El*, . . . since man was made by Him and for Him.' Dante gives five stanzas to the correction of his earlier views, and the difference springs from his new sense of time and history. Here, in the Starry Sphere, near the source of time itself, referred to in the next canto, Dante reflects that 'human choice is renewed with the course of heaven' and 'the usage of mortals is like a leaf on a branch, which goes and another comes.'

PARADISO

'AL Padre, al Figlio, allo Spirito Santo'
   cominciò 'gloria!' tutto il paradiso,
   sì che m' inebriava il dolce canto.
Ciò ch' io vedeva mi sembiava un riso
   dell'universo; per che mia ebbrezza
   intrava per l'udire e per lo viso.
Oh gioia! oh ineffabile allegrezza!
   oh vita integra d'amore e di pace!
   oh sanza brama sicura ricchezza!
Dinanzi alli occhi miei le quattro face   10
   stavano accese, e quella che pria venne
   incominciò a farsi più vivace,
e tal nella sembianza sua divenne,
   qual diverrebbe Giove, s'elli e Marte
   fossero augelli e cambiassersi penne.
La provedenza, che quivi comparte
   vice ed officio, nel beato coro
   silenzio posto avea da ogni parte,
quand' io udi': 'Se io mi trascoloro,
   non ti maravigliar; chè, dicend' io,   20
   vedrai trascolorar tutti costoro.
Quelli ch' usurpa in terra il luogo mio,
   il luogo mio, il luogo mio, che vaca
   nella presenza del Figliuol di Dio,
fatt' ha del cimiterio mio cloaca
   del sangue e della puzza; onde 'l perverso
   che cadde di qua su, là giù si placa.'

CANTO XXVII

St Peter's denunciation of the Church; the ascent to the Crystalline Sphere; Beatrice on human degeneracy

'GLORY be to the Father, and to the Son, and to the Holy Ghost!' all Paradise began, so that the sweet song held me rapt; what I saw seemed to me a smile of the universe, so that my rapture entered both by hearing and by sight. O joy! O gladness unspeakable! O life fulfilled with love and peace! O wealth secure with no craving!

Before my eyes the four torches stood flaming; and the one that had come first began to grow brighter, and its aspect became as would Jupiter's if it and Mars were birds and exchanged plumage. The Providence which here assigns time and duty had imposed silence on the blessed choir on every side, when I heard: 'If I change colour do not marvel, for while I speak thou shalt see the colour change in all of these. He that usurps on earth my place, my place, my place, which in the sight of the Son of God is empty, has made of my tomb a sewer of blood and filth, so that the apostate who fell from here above takes comfort there below.'[1]

Di quel color che per lo sole avverso
   nube dipigne da sera e da mane,
   vid' io allora tutto il ciel cosperso.   30
E come donna onesta che permane
   di sè sicura, e per l'altrui fallanza,
   pur ascoltando, timida si fane,
così Beatrice trasmutò sembianza;
   e tale eclissi credo che 'n ciel fue,
   quando patì la suprema possanza.
Poi procedetter le parole sue
   con voce tanto da sè trasmutata,
   che la sembianza non si mutò piùe:
'Non fu la sposa di Cristo allevata   40
   del sangue mio, di Lin, di quel di Cleto,
   per essere ad acquisto d'oro usata;
ma, per acquisto d'esto viver lieto,
   e Sisto e Pio e Calisto e Urbano
   sparser lo sangue dopo molto fleto.
Non fu nostra intenzion ch'a destra mano
   de' nostri successor parte sedesse,
   parte dall'altra del popol cristiano;
nè che le chiavi che mi fuor concesse
   divenisser signaculo in vessillo   50
   che contra battezzati combattesse;
nè ch' io fossi figura di sigillo
   a privilegi venduti e mendaci,
   ond' io sovente arrosso e disfavillo.
In vesta di pastor lupi rapaci
   si veggion di qua su per tutti i paschi:
   o difesa di Dio, perchè pur giaci?
Del sangue nostro Caorsini e Guaschi
   s'apparecchian di bere: o buon principio,
   a che vil fine convien che tu caschi!   60
Ma l'alta provedenza che con Scipio
   difese a Roma la gloria del mondo,
   soccorrà tosto, sì com' io concipio.
E tu, figliuol, che per lo mortal pondo
   ancor giù tornerai, apri la bocca,
   e non asconder quel ch' io non ascondo.'

With the colour that paints the morning and evening clouds that face the sun I saw then the whole heaven suffused. And as a chaste woman who is sure of herself, and at another's fault, only hearing of it, is put to shame, so Beatrice changed semblance, and such eclipse, I believe, there was in heaven when the Omnipotent suffered.[2]

Then his words continued, in a voice so altered from itself that his looks were not more changed: 'The Bride of Christ was not nurtured with my blood and that of Linus and of Cletus to be used for gain of gold; but for gain of this happy life Sixtus and Pius and Calixtus and Urban shed their blood after many tears.[3] It was not our meaning that on the right hand of our successors should sit one part of Christ's people and the other on the left; nor that the keys which were committed to me should become the device on a standard for warfare on the baptized; nor that I should be the figure on a seal for sold and lying favours, for which I often redden and flash with fire.[4] Ravening wolves in shepherds' clothing are seen from here above through all the pastures. O God of our defence, why sleepst Thou still? Cahorsines and Gascons prepare to drink our blood.[5] O fair beginning, to what base end art thou to fall? But the high Providence which by Scipio saved for Rome the glory of the world[6] will, as I conceive, bring speedy succour. And thou, my son, who, for thy mortal burden, shalt return again below, open thy mouth and do not hide what I hide not.'

389

Sì come di vapor gelati fiocca
   in giuso l'aere nostro, quando il corno
   della capra del ciel col sol si tocca,
in su vid' io così l'etera adorno   70
   farsi e fioccar di vapor triunfanti
   che fatto avean con noi quivi soggiorno.
Lo viso mio seguiva i suoi sembianti,
   e seguì fin che 'l mezzo, per lo molto,
   li tolse il trapassar del più avanti.
Onde la donna, che mi vide assolto
   dell'attendere in su, mi disse: 'Adima
   il viso, e guarda come tu se' volto.'
Dall'ora ch' io avea guardato prima
   i' vidi mosso me per tutto l'arco   80
   che fa dal mezzo al fine il primo clima;
sì ch' io vedea di là da Gade il varco
   folle d'Ulisse, e di qua presso il lito
   nel qual si fece Europa dolce carco.
E più mi fora discoverto il sito
   di questa aiuola; ma 'l sol procedea
   sotto i mie' piedi un segno e più partito.
La mente innamorata, che donnea
   con la mia donna sempre, di ridure
   ad essa li occhi più che mai ardea: 90
e se natura o arte fè pasture
   da pigliare occhi, per aver la mente,
   in carne umana o nelle sue pitture,
tutte adunate, parrebber nïente
   ver lo piacer divin che mi refulse,
   quando mi volsi al suo viso ridente.
E la virtù che lo sguardo m' indulse,
   del bel nido di Leda mi divelse,
   e nel ciel velocissimo m' impulse.
Le parti sue vicinissime e eccelse   100
   sì uniforme son, ch' i' non so dire
   qual Beatrice per loco mi scelse.
Ma ella, che vedea il mio disire,
   incominciò, ridendo tanto lieta,
   che Dio parea nel suo volto gioire:

Even as our air, when the horn of the heavenly Goat is touched by the sun,[7] flakes down frozen vapours, so I saw the ether thus adorned, flaking upwards triumphal vapours which had made their stay with us there. My sight kept following their forms and followed them till the great space between took from it the power of reaching farther.

My Lady, therefore, who saw me freed from gazing up, said to me: 'Cast thy sight down and look how far thou hast revolved.'

From the time when I had looked before[8] I saw that I had moved through the whole arc from the middle to the end of the first clime, so that I saw on the one hand, beyond Cadiz, the mad track of Ulysses, and on the other nearly to the shore where Europa made herself a sweet burden; and more of the space of this little threshing-floor would have been disclosed to me but that the sun was moving on beneath my feet and was a sign and more away.[9]

The enamoured mind that wooes my Lady continually burned more than ever to bring back my eyes to her; and if nature or art have made baits to take the eyes so as to possess the mind, in human flesh or in its portraiture, all these together would seem nothing beside the divine delight that shone on me when I turned to her smiling face. And the virtue that her look granted me drew me forth from the fair nest of Leda[10] and thrust me into the swiftest of the heavens.[11]

Its parts, the nearest and the highest, are so uniform that I cannot tell which Beatrice chose for my place. But she, who saw my desire, began, smiling with such gladness that in her face seemed to be God's own joy: 'The nature of the universe,

'La natura del mondo, che quïeta
  il mezzo e tutto l'altro intorno move,
  quinci comincia come da sua meta;
e questo cielo non ha altro dove
  che la mente divina, in che s'accende   110
  l'amor che il volge e la virtù ch'ei piove.
Luce ed amor d'un cerchio lui comprende,
  sì come questo li altri; e quel precinto
  colui che 'l cinge solamente intende.
Non è suo moto per altro distinto;
  ma li altri son misurati da questo,
  sì come diece da mezzo e da quinto.
E come il tempo tegna in cotal testo
  le sue radici e ne li altri le fronde,
  omai a te può esser manifesto.   120
Oh cupidigia che i mortali affonde
  sì sotto te, che nessuno ha podere
  di trarre li occhi fuor delle tue onde!
Ben fiorisce nelli uomini il volere;
  ma la pioggia continüa converte
  in bozzacchioni le susine vere.
Fede ed innocenzia son reperte
  solo ne' parvoletti; poi ciascuna
  pria fugge che le guance sian coperte.
Tale, balbuzïendo ancor, digiuna,   130
  che poi divora, con la lingua sciolta,
  qualunque cibo per qualunque luna;
e tal, balbuzïendo, ama e ascolta
  la madre sua, che, con loquela intera,
  disïa poi di vederla sepolta.
Così si fa la pelle bianca nera
  nel primo aspetto della bella figlia
  di quel ch'apporta mane e lascia sera.
Tu, perchè non ti facci maraviglia,
  pensa che 'n terra non è chi governi;   140
  onde sì svia l'umana famiglia.
Ma prima che gennaio tutto si sverni
  per la centesma ch'è là giù negletta,
  raggeran sì questi cerchi superni,

which holds the centre still and moves all else round it, begins here as from its starting-point, and this heaven has no other *where* but the Divine Mind, in which is kindled the love that turns it and the virtue which it rains down. Light and love enclose it in a circle, as it does the others, and of that girding He that girds it is the sole Intelligence.[12] Its motion is not determined by another's, but from it the rest have their measures, even as ten from the half and the fifth;[13] and how time should have its roots in that vessel and in the others its leaves, may now be plain to thee.[14]

'O covetousness, who so plungest mortals in thy depths that none has power to lift his eyes from thy waves! The will blossoms well in men, but the continual rain turns the sound plums to withered. Faith and innocence are found only in little children; then, before the cheeks are covered, both are fled. One, still lisping, keeps the fasts, who after, when his tongue is free, devours any food through any month; another, lisping, loves and heeds his mother, who after, when his speech is perfect, longs to see her buried. So the white skin turns black at the first sight of the fair daughter of him that brings morning and leaves evening.[15] That thou marvel not at this, consider that there is no one to govern on the earth, so that the human family goes astray. But before all January leaves the winter, because of the hundredth part that is neglected below,[16] these lofty circles shall shine

che la fortuna che tanto s'aspetta,
  le poppe volgerà u' son le prore,
  sì che la classe correrà diretta;
  e vero frutto verrà dopo 'l fiore.'

forth so that the event so long looked-for shall turn the poops where are the prows; and then the fleet shall run on the straight course and good fruit shall follow the flower.'

1. St Peter's tomb in Rome, traditionally the place of his martyrdom.

2. The darkness at the Crucifixion.

3. Martyr popes of the primitive Church.

4. Pope Boniface kept the Guelfs 'on the right hand' and the Ghibellines 'on the left'; he fought against the Colonna family near Rome, and 'every one of his enemies was Christian' (*Inf.* xxvii); the keys appeared on the Papal standard and Peter's head on the Papal seal for indulgences, etc.

5. Clement V of Gascony and John XXII of Cahors, French popes in Dante's lifetime, trafficked in the Church's patrimony.

6. Scipio Africanus defeated Hannibal in 202 B.C. and 'saved' the future Empire.

7. In mid-winter, when the Sun is in Capricorn.

8. *Par.* xxii.

9. 'The first clime' was a zone of latitude north from the Equator and covering the inhabited world from east to west; 'from the middle to the end' of it was from Jerusalem to Gibraltar. Dante, in Gemini, had been carried west by the Starry Sphere as far as Cadiz, and the Sun, still farther west, showed him the Atlantic, with 'the mad track of Ulysses' (*Inf.* xxvi). In Phoenicia, where Jupiter in the form of a bull carried off Europa on his back to Crete, the Sun was already set, so that Dante saw 'nearly to the shore.'

10. Gemini, the Twins, were the children of Leda by Jupiter.

11. The Crystalline Sphere.

12. The angelic Intelligences control the nine moving spheres; beyond them and outside of space the Empyrean is contained and controlled by the Divine Mind, the supreme Intelligence.

13. The number 10 is 'measured' by its factors 5 and 2. The swift motion of the Crystalline is the standard or measure for that of all the planetary spheres.

14. Time has its starting-point in the motion of the invisible Crystalline, as a plant has its hidden roots in a flower-pot, and time is measured for us by the movements of the planets, which are visible like the leaves of the plant.

15. The innocence of childhood is darkened by the first sight of Circe, daughter of the Sun; she represents the allurement of earthly things, turning men to beasts. The interpretation is much debated.

16. By the Julian calendar then in use the year was nearly a hundredth part of a day too long and January was gradually becoming later in the season.

NOTE

While 'the four torches stood flaming', together the sign of a fulfilled redemption, 'all Paradise', the whole Church Triumphant, burst into the *Gloria Patri*. It is a marked feature of this heaven of All Saints, and a complement of the formality of Dante's theological examination by the three Apostles, that it is full of singing, the chants alternating with the examinations; the truths of the spirit on which Dante has given his answers in formal terms are, for their more perfect utterance, sublimated into song. Then Dante himself, 'rapt'—literally 'intoxicated'—'with the sweet song', follows with one of his great lyric stanzas: 'O joy! O gladness unspeakable! O life fulfilled with love and peace! O wealth secure with no craving!' That is what the Church Triumphant means.

In sudden contrast is the scene that follows, and its strangeness is emphasized in the terms of its description. St Peter's colour changed as if the white sheen of Jupiter had become the fiery glow of Mars and righteousness had turned to wrath. 'The blessed choir' was held silent while he spoke. The whole contrast corresponds with that between the Church of God's purpose, represented by St Peter, and the Church in present earthly fact, the Church of Pope Boniface,—the contrast which is the Church's judgement. The Pope is the head and front of the Church's offending, and he is disowned by Peter himself, who declares that his own place, his place, his place, is 'empty', and that, in Christ's sight, Boniface is no Pope, but a usurper. The whole heaven flushes in sympathy with the Apostle's anger, and Beatrice, the truth of the true Church, changes colour with shame. For it is the peculiar sanctities of the Church that are made the instruments of its wantonness and greed,—the blood of its martyrs, the keys of the Kingdom, the personality of its first head under Christ. Yet Peter, the spokesman of the faith which is the substance of things hoped for, bids Dante expect 'speedy succour' from 'high Providence', the same Providence which once preserved through Scipio the divine order of the world; for Dante, the causes of Church and Empire are one in God's thought and care. The same assurance is expressed by Beatrice in other terms at the end of the canto, the messianic imperial hope now undefined but surviving all disappointment to the last.

When the host of the redeemed has streamed upwards after Christ and the Virgin, like a reversed fall of snow—a comparison the more convincing for its strangeness—Beatrice bids Dante look down on the world far below them, as she did before on their ascent to the eighth sphere. Then, it was in order that he might have his sight clear for earthly and heavenly things in their true proportions; now, it is in order that he may know how far he has revolved with the moving sphere—that he may realize the vastness of the heavens covering the spaces of land and sea and declaring the breadth of God's providence for men. He sees again, from that still greater distance than before, 'this little threshing-floor' of the world he knew,—from the east, where Europa had brought to it from a heathen shore her wantonness and her name, to the west, where the pride of Ulysses had made him trespass beyond the world's appointed bounds in his 'mad track'. So understood, Europa and Ulysses are a kind of parallel by contrast to Francis and Dominic in the eleventh and twelfth cantos,—the forces, encompassing the world, of wantonness and pride, against the heavenly powers of grace and truth.

By the virtue that comes to him from the eyes of Beatrice— by the further enlargement of his mind—he is snatched away from the Starry Sphere and finds himself in the Crystalline, 'the royal mantle of all the world's revolving spheres, which most burns and is most quickened in the breath of God and in His working' (*Par.* xxiii).

This ninth heaven is the boundary of space and time, of all in the created universe that is relative and subject to change, the outermost limit of what Dante means by Nature. Sometimes called the Primum Mobile because it is the first moved of all the spheres, the Crystalline is under the immediate influence of the Empyrean, that influence operating through its controlling order of angels, the Seraphim, the spirits of love, the highest of the angelic orders. The infinite speed of its spin expresses the desire of all its parts to be in contact with the Empyrean, and its motion is distributed to the lower spheres, by whose motions time is measured and given to the world. The whole is as ordered and unquestionable, Dante says characteristically, as that twice five is ten. Thus the co-ordinated movements of all the spheres together represent the divine operations, constant and beneficent, through the nine angelic orders, on the lives of men; and time, the human days and years, springs like a plant, with roots and leaves, from the whole creation and providence of God. 'Time is infinitely more than a mere succession of corporeal movements. It is the procession of the Light and Love of Eternity into the temporal life of man (*J. S. Carroll*).

It is this context that explains Beatrice's outburst against covetousness at the end of the canto. Human degeneracy is the abuse of time—that is, of providence—so that time works for evil instead of good; it is the refusal and reversal of the whole purpose of creation. As sound plums in continual rain turn to withered, so children lose faith and innocence with the passing of the years; and this disregard of the operative grace of God declared in the moving heavens is oddly and characteristically illustrated by the neglect below of the hundredth part of a day—less than fifteen minutes—in the accepted reckoning of the year. The whole passage recalls Virgil's words at the end of *Purgatorio* xiv: 'The heavens call you and wheel about you, showing you their eternal beauties, and your eyes gaze only on the earth; therefore He smites you who sees all', and in *Purgatorio* xix: 'Turn thine eyes to the lure which the Eternal King spins with the great wheels'. Such passages give us the meaning of Dante's astrology. It is part of his astrology, too, to believe that creation is not in vain, and Beatrice ends her speech with an expression of assured confidence: 'Before all January leaves the winter'—as if she had said: 'Before a thousand years are past'—'these lofty circles shall shine forth . . . and good fruit shall follow the flower'. 'Perhaps the Poet, with sublime resignation, now thought only of preparing for the future by his dream of justice and peace, with no more hope of seeing its realization with his mortal eyes' (*E. G. Parodi*).

There is a notable parallel with these lines in Vaughan's *The World*, written, probably, with no reference to Dante, but drawing from the same tradition:

> 'I saw Eternity the other night,
> Like a great Ring of pure and endless light,
>   All calm, as it was bright;
> And round beneath it, Time, in hours, days, years,
>   Driv'n by the spheres,
> Like a vast shadow mov'd; in which the world
>   And all her train were hurl'd.

.   .   .   .

> This Ring the Bridegroome did for none provide,
>   But for His Bride.'

POSCIA che 'ncontro alla vita presente
 de' miseri mortali aperse 'l vero
 quella che 'mparadisa la mia mente,
come in lo specchio fiamma di doppiero
 vede colui che se n'alluma retro,
 prima che l'abbia in vista o in pensiero,
e sè rivolge per veder se 'l vetro
 li dice il vero, e vede ch'el s'accorda
 con esso come nota con suo metro;
così la mia memoria si ricorda   10
 ch' io feci riguardando ne' belli occhi
 onde a pigliarmi fece Amor la corda.
E com' io mi rivolsi e furon tocchi
 li miei da ciò che pare in quel volume,
 quandunque nel suo giro ben s'adocchi,
un punto vidi che raggiava lume
 acuto sì, che 'l viso ch'elli affoca
 chiuder conviensi per lo forte acume;
e quale stella par quinci più poca,
 parrebbe luna, locata con esso   20
 come stella con stella si colloca.
Forse cotanto quanto pare appresso
 alo cigner la luce che 'l dipigne
 quando 'l vapor che 'l porta più è spesso,
distante intorno al punto un cerchio d' igne
 si girava sì ratto, ch'avrìa vinto
 quel moto che più tosto il mondo cigne.
E questo era d'un altro circumcinto,
 e quel dal terzo, e 'l terzo poi dal quarto,
 dal quinto il quarto, e poi dal sesto il quinto. 30

CANTO XXVIII

The Angelic circles

WHEN she that imparadises my mind had declared
the truth as against the present life of wretched
mortals, then, as one that is lighted from behind
sees the flame of a torch in the mirror before he has
it in his sight or thought, and turns round to see
if the glass tells him the truth, and sees that the one
agrees with the other as a song with its measure,
thus my memory records that I did, gazing into the
fair eyes of which love made the noose to take me.
And when I turned again and mine were met by
what appears in that revolving sphere to one that
looks intently on its circling, I saw a point which
radiated a light so keen that the eye on which it
burns must close for its piercing power; and the
star that from here seems the least would seem a
moon if put beside it like star with star in conjunc-
tion. As near, perhaps, as a halo appears to girdle
the light that paints it when the vapour that carries
it is most dense, at such a distance about the point
a circle of fire was wheeling so fast it would have
outstripped the motion that most swiftly girds the
world;[1] and this was encircled by another, and that
by the third, then the third by the fourth, the
fourth by the fifth, and then the fifth by the sixth.

Sopra seguiva il settimo sì sparto
  già di larghezza, che 'l messo di Iuno
  intero a contenerlo sarebbe arto.
Così l'ottavo e 'l nono; e ciascheduno
  più tardo si movea, secondo ch'era
  in numero distante più dall'uno;
e quello avea la fiamma più sincera
  cui men distava la favilla pura,
  credo, però che più di lei s' invera.
La donna mia, che mi vedea in cura   40
  forte sospeso, disse: 'Da quel punto
  depende il cielo e tutta la natura.
Mira quel cerchio che più li è congiunto;
  e sappi che 'l suo muovere è sì tosto
  per l'affocato amore ond'elli è punto.'
E io a lei: 'Se 'l mondo fosse posto
  con l'ordine ch' io veggio in quelle rote,
  sazio m'avrebbe ciò che m'è proposto;
ma nel mondo sensibile si pote
  veder le volte tanto più divine,   50
  quant'elle son dal centro più remote.
Onde, se 'l mio disio dee aver fine
  in questo miro e angelico templo
  che solo amore e luce ha per confine,
udir convienmi ancor come l'essemplo
  e l'essemplare non vanno d'un modo,
  chè io per me indarno a ciò contemplo.'
'Se li tuoi diti non sono a tal nodo
  sufficïenti, non è maraviglia;
  tanto, per non tentare, è fatto sodo.'   60
Così la donna mia; poi disse: 'Piglia
  quel ch' io ti dicerò, se vuo' saziarti;
  ed intorno da esso t'assottiglia.
Li cerchi corporai sono ampi e arti
  secondo il più e 'l men della virtute
  che si distende per tutte lor parti.
Maggior bontà vuol far maggior salute;
  maggior salute maggior corpo cape,
  s'elli ha le parti igualmente compiute.

Beyond followed the seventh, spread now so wide that Juno's messenger,[2] completed, would be too small to contain it; and so the eighth and the ninth. And each moved more slowly as it was farther in order from the first; and that one had the clearest flame which was least distant from the pure spark, because, I believe, most partaking of its truth.[3]

My Lady, who saw me eager and perplexed, said: 'From that point hang the heavens and all nature. See that circle that is closest to it, and know that its motion is thus swift from the burning love by which it is impelled.'[4]

And I answered her: 'If the universe were disposed in the order I see in these wheels I should be satisfied with what thou hast set before me; but in the world of sense we can see that the orbits are more divine the farther they are from the centre. Therefore if my desire is to gain its end in this wondrous temple of the angels which has only love and light for bounds, then I still have to hear why the pattern and the copy do not follow the same plan; for by myself I meditate on this in vain.'

'If thy fingers are unfit for such a knot it is no wonder, so hard has it become from not being tried.' My Lady said this, then continued: 'Take what I shall tell thee if thou wouldst be satisfied, and whet thy wits on it. The material spheres are large or small according as more or less virtue is diffused through all their parts. Greater excellence must make greater blessedness; greater blessedness takes a greater body when the parts are of equal per-

Dunque costui che tutto quanto rape 70
  l'altro universo seco, corrisponde
  al cerchio che più ama e che più sape.
Per che, se tu alla virtù circonde
  la tua misura, non alla parvenza
  delle sustanze che t'appaion tonde,
tu vederai mirabil consequenza
  di maggio a più e di minore a meno
  in ciascun cielo, a sua intelligenza.'
Come rimane splendido e sereno
  l'emisperio dell'aere, quando soffia 80
  Borea da quella guancia ond'è più leno,
per che si purga e risolve la roffia
  che pria turbava, sì che 'l ciel ne ride
  con le bellezze d'ogni sua paroffia;
così fec' io, poi che mi provide
  la donna mia del suo risponder chiaro,
  e come stella in cielo il ver si vide.
E poi che le parole sue restaro,
  non altrimenti ferro disfavilla
  che bolle, come i cerchi sfavillaro. 90
L' incendio suo seguiva ogni scintilla;
  ed eran tante, che 'l numero loro
  più che 'l doppiar delli scacchi s' inmilla.
Io sentiva osannar di coro in coro
  al punto fisso che li tiene alli ubi,
  e terrà sempre, ne' quai sempre foro.
E quella che vedea i pensier dubi
  nella mia mente, disse: 'I cerchi primi
  t' hanno mostrati Serafi e Cherubi.
Così veloci seguono i suoi vimi, 100
  per somigliarsi al punto quanto ponno;
  e posson quanto a veder son sublimi.
Quelli altri amor che dintorno li vonno,
  si chiaman Troni del divino aspetto,
  per che 'l primo ternaro terminonno.
E dei saper che tutti hanno diletto
  quanto la sua veduta si profonda
  nel vero in che si queta ogni intelletto.

fection. This sphere, therefore, which sweeps along with it all the rest of the universe, answers to the circle that loves most and knows most;[6] so that if thou apply thy measure to the virtue, not the appearance, of the spirits that appear to thee as circles, thou wilt see in each heaven a marvellous correspondence with its Intelligence, of greater with more and of smaller with less.'

As the vault of the air is left serene and shining when Boreas blows from his milder cheek[7] and the obscuring fog is dissolved and driven away so that heaven smiles on us with all the beauties of its pageantry, so it was with me when my Lady granted me her clear answer, and, like a star in heaven, the truth was plain. And when she paused in her speech, as iron sparkles when it boils so these circles sparkled; every spark kept to its own fire, and they were so many that their number ran to more thousands than the doubling of the chess-board.[8] I heard from choir to choir *Hosanna* sung to the fixed point, which holds and shall ever hold them in the place where they have ever been.

And she, who saw the uncertain thoughts in my mind, said: 'The first circles have shown thee Seraphim and Cherubim. They follow their bonds[9] thus swiftly to gain all they may of likeness to the point, and this they may in so far as they are exalted in vision.[10] These next loving spirits that circle round them are called Thrones of the divine aspect,[11] and with them the first triad is completed. And thou must know that all have delight in the measure of the depth to which their sight penetrates the truth in which every intellect finds rest; from

Quinci si può veder come si fonda
   l'esser beato nell'atto che vede,   110
   non in quel ch'ama, che poscia seconda;
e del vedere è misura mercede,
   che grazia partorisce e buona voglia:
   così di grado in grado si procede.
L'altro ternaro, che così germoglia
   in questa primavera sempiterna
   che notturno Arïete non dispoglia,
perpetualemente "Osanna" sberna
   con tre melode, che suonano in tree
   ordini di letizia onde s' interna.   120
In essa gerarcia son l'altre dee:
   prima Dominazioni, e poi Virtudi;
   l'ordine terzo di Podestadi èe.
Poscia ne' due penultimi tripudi
   Principati e Arcangeli si girano;
   l'ultimo è tutto d'Angelici ludi.
Questi ordini di su tutti s'ammirano,
   e di giù vincon sì, che verso Dio
   tutti tirati sono, e tutti tirano.
E Dïonisio con tanto disio   130
   a contemplar questi ordini si mise,
   che li nomò e distinse com' io.
Ma Gregorio da lui poi si divise;
   onde, sì tosto come li occhi aperse
   in questo ciel, di sè medesmo rise.
E se tanto secreto ver proferse
   mortale in terra, non voglio ch'ammiri;
   chè chi 'l vide qua su liel discoperse
con altro assai del ver di questi giri.'

which it may be seen that the state of blessedness
rests on the act of vision, not on that of love, which
follows after, and the measure of their vision is
merit, which grace begets and right will. Such is
the process from step to step. The second triad that
flowers thus in this eternal spring which no nightly
Ram despoils[12] sings continual hosannas, the
threefold strain resounding in the three ranks of
bliss that form the triad. In this hierarchy are the
next divine orders,—first Dominions, then Virtues,
and the third are Powers. Then, last but one of the
festal throngs, wheel Principalities and Archangels,
and the last is all of Angels making sport. These
orders all gaze above and so prevail below that all
are drawn and all draw to God. And Dionysius[13]
set himself with such zeal to contemplate these
orders that he named and distributed them as I do;
but later Gregory[14] differed from him, so that as
soon as he opened his eyes in this heaven he
smiled at himself. And if a mortal on earth set forth
truth so secret thou needst not marvel, for he that
saw it here above revealed it to him, with much
more of the truth of these circles.'

1. The Crystalline, or Primum Mobile.

2. Iris, the rainbow.

3. The central point represents the light of God's presence, and the fiery circles the nine angelic orders which respectively control the nine heavenly spheres.

4. 'This is the cause of the extreme swiftness of the motion of the Primum Mobile, that, through the most fervent appetite of each part of that ninth heaven to be united to each part of the most divine and quiet tenth heaven, it revolves within it with such desire that its velocity is almost inconceivable' (*Convito*).

5. The angelic circles, centring on God, are swifter and brighter the nearer they are to Him; but their corresponding spheres, centring on the earth, 'are more divine the farther they are from the centre'.

6. The innermost angelic circle, that of the Seraphim, answers to the outermost sphere, the Crystalline.

7. Old maps sometimes showed the winds as winged heads with inflated cheeks. The north-east wind was regarded as bringing clear weather in North Italy.

8. The Persian inventor of chess is said to have asked the King to reward him with the grains of corn required to cover the squares of the chess-board in geometrical progression: 1-2-4-8, etc., a fabulous number.

9. They keep to the circles to which they are *bound* by their love.

10. 'When he shall appear, we shall be like him; for we shall see him as he is' (1 *John* iii. 2).

11. The Thrones declare the divine judgements. 'Above are mirrors—you call them Thrones—from which God shines on us in judgement' (*Par.* ix).

12. The Ram is seen at night from the autumn to the spring equinox. 'This eternal spring' never passes into autumn and winter, and is never 'despoiled' of its leaves.

13. Dionysius the Areopagite, St Paul's convert at Athens (*Acts* xvii. 34), was supposed to have learned from him about the heavens, which Paul himself had visited (2 *Cor.* xii. 1-4), and to have written *The Celestial Hierarchy*. It was, in fact, written in the 5th or 6th century and became the chief authority on the angels.

14. St Gregory—Pope, A.D. 590-604—gave a different account of the angelic orders.

NOTE

Beatrice is 'she that imparadises my mind'. It is Dante's *mind*, his thinking, his point of view, that is imparadised by Beatrice. The language is at once that of the devout lover and of the learner in divine things; and Dante is both lover and learner all the time. The light of God and of the angel circles he sees first by reflection in her eyes—the demonstration of the truth—just as in the Pageant of revelation on Purgatory he saw the reflection of the human and the divine nature of Christ; and, looking from the reflection to the reality, he finds the one agree with the other 'as a song with its measure'. Dante's praises of Beatrice rise as he rises with her to greater heights of revelation and experience; and now, on the threshold of the true Paradise, she is the song whose measure, whose controlling rhythm, is the glory of God. He is at pains to associate her exceptionally with this sphere of the angels. In all the lower spheres it is the spirits met within them who tell of them; here Beatrice alone is Dante's instructor. In the *Vita Nuova* Beatrice 'is constantly associated with the angels. During her earthly life, when people saw her pass, "crowned and clothed with humility," they said: "This is not a woman, but one of the most beautiful of the angels of heaven." In a dream of her death he saw angels flying heavenward with her soul in the form of a little white cloud. When she really dies he sings:

> "Beatrice is gone up into high Heaven,
> The kingdom where the angels are at peace,
> And lives with them." ' (*J. S. Carroll*).

Here, in the sphere of the Seraphim and in the visionary presence of all the forces of providence, Beatrice is peculiarly at home, declaring the truth as against the present life of wretched mortals and reflecting the light of God's presence.

The Crystalline, still a part of the material universe, although, so to speak, the least earthly and most spiritual part of it, cannot show God and the angelic hosts as they are in their own nature; but it can tell of the functions of the angels as God's immediate agents in transmitting to the world by a great co-operation through the spheres His creative and providential purposes and energies. The vision of the nine fiery circles wheeling about the point of light offers a kind of diagram and summary of the whole system of the divine working in the universe. 'It is a mathematical, systematic, accurate model of rest and motion: of motionless point and circling line' (*K. Vossler*). 'The vision here of the light of God and the angels is introduced, not as Milton introduces his God, as the object of a hymn of adoring angels, but in one of those homely images which at every step, even in the *Paradiso*, almost persuade us that Dante is telling us of what has happened to him, not of what he has dreamed: "As one that is lighted from behind sees the flame of a torch in the mirror before he has it in his sight or thought" ' (*C. H. Herford*).

These angelic orders came of an ancient and varied ancestry. In the Church's tradition and in Dante they derived from the angels, thrones, dominions, principalities and powers of Paul's Epistles,—as these did from the angels of the Jewish Apocalypses and of the Old Testament,—and these, probably, from Persian and Babylonian fancies. Christian tradition had organized them in ranks with their various functions and had associated them according to these ranks and functions with the astronomy, which was also the astrology, of the age. Dante had expounded these matters in some detail in the *Convito*, and it is significant that now, after ten years or more, he is satisfied merely to name the nine orders, which, except the first three, are distinguished nowhere else in the *Divine Comedy* and are not shown to correspond with the character of the several spheres on which they operate. He even jests with the great Pope St Gregory about the order of their ranks,—incidentally jesting with himself, for their order in the *Convito* is not that given here. It is hardly possible to think that Dante took these differences seriously, and by this time he seems to have shed from his mind, or at any rate from his interest, many of the current fancies of the medieval Church on the subject, and to have retained only what he felt to be spiritually significant, especially the assurance that God rules in the heavens by love (the Seraphim), and wisdom (the Cherubim), and judgement (the Thrones). There are, indeed, many references in the poem to the Intelligences which control the spheres, but in such references the angels are simply representative of the one Divine Providence which is continually, variously, harmoniously, operative in the lives of men; and however meaningless in itself is the regimentation of the angelic orders, it is full of Dante's meaning in giving concretely and with objectivity, as of a thing seen, the conception of a vast encompassing spiritual order which quickens and sustains and coordinates the whole of things. The account here may be compared with the words of Beatrice in the first canto, beginning: 'All things whatsoever have order among themselves, and this is the form that makes the universe resemble God', and in the second canto: 'Within the heaven of the divine peace spins a body in whose virtue lies the being of all that it contains.' It is Dante's own large and enduring faith in creation and providence and grace that is expressed in such terms; and when Beatrice has explained the angel circles and the physical spheres in their relations, it is with him, he says, as when 'the vault of the air is left serene and shining' after fog and, 'like a star in heaven, the truth is plain'. It is then that the angels break into hosannas; the diagram has come alive, and 'light and song merge in a cosmic symphony to the Eternal' (*C. Grabher*). The passage is no mere lyrical ornament to relieve a dull account of things, and to take it so is a fundamental misunderstanding of Dante's practice. 'The decorative similitude, so dear to the classic poets, is almost unknown in Dante's art' (*E. G. Parodi*), and there is here a true passion of confidence and praise in the heart of the Poet which is echoed in the angels' song.

The burning point about which the angels wheel has no spatial magnitude and the smallest star 'would seem a moon' beside it; but it has a piercing power which illumines all the angelic circles. It is a symbol of the immateriality and indivisible unity of Him who 'is light'. The circles, seen in their immediate relation to the point of light, are pure spirit, not to be estimated by their size, but only by their nearness to the centre. The Seraphim, the innermost and smallest circle, control the Crystalline, the greatest of the nine spheres, for the centre of the wheeling spheres is the earth, and of the circling angels God. It is a correction of the measurement of spiritual realities by material standards, given as Dante is about to pass beyond all the material spheres into a purely spiritual region of things.

Does love to God spring from knowledge of Him, or knowledge from love? The question was much under debate, and Dante accepts through Beatrice the reply of Aquinas in favour of the former view: 'the state of blessedness rests on the act of vision, not on that of love, which follows after.' The words sum up what has been made plain many times in the *Paradiso*, that the ardour of the saints is kindled by their vision. The question and the answer, which for us are superfluous and unreal, have this reality in the thought of Aquinas and implicit in all his laborious dialectic: that the assurance in God which is both knowledge and love of Him is properly the result, not of wishful thinking and self-persuasion, but of the reasoned and objective consideration of life and reality, and that this answer to this question is essentially an assertion of intellectual integrity as fundamental in the life of the spirit. Aquinas has no nobler lesson, and Dante adopts it. The first necessity, he insists, is *to see*, and *vedere*, with its derivatives, occurs with marked persistency throughout the canto. 'In the angels an intensity of knowledge is love; a less intense love is knowledge' (*Colet, quoted by E. G. Gardner*).

The 'virtues' and functions of the angelic circles are various, but not independent of each other; they are co-ordinated and complementary, passed on from the higher circle to the lower; 'these orders all gaze above and so prevail below that all are drawn and all draw to God'. They are different ranks, but one fellowship and mirrors of the one light. The Divine Providence is manifold, and one.

QUANDO ambedue li figli di Latona,
   coperti del Montone e della Libra,
   fanno dell'orizzonte insieme zona,
quant'è dal punto che 'l cenit i 'nlibra
   infin che l'uno e l'altro da quel cinto,
   cambiando l'emisperio, si dilibra,
tanto, col volto di riso dipinto,
   si tacque Beatrice, riguardando
   fisso nel punto che m'aveva vinto.
Poi cominciò: 'Io dico, e non dimando,   10
   quel che tu vuoli udir, perch' io l' ho visto
   là 've s'appunta ogni ubi e ogni quando.
Non per avere a sè di bene acquisto,
   ch'esser non può, ma perchè suo splendore
   potesse, risplendendo, dir "Subsisto",
in sua etternità di tempo fore,
   fuor d'ogni altro comprender, come i piacque,
   s'aperse in nuovi amor l'etterno amore.
Nè prima quasi torpente si giacque;
   chè nè prima nè poscia procedette
   lo discorrer di Dio sovra quest'acque.   20
Forma e matera, congiunte e purette,
   usciro ad esser che non avia fallo,
   come d'arco tricordo tre saette.
E come in vetro, in ambra od in cristallo
   raggio resplende sì, che dal venire
   all'esser tutto non è intervallo,
così 'l triforme effetto del suo sire
   nell'esser suo raggiò insieme tutto
   sanza distinzïone in essordire.   30

CANTO XXIX

*The creation and functions of the angels; the
foolishness of preachers*

WHEN the two children of Latona, covered by the
Ram and by the Scales, both at once make a belt
of the horizon, as long as from the moment when
the zenith holds them balanced till the one and the
other, changing hemispheres, are unbalanced from
that girdle,[1] for so long, her face illumined with a
smile, Beatrice kept silence, looking fixedly at the
point that had overcome me.

Then she began: 'I tell, not ask, what thou wouldst
hear; for I have seen it there where every *ubi* and
every *quando* is centred.'[2] Not to gain any good for
Himself, which cannot be, but that His splendour,
shining back, might say *Subsisto*,[3]—in His eternity,
beyond time, beyond every other bound, as it
pleased Him, the Eternal Love revealed Himself
in new loves.[4] Nor, before, did He lie as it were
inert; for until God's moving upon these waters
there was no 'before' or 'after'.[5] Form and matter,
united and separate, came into being that had no
defect, like three arrows from a three-stringed
bow.[6] And as a ray shines into glass or amber or
crystal so that from its coming to its completeness
there is no interval, so the threefold creation
flashed into being from its Lord all at once without
distinction in its beginning. With it, order was

Concreato fu ordine e costrutto
  alle sustanze; e quelle furon cima
  nel mondo in che puro atto fu produtto;
pura potenza tenne la parte ima;
  nel mezzo strinse potenza con atto
  tal vime, che già mai non si divima.
Ieronimo vi scrisse lungo tratto
  di secoli delli angeli creati
  anzi che l'altro mondo fosse fatto;
ma questo vero è scritto in molti lati   40
  dalli scrittor della Spirito Santo;
  e tu te n'avvedrai, se bene agguati;
e anche la ragione il vede alquanto,
  che non concederebbe che i motori
  sanza sua perfezion fosser cotanto.
Or sai tu dove e quando questi amori
  furon creati e come; sì che spenti
  nel tuo disïo già son tre ardori.
Nè giugnerìesi, numerando, al venti
  sì tosto, come delli angeli parte   50
  turbò il suggetto de' vostri elementi.
L'altra rimase, e cominciò quest'arte
  che tu discerni, con tanto diletto,
  che mai da circuir non si diparte.
Principio del cader fu il maladetto
  superbir di colui che tu vedesti
  da tutti i pesi del mondo costretto.
Quelli che vedi qui furon modesti
  a riconoscer sè dalla bontate
  che li avea fatti a tanto intender presti;   60
per che le viste lor furo essaltate
  con grazia illuminante e con lor merto,
  sì c' hanno ferma e piena volontate.
E non voglio che dubbi, ma sie certo
  che ricever la grazia è meritorio
  secondo che l'affetto l'è aperto.
Omai dintorno a questo consistorio
  puoi contemplare assai, se le parole
  mie son ricolte, sanz'altro aiutorio.

created and ordained for the spirits, and these were the summit of the universe in whom was produced pure act; pure potency had the lowest place; between, potency and act were held together with such a bond as never is unbound.[7] Jerome wrote for you of the angels being created a long course of ages before the rest of the world was made; but this truth I tell is written in many pages by the scribes of the Holy Ghost, as thou shalt find if thou look carefully;[8] and reason too sees it in some measure, for it would not allow that the movers of the heavens should be so long without their perfection.[9] Thou knowest now where and when these loving spirits were created, as well as how, so that three flames of thy desire are already spent.

'Then, sooner than one might count twenty, a part of the angels convulsed the lowest of your elements;[10] the rest remained and gave themselves with such delight to this art which thou beholdest that they never leave their circling. The beginning of the fall was the accursed pride of him thou sawest, crushed under all the weights of the world. These thou seest here were humble and acknowledged the Goodness that had made them fit for so great intelligence; thus their vision was exalted by enlightening grace and their own merit, so that they have full and steadfast will. And thou must not doubt, but be assured, that there is merit in receiving grace, in the measure that the heart is open to it. Now thou mayst freely contemplate this consistory without more help, if thou hast taken in my words.

Ma perchè in terra per le vostre scole   70
  si legge che l'angelica natura
  è tal, che 'ntende e si ricorda e vole,
ancor dirò, perchè tu veggi pura
  la verità che là giù si confonde,
  equivocando in sì fatta lettura.
Queste sustanze, poi che fur gioconde
  della faccia di Dio, non volser viso
  da essa, da cui nulla si nasconde:
però non hanno vedere interciso
  da novo obietto, e però non bisogna   80
  rememorar per concetto diviso;
sì che là giù, non dormendo, si sogna,
  credendo e non credendo dicer vero;
  ma nell'uno è più colpa e più vergogna.
Voi non andate giù per un sentero
  filosofando; tanto vi trasporta
  l'amor dell'apparenza e 'l suo pensero!
E ancor questo qua su si comporta
  con men disdegno che quando è posposta
  la divina scrittura, o quando è torta.   90
Non vi si pensa quanto sangue costa
  seminarla nel mondo, e quanto piace
  chi umilmente con essa s'accosta.
Per apparer ciascun s'ingegna e face
  sue invenzioni; e quelle son trascorse
  da' predicanti e 'l Vangelio si tace.
Un dice che la luna si ritorse
  nella passion di Cristo e s'interpose,
  per che 'l lume del sol giù non si porse;
ed altri che la luce si nascose   100
  da sè; però all'Ispani e all'Indi,
  come a' Giudei, tale eclissi rispose.
Non ha Fiorenza tanti Lapi e Bindi
  quante sì fatte favole per anno
  in pergamo si gridan quinci e quindi;
sì che le pecorelle, che non sanno,
  tornan del pasco pasciute di vento,
  e non le scusa non veder lo danno.

'But since it is taught in your schools on earth
that it belongs to the nature of the angels to under-
stand and to remember and to will, I shall go on,
that thou mayst see clearly the truth which is
confused down there in such ambiguous teaching.[11]
These beings, since they were made glad with
God's face from which nothing is hid, have never
turned their eyes from it, so that their sight is
never intercepted by a new object and they have no
need to recall the past by an abstract concept.[12]
Thus down there men dream while awake, believing
or not believing that they speak truth; but in the
one case is the greater blame and shame. You
below do not follow a single path in your philo-
sophizing, so much does the love of show and the
thought of it carry you away,[13] and even this is
borne with less anger up here than when the divine
Scripture is neglected or perverted. There is no
thought among you what blood it cost to sow the
world with it or how acceptable he is who approaches
it with humbleness. Each tries for display, making
his own inventions, and these are discoursed on by
the preachers and the Gospel is silent. One says that
at Christ's passion the moon turned back and
interposed itself, so that the sun's light did not
reach below; and others that the light itself hid
itself and therefore for Spaniards and Indians,
as for Jews, that eclipse took place.[14] Florence has
not as many Lapo's and Bindo's[15] as tales like
these that are proclaimed in the pulpit on all hands
through the year, so that the poor sheep that
know nothing return from pasture fed on wind;
and not to see their loss does not excuse them.

421

Non disse Cristo al suo primo convento:
   "Andate, e predicate al mondo ciance";   110
   ma diede lor verace fondamento.
E quel tanto sonò nelle sue guance,
   sì ch'a pugnar per accender la fede
   dell' Evangelio fero scudo e lance.
Ora si va con motti e con iscede
   a predicare, e pur che ben si rida,
   gonfia il cappuccio, e più non si richiede.
Ma tale uccel nel becchetto s'annida,
   che se 'l vulgo il vedesse, vederebbe
   la perdonanza di ch'el si confida;   120
per cui tanta stoltezza in terra crebbe,
   che, sanza prova d'alcun testimonio,
   ad ogni promission si correrebbe.
Di questo ingrassa il porco sant'Antonio,
   e altri assai che sono ancor più porci,
   pagando di moneta sanza conio.
Ma perchè siam digressi assai, ritorci
   li occhi oramai verso la dritta strada,
   sì che la via col tempo si raccorci.
Questa natura sì oltre s' ingrada   130
   in numero, che mai non fu loquela
   nè concetto mortal che tanto vada;
e se tu guardi quel che si revela
   per Danïel, vedrai che 'n sue migliaia
   determinato numero si cela.
La prima luce, che tutta la raia,
   per tanti modi in essa si recepe,
   quanti son li splendori a ch' i' s'appaia.
Onde, però che all'atto che concepe
   segue l'affetto, d'amar la dolcezza   140
   diversamente in essa ferve e tepe.
Vedi l'eccelso omai e la larghezza
   dell'etterno valor, poscia che tanti
   speculi fatti s' ha in che si spezza,
uno manendo in sè come davanti.'

Christ did not say to His first fellowship: "Go and preach idle tales to the world", but gave them a true foundation; and that alone sounded on their lips, so that in fighting to kindle the faith they made of the Gospel shield and spear. Now they go to preach with jests and gibes, and if only there is a good laugh the cowl inflates and they ask no more. But such a bird nests in the hood's tail[16] that if the people saw it they would see what pardons they are trusting to; from which such folly has grown on earth that with no warrant for it they will flock to every promise. By this the swine of Saint Anthony wax fat, with many others that are still more swinish, paying with unstamped coin.[17]

'But, since we have digressed enough, turn thine eyes now back to the straight road, that the way may be shortened with the time.

'This kind[18] mounts to such a number that no mortal speech or thought ever went so far, and if thou consider what is revealed by Daniel thou shalt see that in his thousands no determinate number is to be found.[19] The primal light that irradiates them all is received by them in as many ways as are the splendours with which it is joined, and therefore, since the affections follow the act of conceiving, love's sweetness glows variously in them, more and less. See now the height and the breadth of the Eternal Goodness, since it has made for itself so many mirrors in which it is broken, remaining in itself one as before.'

1. In the spring equinox, with the Sun (Apollo) in the Ram and the Moon (Diana) in the Scales, when one is rising and the other setting in the east and west horizons, which divide each of them in half like a girdle, and they are, as it were, held 'balanced' for a moment.

2. In God's eternity every *where* is here and every *when* is now.

3. 'I am.'

4. The divine motive in the creation of the angels was that God's 'splendour'—His reflected light—should 'shine back' to Him from their self-conscious existence. 'The Divine Goodness which spurns all envy from itself, burning within itself, so sparkles that it displays its eternal beauties' (*Par.* vii).

5. 'In the beginning ... the Spirit of God moved upon the face of the waters' (*Gen.* i. 1–2). There is no *before* and *after* in eternity.

6. Pure form without matter = pure mind, the angels; pure matter without form = the primal undifferentiated stuff of the elements; form and matter united = the heavenly bodies.

7. 'Pure act' = the condition of the angels, their powers always in perfect operation; 'pure potency' = the condition of primal matter, wholly passive and only capable of *becoming* something; 'potency and act held together' = the condition of the heavens and the elements. 'The angels, brother, and the pure country where thou art', etc. (*Par.* vii).

8. 'In the beginning God created the heaven and the earth' (*Gen.* i. 1).

9. The angels, as 'the movers of the heavens', would not have had their 'perfection', their activity, unless the heavens had been created along with them.

10. The angels that fell with Satan convulsed the earth in their fall (*Inf.* xxxiv). Earth is the lowest of the four 'elements': earth, water, air and fire.

11. It is ambiguous to speak of 'memory' in the angels.

12. Looking into God's face, they have the past always present to them and have no need to recall it 'by an abstract concept', a mental impression which is detached from sight.

13. 'There are many who love rather to be called, than to be, masters' (*Convito*).

14. So that the darkness would extend to the extremities, east and west, of the inhabited world.

15. Lapo and Bindo, short for Jacopo and Ildobrando, were common names for boys in Florence.

16. The devil was popularly likened to a crow.

17. St Anthony of Egypt (3rd and 4th centuries), regarded as the founder of monasticism, is usually represented with a hog at his feet in sign of his conquest of sensual appetite; the swine belonging to his monks were considered sacred and were allowed to feed where they pleased. The monks 'paid' by granting unauthorized pardons.

18. The angels.

19. 'The Ancient of days did sit, ... thousand thousands ministered unto him, and ten thousand times ten thousand stood before him' (*Dan.* vii. 9–10).

NOTE

When Beatrice has ended her talk about the angelic hierarchy and is to tell of the divine act of creation, in eternity, at the beginning of time, Dante describes her as gazing, 'her face illumined with a smile', into the eternal light of God,—rapt, like Wordsworth's 'nun, breathless with adoration'. The scene presented in the first lines of the canto, of the sun and moon as if girt and held for an instant by the east and west horizons and standing on opposite scales of a balance hung from the zenith, the one scale rising as the other falls, is no mere picturesque irrelevance and superfluous elaboration in the account of Beatrice. That vast momentary poise of the two great luminaries is emphasized, in Dante's manner, by the triple rhyme: *Libra, i'nlibra, si dilibra* ('the Scales', 'holds them balanced', 'is unbalanced'), in which the two verbs are Dante's own coinage. The whole imagined scene, by its strangeness and silence and immensity, as if the heavens—and Beatrice and Dante—were held by a spell, suggests a mood that Dante surely knew, for which time all but stands still and the 'moment, one and infinite,' seems eternity. The scene brings the reader into sympathy with Beatrice's silent gaze, and her silences, throughout the *Paradiso*, are significant; she means more, herself, than all her words, and something of that deeper, more intimate significance is given to her discourse that follows.

In trying to express the inexpressible act of creation Beatrice repeats in her own terms the account given by Aquinas in the thirteenth canto: 'That living Light which so streams from its shining Source that it is not parted from Him nor from the Love which with them makes the Three, of its own goodness gathers its beams, as it were mirrored, in nine subsistences, remaining forever one.' He dwells on the Creator in the act of creating; she on the angels and the spheres, the creation itself.

The same creative act produces with the angels the heavenly
spheres and the primal matter, so that the whole working appara-
tus of the universe, so to speak, is in being, and time, having
its roots in the Crystalline and its branches in the other spheres
(*Par.* xxvii), issues from eternity. In eternity 'every *ubi* and
every *quando* is centred'; it is an unbroken here and now. This
conception of the life of God and of all created spirits in the
measure of their approach to God, as holding the knowledge of
past and future in an enduring present, and of near and far as
here, is a conception which has a very long history,—from
ancient oriental cults to Plato and the Fourth Gospel and from
Augustine to Aquinas, and the *Paradiso* is full of the idea that it
belongs to the soul's perfection to see all, at once,—*totum simul*—
in God, the Eternal. Time begins with the angels and the moving
of the spheres, and for Dante the angels are, not symbolically
but in fact, God's agents in the whole system of secondary
causes which is Nature. They are called here a 'consistory',
and the word meant, in common use, the Pope and Cardinals
in council, charged with divine authority for the spiritual order-
ing of humanity; for the angels, in their own orders, are created
and appointed for the spiritual ordering of the universe. They
operate an order and control in the heavens which is at once
spiritual and physical, and all creation in their hands is an
effulgence and then a reflection of the Eternal Love. The one
inclusive merit of angels and men is the humble acceptance of
grace, the reward of that merit is more grace, and the root and
essence of sin is the pride that refuses the bonds of grace and
rebels against the divine order of the universe. The whole is a
spiritual conception in a mythical frame, not Dante's invention
but an inheritance glorified by his imaginative realization, and
it is the solution adopted by medieval Christianity of the
problem that is still with us, the relation of the natural world
to the spiritual values which are our life.

Then, still speaking through Beatrice, Dante turns from these
high contemplations, as is his way, to the earth, to the teachers
and preachers whose proper function it is to declare and main-
tain these values among men. He charges them, in what seems
a deliberate crescendo of severity, with irresponsible and
sometimes dishonest speculations, love of display, neglect and

perversion of Scripture, jests and gibes in the pulpit, impo-
sitions on popular ignorance by false pardons and monkish
greed; and here, as always with Dante, the Church is judged
by the standard of Christ and the Gospel. 'The form of the
Church is nothing else but the life of Christ, including both
His words and His deeds' (*De Monarchia*). It is highly charac-
teristic of him that alongside of these flagrant offences of the
Church he puts slackness of thinking and futile discussion:
the prevalent 'ambiguous teaching' about memory in the angels,
the confusion between their *retaining* of the past because, for
them, it never passes and our human *recalling* of it; the failure
to 'follow a single path', a deliberate and consistent course of
thinking, in their philosophizing; the proclaiming in the
pulpit of 'tales like these' about the darkness at the Crucifixion.
The laws of thought are the laws of God, and the Church's
heedlessness of mental integrity he regarded as akin to all its
offences. It is a judgement in which he proved himself a true
pupil of the great Scholastics.

We have here the last of the many denunciations in the *Para-
diso* of the sins of the time, and if we glance back on these
passages we shall see that they are not mere general outcries
by the saints, but charges made with peculiar appropriateness
by those who make them. Justinian, the representative of uni-
versal Roman law, rebukes the partisan passions of the Guelfs
and Ghibellines (*Par.* vi); Folco, the bishop zealous to slaying
for the Church's purity, condemns the gross worldliness that
corrupts the Church (*Par.* ix); Aquinas, the great Dominican,
passes judgement on his own order, and Bonaventura, the
Franciscan General, on his (*Par.* xi and xii); Cacciaguida, the
noble Florentine and martyr, makes his bitter comment on
modern Florence (*Par.* xv, xvi and xvii); the heavenly Eagle
of just rulers judges the kings of Europe (*Par.* xix); Damian,
the ascetic bishop and cardinal, exposes the wantonness and
luxury of the higher clergy (*Par.* xxi); Benedict, the monastic
founder, denounces the abuses of monasticism (*Par.* xxii);
St Peter, the Church's first earthly head under Christ, cries
out on the corruptions of the Papacy (*Par.* xxvii); and Beatrice,
the 'true praise of God', challenges the preachers and teachers
of the time. In not one of such cases does Dante speak in his

427

own person; and in each case the challenger speaks with the peculiar authority that belongs to those who are themselves wholly and unquestionably identified with the cause for which they speak, and whose attack is the defence of that which is their life.

From that diversion Beatrice returns to the angels. They are numberless; but their number is no mere multiplication of identities. Aquinas had taught that each one of all their host has his own distinctive quality and degree and is so individual as to be a species by himself; 'the primal light that irradiates them all is received in them in as many ways as are the splendours with which it is joined'. Their eternal function is the fulfilment of 'the manifold wisdom of God' which, in St Paul's language, is 'known to the principalities and powers in heavenly places'. And with all that dispensing of His being, with all the vastness and diversity of nature and of providence, that light of God is forever one.

PARADISO

FORSE semilia miglia di lontano
   ci ferve l'ora sesta, e questo mondo
   china già l'ombra quasi al letto piano,
quando il mezzo del cielo, a noi profondo,
   comincia a farsi tal, ch'alcuna stella
   perde il parere infino a questo fondo;
e come vien la chiarissima ancella
   del sol più oltre, così 'l ciel si chiude
   di vista in vista infino alla più bella.
Non altrimenti il triunfo che lude   10
   sempre dintorno al punto che mi vinse,
   parendo inchiuso da quel ch'elli 'nchiude,
a poco a poco al mio veder si stinse;
   per che tornar con li occhi a Beatrice
   nulla vedere ed amor mi costrinse.
Se quanto infino a qui di lei si dice
   fosse conchiuso tutto in una loda,
   poco sarebbe a fornir questa vice.
La bellezza ch' io vidi si trasmoda
   non pur di là da noi, ma certo io credo   20
   che solo il suo fattor tutta la goda.
Da questo passo vinto mi concedo
   più che già mai da punto di suo tema
   soprato fosse comico o tragedo;
chè, come sole in viso che più trema,
   così lo rimembrar del dolce riso
   la mente mia di sè medesmo scema.

CANTO XXX

The ascent to the Empyrean; the river of light;
the Celestial Rose

SOME six thousand miles away the sixth hour
burns and already this world inclines its shadow
almost to a level bed, when the mid-sky, deep
above us, begins to change so that a star here and
there is lost to sight at this depth; and as the bright-
est handmaid of the sun advances the sky then
shuts off its lights one by one, even to the loveliest.[1]
In like manner, the triumph that sports forever
round the point which overcame me and which
seems enclosed by that which it encloses[2] was
extinguished little by little from my sight, so that
my seeing nothing and my love constrained me to
return with my eyes to Beatrice. If all that is said
of her up to this were gathered in one meed of
praise, it would be little to serve this turn; the beauty
I saw not only surpasses our measures, but I surely
believe that only its Maker has all the joy of it.
I own myself beaten at this pass more than ever
comic or tragic poet was baffled by a point in his
theme; for, like the sun in the most wavering sight,
the remembrance of the sweet smile deprives
my mind of its very self. From the first day I saw

Dal primo giorno ch' i' vidi il suo viso
  in questa vita, infino a questa vista,
  non m'è il seguire al mio cantar preciso;   30
ma or convien che mio seguir desista
  più dietro a sua bellezza, poetando,
  come all' ultimo suo ciascuno artista.
Cotal qual io la lascio a maggior bando
  che quel della mia tuba, che deduce
  l'ardüa sua matera terminando,
con atto e voce di spedito duce
  ricominciò: 'Noi siamo usciti fore
  del maggior corpo al ciel ch'è pura luce:
luce intellettüal, piena d'amore;   40
  amor di vero ben, pien di letizia;
  letizia che trascende ogni dolzore.
Qui vederai l'una e l'altra milizia
  di paradiso, e l'una in quelli aspetti
  che tu vedrai all' ultima giustizia.'
Come subito lampo che discetti
  li spiriti visivi, sì che priva
  dall'atto l'occhio di più forti obietti,
così mi circunfulse luce viva;
  e lasciommi fasciato di tal velo   50
  del suo fulgor, che nulla m'appariva.
'Sempre l'amor che queta questo cielo
  accoglie in sè con sì fatta salute,
  per far disposto a sua fiamma il candelo.'
Non fur più tosto dentro a me venute
  queste parole brievi, ch' io compresi
  me sormontar di sopr'a mia virtute;
e di novella vista mi raccesi
  tale, che nulla luce è tanto mera,
  che li occhi miei non si fosser difesi.   60
E vidi lume in forma di rivera
  fulvido di fulgore, intra due rive
  dipinte di mirabil primavera.
Di tal fiumana uscìan faville vive,
  e d'ogni parte si mettìen ne' fiori,
  quasi rubin che oro circunscrive.

her face in this life until this sight the pursuit
in my song has not been cut off; but now must my
pursuit cease from following longer after her
beauty in my verse, as with every artist at his limit.

Such that I leave her to a greater heralding than
that of my trumpet which approaches the end of
its hard theme, she began again with the voice and
bearing of a guide whose task is done: 'We have
come forth from the greatest body to the heaven
that is pure light,[3]—light intellectual full of love,
love of true good full of joy, joy that surpasses
every sweetness. Here thou shalt see the one and the
other soldiery of Paradise, and the one in that
aspect in which thou shalt see them at the last
judgement.'[4]

Like sudden lightning that scatters the visual
spirits and deprives the eye of the action of the
clearest objects,[5] a vivid light shone round about
me and left me so swathed in the veil of its effulgence
that nothing was visible to me.

'The love that calms this heaven always welcomes
to itself with such a greeting, to prepare the candle
for its flame.'[6] No sooner had these brief words
reached my mind than I was conscious of rising
beyond my own powers, and such new vision
was kindled in me that there is no light so bright
my eyes would not have borne it. And I saw light
in the form of a river pouring its splendour between
two banks painted with marvellous spring. From
that torrent came forth living sparks and they
settled on the flowers on either side, like rubies set

Poi, come inebriate dalli odori,
   riprofondavan sè nel miro gurge;
   e s'una intrava, un'altra n'uscìa fori.
'L'alto disio che mo t' infiamma e urge,   70
   d'aver notizia di ciò che tu vei,
   tanto mi piace più quanto più turge;
ma di quest'acqua convien che tu bei
   prima che tanta sete in te si sazii.'
   Così mi disse il sol delli occhi miei.
Anche soggiunse: 'Il fiume e li topazii
   ch'entrano ed escono e 'l rider dell'erbe
   son di lor vero umbriferi prefazii.
Non che da sè sian queste cose acerbe;
   ma è difetto dalla parte tua,   80
   che non hai viste ancor tanto superbe.'
Non è fantin che sì subito rua
   col volto verso il latte, se si svegli
   molto tardato dall'usanza sua,
come fec' io, per far migliori spegli
   ancor delli occhi, chinandomi all'onda
   che si deriva perchè vi s' immegli;
e sì come di lei bevve la gronda
   della palpebre mie, così mi parve
   di sua lunghezza divenuta tonda.   90
Poi come gente stata sotto larve
   che pare altro che prima, se si sveste
   la sembianza non sua in che disparve,
così mi si cambiaro in maggior feste
   li fiori e le faville, sì ch'io vidi
   ambo le corti del ciel manifeste.
O isplendor di Dio, per cu' io vidi
   l'alto triunfo del regno verace,
   dammi virtù a dir com' io il vidi!
Lume è là su che visibile face   100
   lo creatore a quella creatura
   che solo in lui vedere ha la sua pace.
E' si distende in circular figura,
   in tanto che la sua circunferenza
   sarebbe al sol troppo larga cintura.

in gold; then, as if intoxicated with the odours, they plunged again into the wondrous flood, and as one entered another came forth.

'The high desire that is now aflame and urgent in thee to have knowledge of that which thou seest pleases me more the more it swells; but first thou must drink of these waters before this great thirst of thine can be satisfied.' Thus she spoke to me who was the sun of my eyes; then she continued: 'The river and the topazes that pass into it and out and the laughter of the flowers are shadowy forecasts of their truth; not that these things are imperfect in themselves, but the defect is in thyself, that thy vision is not yet so exalted.'

No infant, waking long after its hour, throws itself so instantly with its face to the milk, as I, to make still better mirrors of my eyes, bent down to the water that flows forth for our perfecting; and no sooner did the eaves of my eyelids drink of it than it seemed to me out of its length to have become round. Then, like people who have been under masks and seem other than before if they put off the semblance not their own in which they were hid, the flowers and the sparks changed for me into a greater festival, so that I saw both the courts of heaven made plain.

O splendour of God by which I saw the high triumph of the true kingdom, give me power to tell of what I saw there!

Light is there above which makes the Creator visible to every creature that has his peace only in seeing Him, and it spreads to so wide a circle that the circumference would be too great a girdle

Fassi di raggio tutta sua parvenza
   reflesso al sommo del mobile primo,
   che prende quindi vivere e potenza.
E come clivo in acqua di suo imo
   si specchia, quasi per vedersi adorno,   110
   quando è nel verde e ne' fioretti opimo,
sì, soprastando al lume intorno intorno,
   vidi specchiarsi in più di mille soglie
   quanto di noi là su fatto ha ritorno.
E se l' infimo grado in sè raccoglie
   sì grande lume, quanta è la larghezza
   di questa rosa nell'estreme foglie!
La vista mia nell'ampio e nell'altezza
   non si smarriva, ma tutto prendeva
   il quanto e 'l quale di quella allegrezza.   120
Presso e lontano, lì, nè pon nè leva;
   chè dove Dio sanza mezzo governa,
   la legge natural nulla rileva.
Nel giallo della rosa sempiterna,
   che si dilata ed ingrada e redole
   odor di lode al sol che sempre verna,
qual è colui che tace e dicer vole,
   mi trasse Beatrice, e disse: 'Mira
   quanto è 'l convento delle bianche stole!
Vedi nostra città quant'ella gira: 130
   vedi li nostri scanni sì ripieni,
   che poca gente più ci si disira.
E 'n quel gran seggio a che tu li occhi tieni
   per la corona che già v'è su posta,
   prima che tu a queste nozze ceni,
sederà l'alma, che fia giù agosta,
   dell'alto Arrigo, ch'a drizzare Italia
   verrà in prima ch'ella sia disposta.
La cieca cupidigia che v'ammalia
   simili fatti v' ha al fantolino   140
   che muor per fame e caccia via la balia.
E fia prefetto nel foro divino
   allora tal, che palese e coverto
   non anderà con lui per un cammino.

for the sun. Its whole expanse is made by a ray
reflected on the summit of the Primum Mobile,
which draws from this its life and potency; and as
a hillside is mirrored in water at its foot as if to
see itself adorned when it is rich with grass and
flowers, I saw, rising above the light all round in
more than a thousand tiers, as many of us as have
returned there above. And if the lowest rank encloses
within it so great a light, what is the expanse of this
rose in its farthest petals? My sight did not lose
itself in the breadth and height, but took in all the
extent and quality of that rejoicing; there, near and
far neither add nor take away, for where God rules
immediately natural law is of no effect.

Into the yellow of the eternal rose, which expands
and rises in ranks and exhales odours of praise to
the Sun that makes perpetual spring, Beatrice
drew me, as one who is silent and fain would speak,
and she said: 'Behold how great is the assembly of
the white robes! See our city, how great is its
circuit! See our seats so filled that few souls are
now wanting there![7] And in that great chair on
which thy eyes are held by the crown that is already
set over it, before thou shalt sup at these nuptials
shall rest the soul, which shall be imperial below,
of lofty Henry, who shall come to set Italy straight
before she is ready.[8] The blind greed that bewitches
you has made you like the infant that is dying of
hunger and drives away his nurse, and at that time
one shall be president of the divine court who shall
not take the same course with him openly and

Ma poco poi sarà da Dio sofferto
  nel santo officio; ch' el sarà detruso
  là dove Simon mago è per suo merto,
  farà quel d'Alagna intrar più giuso.'

secretly.[9] But not long shall God then suffer him
in the holy office; for he shall be thrust down where
Simon Magus gets his dues, and shall make him of
Anagni go deeper still.'[10]

1. When it is noon, 'the sixth hour', 6,000 miles eastward from us, it is, in Dante's reckoning, near sunrise where we are, and the earth's shadow is 'almost level' from our point of view; when Aurora, the sun's 'handmaid', approaches, the stars gradually disappear.

2. 'Uncircumscribed circumscribes all' (*Par*. xiv).

3. From the Primum Mobile, the greatest of the material spheres, to the Empyrean.

4. The saints and the angels. The saints will appear to Dante as in the flesh, which they are to recover at the general resurrection.

5. Cp. 'The visual spirit runs to meet the brightness' (*Par*. xxvi).

6. 'The spirit of man is the candle of the Lord' (*Prov*. xx. 27).

7. 'We are already in the last age of the world' (*Convito*).

8. The Emperor Henry VII, elected in 1308, in Italy in 1310, crowned at Rome in 1312, died in 1313; cp. Note on *Purg*. xxxiii.

9. Pope Clement V. Cp. *Inf*. xix and *Par*. xvii.

10. Pope Boniface VIII was born in Anagni, S. Italy.

NOTE

Approaching the end of his hard theme and entering the Empyrean, Dante is made conscious of the inevitable gradualness of revelation, and by the successive stages of his imagery he strives to set the ultimate realities of the spirit apart from all lesser experience. The coming of dawn on earth, described in cosmic terms, opens the canto that is to tell of his passing beyond all the spheres into the heaven that is all light. The sun has not yet reached its rising, and the earth's shadow—from an imaginary observer's point of view—is 'almost' in its level bed; then Aurora, coming nearer, shuts off the stars one by one till the last is gone. And still it is not the dawn, only the preparation for it. Like the stars in the morning, the formal imagery of the dazzling point and the fiery circles fades from his sight. The point only *seems* 'enclosed by that which itself encloses', and point and circles must make way for a truer vision. Dante may have had Hosea's words in mind: 'His going forth is prepared as the morning.'

Here, more than ever before, Beatrice, the truth of God, is found unspeakable: 'only her Maker has all the joy' of her beauty. But she is no less Beatrice. In the Empyrean at the end of his journey—but in fact while he writes in Ravenna, twenty years after the assumed date of his vision and near his last days on earth—, his mind is carried back over the stormy years to 'the first day I saw her face in this life' when both were children, just as it had been on the summit of Purgatory when he knew her again and 'felt old love's great power'. So identical were Dante's life and his vision, both of them the record of his love and the discovery of its meaning.

In a single stanza Beatrice describes to him the perfected life of the redeemed as light, love and joy,—in that order. The first element of its perfection is 'light intellectual'. It is the

441

teaching again of the twenty-eighth canto, that 'the state of
blessedness rests on the act of vision', and of the twenty-ninth,
that 'the affections follow the act of conceiving', the seeing of
things as they are and as we can and the thinking *so* of God
and of creation and of ourselves. From such vision springs the
love of true good, and from such love joy surpassing every
sweetness. (The suggestion of Mr. C. S. Lewis, made in another
connection, is relevant here: 'The joys of heaven are for most
of us, in our present condition, an acquired taste.') In this canto,
as in the last, the references to vision are persistent and cumu-
lative; and when his faith passes into sight and at last his eyes
are cleared and he exclaims at the courts of heaven made plain,
Dante takes *vidi* for the triple rhyme—'I saw . . . I saw . . .
I saw.' Is this verbal insistence an echo of 1 *John* i. 1–3: 'That
which we have seen . . . we have seen . . . we have seen
. . . declare we unto you'?

Before that he was for a moment blinded by the sudden light
that 'shone round about me'. The incident may well have been
suggested by St Paul's experience on the Damascus road when
he was blinded by a light from heaven and in his blindness
gained a new enlightenment; and it is perhaps significant that
the unusual word *circunfulgere*, to shine round about, which is
used here, occurs, in its Latin form, in each of the three Vulgate
accounts of Paul's vision.

The first vision here is easily interpreted in relation to the
other that follows. A river is a familiar image in Scripture for
divine grace, and the living sparks and the flowers represent
the angels and the souls to which they minister. Dante drinks
of the stream with his eyes at the bidding of Beatrice, with an
eagerness like an infant's for its mother's milk when it has
wakened 'long after its hour'—do the words carry Dante's per-
sonal confession?—; and then the vision is, as it were, unmasked,
changing dreamlike, and the stream of time becomes the circle
of eternity and grace becomes glory. His strengthened sight
pierces these 'shadowy forecasts' to 'their truth'. For 'grace
and glory are the same in kind, since grace is nothing but a
certain beginning of glory in us' (*Aquinas, quoted by J. S.
Carroll*). The passage is Dante's version of the language of the
thirty-sixth Psalm: 'Thou shalt make them drink of the river

of thy pleasures. For with thee is the fountain of life: in thy light shall we see light.'

The truth as it is known at each stage of the soul's enlightenment is only a forecast of the truth itself; but it is only by the absorption of that imperfect vision—'first thou must drink of these waters'—that the soul's 'great thirst' can ever be satisfied.

The great shining circle is the eternal light of God's presence reflected on the convex surface of the Primum Mobile and giving to it that life and potency which is distributed by the angelic orders through the spheres to the earth and the life of men. The same circle forms 'the yellow of the eternal rose', whose white petals, 'rising in more than a thousand tiers', show all the ranks of the redeemed; and these are given to Dante's sight without any hindrance from distance, because he is now beyond the limiting conditions of time and space. Twice in this canto and three times in the cantos following the Empyrean is described as a rose.. 'The old French *Roman de la Rose*, the great literary success of the 13th century, made all western Europe familiar with the rose as a symbol of earthly love; Dante's white flower is the rose of heavenly love' (*C. H. Grandgent*).

When Dante, awe-struck and wondering, 'as one who is silent and fain would speak', is brought by Beatrice into the heart of the rose, she tells him of 'the noble Henry, who shall come to set Italy straight before she is ready'. This is her prevision in 1300 of the events of thirteen years later, Henry's gallant and vain struggle in Italy and his death. For Dante himself, writing probably seven years later still, it is the memorial of a great hope. 'The ideal of the Empire fills the whole of the *Paradiso*, but there is no longer any allusion to its near restoration, to a coming king, to a new dawn. The last reference to human affairs is at the end of the thirtieth canto of the *Paradiso*, the apotheosis of Henry, under whose chair opens the unlooked-for vision of the infernal abyss where lie, head downward and licked by the red flame, Boniface and Clement; but not one word of surviving hope escapes from the lips of the stern and disdainful Poet' (*E. G. Parodi*). These two popes, both of them Dante's contemporaries, are frequently referred to in the course of the *Divine Comedy*, but neither of

443

them is ever named, with the single and significant exception
that their predecessor in papal simony calls on Boniface from
the pit in the Malebolgia that awaits him: 'Standest thou
there already, Boniface?' The nineteenth canto of the *Inferno*
is a vivid commentary on the last lines of this. It is thus that
the two popes are dismissed from the poem, like Philip of
France at the end of the nineteenth canto. In the whole
passage Dante makes use of extreme dramatic contrast—
and by no other means could it have been made more con-
vincing than through the lips of Beatrice—, on the one hand
exalting the Empire, the divine order of the world, by the unique
honour shown to the ideal Emperor in the glory of Paradise,
and on the other declaring the measure of his scorn and repro-
bation of the Church's recreant heads who have refused and
thwarted the high providence of God. In these last words of
Beatrice 'there seems to be summed up that holy wrath which
we have felt increasing in force from heaven to heaven, up to
Peter's invective in *Paradiso* xxix and this of Beatrice against the
false preachers; for the nearer approach to God as it were
intensifies the struggle between holiness and sin and makes
more severe "the cords of the scourge"' (*C. Grabher*). The
ultimate realities are beyond Dante's language or conceiving,
and the static and formal glory of the heavenly rose, as it is
described more particularly in the thirty-second canto, fails
notably in comparison with the living beauty of the river of
light; but it is in the light of that perfected fellowship of men
with God of which he thus tries to tell that he judges the glory
and the shame of Emperor and Pope on earth.

IN forma dunque di candida rosa
   mi si mostrava la milizia santa
   che nel suo sangue Cristo fece sposa;
ma l'altra, che volando vede e canta
   la gloria di colui che la innamora
   e la bontà che la fece cotanta,
sì come schiera d'ape, che s' infiora
   una fïata e una si ritorna
   là dove suo laboro s' insapora,
nel gran fior discendeva che s'adorna   10
   di tante foglie, e quindi risaliva
   là dove 'l suo amor sempre soggiorna.
Le facce tutte avean di fiamma viva,
   e l' ali d'oro, e l'altro tanto bianco,
   che nulla neve a quel termine arriva.
Quando scendean nel fior, di banco in banco
   porgevan della pace e dell'ardore
   ch'elli acquistavan ventilando il fianco.
Nè l' interporsi tra 'l disopra e 'l fiore
   di tanta plenitudine volante   20
   impediva la vista e lo splendore;
chè la luce divina è penetrante
   per l'universo secondo ch'è degno,
   sì che nulla le puote essere ostante.
Questo sicuro e gaudïoso regno,
   frequente in gente antica ed in novella,
   viso e amore avea tutto ad un segno.
Oh trina luce che 'n unica stella
   scintillando a lor vista, sì li appaga!
   Guarda qua giuso alla nostra procella!   30

CANTO XXXI

The angels in the Rose; the ascent of Beatrice;
St Bernard; the Virgin

IN form, then, of a white rose was shown to me the
saintly host which Christ, with His own blood,
made His bride. But the other host—who, as they
fly, see and sing the glory of Him who holds their
love and the goodness that made them what they
are,—like a swarm of bees that one moment dip in
the flowers and the next go back where their toil
turns to sweetness, descended into the great flower
that is decked with so many petals, and thence
re-ascended where their love abides forever.
Their faces were all of living flame and their wings
of gold; and, for the rest, they were of such white-
ness as no snow would match. When they descended
into the great flower they imparted to it, from
rank to rank, of the peace and the ardour which they
had gained fanning their sides. Nor did such
plenitude of flight coming between the height and
the flower obstruct the sight or the splendour; for
the divine light penetrates the universe according
to the fitness of its parts so that nothing can hinder
it. This secure and joyful kingdom, thronged
with people of old times and new, had sight and
love all on one mark. O threefold Light, which, in
a single star sparkling on their sight, so satisfiest
them, look upon our tempest here below. If the

447

Se i barbari, venendo da tal plaga
   che ciascun giorno d' Elice si copra,
   rotante col suo figlio ond'ella è vaga,
veggendo Roma e l'ardüa sua opra,
   stupefacìensi, quando Laterano
   alle cose mortali andò di sopra;
ïo, che al divino dall' umano,
   all'etterno dal tempo era venuto,
   e di Fiorenza in popol giusto e sano,
di che stupor dovea esser compiuto!   40
   Certo tra esso e 'l gaudio mi facea
   libito non udire e starmi muto.
E quasi peregrin che si ricrea
   nel tempio del suo voto riguardando,
   e spera già ridir com'ello stea,
su per la viva luce passeggiando,
   menava ïo li occhi per li gradi,
   mo su, mo giù, e mo recirculando.
Vedea visi a carità süadi,
   d'altrui lume fregiati e di suo riso,   50
   e atti ornati di tutte onestadi.
La forma general di paradiso
   già tutta mïo sguardo avea compresa,
   in nulla parte ancor fermato fiso;
e volgeami con voglia rïaccesa
   per domandar la mia donna di cose
   di che la mente mia era sospesa.
Uno intendea, e altro mi rispose:
   credea veder Beatrice, e vidi un sene
   vestito con le genti glorïose.   60
Diffuso era per li occhi e per le gene
   di benigna letizia, in atto pio
   quale a tenero padre si convene.
E 'Ov' è ella?' subito diss' io.
   Ond'elli: 'A terminar lo tuo disiro
   mosse Beatrice me del loco mio;
e se riguardi su nel terzo giro
   dal sommo grado, tu la rivedrai
   nel trono che suoi merti le sortiro.'

barbarians, coming from the region that is covered every day by Helice, wheeling with her son whom she delights in,[1] were struck dumb at the sight of Rome and her mighty works, when the Lateran rose above all mortal things,[2] I, who had come to the divine from the human, to the eternal from time, and from Florence to a people just and sane, with what amazement must I have been filled! Truly between that and the joy I was content to hear nothing and to remain silent. And like a pilgrim who is refreshed in the temple of his vow as he looks round it and hopes some time to tell of it again, so, taking my way up through the living light, I carried my eyes through the ranks, now up, now down, and now looking round again. I saw faces persuasive to charity, adorned with Another's light and with their own smiles, and every movement graced with dignity.

Already my glance had taken in the whole general form of Paradise but had not yet dwelt on any part of it, and I turned with new-kindled eagerness to question my Lady of things on which my mind was in suspense. One thing I intended, and another encountered me: I thought to see Beatrice, and I saw an old man, clothed like that glorious company. His eyes and his cheeks were suffused with a gracious gladness, and his aspect was of such kindness as befits a tender father. And 'Where is she?' I said in haste; and he replied: 'To end thy longing Beatrice sent me from my place; and if thou look up to the third circle from the highest tier thou shalt see her again, in the throne her merits have assigned to her.'

Sanza risponder, li occhi su levai,   70
  e vidi lei che si facea corona
  reflettendo da sè li etterni rai.
Da quella regïon che più su tona
  occhio mortale alcun tanto non dista,
  qualunque in mare più giù s'abbandona,
quanto lì da Beatrice la mia vista;
  ma nulla mi facea, chè sua effige
  non discendea a me per mezzo mista.
'O donna in cui la mia speranza vige,
  e che soffristi per la mia salute   80
  in inferno lasciar le tue vestige,
di tante cose quant' i' ho vedute,
  dal tuo podere e dalla tua bontate
  riconosco la grazia e la virtute.
Tu m' hai di servo tratto a libertate
  per tutte quelle vie, per tutt' i modi
  che di ciò fare avei la potestate.
La tua magnificenza in me custodi,
  sì che l'anima mia, che fatt' hai sana,
  piacente a te dal corpo si disnodi.'   90
Così orai; e quella, sì lontana
  come parea, sorrise e riguardommi;
  poi si tornò all'etterna fontana.
E 'l santo sene 'Acciò che tu assommi
  perfettamente' disse 'il tuo cammino,
  a che priego e amor santo mandommi,
vola con li occhi per questo giardino;
  chè veder lui t'acconcerà lo sguardo
  più al montar per lo raggio divino.
E la regina del cielo, ond' io ardo   100
  tutto d'amor, ne farà ogni grazia,
  però ch' i' sono il suo fedel Bernardo.'
Qual è colui che forse di Croazia
  viene a veder la Veronica nostra,
  che per l'antica fame non sen sazia,
ma dice nel pensier, fin che si mostra:
  'Signor mio Gesù Cristo, Dio verace,
  or fu sì fatta la sembianza vostra?';

Without answering, I lifted up my eyes and saw her where she made for herself a crown, reflecting from her the eternal beams. From the highest region where it thunders no mortal eye is so far, were it lost in the depth of the sea, as was my sight there from Beatrice; but to me it made no difference, for her image came down to me undimmed by aught between.

'O Lady in whom my hope has its strength and who didst bear for my salvation to leave thy footprints in Hell, of all the things that I have seen I acknowledge the grace and the virtue to be from thy power and from thy goodness. It is thou who hast drawn me from bondage into liberty by all those ways, by every means for it that was in thy power. Preserve in me thy great bounty, so that my spirit, which thou hast made whole, may be loosed from the body well-pleasing to thee.' I prayed thus; and she, so far off as she seemed, smiled and looked at me, then turned again to the eternal fount.

And the aged saint said: 'In order that thou mayst complete thy journey to the very end, for which prayer and holy love have sent me, fly with thine eyes through this garden, for seeing it will prepare thy sight to mount higher through the divine radiance; and the Queen of Heaven, for whom I am all on fire with love, will grant us every grace, since I am her faithful Bernard.'[3]

Like one that comes, perhaps, from Croatia to see our Veronica[4] and whose old hunger is never satisfied, but he says within himself, as long as it is shown: 'My Lord Jesus Christ, very God, was this then your true semblance?', such was I, gazing

451

tal era io mirando la vivace
  carità di colui che 'n questo mondo, 110
  contemplando, gustò di quella pace.
'Figliuol di grazia, quest'esser giocondo'
  cominciò elli 'non ti sarà noto,
  tenendo li occhi pur qua giù al fondo;
ma guarda i cerchi infino al più remoto,
  tanto che veggi seder la regina
  cui questo regno è suddito e devoto.'
Io levai li occhi; e come da mattina
  la parte orïental dell'orizzonte
  soverchia quella dove 'l sol declina, 120
così, quasi di valle andando a monte
  con li occhi, vidi parte nello stremo
  vincer di lume tutta l'altra fronte.
E come quivi ove s'aspetta il temo
  che mal guidò Fetonte, più s' infiamma,
  e quinci e quindi il lume si fa scemo,
così quella pacifica oriafiamma
  nel mezzo s'avvivava, e d'ogni parte
  per igual modo allentava la fiamma.
E a quel mezzo, con le penne sparte, 130
  vid' io più di mille angeli festanti,
  ciascun distinto di fulgore e d'arte.
Vidi a' lor giochi quivi ed a' lor canti
  ridere una bellezza, che letizia
  era nelli occhi a tutti li altri santi.
E s' io avessi in dir tanta divizia
  quanta ad imaginar, non ardirei
  lo minimo tentar di sua delizia.
Bernardo, come vide li occhi miei
  nel caldo suo calor fissi e attenti, 140
  li suoi con tanto affetto volse a lei,
che i miei di rimirar fè più ardenti.

on the living charity of him who in this world tasted by contemplation of that peace.

'Child of grace,' he began 'this joyful state will not be known to thee if thou keep thine eyes only down here at the foot; but look at the circles up to the farthest till thou see in her seat the Queen to whom this realm is subject and devoted.'

I lifted up my eyes; and as in the morning the eastern part of the horizon outshines that where the sun goes down, so, as it were climbing with my eyes from valley to mountain-top, I saw a part of the extreme verge surpassing with its light all the rest of the rim; and as the point where we await the shaft that Phaeton misguided is most aflame and on this side and on that the light shades off,[5] so that peaceful oriflamme[6] showed brightest in the middle and on each side the flaming diminished equally. And at that middle point I saw more than a thousand angels with outspread wings making festival, each distinct in brightness and in function. I saw there, smiling at their sports and songs, a beauty which was joy in the eyes of all the other saints; and if I were as rich in speech as in imagining I should not dare attempt the least part of her delights. Bernard, who saw my eyes fixed and intent on the fire that warmed him, turned his own on her with so great affection that he made mine more eager in their gazing.

1. The nymph Helice, seduced by Jupiter, was transformed by Juno into a bear, then raised by Jupiter to the sky as the constellation of the Great Bear, along with her son, who became the Little Bear.

2. 'The Lateran', the Papal Palace in Rome, believed to have been Nero's; St John Lateran, for many centuries regarded as the mother-church of Christendom, was almost entirely destroyed by fire in 1308.

3. St Bernard (12th century), first Abbot of Clairvaux, founder of many monasteries, theologian and contemplative; for his devotion to the Virgin she was believed to have granted him a vision of herself.

4. The name, meaning 'true likeness', given to a handkerchief with which a woman wiped the brow of Christ on His way to Calvary and which afterwards bore His likeness. It was kept as a sacred relic at Rome and shown to the faithful twice a year.

5. At sunrise; for Phaeton see *Par.* xvii.

6. The Oriflamme was the war-flag of France, a red pennon on a golden staff; it was believed to have been given by the Archangel Gabriel to the early French kings.

NOTE

This canto and the next are occupied with the fellowship of the saints in the light of God, and first Dante pictures the ministry of peace and ardour given them by the angels; for 'passion is here peaceful and peace passionate' (*P. H. Wicksteed*). Standing with Beatrice in the golden centre of the white rose he observes that the flying hosts cast no shadow; in the purity of their nature they are transparent to the divine light and they are seen by Dante without hindrance from dimness or distance. This is one of the devices in which Dante suggests by sensible imagery the conditions of a super-sensible world. 'Through all Dante's *Paradiso* there has been little thought of matter. Sound and light have been the main ingredients of his marvellous effects, even in the physical heavens. And now, in the last four cantos, he achieves what no other poet, before or since, has attempted with so much as a shadow of success: the presentation of a world beyond the perceptions of sense. Discreet omission and subtle suggestion, insistence on a progressive sharpening of spiritual insight, repeated warning that the increasingly exalted vision can be expressed only in ever more inadequate symbols,—these are the elements from which the master creates an atmosphere of supersensual grandeur, love and joy' (*C. H. Grandgent*). And yet, for all its vastness and splendour, the scene here is made, as it were, near and real to us by the familiar image of a swarm of bees, busy between the flowers and the hive. With all their active dispersion in the vast spaces of the saints the angels 're-ascended where their love abides forever', the immediate divine presence from which they had never been absent. They have a 'heart untravell'd', like Goldsmith's Traveller. They are 'ministering spirits, sent forth to minister', and they are still with God. All their being is given in three words: 'as they *fly*' they '*see* and *sing*', service, vision and praise. Dante would remind us that the spatial account of the true heaven, the Empyrean, which is in fact beyond space and its conditions, is a mere accommodation to our earthly minds, and that in this unimaginable fellowship full activity and perfect peace are one.

'This secure and joyful kingdom'—the 'wealth secure with no craving' of Canto xxvii—having its 'sight and love all on one mark', recalls to Dante, by extreme contrast, 'our tempest here below'; and that contrast suggests another, between the country of the barbarians in the far north 'covered every day by Helice'—the reference suddenly making it not merely distant but strange and outlandish—and the glory of Rome, with its great church that was the heart of Christendom 'when the Lateran rose', not merely in bulk, 'above all mortal things'. It is the contrast between the heathen and the Christian worlds; and by this succession of contrasts he is led to its culmination in his last reference to Florence, the bitterer because ostensibly casual and matter-of-fact,— 'from Florence to a people just and sane'. Scorn can go no farther. Gardner notes the grave, deliberate rhythm of the line, with every vowel sounded separately—*io, che al divino dall'umano*, as if it was spoken by Dante in solemn wonder at his experience. 'No one who makes much of inspiration at the expense of knowledge, judgement and calculated art, need hope for any success with Dante. While his inventive genius, the triumph of his poetry in vision, music, and story, is as safe beyond challenge as Homer's, yet in every line you can trace him taking thought and making sure of every syllable' (*W. P. Ker*). In connection with this passage, Croce comments: 'What is not found in the *Paradiso*, for it is foreign to the spirit of Dante, is flight from the world, absolute refuge in God, asceticism. He does not seek to fly from the world, but to instruct it, and correct it, and reform it, and give to it the fulness of heavenly blessedness. Of this he knew assuredly the beauty and the joy, but he knew, at the same time, the world and its doings and passions; not even in the Empyrean, declaring his amazement at finding himself transported from the human to the divine, is he forgetful of Florence, and humanity is particularized and belittled for him in Florentine society.' It is important for the reader of Dante to remember—especially in the *Paradiso* where it is easy to forget it—that, not only in point of fact but in the whole conception of the poem, he tells his story in Italy and addresses his fellow-countrymen. No poet is more constantly aware of his audience or of the world in which he and they are living.

'It is profoundly significant that in this kingdom of the ideal the determination of the personality, the individual, attains its culmination; the supreme ideal is the supremely real. Even the angels, who in the Primum Mobile were only sparks in one vast conflagration, appear to us in their personal form, with their "faces of living flame"; but, more particularly, the souls of the blest, who in the planets were confounded together in a common uniformity of splendours, are shown here with unveiled face in the aspect of their earthly individuality. It may be said that there they were groups, virtues, and here each shines with his own distinct individual quality.... That corporeal aspect of the souls is the light of their individual life, which Dante sees and distinguishes in the divine light, the eternal stamp which they have borne on themselves, the impress of their painful but dear and unforgettable earthly prison, by which they have won the exercise of their conscience and from the generality of the species have been transformed into individuals. . . . The dogma of the resurrection of the body has never had a more lofty or poetical interpretation. The Christian poet succeeds thus in taking with him even to the supreme height of the Empyrean his dear earth, symbolizing a state of human perfection in which the body, the earth, and all the beauty of sensible things vindicate their rights alongside those of pure spirit' (*E. G. Parodi*).

The middle part of the canto tells of Beatrice's parting from Dante, in a passage of singular imaginative conviction, an outstanding instance of the restraint and the dramatic intensity of which Dante is the master. As much is told by silence as by speech. He is silent, first, with wonder at the great sight before him, then with bewilderment at the absence of Beatrice, and, except for his sudden question, 'Where is she?', still silent as he looks up, at the bidding of St Bernard, to see her. Seeing her, he breaks into speech that sums up all his story; and the passage ends with a strangely moving stanza, Dante's last words on Beatrice: 'I prayed thus; and she, so far off as she seemed, smiled and looked at me, then turned again to the eternal fount.' The brevity and simplicity and silence of the scene make us conscious, as we read, of Dante at gaze and oblivious, for an instant, of all the glories of Paradise. There is no more to say. He has fulfilled the promise recorded long ago on the last page of the story of his love: 'I hope to say of her that which was never said of any woman.' It is significant that here the honorific *voi*, with which he has addressed Beatrice up to this point, is changed for the more intimate and personal *tu*. She has shed her veil of symbolism and her task is done; now she is simply herself. To his still imperfect mortal sight she seems far away, but only seems; for in the realm of the spirit there is no near and far, and nothing separates. Here, if anywhere, Dante is faithful to his own standard of poetry: 'I am one who, when love breathes in me, take note, and in that manner which he dictates within go on to set it forth' (*Purg.* xxiv).

The scene inevitably recalls the other, in *Purgatorio* xxx, of Dante's parting with Virgil, with which it corresponds both in dramatic quality and in allegorical sense. On the summit of Purgatory Dante had been brought by Virgil to the Earthly Paradise, the recovered Eden, where he had met Matilda (*Purg.* xxvii and xxviii). The soul's difficult obedience to the demands of reason and conscience had flowered at last into the free delight in good which is the perfection of the active life, and which is symbolized in Matilda. Then, having watched the Pageant, he had passed from the guidance of Virgil to that of Beatrice, from reason to revelation. So here, in the Heavenly Paradise, he passes from the instructions of Beatrice in spiritual things, her lessons in obedience to the truth, that obedience of the mind which is faith and hope and love, and, under Bernard's directions, these lessons in the ordered knowledge of God come to flower in mystic contemplation, by which, through many 'shadowy forecasts', he attains at last to the Beatific Vision. 'Reason, Revelation, Contemplation represent the three stages of approach to God' (*C. H. Grandgent*). The scheme, in mere outline, is formal and abstract; but it was plainly adopted by

Dante as no mere conventional framework for his poem, but as a verifiable and valid account of the soul's experience of redemption, and all the wealth and passion of his narrative is evidence of his conviction. No man was ever better equipped than Dante with that 'effectiveness of assertion' which Mr. Bernard Shaw calls 'the alpha and omega of style'. 'The medieval man thought and felt in symbols, and the sequence of his thought moved as frequently from symbol to symbol as from fact to fact' (*A. E. Taylor*). Fundamentally, Dante was a medieval man; but he was much more besides, and Virgil and Beatrice and Bernard, for being severally reason and revelation and contemplation, are no less personalities in the real world and in Dante's mental and spiritual experience. 'St Bernard, probably more than any other great teacher of the Christian society, influenced the moral and spiritual life of Dante' (*F. M. Powicke*). His semi-allegorical figures are unlike the allegorically named people of Bunyan in being drawn from history or mythology or contemporary life; but they are like Bunyan's in being alive and real, and in telling of them and of what they were to him Dante tells his own story. 'Love ceased to be a passion and became the energy of contemplation; it diffused over the universe, natural and ideal, that light of tenderness and that faculty of worship which the passion often is first to quicken in a man's heart' (*G. Santayana*).

St Bernard was the most commanding figure in the Church of his time; his eloquence and his fame were main factors in the launching of the Second Crusade, that in which Cacciaguida died (*Par.* xv). 'His face glowed with a brightness that was not earthly but heavenly, and his eyes were radiant with a certain purity and the simplicity of the dove. The skin of his cheeks, which were somewhat ruddy, was of the finest delicacy' (quoted from a contemporary of the saint by *A. J. Butler*). 'Few men contributed more than the Saint of Clairvaux did to the *cultus* of the Virgin, which spread over Europe in the 12th, 13th and 14th centuries, and left its mark in the hymnology, the painting, the sculpture, and the architecture of Western Christendom. The lady-chapels of this period were the outcome of the teaching of the *Praises of the Blessed Virgin Mary*' (*E. H. Plumptre*). Dante gazes at him, like a foreign pilgrim before the Veronica,

as at a 'true image' of Christ, for his 'living charity'; and here
again, as in telling of the 'faces persuasive to charity' and
elsewhere in the poem, he uses the word for a love that is not
merely personal and selective, but fundamental and compre-
hensive. The whole account of Bernard is not merely that of
an image of contemplation; it is a portrait of the man.

But Bernard himself tells Dante that he must look higher,
'as it were climbing with his eyes', to come nearer to the final
vision; and he sees, at first, a diffused radiance like the dawn,
and then, in the heart of it, the glory of the Virgin.

The problem for the poet of representing Beatrice and the
Virgin in the same scene is solved by the extreme restraint of
his portrayal of Beatrice, on the one hand, and, on the other,
by his account of the glory of the Virgin, a glory so little per-
sonal that the two do not come into any real comparison. The
Virgin is described in rich imagery, as if all but divine,—'the
Queen to whom this realm is subject and devoted'; but that
imagery itself seems as if expressly devised to show her in the
ranks of redeemed humanity,—with 'all the other saints', at
'a part of the extreme verge' of their circles, not beyond them,
not excelled and not equalled, but approached on this side and
on that by other souls in the one fellowship, and, like all the
rest, 'adorned with Another's light', the Queen of Heaven
and still the handmaid of the Lord.

AFFETTO al suo piacer, quel contemplante
   libero officio di dottore assunse,
   e cominciò queste parole sante:
'La piaga che Maria richiuse e unse,
   quella ch'è tanto bella da' suoi piedi
   è colei che l'aperse e che la punse.
Nell'ordine che fanno i terzi sedi
   siede Rachel di sotto da costei
   con Beatrice, sì come tu vedi.
Sara e Rebecca, Iudìt e colei   10
   che fu bisava al cantor che per doglia
   del fallo disse *"Miserere mei"*,
puoi tu veder così di soglia in soglia
   giù digradar, com' io ch'a proprio nome
   vo per la rosa giù di foglia in foglia.
E dal settimo grado in giù, sì come
   infino ad esso, succedono Ebree,
   dirimendo del fior tutte le chiome;
perchè, secondo lo sguardo che fee
   la fede in Cristo, queste sono il muro   20
   a che si parton le sacre scalee.
Da questa parte onde 'l fiore è maturo
   di tutte le sue foglie, sono assisi
   quei che credettero in Cristo venturo;
dall'altra parte onde sono intercisi
   di voti i semicirculi, si stanno
   quei ch'a Cristo venuto ebber li visi.

CANTO XXXII

The saints in the Rose; the children among the elect

ABSORBED in his delight, that contemplative freely undertook the office of a teacher and began with these holy words: 'The wound that Mary closed and anointed, she at her feet who is so fair it was that opened it and pierced it.[1] Below her, in the seats of the third row, sits Rachel with Beatrice, as thou seest. Sarah and Rebecca, Judith and her that was great-grandmother of the singer who, in grief for his sin, cried: "*Miserere mei*",[2] thou canst see, one thus below the other from rank to rank, as I, giving each her name, go down through the rose from petal to petal. And from the seventh grade, just as down to that point, follow Hebrew women, parting all the tresses of the flower. For these are the wall by which the sacred stairway is divided according to the look which their faith turned to Christ; on the one side, where the flower is in full bloom with all its petals, are seated those who believed in Christ yet to come,—on the other, where the half-circles are broken by vacant places, those who held their eyes on Christ already come. And

463

E come quinci il glorïoso scanno
    della donna del cielo e li altri scanni
    di sotto lui cotanta cerna fanno,   30
così di contra quel del gran Giovanni,
    che sempre santo 'l diserto e 'l martiro
    sofferse, e poi l' inferno da due anni;
e sotto lui così cerner sortiro
    Francesco, Benedetto e Augustino
    e altri fin qua giù di giro in giro.
Or mira l'alto proveder divino;
    chè l'uno e l'altro aspetto della fede
    igualmente empierà questo giardino.
E sappi che dal grado in giù che fiede   40
    a mezzo il tratto le due discrezioni,
    per nullo proprio merito si siede,
ma per l'altrui, con certe condizioni;
    chè tutti questi son spiriti assolti
    prima ch'avesser vere elezïoni.
Ben te ne puoi accorger per li volti
    e anche per le voci puerili,
    se tu li guardi bene e se li ascolti.
Or dubbi tu, e dubitando sili;
    ma io dissolverò 'l forte legame   50
    in che ti stringon li pensier sottili.
Dentro all'ampiezza di questo reame
    casüal punto non puote aver sito,
    se non come tristizia o sete o fame;
chè per etterna legge è stabilito
    quantunque vedi, sì che giustamente
    ci si risponde dall'anello al dito.
E però questa festinata gente
    a vera vita non è *sine causa*
    intra se qui più e meno eccellente.   60
Lo rege per cui questo regno pausa
    in tanto amore ed in tanto diletto,
    che nulla volontà è di più ausa,
le menti tutte nel suo lieto aspetto
    creando, a suo piacer di grazia dota
    diversamente; e qui basti l'effetto.

just as here the glorious seat of the Lady of Heaven and the other seats below it make that great division, so, opposite, does that of the great John, who, ever holy, bore the wilderness and martyrdom and, for two years, Hell;[3] and below him, continuing the division, were assigned Francis and Benedict and Augustine and others from circle to circle down to here. Behold now the depth of the divine foresight; for the one and the other aspect of the faith shall fill this garden equally. And note that downward from the grade which cuts midway the two dividing lines they have their seats for no merit of their own, but for that of others, under certain conditions; for all these are spirits released before they had real choice. This, indeed, thou mayst observe for thyself by their faces and also by their childish voices, if thou look well and listen to them.

'Now thou art perplexed and silent in thy perplexity; but I will loose the hard knot with which thy subtle thoughts are holding thee. In all the breadth of this kingdom nothing of chance can find a place any more than sorrow or thirst or hunger, for all thou seest is ordained by eternal law, so that here the ring exactly fits the finger; and therefore this company who were hastened to true life are not *sine causa*[4] higher and lower here among themselves. The King through whom this kingdom rests in such love and delight that desire can dare no farther, creating all minds in His glad sight, bestows His grace variously at His pleasure; and for this let the fact suffice. And it is

465

E ciò espresso e chiaro vi si nota
  nella Scrittura santa in quei gemelli
  che nella madre ebber l' ira commota.
Però, secondo il color de' capelli   70
  di cotal grazia, l'altissimo lume
  degnamente convien che s' incappelli.
Dunque, sanza merzè di lor costume,
  locati son per gradi differenti,
  sol differendo nel primiero acume.
Bastavasi ne' secoli recenti
  con l' innocenza, per aver salute,
  solamente la fede de' parenti.
Poi che le prime etadi fuor compiute,
  convenne ai maschi all' innocenti penne   80
  per circuncidere acquistar virtute.
Ma poi che 'l tempo della grazia venne,
  sanza battesmo perfetto di Cristo,
  tale innocenza là giù si ritenne.
Riguarda omai nella faccia che a Cristo
  più si somiglia, chè la sua chiarezza
  sola ti può disporre a veder Cristo.'
Io vidi sopra lei tanta allegrezza
  piover, portata nelle menti sante
  create a trasvolar per quella altezza,   90
che quantunque io avea visto davante
  di tanta ammirazion non mi sospese,
  nè mi mostrò di Dio tanto sembiante;
e quello amor che primo lì discese,
  cantando 'Ave Maria, gratïa plena,'
  dinanzi a lei le sue ali distese.
Rispuose alla divina cantilena
  da tutte parti la beata corte,
  sì ch'ogni vista sen fè più serena.
'O santo padre, che per me comporte   100
  l'esser qua giù, lasciando il dolce loco
  nel qual tu siedi per etterna sorte,
qual è quell'angel che con tanto gioco
  guarda nelli occhi la nostra regina,
  innamorato sì che par di foco?'

clearly and expressly noted for you in Holy Scrip-
ture in those twins who were moved to anger in
their mother's womb. Therefore according to the
colour of the hair given by such grace the supreme
light must fittingly crown them.[5] Without merit
for their doings, then, they are placed in different
ranks, differing only in their original keenness of
vision. In early times their parents' faith alone,
with their own innocence, sufficed for their salva-
tion; when the first ages were completed, male
children must find strength for their innocent
wings by circumcision; but when the time of grace
was come such innocence, without the perfect
baptism of Christ, was held there below.[6]

'Look now on the face that most resembles
Christ, for only its brightness can fit thee to see
Christ.'

I saw such gladness rain down upon her, borne
in the holy minds created to fly through those
heights, that all I had seen before had not held me
in such wonder and suspense nor shown me such
likeness to God, and that loving spirit which had
first descended on her singing '*Ave Maria, gratia
plena*'[7] spread his wings before her. On all sides
the blessed court sang responses to the divine
canticle, so that every face turned brighter for it.

'O holy father, who bearest for my sake to be
here below, leaving the sweet place where by
eternal lot thou hast thy seat, who is that angel
that gazes with such rapture on the eyes of our
Queen, so enamoured that he seems on fire?' Thus

467

Così ricorsi ancora alla dottrina
   di colui ch'abbelliva di Maria
   come del sole stella mattutina.
Ed elli a me: 'Baldezza e leggiadria
   quant'esser puote in angelo ed in alma,   110
   tutta è in lui; e sì volem che sia,
perch'elli è quelli che portò la palma
   giuso a Maria, quando 'l Figliuol di Dio
   carcar si volse della nostra salma.
Ma vieni omai con li occhi sì com' io
   andrò parlando, e nota i gran patrici
   di questo imperio giustissimo e pio.
Quei due che seggon là su più felici
   per esser propinquissimi ad Augusta,
   son d'esta rosa quasi due radici: 120
colui che da sinistra le s'aggiusta
   è il padre per lo cui ardito gusto
   l'umana specie tanto amaro gusta;
dal destro vedi quel padre vetusto
   di Santa Chiesa a cui Cristo le chiavi
   raccomandò di questo fior venusto.
E quei che vide tutti i tempi gravi,
   pria che morisse, della bella sposa
   che s'acquistò con la lancia e coi chiavi,
siede lungh'esso, e lungo l'altro posa   130
   quel duca sotto cui visse di manna
   la gente ingrata, mobile e retrosa.
Di contr'a Pietro vedi sedere Anna
   tanto contenta di mirar sua figlia,
   che non move occhio per cantare osanna;
e contro al maggior padre di famiglia
   siede Lucia, che mosse la tua donna,
   quando chinavi, a ruinar, le ciglia.
Ma perchè 'l tempo fugge che t'assonna,
   qui farem punto, come buon sartore   140
   che com'elli ha del panno fa la gonna;
e dirizzerem li occhi al primo amore,
   sì che, guardando verso lui, penetri
   quant'è possibil per lo suo fulgore.

I sought again the lessons of him who drew beauty from Mary as from the sun the morning star.

And he answered me: 'All confidence and gallant bearing that can be found in angel or in any soul are in him; and we would have it so, for it is he that brought the palm down to Mary when the Son of God would take on Himself the burden of our flesh.

'But follow my words now with thine eyes as I continue, and note the great nobles of this most just and merciful empire. These two who are seated there above, most happy to be so near the Empress, are as it were two roots of this rose: he that is beside her on the left is the father for whose rash tasting the human kind tastes such bitterness,—on the right see that ancient father of Holy Church to whom Christ committed the keys of this beauteous flower. And he who saw before he died all the grievous times of the fair bride that was won with the lance and the nails[8] sits beside him, and beside the other rests that leader under whom the thankless, fickle and stiff-necked people lived on manna. Opposite Peter see Anna sitting,[9] so well content to gaze on her daughter that she does not move her eyes while singing hosanna; and opposite the greatest father of a family sits Lucy, who sent thy Lady when thou didst bend thy brow downward to destruction.[10]

'But since the time flies that holds thee sleeping we shall stop here, like a good tailor that cuts his coat according to his cloth; and we shall direct our eyes to the Primal Love, so that, looking towards Him, thou mayst penetrate, as far as that

Veramente, ne forse tu t'arretri
  movendo l'ali tue, credendo oltrarti,
  orando grazia conven che s' impetri,
grazia da quella che puote aiutarti;
  e tu mi seguirai con l'affezione,
  sì che dal dicer mio lo cor non parti.'   150
E cominciò questa santa orazione:

can be, into His effulgence. But lest perchance thou fall back, beating thy wings and thinking to advance, grace must be gained by prayer, grace from her who has power to help thee; and do thou follow me with thy love so that thy heart may not separate from my words.'

And he began this holy supplication:

1. Eve 'took of the fruit',—'opening' the wound—and she 'gave also unto her husband'—'piercing' it (*Gen.* iii. 6).

2. Ruth, great-grandmother of David. 'Have mercy upon me' (*Ps.* li. 1).

3. John the Baptist, who died two years before the Crucifixion and the Harrowing of Hell.

4. 'Without cause.'

5. Esau and Jacob 'struggled together within her, . . . and the first came out red, all over like an hairy garment' (*Gen.* xxv. 22, 25). The metaphor, 'the colour of the hair given by such grace', seems to mean that the physical difference in the twins corresponds, inscrutably, with their pre-natal spiritual difference, grace being given to Jacob and not to Esau.

6. In Limbo (*Inf.* iv). Circumcision is here regarded as *im*perfect baptism, sufficient for its time.

7. 'Hail Mary, full of grace'; Gabriel's greeting at the Annunciation.

8. John the Evangelist, as author of the Apocalypse, foreseeing the Church's sufferings.

9. St Anna, legendary mother of Mary.

10. 'When I was rushing down to the place below' (*Inf.* i). 'Lucy, enemy of all cruelty, rose and came to the place where I was seated beside the ancient Rachel and said: "Beatrice, true praise of God, why dost thou not succour him who so loved thee?"' (*Inf.* ii).

NOTE

In his account of the saints in the Empyrean St Bernard begins with Mary and Eve, who were so constantly coupled and contrasted in medieval religious thinking as the historical fountainheads of human sin and of divine redemptive grace; and in so beginning he gives the keynote and the character of the whole assembly. All the saints he names are connected in one way or other with the history of human redemption, so that the Empyrean, the fulfilment of God's purposes for men, is represented by them not only as a state of glory but as a life redeemed, healed by grace of a wound that is not forgotten. 'Here we do not repent; nay, we smile, not for our fault, which does not come back to mind, but for the Power which ordained and foresaw. Here we contemplate the art that makes beautiful the great result, and discern the good for which the world above wheels about the world below' (*Par.* ix). David is mentioned, not as king but as a sinner who begged for mercy, and found it. In the line down from the Baptist, the Forerunner, are three who conspicuously continued his work of preparing the way of Christ: Francis, the most Christlike among the saints, Benedict, the founder of western monasticism, and Augustine, the greatest of Christian theologians. St Benedict is named, not only on his merits, so to speak, but also for the fulfilment of his promise that Dante would see him in the Empyrean 'with unveiled face' (*Par.* xxii). Adam is there as the partner in Eve's transgression who was yet the first soul redeemed from Limbo, Peter as the first head of the Church of the redeemed, John as recorder of the Church's sufferings, Moses as the leader of the chosen race, Anna as mother of the Virgin and now her devotee. Lucy is named in each part of the *Comedy* (*Inferno* ii, *Purgatorio* ix and here), each time as a chief agent in Dante's own redemption.

473

Bernard finds evidence of 'the depth of the divine foresight' in the formally balanced numbers and arrangement of the saints, the believers before Christ in the one half-circle and those after Christ in the other, with the adults above the middle line and the children below. 'Mary who had faith in Christ before he was conceived ranks as a Hebrew, and John Baptist who, when still in the womb, greeted him and afterwards proclaimed him as already come, ranks as a Christian' (*P. H. Wicksteed*). It is a plan which must seem to us pedantic and unimaginative and out of keeping with the visionary rapture of this part of Dante's pilgrimage. And yet this deliberate and formal account —which is in line with his frequent use of mathematical and arithmetical certainties in illustration of the ultimate realities and the knowledge of them—may fairly be regarded as Dante's way of keeping his feet on the ground of reality in the very height and ecstasy of his vision. This perfected life in God, to have meaning at all, must be a consummation for actual human souls, for men and women who can be named and known and whose several parts in it are determined by what, individually and historically, they have been; and this perfect life is not merely the lives of so many individuals, but an ordered fellowship in which 'nothing of chance can find a place any more than sorrow or thirst or hunger.'

'Dante's intellect is first engaged in emphasizing the perfect construction of his edifice, i.e., the relation of the parts of it to one another and to the whole, an intellectual process resulting in a static formal image, mercilessly formal in its absolute symmetry, a mere geometrical design, lifeless, but, to the intellect or scientific understanding, satisfying. But it is not poetry, for it does not touch the heart, any more than does the language employed in expressing it. This is the first phase; but that completed, the moment he passes to the second phase (and the reader with him) and from the formal pattern proceeds to the heart and soul of the pattern, i.e., that which accounts for it and explains why it is what it is, namely to Mary, his love for her transfigures and makes alive what has up to now been a mere pattern of names. The names become persons, the two-dimensional design becomes a living three-dimensional reality. With Dante, you must have the intellectual vision with its appropriate symbol, *before* emotional vision with *its* appropriate symbol, the counterpointing, as it were, of the second upon the first' (*G. L. Bickersteth*).

The scene recalls the great fresco of The Last Judgement in the Chapel of St Thomas Aquinas in Santa Maria Novella in Florence. It was painted by the Orcagna brothers nearly forty years after this canto was written and it is planned, in many respects, in accordance with the *Divine Comedy*. Among the recognizable saints in the Paradise on the right hand of Christ who is on the judgement-seat is Dante, gazing up in absorbed reverence at the Madonna. Was this a repudiation, with the authority as it were of Aquinas himself, of the old charges of heresy? Some years earlier, a portrait of Dante as he had been in his happier years in Florence was painted— probably by a follower of Giotto—in the chapel of the Governor's palace, as part of a group of the notables of the city at that still earlier time. Church and State had cast him, living, out of Florence; dead, they made him these poor amends.

Especially in the *Paradiso* Dante delights in intimate references to the ways of children, and his lines here about 'their faces and also their childish voices' which he saw and heard are the more characteristic because they are a departure from the teaching of both Augustine and Aquinas that the redeemed children would rise from their graves in mature manhood and womanhood, as they are generally represented in medieval art. It would seem that Dante could not conceive of Paradise without children, remembering, surely, that 'of such is the kingdom of heaven'.

It was not *sine causa* that the children are 'higher and lower here among themselves'. When Dante uses a Latin expression without other obvious reason, we may take it as having some more or less legalistic significance; as *et coram padre* in *Paradiso* xi, and *non decimas, quae sunt pauperum Dei* in *Paradiso* xii.

The reference to the children re-awakens in him his old unsolved perplexities about election and predestination, and the word is repeated for emphasis, *dubbi, dubitando*. These perplexities are not solved here, only silenced, as they are in St Paul's harsh logic, with its rabbinical argument from the patriarchal story: 'Jacob have I loved, but Esau have I hated', and 'therefore hath he mercy on whom he will have mercy, and whom he will he hardeneth' (*Rom.* ix. 13, 18). The twins were so opposite that they 'were moved to anger in their mother's womb'. The primal elective gift of grace is as inscrutable as the colour of the hair; 'and in this let the fact suffice'. It is a logic from which Dante finds no escape and which belongs to the legalistic conceptions which conditioned the whole western theology of redemption; 'all thou seest is ordained by eternal law, so that here the ring exactly fits the finger'. Under that compulsion he concludes that even the innocence of uncircumcized and unbaptized infants 'was held there below'. It is the more remarkable that Dante should have put this grim conclusion into the mouth of St Bernard, who, in fact, expressly refrained from it: 'It is in God's hands; not mine be it to set the limit' (*quoted by P. H. Wicksteed*).

Here, at the end of this course of reasoning, the name of Christ occurs in the triple rhyme, as before in the twelfth, fourteenth and nineteenth cantos. In the spheres of the Sun, Mars and Jupiter—of wisdom, courage and justice—and now on the eve of the last vision, Christ, as Dante must conceive of Christ within the terms of his theology, is the measure and sum of the truth.

The canto tells of Dante's third vision of the Virgin. In the twenty-third we are told that the souls in the Church Triumphant 'reached upward' after her as she 'rose after her seed', and they sang the *Regina coeli* in her praise. In the thirty-first, she appears in the Empyrean in the fellowship of the redeemed, the brightest of them all, in 'a part of the extreme verge surpassing with its light all the rest'. Here, she is 'the Empress', and the immediate preparation, by her likeness to Him, for the vision of Christ Himself, and in chief attendance on her is Gabriel, the angel of the Annunciation, the herald of human redemption. It is by this cumulative and heightened celebration of Mary, the chosen medium and unique embodiment, for Dante and his readers, of redeeming grace, that he prepares our minds for the final vision.

The traditional literary form of an imaginary visit to the world of the dead is the record of a dream, and although there is no clear reference to the idea elsewhere in the poem it seems to be taken for granted by St Bernard when he says to Dante: 'The time flies that holds thee sleeping.' Perhaps it is meant to be enough that Dante tells us at the beginning of his story that he came to himself in a dark wood and that he cannot rightly tell how he entered there, he was so full of sleep at that moment (*Inf.* i); that entering the substance of the Moon he does not know if he was body (*Par.* ii); and that Cacciaguida bids him tell all his vision (*Par.* xvii). A hint, an implication, is often sufficient for Dante's purpose, and the framework of a dream makes the reader more tolerant of the occasional and inevitable incongruities in the mechanism of his story. There is, indeed, something curiously dreamlike in the way in which the first simile for the Empyrean of a great white rose seems to melt and disappear in the account of it. The rose becomes a garden, a city, a kingdom, an empire; it has two roots, a stairway, and keys; and it might almost seem as if in this canto Dante deliberately let the splendour of the rose be lost and forgotten, and made his detailed description matter-of-fact and pedestrian —Mr. Melville B. Anderson happily describes it as a recitative— in contrast with the glowing passage on the Virgin and with the glory that is to follow. The contrast was surely as plain to Dante as it is to his commentators, between St Bernard's homely proverb of the tailor with his cloth and the 'holy supplication' that begins the final canto. Now above all he must persuade us that these things happened.

'VERGINE madre, figlia del tuo figlio,
    umile e alta più che creatura,
    termine fisso d'etterno consiglio,
tu se' colei che l'umana natura
    nobilitasti sì, che 'l suo fattore
    non disdegnò di farsi sua fattura.
Nel ventre tuo si raccese l'amore
    per lo cui caldo nell'etterna pace
    così è germinato questo fiore.
Qui se' a noi meridïana face   10
    di caritate, e giuso, intra i mortali,
    se' di speranza fontana vivace.
Donna, se' tanto grande e tanto vali,
    che qual vuol grazia ed a te non ricorre,
    sua disïanza vuol volar sanz'ali.
La tua benignità non pur soccorre
    a chi domanda, ma molte fïate
    liberamente al dimandar precorre.
In te misericordia, in te pietate,
    in te magnificenza, in te s'aduna   20
    quantunque in creatura è di bontate.
Or questi, che dall' infima lacuna
    dell'universo infin qui ha vedute
    le vite spiritali ad una ad una,
supplica a te, per grazia, di virtute
    tanto, che possa con li occhi levarsi
    più alto verso l'ultima salute.
E io, che mai per mio veder non arsi
    più ch' i' fo per lo suo, tutti miei preghi
    ti porgo, e priego che non sieno scarsi,   30

CANTO XXXIII

St Bernard's prayer; the Beatific Vision

'VIRGIN Mother, daughter of thy Son, lowly and
exalted more than any creature, fixed goal of the
eternal counsel, thou art she who didst so ennoble
human nature that its Maker did not disdain to be
made its making. In thy womb was rekindled the
love by whose warmth this flower has bloomed thus
in the eternal peace; here thou art for us the noon-
day torch of charity, and below among mortals
thou art a living spring of hope. Thou, Lady, art
so great and so prevailing that whoso would have
grace and does not turn to thee, his desire would
fly without wings. Thy loving-kindness not only
succours him that asks, but many times it freely
anticipates the asking;[1] in thee is mercy, in thee
pity, in thee great bounty, in thee is joined all
goodness that is in any creature. This man, who
from the nethermost pit of the universe to here has
seen one by one the lives of the spirits, now begs
of thee by thy grace for such power that with
his eyes he may rise still higher towards the last
salvation; and I, who never burned for my own
vision more than I do for his, offer to thee all my
prayers, and pray that they come not short, that

perchè tu ogni nube li disleghi
di sua mortalità co' prieghi tuoi,
sì che 'l sommo piacer li si dispieghi.
Ancor ti priego, Regina, che puoi
ciò che tu vuoli, che conservi sani,
dopo tanto veder, li affetti suoi.
Vinca tua guardia i movimenti umani:
vedi Beatrice con quanti beati
per li miei preghi ti chiudon le mani!'
Li occhi da Dio diletti e venerati,   40
fissi nell'orator, ne dimostraro
quanto i devoti prieghi le son grati;
indi all'etterno lume si drizzaro,
nel qual non si dee creder che s' invii
per creatura l'occhio tanto chiaro.
E io ch'al fine di tutt' i disii
appropinquava, sì com' io dovea,
l'ardor del desiderio in me finii.
Bernardo m'accennava e sorridea
perch' io guardassi suso; ma io era   50
già per me stesso tal qual ei volea;
chè la mia vista, venendo sincera,
e più e più intrava per lo raggio
dell'alta luce che da sè è vera.
Da quinci innanzi il mio veder fu maggio
che 'l parlar nostro, ch'a tal vista cede,
e cede la memoria a tanto oltraggio.
Qual è colui che somnïando vede,
che dopo il sogno la passione impressa
rimane, e l'altro alla mente non riede,   60
cotal son io, chè quasi tutta cessa
mia visïone, ed ancor mi distilla
nel core il dolce che nacque da essa.
Così la neve al sol si disigilla;
così al vento nelle foglie levi
si perdea la sentenza di Sibilla.
O somma luce che tanto ti levi
da' concetti mortali, alla mia mente
ripresta un poco di quel che parevi,

by thy prayers thou wilt disperse for him every cloud of his mortality so that the supreme joy may be disclosed to him. This too I pray of thee, Queen, who canst what thou wilt, that thou keep his affections pure after so great a vision. Let thy guardianship control his human impulses. See Beatrice and so many of the blest who clasp their hands for my prayers.'

The eyes by God beloved and reverenced,[2] fixed on the suppliant, made plain to us how dear to her are devout prayers; then they were directed to the Eternal Light, into which it is not to be believed that any creature should penetrate with so clear an eye. And I, who was drawing near to the end of all desires, ended perforce the ardour of my craving. Bernard signed to me with a smile to look upward, but already of myself I was doing what he wished; for my sight, becoming pure, was entering more and more through the beam of the lofty light which in itself is true.[3]

From that moment my vision was greater than our speech, which fails at such a sight, and memory too fails at such excess. Like him that sees in a dream and after the dream the passion wrought by it remains and the rest returns not to his mind, such am I; for my vision almost wholly fades, and still there drops within my heart the sweetness that was born of it. Thus the snow loses its imprint in the sun; thus in the wind on the light leaves the Sibyl's oracle was lost.[4]

O Light Supreme that art so far exalted above mortal conceiving, grant to my mind again a little of what thou appearedst and give my tongue such

481

e fa la lingua mia tanto possente,   70
  ch' una favilla sol della tua gloria
  possa lasciare alla futura gente;
chè, per tornare alquanto a mia memoria
  e per sonare un poco in questi versi,
  più si conceperà di tua vittoria.
Io credo, per l'acume ch' io soffersi
  del vivo raggio, ch' i' sarei smarrito,
  se li occhi miei da lui fossero aversi.
E mi ricorda ch' io fui più ardito
  per questo a sostener, tanto ch' i' giunsi   80
  l'aspetto mio col valore infinito.
O abbondante grazia ond' io presunsi
  ficcar lo viso per la luce etterna,
  tanto che la veduta vi consunsi!
Nel suo profondo vidi che s' interna,
  legato con amore in un volume,
  ciò che per l'universo si squaderna:
sustanze e accidenti e lor costume,
  quasi conflati insieme, per tal modo
  che ciò ch' i' dico è un semplice lume.   90
La forma universal di questo nodo
  credo ch' i' vidi, perchè più di largo,
  dicendo questo, mi sento ch' i' godo.
Un punto solo m'è maggior letargo
  che venticinque secoli alla 'mpresa,
  che fè Nettuno ammirar l'ombra d'Argo.
Così la mente mia, tutta sospesa,
  mirava fissa, immobile e attenta,
  e sempre di mirar facìesi accesa.
A quella luce cotal si diventa,   100
  che volgersi da lei per altro aspetto
  è impossibil che mai si consenta;
però che 'l ben, ch'è del volere obietto,
  tutto s'accoglie in lei, e fuor di quella
  è defettivo ciò ch'è lì perfetto.
Omai sarà più corta mia favella,
  pur a quel ch' io ricordo, che d'un fante
  che bagni ancor la lingua alla mammella.

power that it may leave but a gleam of thy glory to the people yet to come;[5] for by returning somewhat to my memory and by sounding a little in these lines the better conceived will be thy victory.

I think, from the keenness I endured of the living ray, that I should have been dazzled if my eyes had been turned from it; and I remember that for this cause I was the bolder to sustain it until I reached with my gaze the Infinite Goodness. O abounding grace, by which I dared to fix my look on the Eternal Light so long that I spent all my sight upon it! In its depth I saw that it contained, bound by love in one volume, that which is scattered in leaves through the universe, substances and accidents and their relations[6] as it were fused together in such a way that what I tell of is a simple light. I think I saw the universal form of this complex,[7] because in telling of it I feel my joy expand. A single moment makes for me deeper oblivion than five and twenty centuries upon the enterprise that made Neptune wonder at the shadow of the Argo.[8] Thus my mind, all rapt, was gazing, fixed, still and intent, and ever enkindled with gazing. At that light one becomes such that it is impossible for him ever to consent that he should turn from it to another sight; for the good which is the object of the will is all gathered in it, and apart from it that is defective which there is perfect.[9]

Now my speech will come more short even of what I remember than an infant's who yet bathes his tongue at the breast. Not that the living light

Non perchè più ch' un semplice sembiante
   fosse nel vivo lume ch' io mirava,   110
   che tal è sempre qual s'era davante;
ma per la vista che s'avvalorava
   in me guardando, una sola parvenza,
   mutandom' io, a me si travagliava.
Nella profonda e chiara sussistenza
   dell'alto lume parvermi tre giri
   di tre colori e d'una contenenza;
e l'un dall'altro come iri da iri
   parea reflesso, e 'l terzo parea foco
   che quinci e quindi igualmente si spiri.   120
O quanto è corto il dire e come fioco
   al mio concetto! e questo, a quel ch' i' vidi,
   è tanto, che non basta a dicer 'poco'.
O luce etterna che sola in te sidi,
   sola t' intendi, e da te intelletta
   e intendente te ami e arridi!
Quella circulazion che sì concetta
   pareva in te come lume reflesso,
   dalli occhi miei alquanto circunspetta,
dentro da sè, del suo colore stesso,   130
   mi parve pinta della nostra effige;
   per che 'l mio viso in lei tutto era messo.
Qual è 'l geomètra che tutto s'affige
   per misurar lo cerchio, e non ritrova,
   pensando, quel principio ond'elli indige,
tal era io a quella vista nova:
   veder volea come si convenne
   l'imago al cerchio e come vi s'indova;
ma non eran da ciò le proprie penne:
   se non che la mia mente fu percossa   140
   da un fulgore in che sua voglia venne.
All'alta fantasia qui mancò possa;
   ma già volgeva il mio disio e 'l velle,
   sì come rota ch' igualmente è mossa,
l'amor che move il sole e l'altre stelle.

at which I gazed had more than a single aspect—
for it is ever the same as it was before—, but by my
sight gaining strength as I looked, the one sole
appearance, I myself changing, was, for me, trans-
formed. In the profound and clear ground of the
lofty light appeared to me three circles of three
colours and of the same extent, and the one seemed
reflected by the other as rainbow by rainbow, and
the third seemed fire breathed forth equally from
the one and the other.[10] O how scant is speech
and how feeble to my conception! and this, to
what I saw, is such that it is not enough to call it
little. O Light Eternal, that alone abidest in Thy-
self, alone knowest Thyself, and, known to Thyself
and knowing, lovest and smilest on Thyself![11]
That circling which, thus begotten, appeared in
Thee as reflected light, when my eyes dwelt on it
for a time, seemed to me, within it and in its own
colour, painted with our likeness, for which my
sight was wholly given to it. Like the geometer who
sets all his mind to the squaring of the circle[12] and
for all his thinking does not discover the principle
he needs, such was I at that strange sight. I wished
to see how the image was fitted to the circle and
how it has its place there; but my own wings were
not sufficient for that, had not my mind been
smitten by a flash wherein came its wish.[13] Here
power failed the high phantasy;[14] but now my
desire and will, like a wheel that spins with even
motion, were revolved by the Love that moves
the sun and the other stars.

1. Compare the language of Beatrice in *Inf*. ii: 'There is a gentle lady in heaven', etc.

2. Beloved by the Father, reverenced by the Son.

3. 'In Thy light shall we see light' (*Ps*. xxxvi. 9). 'That was the true light'—*vera lux* in the Vulgate—(*John* i. 9).

4. The Cumean Sibyl, prophetess of Apollo, wrote the oracles on tree-leaves, which were scattered by the wind (*Aeneid* iii).

5. Cp. *Par*. i: 'O power divine, if thou grant me so much of thyself that I may show forth the shadow of the blessed kingdom imprinted in my brain', etc.

6. 'Substances', things existing in themselves; 'accidents', qualities and relations existing not in themselves but in substances.

7. The divine idea of all things, 'the unity of creation in the Creator' (*C. E. Norton*).

8. The Argo on its voyage to Colchis for the Golden Fleece in the 13th century B.C., believed to be the first ship that ever sailed.

9. 'The true light that gives them peace does not let them turn their steps from itself' (*Par*. iii). 'The end of all desires'; 'the eternal light which, seen, alone and always kindles love; and if aught else beguiles your love it is nothing but some trace of this, ill-understood, that shines through there' (*Par*. v); 'that Essence in which is such pre-eminence that every good found outside of it is nothing but a light from its radiance' (*Par*. xxvi).

10. In the Western doctrine of the Trinity the Son is 'begotten' of the Father, and the Spirit 'proceeds' from the Father and the Son. Cp. 'Looking on His Son with the Love which the One and the Other eternally breathe forth', etc. (*Par*. x). The Father, the eternal Begetter of the Son,—the Son, the eternal Word of the Father,—the Spirit, the eternal Love, at once the Father's and the Son's.

11. 'No man knoweth the Son, but the Father; neither knoweth any man the Father, save the Son, and he to whomsoever the Son will reveal him' (*Matt*. xi. 27).

12. 'The squaring of the circle', the reckoning of a square that shall be equal in area to a given circle, an ancient and mathematically insoluble problem.

13. Cp. *Par*. ii: 'There will be seen that which we hold by faith, not demonstrated but known in itself.'

14. *Fantasia* is defined in the *Convito* as 'the power by which the intellect represents what it sees'.

NOTE

Nowhere else does Dante attain to the greatness of the last canto of the *Paradiso*, and in it more than any other it must be remembered that a *canto* is a *song*. Here his reach most exceeds his grasp, and nothing in all his work better demonstrates the consistency of his imagination and the integrity of his genius. In the culmination of his story he reports his experience with such intensity of conviction, in a mood so docile and so uplifted, and in terms so significant of a vision at once cosmic and profoundly personal, that we are persuaded and sustained to the end. The hosts of the redeemed are forgotten in the approach to a greater vision, the vision that is the blessedness of all the saints. Throughout the canto Dante is silent, and except for St Bernard's prayer heaven is silent too, and all that happens in that hush of wonder and worship and expectancy happens to himself. Here if anywhere it is true, as has been said, that 'to read the *Divine Comedy* is to be less aware of Dante presenting his ideas about God, than of God Himself.' The theology of the schools has little place, here it is transformed to vision; and the canto tells of a purely mystical experience, an immediate apprehension of spiritual things which issues in the final assurance of love. 'Scholasticism is the body of Dante's religion, Mysticism is the soul, and Love the animating spirit of both' (*E. G. Gardner*).

St Bernard's prayer to the Virgin is at once studied and spontaneous, studied for the Poet, spontaneous for the Saint. It passes from the greatness of Mary as the chosen medium for the coming of Christ and the redemption of humanity, to her incomparable graciousness and her bounty to 'this man's' need and his aspiration after 'the last salvation' and 'the supreme joy', and finally to the guarding of his affections and human 'impulses' from unworthiness 'after so great a vision'.

In the prayer and its context Mary is three times compared with 'any creature', angel or human. She excels them all in lowliness, in goodness, in the vision of God, and, as the consummation of all creaturely worth, she is in effect the one mediator of the divine favour: 'Whoso would have grace and does not turn to thee, his desire would fly without wings.' Here and throughout the *Divine Comedy* Christ is not the Christ we know in the Gospel story. The Man of Nazareth and Bethany and Olivet is lost in the unspeakable glory of the second Person of the Godhead, the Divine Word and Wisdom, the Judge of all the earth. Christ is, indeed, the appointed means of human salvation; but the immediate and operative Divine Grace for men is found by men in the 'gentle lady in heaven who is so moved with pity . . . that she breaks the stern judgement there on high' (*Inf.* ii). Abelard, two centuries before Dante, wrote in a hymn to the Virgin:

> 'They flee to the Judge's mother
> Who flee from the Judge's wrath.'

The Church, through many generations, was so bound by the absolute requirements of a ruthless dialectic concerned with the divine unity in trinity that it could find its liberation and assurance only in the 'Virgin Mother, daughter of thy Son'; and Dante was a medieval Christian.

At the end of the prayer its ardour is emphasized, in Dante's manner, by its harping on the word *prayer* itself. Bernard offers his own prayers and prays that they come not short; he prays for Mary's prayers for Dante, and notes how 'Beatrice and so many of the blest clasp their hands for my prayers.' It is Dante's final demonstration of the vast fellowship of aspiration and intercession which is the life of the saints in heaven and earth and which avails for a single soul. The conception belongs to the whole texture of the *Divine Comedy*, from the intervention of the 'three blessed ladies in the court of heaven' at the beginning of the *Inferno* to this silent pleading of Beatrice and so many of the saints in the Empyrean, where he has his last sight of her.

It has often been remarked that St Bernard's prayer in the poem is cast much in the manner and language of the historical Bernard; but, that being so, it is the more significant that it entirely avoids one aspect of the Virgin-cult as St Bernard represented it. 'After Bernard, and influenced by him, the erotic note grows ever clearer in medieval mysticism. Lover-like devotion commingles with worship of Mary. Out of the glowing language of the Song of Songs, out of the lighter tones of the popular love-ballads and the gallant forms of knightly madrigals, new forms of religious expression take shape, whose unmanly and frivolous sensuousness was less pleasing to the taste of our poet. . . . The prayer to the Virgin Mary, as uttered by St Bernard, sounds like solemn and biblical adoration. Here there is nothing dainty, no languors; I would almost say, nothing personal' (*K. Vossler*). 'Of Mary, in that supreme moment, Dante says the least that is possible. . . . Not even Dante could imagine an answer spoken by the Virgin Mother. She holds her eyes steadily on Bernard to signify her consent, then directs them on the Eternal Light. . . . They do not even smile; after so many smiles of Beatrice that would be at once too much and too little' (*E. Pistelli, L.D.*). There is again the same sensitive restraint and measure as we found in the account of Beatrice's departure in the thirty-first canto, 'the curb of art' which sets Dante's work out of all comparison with the medieval exuberance of his fore-runners in apocalyptic.

Just as Beatrice, after Dante's last words to her, smiled and looked at him, 'then turned again to the eternal fount', so the Virgin, having looked her acceptance of Bernard's prayer, directed her eyes on 'the Eternal Light'; and it is by his steadfast gazing into the same light, which before he could not bear, that his last vision is given to him and the Saint's prayer and his own are answered. Light, with no shadow and little even of colour, is the most constant visible feature of the *Paradiso*, and Dante taxes all his skill in exploiting this single element,— its sweet dispersion in the Moon, its envelopment of the saints in the higher spheres, its blazing splendour in the angelic circles and its dazzling brightness in the central point; and this treatment of light reaches its consummation in the Empyrean and chiefly in the last scene of all. Here light—*luce* or *lume*, light in its source or light diffused—is named ten times, and here God is light and is addressed as 'Light Supreme' and 'Light Eternal'. In the last vision Dante's sight 'was entering through the beam of the lofty light which in itself is true'—or 'real'—, the light of which every other light is either the radiation or the reflection.

After the prayer the rest of the canto is occupied with its answer. Dante, not as the pilgrim in Paradise but as the poet in Ravenna handling his 'weighty theme' and feeling the burden on his 'mortal shoulder', reports his experience as he can, searching his memory as for a forgotten dream, praying for the help of the Supreme Light, and giving thanks for the 'abounding grace' by which he has been enabled to fix his gaze on the light so long as to reach the Infinite Goodness.

In answer to his prayer there comes back to him what is less a vision than a mystic sense and assurance of all created things as one creation, the scattered pages 'bound by love in one volume', merged together as 'a simple light'. In the thirtieth canto he said, with a triple emphasis: 'I saw the courts of heaven, . . . I saw the high triumph of the true kingdom, . . . grant me the power to tell of what I saw.' With more diffidence he speaks here of a deeper vision: 'I think I saw the universal form of this complex',—the meaning of the whole, the universe of things *sub specie aeternitatis*, the divine order which penetrates and controls the world's confusions and resolves its contradictions. He thinks he sees it for a moment, and in a moment it is lost as if in the lapse of ages, like the first ship's shadow that fell on the amazed sea-god in the depth beneath, twenty-five centuries ago. So passing and so indubitable, so intangible and so real, so apart from all experience of the world we know and so profoundly significant for it, was this moment of revelation, the impact of another world on this. Dante's repeated insistence on the unspeakableness of the final vision as it were compels and justifies his cumulative imagery for it: an almost forgotten dream, melting shapes in snow, the Sibyl's oracle in the wind, an ancient, momentary shadow in the sea; and the failure of his utterance is the means and the measure of his success. His experience is the reward and the fulfilment of his faithful thinking; but it is also much more,—'exceeding abundantly above all that we ask or think, according to the power that worketh in us'. In the end the scholastic, from very faithfulness in his thinking, becomes the mystic, and thought is wholly surpassed and superseded in vision.

As he gazes, 'still and intent', 'the one sole appearance, I myself changing, was, for me, transformed'. The verb *si travagliava* in line 114 might mean 'was sifted out', and this, at least as a secondary sense, may well have been in Dante's mind, commending itself, as it does, by its bold and peculiarly Dantesque quality,—God's being, as he gazed, *was sifted out*, for him, into its elements. The being of God was represented to him in strange and abstract terms, the compression into a few lines of much of the teaching of Aquinas; and when he saw there 'our human likeness', his 'sight was wholly given to it'. Before that imaged mystery of God in Christ and Christ in God—the very humanness of God—his mind can only ask unanswerable questions. But a flash of inward illumination, beyond all reach not only of thought but even of phantasy, fills him with conviction and peace, and he rests in the Love that moves the sun and stars and now masters his soul.

The manifestations of Christ in the course of the poem stand in significant sequence. In the pageant of human redemption, still on the earth (*Purg.* xxix–xxxii), the Griffin, described as 'the two-fold beast', 'the twice-begotten animal', and 'the biformed beast', is surely not Christ, but the symbolical representation of the Church Militant's *doctrine* of Christ, whose two natures are reflected in the eyes of Beatrice,—as it were in the Sacred Host, if that interpretation is adopted. In the heaven of Mars (*Par.* xiv), the great white cross filled with the light of the warrior saints 'flamed forth Christ', while the saints sang 'Arise' and 'Conquer', and Christ is declared in their fellowship. In the vision of the Church Triumphant (*Par.* xxiii), Christ is the Sun that kindles all the saints as through His living light shows the shining substance of His person, and He passes, and the Virgin after Him, out of their sight. Here, in the final vision, Christ is known as, fundamentally, He is, one with the eternal being of the Godhead.

It should be noted, for it is fundamental in Dante, that, while his pilgrimage ends in rapture, it is not mere rapture, but, expressly, a vision which controls his desire and will, a final persuasion to an inward and complete obedience, the fulfilment of Bernard's prayer for him that his affections may be kept pure and his human impulses guarded from above. Dante is in the true succession of the Prophets and Apostles when he reckons the value of the Beatific Vision itself in terms of the good life, the life in which desire and will are perfected and made one. His claim here is that of St. Paul: 'I was not disobedient unto the heavenly vision'. The contemplative life in its consummation, so conceived, includes within itself, so to

speak, the lesser active life, as the *Paradiso* includes, by impli-
cation, all the meaning of the *Inferno* and the *Purgatorio*. The
soul, in all its functions, is subdued to what it sees, and 'this is
life eternal, that they might know thee'.

The whole account might seem to suffer from an incoherence
which is emphasized by the repeated exclamations in the course
of it that only a little can be recalled and that that little cannot
be told except in the broken utterance of an infant, were it
not that that very incoherence and these exclamations so demon-
strate the conditions of such a visionary experience that it
becomes for us no mere poetic invention but a true report, as
true as Wordsworth's when he knew

> 'A motion and a spirit, that impels
> All thinking things, all objects of all thought,
> And rolls through all things',

and Isaiah's when he 'saw the Lord sitting upon a throne, high
and lifted up, and his train filled the temple'. A modern psycho-
logist will make his own analysis of the record in terms which
would be strange to Dante; but he will not find reason to doubt
that such a vision, or 'ecstasy', did happen to Dante, or that it
had for him a fundamental and lasting significance.

For those who share the view offered in these notes with
regard to the large measure of spiritual autobiography through-
out the *Divine Comedy*, this closing canto will be an authentic
record of the fulfilment in Dante's last quiet years of the words
he gave to Piccarda: 'In His will is our peace.' The *Paradiso*,
like the *Inferno* and the *Purgatorio*, ends with the stars, 'the
organs of the universe' (*Par*. ii) which are driven by the angelic
powers in their courses round the world and work out the high
ends of providence in the lives of men. It is so that Dante
gives his final testimony, out of a life of passionate contention
and great hopes and bitter defeat and humiliation, and out of
the obedience and peace to which he attained, 'like a wheel that
spins with even motion'—the union of swiftness and perfect
rest; and his testimony is the sum of all the lessons of his journey.
The last line of the *Paradiso* recalls and expounds the first.
'The glory of Him who moves all things' *is* 'the Love that
moves the sun and the other stars'; and these are Dante's
last recorded words.

INDEX OF PERSONS AND PLACES
NAMED IN THE DIVINE COMEDY

LITERATURE: Criticism

PHILOSOPHY

POLITICAL SCIENCE